A HOPSCOTCH SUMMER

In the impoverished area of Nechells in Birmingham in the 1930s, Emma Brown's life is turned upside down when her mother, Cynthia, has another baby. When the baby is born Cynthia doesn't seem able to cope and eventually has to go and stay with her tyrannical older sister across the city. Life gets even tougher for poor Em with her mother away; her best friend ostracizes her, and she's got the Board Man calling about her lack of attendance at school. When she decides to travel across Birmingham and bring her mother home, the woman she discovers is very different from the mother she remembers...

A HOPSCOTCH SUMMER

A HOPSCOTCH SUMMER

by

Annie Murray

Magna Large Print Books
Long Preston, North Yorkshire,
BD23 4ND, England.

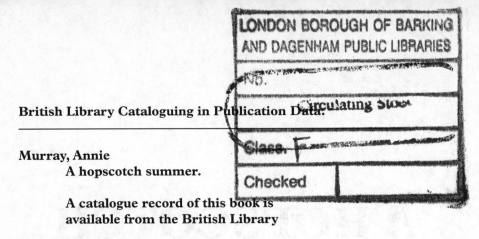
British Library Cataloguing in Publication Data.

Murray, Annie
    A hopscotch summer.

A catalogue record of this book is
available from the British Library

ISBN   978-0-7505-3201-3

First published in Great Britain in 2009 by Pan Books
an imprint of Pan Macmillan Ltd.

Published in Large Print 2010 by arrangement with
Pan Macmillan Publishers Ltd.

Magna Large Print is an imprint of Library Magna Books Ltd.

Printed and bound in Great Britain by
T.J. (International) Ltd., Cornwall, PL28 8RW

For Ruth Mary
With love and gratitude
RIP

Hopscotch

One

1931

'That's it, Joycie!' Em was jumping up and down, clapping her hands with excitement. 'You can do it!'

Her four-year-old sister Joyce was hopping along the wonky grid chalked on the pavement, the tip of her tongue sticking out and her eyes fixed on her feet in her eagerness to get it right. A pale blue ribbon bounced up and down in her hair as she hopped, avoiding the third square with the stone in it, and landed in square two, then square one, and finally, beaming like a cheeky angel, fell into Em's waiting arms.

'I done it, Em! I can do it!'

Em laughed in delight at the sight of her little sister's face. It was quite similar to her own, though Joyce's face was pudgier, like a puppy's, and without Em's sprinkling of freckles across the nose. But they both had the same bobbed brown hair and fringe, regularly chopped by their mother, Cynthia. 'I never said I was born to be a hairdresser,' she'd say, snipping the scissors across.

'You done it, Joycie. Told you I'd teach you, didn't I?'

It was August, and the sound of playing children could be heard all along the street, their voices and laughter echoing against the tired, sooty bricks of terraced houses. A gaggle of kids squatted over pocketfuls of marbles, there were lads swinging from ropes on the lamp posts and three of them were prodding the metal rim of a cycle wheel, cajoling it along the road in a sinuous course. And all across the pavements was smudged evidence of the latest craze: chalked hopscotch grids where boys and girls, but mostly girls, went skip-hopping up and down in the broiling afternoon sun.

'My turn again!' Joyce was shouting ecstatically, when a commanding cry cut through all the chatter and hubbub of the street.

'Em! Emma Brown. Get in 'ere quick, bab – your mom needs yer!'

'Mrs Wiggins is calling,' Joyce said, unnecessarily, because when Mom's best pal, Dot Wiggins, opened her mouth to shout, the whole street could always hear her. And they could see Dot's dark-haired, rangy figure waving her arms at them from their front door.

'Gotta go!' Em called to her friends. 'C'mon, Joycie.'

They dashed along past other women in the street who were settled on their front steps or on broken-backed chairs, gossiping and peeling spuds or shelling peas into their aprons, escaping the heat of all the cooking ranges blasting away indoors.

'She 'aving it?' one of them yelled down to Dot Wiggins.

'Looks like it!'

'Rather 'er than me!' A ripple of sympathetic laughter ran along the street.

Em ran into number eighteen Kenilworth

12

Street, still clutching Joyce's hand. It was dark inside after the bright outdoors, but already Em could hear her mother's gasps of pain. Cynthia was leaning over the table.

'That's it, Cynth – keep going, you're all right,' Dot encouraged her confidently. Dot had three kids of her own and was a widow. She was strong and stringy, a workhorse of a woman because she'd had to be.

'Oh, Lord God!' Cynthia Brown cried as the worst of it passed. 'Go and get Mrs Hibbert from number thirty-six, Em. Hurry up!'

'I'll stay with yer mom and get things ready,' Dot said. 'Go on, bab – do as your mother says!'

'Are you having the babby?' Em asked, excited but scared as well.

'*Yes* – go *on!*'

Em dashed out, Joyce hurrying along behind. She could tell Mom was in a bad state because she didn't say 'Where's Sid?' or 'I don't want to see you playing with that Molly Fox – she's common.' Mom hadn't seen that Molly Fox had been hanging around them as usual, always trying to join in. And she was the one who had some chalk so they'd had to let her play. Otherwise they'd have had to scrape out a grid with any old stone, or an old bit of slate off a roof. Molly had most likely nicked the chalk from somewhere, Em thought. The whole family were known to be light-fingered. Mom also didn't know that Em's six-year-old brother Sid was at this moment kicking a pig's-bladder football with Molly's brother Bert, who was nine. If she'd known she'd have been after him. Bert was a truly nasty piece

13

of work.

Mrs Hibbert lived in a little cottage next to the timber yard, a noisy place because of all the sawing and banging. But the sweet smell of sawdust which floated along that part of the street helped cover up the stench of drains, the manure in the horse road and miskins full of maggoty refuse festering in the summer heat.

There was a straggling pot of parched lobelia outside the door of Mrs Hibbert's. In too much of a panic to be shy, Em flung herself at the door knocker, then she and Joyce retreated. Mom always said it was rude to stand too close to the door when someone was opening it.

In a moment the rounded figure and kindly face of Mrs Hibbert appeared. She was a woman in her mid-forties, very plump and rosy-cheeked, her mousy hair escaping from its bun in curling strands.

'Please, Mrs Hibbert – our mom said to come,' Em gasped.

Mrs Hibbert took one look at Em and Joycie with their pudding-basin haircuts and grubby gingham frocks and gave a broad smile.

'So it's you two, is it? And your mother's come on with the pains, has she, bab? Lucky you came now, I was about to go out. But I'm ready.' She picked up her bag and they all hurried along. 'Goodness, I remember bringing all of you into the world. How old are you now, Emma?'

'Eight,' Em panted, thinking how calm Mrs Hibbert was.

'Eight already. Well, fancy that.'

Cynthia Brown clutched at the edges of the stained oilcloth on the table, bracing herself as another racking pain tore through her abdomen. She always tried to be respectable, but she couldn't help crying out as each contraction reached its climax, burned through her, then receded again, and she heard Dot's reassuring voice telling her it was going to be all right as she filled the kettle, tidied and set things ready for the midwife.

Dot, nine years older than Cynthia, had lost her beloved Charlie in 1916, and had been left struggling to bring up her twin boys and then little Nancy. Cynthia could remember the times when Dot was up before dawn to go out cleaning, taking on work in factories, carding buttons or hooks and eyes at home as well as taking in washing, often doing several jobs at once to make ends meet. Now her boys, David and Terry, were old enough to work so things were so much easier. But Dot had always had more energy than anyone else Cynthia knew. In an already poor district, where the Depression was biting hard, so many others around them were barely keeping their heads above water. Of course, Cynthia and Bob had given Dot help over the years, plenty of it. They'd always been in each other's pockets. And it was such a comfort to have Dot there now. She was like a sister and friend in one. There wasn't anyone else except her real sister, Olive, two years younger, and they'd never been close. Olive was far too hard-faced and tied up with her own life, even though she didn't have any children of her own.

'Dear God, I feel weary!' Cynthia said, sinking down onto a chair between one pain and another.

'Well, you overdid it this morning – didn't I warn yer?' Dot reproached, turning to look at her friend.

Cynthia nodded, cupping her chin wearily in her hands. 'I couldn't seem to help it!'

All morning she'd been hot and scratchy, frantic to get everything done before the baby arrived: clean cupboards and stove the upstairs. The house still stank of disinfectant and of the sulphur she'd burned to chase out the bugs. She'd worked like a Trojan, setting everything right, like a bird building a nest.

Come dinner time, she gave the kids their piece of bread and margarine and a wafer of cheese each before they scurried off into the sunshine again. Then she'd come over all funny and the pains had started. She should have rested, she knew. Bob was forever telling her to rest. She didn't want to go the way of her own mother, did she, her heart giving out on her at thirty-one? Cynthia had been only five then. Sometimes she broke her heart over it, the way her mother had never lived to see her grandchildren – or even much of her children for that matter. Nothing had been right after that, not for years. Until she met Bob, and life began again, and love.

It was so hot. Sweat collected between her breasts and under her arms. Flies were buzzing dreamily round the sticky fly paper hanging in the middle of the room as if they were too lazy to decide to land on it.

'I didn't feel this done in when I started with

16

the other three,' she murmured. 'God, I hope I'll have the strength to push it out!'

'Oh, nature'll take her course like she always does,' Dot said.

'Bob wants another boy – start a football team...'

'Well, he'll have to take what comes,' Dot said with a chuckle, leaning over her to wipe the table.

Cynthia grasped her wrist suddenly. 'I'm so frightened, Dot.'

'Eh – what's up, bab?' Dot said, startled. She gave Cynthia's hand a squeeze. 'You'll be all right – you've done it all before! You'll just be a couple more teeth short, that's all!' Dot gave a grin which revealed several gaps at the side of her mouth.

But Cynthia was deadly serious. 'What if there's summat wrong with the babby?' She struggled to put into words the fears that had flapped in her head all morning like ugly black birds. 'What if...'

But the next wave of pain start to swell in her.

What if she gave birth to a monster, like that lad down the park who walked like an ape and could not speak, who was fifteen and still in napkins? Or what if Bob was taken bad? If they couldn't feed the children? That Mrs Brand in Rupert Street gassed herself after her husband left her...

Then she let out a cry of pain so sharp that she didn't hear the midwife knocking on the door.

'Oh dear, it's like that, is it!' Mrs Hibbert said cheerfully as she entered the room to find Cynthia braced and panting over the table. 'It's all right, dear. Soon be over now. I'll look after you. Oh and look at you,' she said to Dot. 'You've already got the water on the boil! Bless you, Mrs Wiggins – we can always count on you!'

As the pain receded, Cynthia smiled weakly, her brown eyes softening with relief at the sight of Nancy Hibbert.

'Thank God you're here...'

'Oh, I'm here. Always turn up like a bad penny, me!'

Then Cynthia caught sight of Em and Joyce watching timidly from the door.

'There's a halfpenny or two.' She pointed to a jug on the mantel. 'You go and get some sweets. Oh – and my ticket's in there. Go to Mrs Larkin.'

Em ran to the old cracked jug which, as well as the pawn ticket, held some coppers, a few old nails and a couple of feathers. She pocketed the pawn ticket and the coins before Cynthia could change her mind. 'Ta, Mom. I'll get the bundle and I'll get a gobstopper for Sid an' all.'

She and Joyce fled the dark house, glad to be back out in the sun and away from the disturbing events going on in there. She could just about remember when Joyce was born, but a baby arriving was a new experience for Joyce.

'Why's Mom looking all queer?' she asked as they hurried along the street to the sweet shop.

'The babby'll be born soon,' Em told her, importantly. 'After we've ate our sweets. Come on, let's be birds!'

They held out their arms and began their flight along the street, swooping from side to side like the pigeons that flapped lazily between rooftops. Had they been real birds they might have looked down on themselves, two slight girls in cotton frocks running along the grimy street of a poor quarter of town, amid a densely packed ward of other such streets where houses and works and foundries shouldered up against the railway goods yard to the north. Looming over the wider neighbourhood were the fat gasometers of the Windsor Street gas and coking works. To Em and Joyce these were 'Dad's works', from where he arrived home after a day shovelling coal off the canal boats to feed the roaring, sulphurous maw of the furnaces. In the distance rose the majestic towers of the 'Princes' power station, known as such because the Prince of Wales had come to open it in 1923, since when it had created a permanent haze above their heads unless the wind blew hard enough to chase away the clouds. If they scanned far enough they might have picked out the spire of St Martin's Church, just a few miles away in the heart of Birmingham, and, winding through the district like a tarnished silver strip, they would have seen segments of canal. This dark artery sidled under bridges and into factory loops, appearing along the sides of the goods yard and works turning out anything from buttons and machine tools to pistols and parts for bicycles. As little girls instead of birds, they could see only the street, the familiar pavement world of school and shops and neighbours, and the nooks which were the favoured backdrop to their games, the narrow entries, coal cellars and back yards.

They fluttered along to Mrs Larkin's to retrieve the week's little bundle of clothes. Her cramped shop was in the front room of her house, and stank of moth balls and the frowsty old clothes which were folded on shelves at the back. Cynthia, like most of the women in a district where wages were low or non-existent, pawned every week to make ends meet: Bob's Sunday jacket and anything else they could spare. Bob's pay from the gas works was far from enough to feed a growing family. Mrs Larkin, a thin, hard-faced crone with loose-fitting false teeth, surrendered the bundle to them with her usual resentful muttering, her teeth clacking like castanets.

Then it was time for the sweet shop and the Miss Prices, twin sisters both dressed in black, their grey hair Marcel-waved in just the same length and style. The only way you could tell them apart was that one was slightly taller and had a dark brown mole on her cheek to the left of her mouth. Em and Joyce soon forgot everything that was going on at home when surrounded by jars of sherbet lemons, strawberry bonbons, chocolate limes and troach drops.

Em picked out a giant gobstopper for Sid, and decided that since he wasn't doing anything else to help, that would do for him. She and Joyce spent ages deliberating over sherbet dips and liquorice and toffee, while the Miss Prices smiled like benign gargoyles. In the end Em chose her favourite: a fistful of liquorice laces.

'Made your choice, have you?' Miss-Price-with-the-mole said, taking the pennies to the big till.

'Yes, ta,' Em said politely. She had been brought up to be respectful to adults and do as she was told.

'I s'pect our mom's had the babby by now,' Joyce said once they were outside, sticking her finger into her little twist of yellow kali. She transferred it rapturously to her mouth.

Em grinned, sucking the sweet liquorice from round her teeth. 'Let's go back and play hopscotch!'

They skipped back along the road, full of the joys. It was the holidays, the sun was shining, they had long, free days to play and their dad had promised that this weekend he would show them how to make a kite. To crown it all, Mom was about to give them a new brother or sister and Em, the big sister, had taught Joycie to play hopscotch. What could be better?

Two

'Christ Almighty, woman – how much longer's this going on?'

Bob Brown crouched like a coiled spring at the edge of his chair beside the range, sleeves rolled up his thick, muscular arms, the remains of a cigarette nipped between finger and thumb. On the floor between his feet a saucer contained the blackened remains of many more, and near it what had been a full jug of ale.

This was not a quick birth. It was almost dark, and still the agony was going on and on.

'I can't tell yer how long, I'm afraid,' Mrs Hibbert said. Each time she came down she looked more exhausted; there was a sheen of sweat on her skin and her soft curls now hung straight and lank. She went to the scullery for a cup of water and drank thirstily, then came in to speak to him again, resting the blue and white cup against her hot cheek. 'She's having it hard this time. You can't hurry Mother Nature.'

'Well, she's a brute!' Bob sprang to his feet. He was a broad-shouldered man, hardened to physical labour, with wavy brown hair and a gentle, large-featured face, his wide mouth tending towards a smile. He was good natured and popular in the district, but now his blue eyes, so often full of twinkling laughter, were flinty from the tension of waiting.

'It shouldn't have to be like this.' In his powerlessness he ranted at the very source of life. 'My poor Cynth. If I could do it for her!'

He sank back down, wiping his forehead and patting his breast pocket in search of another cigarette. There was nothing to be done. Another thin wail came from upstairs.

'Will 'er be all right?' His voice was pleading.

'I hope so, bab,' Mrs Hibbert replied. 'She's a strong'un, but she's taking it hard this time. I must go back to her. You keep those kettles on the boil.'

Em, Sid and Joyce had all come in as the hot day faded, and sat at the table, their frightened gaze turning to the ceiling at every sound from upstairs. Dot, calling in to see how things were progressing, had taken them all next door once they'd had their tea.

'No need for them all to sit listening,' Dot said quietly to Bob. 'I'll have them round at mine. Come on, little'uns, you can go up the wooden hill in my house tonight!' They went eagerly, the girls excited about bunking up with Nancy, who was the same age as Joyce. And when they woke up the next morning, Dot told them, there'd be a new brother or sister.

Bob took out the last Woodbine from the packet, which he chucked into the fire. It might be the last but he bloody needed it. He sat hunched into the little lead fireplace, arms resting on his knees, so tightly wound up he could never have sat back and relaxed.

He breathed in a lungful of smoke, let it out, clouding the air with it. It seemed strange and quiet without the kids about. Cheeky little bleeders, he thought fondly. Specially that Joycie. Something about her made him feel fiercely protective. She was like a tiny version of her mother and Cynthia made him feel protective too, always had. He'd lit the fire in the bare front room to keep out of Mrs Hibbert's way and be further from the noise of birthing. There was just the chair, a stool, and a peg rug by the grate. Cynthia liked the idea of a front room, but they couldn't afford to furnish it. Mostly they lived round the range at the back.

Another long groan came from upstairs and Bob winced, shaking his head. He couldn't bear her distress and forced himself to look on the bright side.

'God, when will it be over?' He addressed the question to the wide, sweet face of the woman looking down at him from a frame on the mantelpiece, with a shawl softly arranged round her shoulders. It was the only trace he had of his mother, who died when he was a boy. She seemed to look down reassuringly at him. Soon it would be over and Cynthia was having their fourth child. It was marvellous, course it was, even with the daily struggle to make ends meet. It seemed like a miracle to him, that he had this life and family after the start he'd had, he and his brothers left to grow up in the Boys' Home, where they were nothing to anyone. He looked up at the other precious picture above his head, their wedding photograph. April 1922 they'd married, and Cynthia caught for Em almost straight away.

'Nine years,' Bob said to himself. 'Already!' What a picture she looked, in her pretty frock, flowers in her hair and her eyes twinkling out of the picture. And he beside her, hair slicked back, suit on and boots blacked, smiling at her as if he was about to burst with pride.

'That's my girl,' he murmured, reaching down to flick ash from his cigarette.

She was his missis and that was that. The sight of her still got him going, oh yes! Ever since the first time he'd laid eyes on her on the tram down on Nechells Park Road, he'd felt just the same. He'd seen those lively brown eyes peeping across at him from under her curling fringe, her sweet, shy smile. He couldn't help noticing her left hand, scarred by falling in the fire when she was an infant so that the skin was shiny and puckered. And she just seemed to call out to him, not with her voice or anything, she wasn't forward like that – quite prim and correct, in fact – but something of her, her body, the way she moved. As if he recognized her. His desire for her had never died.

And when there was a babby – Christ, she was lovely, milk coming from her, oh boy, that was bliss! It was life. He felt a strong pulse in his groin just thinking about it. Women were something, that they were, and she was his woman. Nothing better. The only things that came close were a win for the Villa and a pint of Ansells with his pals. But they didn't measure up the same, didn't touch it, not when you came down to it.

'Nothing like it.' He found himself speaking out loud again. 'Me and my missis and the kids, that's the thing, more the merrier.'

He looked up as Cynthia gave a cry which faded to a wail, and clenched his fists.

'That's it, wench, you can do it. That's my little woman!'

It was ten past four before Cynthia managed to push out the child. Bob heard the muffled cries of pain and gripped the arms of the chair until his knuckles almost cracked. When he heard the baby's dry wail he lay back in the chair and, to his bewilderment, felt panting sobs of relief rising in him.

'Thank Christ it's over!' he whispered. 'What a business. What a bloody terrible business.'

When he heard Mrs Hibbert coming downstairs, he hurriedly wiped his eyes with the back of his hands and stood up. Her face sagged with exhaustion.

'You've got another little wench.' He couldn't tell if the flatness of her tone was worry or just tiredness.

'Cynth?' He stepped forward.

'She's all right. Knocked out, of course, after all that. And the babby's very small. I don't know if...' She trailed off, sorrowfully.

He hesitated. 'Should I go to her?'

She stood back, smiling faintly. 'Go on, then.'

Em's rag doll with yellow hair and pink embroidered features on her grubby face was called Princess Lucy. Em had her tucked under her arm that morning as she led the others, creeping upstairs, to see their little sister, and they found their father sitting by the bed, the baby in his arms. Em's hand went to her mouth.

'Oh – she's *tiny!*'

'She is that,' Bob said, looking down at her with tired, yet excited eyes. 'She's had a tough time, her and your mother, but she's a fighter, you can see. But you've all got to look after your mom. She needs to get her strength back.' He loosed his arm for a moment and laid a hand on his wife's head.

Cynthia looked terribly pale and ill and had barely found the strength to smile as her three children came tiptoeing into the room. Even cheeky Sid, with his dark hair and prominent ears like his father's, looked overawed. Joyce crept close and touched the baby's cheek, very nervously at first as if she might bite. Bob laughed.

'You're all right, our Joycie. The babby won't hurt yer!'

Em propped Princess Lucy up nearby to watch, then had a turn at stroking the velvety little cheek with her finger. She was surprised how warm it felt, how much life seemed to be in this tiny creature. She felt like a friend already.

'Her name's Violet,' Bob said, 'after your mom's mother. Violet Ivy.'

The three of them all said, 'Violet', trying the name out on their tongues.

'Well,' Sid said disgustedly, after considering the squashed little face of the sleeping baby – yet another sister. 'She ain't going to be any good at playing football neither, is she?'

Three

'Are you coming to play out, Em?'

Katie O'Neill stood on the front step, a tall, skinny girl with soft black hair tied in plaits which swung almost to her waist. Her face was long and pale, her eyes deep blue and dancing, as if she was trying nervously to keep a watch on everything at once. When Em hesitated, she came back with, 'Don't you want to, then?'

'Yes, I do, only...'

Em glanced back into the house. It was a week since Violet's birth and Em was taking Bob's words very seriously: she was to look after Mom and the others. Cynthia was still knocked back by the birth. She lay in bed, with hardly the will to smile and her face was white and drawn. Em was doing all she could to help, but everything was quiet just now. Joyce and Sid were playing out the front and the baby was fast asleep on her soft white blanket in the drawer next to Mom's bed. Em, ever biddable, had felt very grown up being asked to help, but now it was the last week of the summer holidays and she craved being out with her friends. She just wanted Mom to be up and back to normal.

'S'pose I could – for a bit.'

'Can I see the babby again?'

'Not now – she's asleep in Mom's room.'

Katie had already had a glimpse of Violet on her second day in the world. She'd looked with big eyes into the tiny, puckered face and sighed, 'Oh you're so lucky, Em!' Katie didn't have any brothers or sisters. Her mom was a widow and Katie lived only with her and with her dead father's brother, Uncle Patrick, who, by all accounts, was odd and unpredictable.

'He's got the doolally-taps,' she'd heard Bob say when they mentioned him, and he usually rolled his eyes and tapped his temple when he said it even though he didn't speak unkindly. She never said anything, but Em knew this was why Katie never invited anyone home to her house. Mrs O'Neill lived in a front house, three rooms stacked one above another, back to back with a house on a yard, whereas Em's family had a two-up, two-down house, with a tap in the scullery, and there was a proper family life going on.

'My mom doesn't like visitors,' Katie said airily. 'She likes a bit of peace and quiet.' By now Em never gave it a thought. It was long taken for granted that if they were going to play out, Katie would call round. So she only ever saw Mrs O'Neill in the street, and she was a remote, cold-seeming woman.

Em had been delighted when the O'Neills

moved into the street a year ago and Katie came to Cromwell Street School. Two of Em's other friends had moved away and Katie arrived in time to fill the gap. Everyone wanted to be her friend. Katie was one of those girls who had a magnetic effect. She was pretty and commanding, as if surveying the world from a height, and when she picked her friends – and she was the one who picked, not the other way round – she lit on Em. Em felt honoured, and happy to be in Katie's orbit. Both of them were top of the class, they played out together and lately they had begun to go every week to the chapel round the corner where they were cadets in the Girls' Life Brigade. Em was proud as anything, going off in her uniform with Katie.

With a last glance behind her, she closed the door quietly and hurried thankfully along the street with Katie. She caught sight of Joyce's blue hair ribbon bouncing up and down among a group of other girls from the street, playing hopscotch again.

'Oh, I see old pongy-drawers is hanging round again,' Katie said spitefully, spotting Molly Fox at the edge of the group.

'I s'pect she's got chalk,' Em said. It was so much better if they could get hold of chalk, if someone had filched a bit from the classroom when the teacher had her back turned. But they hadn't been to school for weeks, so Molly couldn't have got it there. 'She says she's got a whole packet of it!'

'Bet she *stole* it,' Katie said, wrinkling her nose.

Molly was watching the two of them come along the road. She was a large-boned girl, with a head of thick, blonde hair, tied back today with a grubby yellow-rag ribbon that had seen better days. As usual, she was dressed up like a four-penny rabbit. Barely any of the girls in the street had ever possessed a new frock, but wore hand-me-downs or women's dresses cut down to size. Molly's frock, although not new and very grubby, was an odd, fancy item in red with frills on the bodice and sleeves trimmed with red ribbon. It was far too grown-up for her and made her look ridiculously over-dressed. It must have been a party dress from the Rag Market.

'You coming to play?' Molly boomed at them from afar. As soon as Em appeared she always made a beeline for her.

'Might be,' Em said, heart sinking. Molly was like her flaming shadow! She was forever sucking up to Em and Katie, offering them sweets, begging to tag along. Katie was downright nasty to her, but Em couldn't bring herself to be like that. Molly was smelly, it was true. There was always a stink of wee about her, and she drove you mad, always keeping on, trying to buy favour. But Em, who had always made friends easily, felt sorry for Molly because no one wanted her. And because of what she'd seen that one time she went to Molly's yard.

'You can come to my house,' Molly had said, hauling Em by the arm. They'd just come home from school, shortly after Molly's family had moved into the yard, a few months before Katie arrived. Molly had fixed on Em straight away, as she was one of the most popular, good-hearted girls in the class.

Em didn't want to go. For a start she was scared stiff of Molly's mom. Iris Fox was a huge, fierce woman who wore her black hair scraped up high in a bun on top of her head and always seemed on the point of bursting out of her dresses, especially over the bust line. Bob said she looked like a prizefighter and on top of that she had a voice like a foghorn. Cynthia was always warning her children off the place. The yard Molly lived on was just along the road, reached by a narrow entry which never saw the sun, and although she'd lived in the same street all her life, Em had never ventured into the yard until that day.

'You just keep out of there,' Cynthia had instructed. 'You'll catch summat – there's dirty people there.'

When she went along the entry, Em felt she was venturing somewhere foreign and forbidden. The walls oozed green slime and the yard, overshadowed by the high wall of the Cycle Finishing Works, was dark and smelly. Three of the six dwellings squeezed round it were built right up against the works' wall, and Molly lived in one of them, number four. Opposite her house was a wall on which dripped the tap shared by all the houses, none of which had running water. Nearby, a wavering plume of smoke rose from a heap of stinking rubbish which someone had tried to set fire to. A lamp in the middle of the yard had been knocked askew so that it looked as drunken as some of the yard's inhabitants, and there was a little building at the end called the brew house, which housed the copper for heating water for washing. Close by were three stinking

31

toilets, their doors left swinging open.

Molly dragged Em along the yard, and Em wrinkled her nose at the stench of the place. It was a drizzly day and Bert Fox, backside hanging out of his shorts as usual, was out in the yard messing with the mangle. When the girls went closer he showed them he was feeding worms between the rollers and flattening them. He came running at Em, thrusting a handful of writhing pink and grey worms into her face.

'There you go. These're for you!'

'Ugh!' Em thought she was going to gag and she nearly tripped over backwards trying to get away.

'Stupid, sissy *girls*,' Bert snarled viciously. He had his mother's bullish face and narrow, calculating eyes and Em loathed him. She just wanted to run out of the horrible yard, back to the friendly games of the street.

The house was one of the most cheerless places Em had ever seen. There was no covering of any sort on the bare floorboards or on the table and everything looked dirty and uncared for. On the table stood a milk bottle, with the dregs of black tea in it, a stale heel of bread and sugar and other spills all over the surface. The whole downstairs room – and there was only one room with a tiny scullery – was dominated by the presence of two old men, or at least they seemed old to Em, camped either side of the range on two tatty chairs. One of them, who had greasy, grizzled hair and mutton-chop whiskers, kept staring at her all the time over the bowl of his pipe, and the other, who had his back to Em, simply sat hunched, staring ahead of him as if there was no one else there. His hair was brown and thin, with a bald patch at the back, pale as an egg. Later she was to learn that the grizzle-haired man with the pipe and whiskers was Molly's grandfather, and the other was Molly's dad. He'd been shell-shocked in the war and couldn't do anything much now, his nerves had given way over the years.

As soon as they set foot inside, Iris bawled at them from upstairs.

'Molly – is that you? 'Bout bloody time!'

Her fury-fuelled tread was heard thudding down the twisting staircase. Em shrank inside at the sight of her, but Iris took no notice of Em at all; clutching a greyed sheet in front of her she went straight for Molly.

'What's this, then, yer dirty little bugger?'

She held out the offending article, with its unmistakable yellow stains.

'Come 'ere, yer filthy bleeder...' She grabbed Molly and shoved the urine-soaked sheet hard into her daughter's face.

'There, see how yer like that, yer little vermin!'

'Ow, Mom, gerroff!' Molly wailed. Iris had seized her by the back of the neck and she was struggling to get away, but to no avail.

'Gerroff be damned! What's that, then, eh? What did yer do – go on, tell us – what's them stains, eh?'

'It ain't nothing!' Molly cried, starting to sob.

Iris dealt her a ringing slap round the face.

'I'll give yer nothing! I said, what is it?'

Iris's viciousness made Em sick at heart. No one in her life had ever spoken to her like that.

'It's...' Molly whispered. 'I had a bit of an accident.'

'A bit of an accident!' Iris mocked. Then she shouted. 'You 'ave another "bit of an accident" and yer'll be out on yer ear on the bloody street to fend for yerself, d'you 'ear, yer dirty little bastard!'

'I never meant to. I couldn't help it.'

'Well, yer'd better start helping it. You're just as cowing bad as him!' Iris pointed disgustedly at the old man, who was leering at all of them through clouds of pipe smoke. 'And I ain't fetching and carrying for the lot of yer. Now take this and go and wring it out!'

She hurled the sheet at Molly, whose round face was crumpled into lines of utter misery. The pungent stink of Molly's sheet reached Em's nostrils and she just wanted to run back home. She was relieved that Iris didn't even seem to have noticed she was there.

'Come on, Em,' Molly said. She went to the scullery and picked up a bucket.

As they went, Em heard the old man say in a wheedling voice, 'Make us a nice cuppa tea, Iris, there's a girl.'

To Em's surprise, as soon as she and Molly got out into the yard, Molly's demeanour changed immediately. All her lip-trembling misery dissappeared and she went back to normal, as if what had just happened in the house was nothing and she had forgotten it.

'Come on – I'll 'ave to get this hung out and then we can play summat,' she said.

But after that, Em hadn't been in the mood for playing anything.

Just as the girls got ready for their game of hopscotch, a raucous burst of laughter broke out in the horse road. A group of lads ran out from the entry to another yard, led by Molly's brother Bert, who was making a loud show of guffawing mockingly at another lad. The boy, a sad little orphaned lad called Johnny, was bent over, a desperate, mortified expression on his face.

'Look at him, the dirty sod!' Bert Fox blared, making sure the whole street could hear. He made his finger and thumb into a peg for his nose. 'He's just gone and crapped 'isself! Stand back, everyone!'

The boy's thin face crumpled and he started to snivel.

'I never,' he sobbed brokenly. 'They was hurting me... I never...' He hobbled off along the street, in obvious discomfort at his rear end, with Bert's taunts raining down on him like stones.

'He's vile, that Bert,' Em whispered to Katie. She felt sorry for poor little Johnny, but she knew better than to challenge Bert, who was as vicious a bully as his mother.

'You coming to play?' Molly was by them now. 'I've got chalk, look.'

From inside the elastic of her knicker leg she produced several broken, but otherwise presentable-looking bits of chalk.

'Don't know,' Em snapped. She felt like punishing Molly for the cruelty she'd just seen in her brother, even though she knew it wasn't Molly's fault.

She did join in, of course. It was too much fun

to resist, and soon she and Katie were caught up in the game with Molly and Joyce and the others, trying to put the bullying they had seen out of their minds.

They'd not been playing long, though, when she saw Bob advancing along the street towards them on his way home from work, black from head to foot, his jacket slung over one shoulder. She saw the weariness in his face, but catching sight of her, he waved and smiled.

'Dad!'

She and Joycie ran to him, proud to be seen out with him. They knew he was seen as one of the best dads in the neighbourhood.

'Can we make that kite tomorrow?' Em asked. It had all been put off because of the baby.

'I don't know, wench,' Bob said. Close up she saw the coal dust caught in the creases of his face. 'Look, Em – you'd better come in now. Your mother's not well and I'll need your help.'

Sorry to leave the game, but feeling important because of this summons, Em went with him. He took her hand, and she felt safe with him tall and strong beside her.

'I don't know why your mom's not picking up better,' he said, and now he sounded sad. 'It's never been as bad as this before, but we'll have to muck in and help. I can count on you, can't I, Em?'

She nodded as hard as she could. 'Yes, Dad. Course you can.'

He raised a smile and a wink. 'Good kid.'

Hide and Seek

Four

Cynthia did not know how long she had been sitting on the edge of the bed, staring out at the hazy sky. At last she rocked forward, covering her face with her hands. Her lips moved but only the faintest sound issued between them.

'Dear God ... help me...'

Outwardly she appeared recovered from the baby's birth. The pallor had gone from her cheeks and she had washed her hair, which was hanging loose in pretty chestnut curls. The strap of her white nightdress had slipped to reveal her strong shoulder and more than a hint of a breast swollen with milk. She looked a healthy young woman, sitting in a shaft of sunlight on the rumpled bed, her baby daughter asleep at her feet in the bottom drawer of the bedroom chest which just fitted in at the end of the bed.

But the lifeless look of despair in her eyes told a different story.

Violet was now a fortnight old, and though only just over five pounds at birth, was feeding well and thriving. She lay pink-cheeked and sated with a ragged piece of sheet over her, oblivious to her mother's desperation.

Bob had already gone to work. Em and Sid were back at school. But Cynthia could not seem to move, as if her limbs had been filled with wet sand.

'You'll be back to normal soon,' Bob kept

saying, cheerily. 'You know you sometimes feel a bit down after a babby, just for a few days.'

And she would nod at him in a vague way, trying to wrench her lips into a smile, to make him feel better. She didn't feel as if she'd ever be all right again, as if she'd been locked into this dark, despairing place and someone had thrown away the key. No one could reach her nor she them. It was blackness far worse than the 'blue' days she had known before. She felt utterly cut off from everyone.

It was only then that she saw it was a nice day and thought to open the window and let in the warm air, but she just couldn't find the will to budge from the bed. She ought to be heating up the copper in the scullery so that by mid-morning she would have a line of clean washing drying in the balmy September breeze. But what would have been normal routine before now felt an impossible task. All she wanted was to lie down and slip back into oblivion, away from everything. Just sleep and more sleep. That was all she could manage.

Nothing felt the same. Until now she had loved this simple room where she and Bob slept each night. They couldn't afford much; the floorboards were bare and there was nothing but the bedstead and an old chest of drawers and a chair, but it was theirs, and cosy with the colourful patchwork quilt she had stitched in preparation for marriage. They were not living on a yard, they'd not sunk that low. Now, though, everything had changed in her eyes. Even in the sunlight the room looked poor and mean, the quilt tatty, the floorboards wormed and rough. The grime on the windows blown from countless chimneys around them, and the endless battle with bugs and vermin, oppressed her. Everything screamed of tasks undone and it was all more than she could manage. And the child... Her eyes filled with tears as she looked down at Violet, so sweet and pretty with her down of soft, brown hair.

'I don't want you,' she whispered. Hearing her own words, she was horrified that she should say such a thing out loud. 'You're too much. I can't look after you. I'm no good as a mother, no good to anyone. Someone should take you away...'

For a moment she imagined pressing something over Violet's innocent face: so quiet it would be, stopping her breathing, no more noise, no more crying. She could sleep, just sleep... Her hand even strayed to the pillow, as if daring herself, then she pulled back with a sharp gasp, starting to tremble all over. God in heaven, what had she come to? A child murderer?

She was about to give way to the desperate tears that seemed to well up so often when she tensed, hearing cautious footsteps on the stairs. Joyce came tiptoeing in, then, seeing her mom sitting up, relaxed and ran excitedly towards her.

'I been sitting quiet in my room like Dad told me but you're awake now! Can I help with the babby?'

Joyce looked so sweet in her gigantic frock, some of her hair caught up and tied with a strip of rag into a little topknot. Em must have done it before she went to school. She had her shoes on, little T-bars, and her face shone with eagerness, but Cynthia found that the child's presence filled

41

her with overwhelming panic. Joyce's energy was too much for her, her sheer vitality seemed to drink Cynthia dry. She stared at her little girl and said, 'Oh Joycie, look at you, your ribbon's filthy and your shoes are all scuffs.' Her dress had dried porridge spilled down the front, and at the sight of all this Cynthia dissolved into tears.

'What's the matter, Mom?' Joyce asked, eyes wide with alarm.

Cynthia felt like two different people in one. Her real self that wanted to be kind, to let Joycie help her, had been locked away somewhere. The witch she had become snarled at her, full of irritation.

'Just go on downstairs, Joycie. I can't be doing with all yer noise up here. You'll wake the babby and I need to get myself dressed.'

Joyce put her hands behind her back and swung herself from side to side for a moment, her face pulled into a hurt, angry pout. She was trying to decide whether to argue but she didn't dare say anything. All excitement wiped away, she sidled off towards the stairs again.

'Go and see Nance,' Cynthia called after her. 'Just go and play. Or go and see Mrs Button. She might have a cake for you.'

There was no reply. She heard Joyce pause half-way down the stairs and stand kicking her feet resentfully against the wall, until Cynthia thought she'd stream.

'I said go down, will you!' she yelled. 'For heaven's sake, let me be!'

As Joyce thumped furiously down the rest of the stairs, Cynthia fell sideways on the bed, sobbing her heart out.

'If only I could sleep, I'd feel better.' It wasn't just the baby waking her. She felt so wound up all the time she just couldn't settle, and she'd lost her appetite and could hardly get anything down her, despite Bob saying, 'You need to keep your strength up, what with feeding and that. Come on, love, try a bit more.' But she felt queasy and the smell of food repelled her.

Once again she found herself just lying there for she didn't know how long. Time swam by, her thoughts turning like a cruel wheel. She found herself dwelling on things long in the past, on those weeks only a few months after Mom died. Her father, desperate for someone to care for his three children, Geoff, herself and Olive, had brought Mary Jones to live with them, saying she was going to be their new mother.

She'd never liked Mary, not even for a second. And with her came three sons, all older than Cynthia. Percy and Joe were thirteen and eleven, and Albert nine. She squeezed her eyes tightly shut, trying to block out the memory of when they'd arrived with their gross habits. Mary Jones was never much of a housekeeper, and the boys! Cynthia recoiled at the thought. Their loud, battering voices, the crude teasing, the skeins of snot and all the smells that came with them had filled her with the deepest loathing. They had bullied Geoff, her sweet-natured brother. And it was Albert's fault she had burned her hand. One day he was clowning around in the back room, in a space far too small. His teasing always had a threat in it and he grabbed Cynthia and started to swing her round and round by her hands, too fast, while she shrieked at him to let go. Suddenly she was whirling across the room, unable to stop, and broke her fall by plunging her hand into the grate.

Mary Jones, a small, mean woman, had come running at her screams.

'What in hell's name are you doing, you stupid girl?' She dragged Cynthia back from the fire and slapped her cheek for the racket, before realizing that her screams of agony were rooted in a genuine, terrible injury. She dressed Cynthia's hand but she never said a word of reproach to Albert.

Those years of misery and fear, feeling so helpless with her mother gone, a father who didn't care and the rough slovenliness of Mary Jones, all came back to haunt her. She had always tried so hard never to think of it, but now it all welled up, raw and agonizing, however hard she tried to push the memories away. All she had wanted was a place that was safe and clean and loving. All! That had been everything she yearned for!

As soon as she was old enough, Cynthia had got a job at a button factory on the edge of the Italian quarter in Duddesdon and moved into a bug-infested room. Anything was better than living with Mary Jones. Eventually, that day on the tram when she was eighteen and she had seen Bob's dancing eyes fixed on her, and she'd looked back into his generous, open face, life had begun in earnest, with someone to love her.

They'd been so happy, in their cosy little house, making a family. Cynthia knew Bob was proud of her and relied on her. She loved the way he called her 'my girl' even now, or 'my wench', to tease her.

'Girl sounds better,' she'd say archly. 'Wench is common.'

'Oh, you're not common,' Bob might say, sidling up to kiss her, then pinch her bottom, making her squeal with laughter. 'You're queen of the household, that's what you are, missis.'

Who was that person who could laugh, she wondered now, remembering all her happiness with him. And she'd had Dot to share everything with. Everyone respected Dot for managing the way she had after Charlie was killed without ever once turning to the parish. Dot had always been a staunch friend. Together, they'd been two of the most energetic and capable mothers in the street. She certainly didn't feel up to much these days.

'Oh, Bob, I'm sorry,' she whispered, pressing her face against the pillow. 'I don't know what's the matter with me.' She was letting him down, letting Dot and all of them down. The way she felt now, they'd all be better off without her.

Five

'Emma Brown!' *Thwack!*

A sharp slap across the side of her head forced out a whimper between Em's lips.

'What d'you think you're doing?' Miss Lineham towered over her. She was a young teacher, with pale, washed-out looks and a very strict, spiteful personality. 'All this time and there's nothing on your slate. Stop biting your nails, it's

45

a disgusting habit. I don't know what's come over you this term.'

The class all watched in amazement. It was almost unheard of for Emma Brown to get a telling-off.

They'd been back at school a week. The heavy, metal-framed wooden desks were arranged in lines, two children at each, and Em and Katie were seated side by side. In front of every pupil lay a slate and on the blackboard was a set of subtraction sums. The sound of the squeak of pencils on the slates filled the room as the children attempted the calculations.

Em and Katie had walked to school together, down Kenilworth Street and along to the big red-brick school which crouched there waiting for them. The doors which had been locked all summer were flung open now. Across the road was the big goods yard next to Windsor Street Wharf and behind, belching out steam, the power station. School did not normally hold too much fear for Em and Katie, as they were able girls and most people wanted to be their friends.

Em's cheeks burned and tears stung her eyes at Miss Lineham's attack on her. She wasn't used to being in trouble. She had always tried her best at school, but today she couldn't keep her mind on anything, was barely conscious of the classroom's panelled walls, the wilting aspidistra in its pot on a little table at the side or the vase of pinks on the teacher's desk. She sat dreamily chewing away at her nails.

'You'd better get working or it'll be the cane for you!' Miss Lineham threatened.

Hurriedly Em took up her slate pencil and started to copy a sum from the board. Katie nudged her in sympathy but Em ignored it. Out of the corner of her eye she saw Molly Fox glance round and mouth something at her when Miss Lineham's back was turned. There was an odd number of children in the class and Molly was the only one sitting at a double desk on her own as no one wanted to sit with her. Em felt her cheeks go even redder. She didn't want Molly's sympathy either.

A while later her left hand automatically strayed back to her mouth and she was nibbling at her nails again. She pulled her hand away and stared at them; they looked raw and ugly now she had bitten them down to the quicks. How did that happen? She never used to bite them.

Lost in her own thoughts, she didn't notice Miss Lineham approaching until another cuff across the head slammed her back to the present.

'What did I tell you? Go and stand by my desk!'

Miss Lineham followed her up to the front, frowning in anger. Em felt her legs turn to jelly as the teacher picked up the thin cane which lay across her desk.

'Hold out your hand.'

Em obeyed, reluctantly, trying to be brave, but she was already trembling with fear and hurt pride and it took her all her will power to keep the hand there as Miss Lineham whisked the cane through the air and delivered six stinging lashes with it to Em's palm.

'Now you can stand there until I tell you to move, d'you hear?'

'Yes, Miss,' Em said, so close to tears she had to swallow hard to keep them back. She clenched her smarting hand and nursed it under her other arm. Her head was throbbing from Miss Lineham's slaps and she felt the eyes of the whole class fixed on her. Many, she knew, would be on her side, but others would be enjoying seeing her brought down a peg. She didn't look at anyone, but stared down at her slate through her swimming eyes.

Out in the playground at break time, Katie was at her side immediately.

'Bad luck!' Em wasn't sure if she imagined the smug edge to Katie's voice. 'She was after *you* this morning, wasn't she?'

Em shrugged, still trying not to cry. Everything was changing too fast and she didn't understand what was going on. This wasn't meant to happen, not to her – Emma Brown getting the cane! Nothing felt right at home, with Mom still so quiet and strange. It all felt wrong, and even the new baby seemed like an intruder now, because, lovely as she was, she was the one who'd made Mom poorly. Em just wanted her to be back how she usually was when they got home from school, standing on the step canting to Dot, or cooking tea, singing 'Cherry Ripe' or 'Down Yonder Green Valley', songs she'd learned at school, while she bustled about the kitchen, shooing Sid and Joyce out from under her feet. Now she was always upstairs having a lie-down and the house felt silent and deserted, as if Violet had stolen their mom.

'Oh-oh.' Katie nudged her. 'Here comes old smelly.'

Molly hove into view, in a grey frock which was too big for her, her thick hair scraped back untidily into a bunch. They saw one of the others shout a nasty remark at her, and Molly scowled and retorted in kind.

Em waited for Molly to say something irritating in her sucking-up way but, to her surprise, she said matter-of-factly, 'That Miss Lineham's a cow. You don't want to take no notice of her. Bet yer hand's smarting, ain't it?'

Em nodded miserably.

'Here, what you wunna do is go and put it on the railings – they're nice and cold,' Molly said.

'Who asked you, then?' Katie said with a sneer, but Em could see that Molly meant well. She tried it, reluctantly, but she found Molly was right. Even though they were a bit rusty, the iron struts felt cool and soothing against her stinging flesh.

'Bet that feels better, eh?' Molly spoke in a motherly way, very pleased with herself for having been able to show Em something. She was used to dealing with canings. 'D'you wunna play statues?'

Em looked at Katie, who rolled her eyes and said, '*No!*'

But Em was grateful to Molly. 'Go on, then,' she said.

On the way home Em thought: Let our Mom be all right, let her be up and making tea for us.

She was with Katie, and Molly, who was now determinedly glued to their side.

'I've got three 'alfpence,' Molly boasted. 'Let's

49

go to Prices' and I'll get yer some rocks. Yer can have an 'alfpenny each.'

It was too good an offer to resist, even for Katie, and soon they were in the Price sisters' palace of sugar and Em chose her usual favourite of liquorice laces. The sweet taste was a comfort.

'Ta, Molly,' she said, and Katie grudgingly said thanks too, sucking on her sweets.

'You playing out after tea?' Molly wanted to know.

'Dunno,' Em said. 'Our dad said he'd make us a kite.'

The envy was naked on Molly's face. 'Oh,' she said. 'Can I come and watch?'

'Dunno,' Em said evasively. 'I'd have to ask our mom.'

It was true about the kite. Bob had been promising and now that it was Friday he said he'd make the kite and they'd have a proper day out tomorrow while the weather was still fine, right up to the Lickey Hills or somewhere, and fly it. That was a big outing and they were all excited. Em had only ever been to the Lickeys once before.

But would Mom be well enough? Parting with Katie and Molly she went home, still tasting the last of the liquorice in her mouth. Nervously she pushed the door open. Yesterday when she got home, she'd found Joyce looking very down in the mouth, Mom upstairs, no dinner on. But tonight, relief flooded through her. Mom was downstairs and there was a delicious smell which made her mouth water!

Sid was already home. She was supposed to look out for him but he always ran off with his mates and as the school was so near it didn't matter. He and Joyce were waiting at the table. Cynthia, with Violet resting in one arm, was beside them.

'Our mom's got us fish and chips!' Joyce yelled importantly as soon as Em appeared.

And Mom was up and about, even though she looked pale, and she tried to smile as Em came in.

'Come and have your tea now,' Cynthia ordered Em. 'Get your hands washed. I've got some kept warm for your dad when he comes in.'

They all sat round the table and Em felt something give inside her, as if her emotions had all been twisted up like tangled wool and they'd suddenly been released. Things felt right, back to normal and life was good. The kids ate their bit of fish and chips out of the newspaper, the air tangy with vinegar, and when Bob came in from work his face lit up at the sight of all the family round the table. Em saw how relieved he was too.

'Well!' Bob said. 'This looks like a celebration!' He rolled up his sleeves and went to wash his hands and face in the scullery.

'Can we make the kite, Dad?' Sid boomed, jumping up and down on his chair.

'Let your dad get his tea down him before you start on him,' Cynthia said.

'Steady on, son, or that chair'll be matchwood,' Bob said, emerging, wiping his face.

He went to Cynthia, smiling at the sight of Violet plugged in at her breast and feeding contentedly.

'You all right, love? Had summat to eat yourself?'

51

'Yes, ta, I've had all I want – the rest's for you,' Cynthia said.

Em frowned for a moment. She hadn't seen Mom eat any of the fish and chips, had she? Maybe she'd had some before they got home.

They spent an absorbing evening watching Bob carefully make a little kite out of thin strips of plywood, a frame onto which he glued thick paper. The smell of glue soon filled the room. It was a blue kite and he knotted on a thin string as a tail with little bits of coloured paper along it.

'Can we fly it now?' Joyce said, wriggling with anticipation.

'No, it needs to dry,' Bob said. 'And d'you need a wee-wee, Joycie?'

Joyce shook her head vigorously. She wasn't going out back to the privy and missing the fun!

'Now, don't touch it or it'll break.' Bob twinkled at his eager children. 'I'll put it above the stove and if it's a nice day we'll all go out and fly it tomorrow.'

The four of them were so caught up in the excitement of the kite that they didn't see Cynthia, sitting over on the other side of the room, very still. The supreme effort she'd made to be there for her family when they came home, to get back to normal, had taken every ounce of her strength. Now, in the half dark, her face was a blank mask of despair.

Six

Molly lay in bed that night, the smelly blanket pulled up to her chin, for once thinking back happily on her day. The look of gratitude on Em's face as Molly had soothed the burns from the cane against the cool railings had made it one of the best days she could remember. She had done something for Em, and Em had looked pleased and grateful!

Looking up into the darkness she wove dreams about being Em's friend, how Em and Katie would invite her into all their games without begrudging it or rolling their eyes when she came near. Maybe she could even share a desk with Em instead of sitting on her own. But Em was always with Katie O'Neill, the stuck-up little bitch, wrinkling her nose whenever Molly came near. Molly knew the nicknames the others called her – Moll the Pong, Yellow Drawers, Wee Wee Molly... She tried not to notice. Every day she tried to join in, hanging around her classmates and trying to make them like her, until their ganging up and name-calling got too much and she burst out in a temper and yelled at them all. But today Em had smiled at her – actually smiled!

Her reverie was shattered by the sound of the springs of the other bed creaking, and she tensed with dread. Not tonight... Oh please, not tonight... Molly felt the terrible pulse between her legs, a reflex. She clenched herself, pressing her hand over her private parts to stop it. She couldn't get out and sit on the bucket now! He was coming, in his thick socks, round the bed, shuffle, shuffle.

Mom had divided the room with a curtain, tied up between two nails. There were only two upstairs rooms in the house and she had to share with *them*.

'There,' Iris had said with one of her odd, cruel laughs. 'There's your room now – you've got a wall between yer!'

Molly's metal bedstead was tucked in close to the window. On the other side of the curtain, in the big bed, her brother Bert slept top to tail with her grandfather, William Rathbone: Iris's father and Molly's tormentor.

She didn't speak, but he knew she was awake. He always knew. Not that he cared if she was or not when he wanted to do his dirty things. Bert would be listening too; he would say dirty things to her tomorrow, nudging, poking her. All she could do was play dead until it was over.

Screwing her eyes tightly shut, she pulled the blanket in closer, with its reek of stale urine. It was no use doing anything but lie still. He was a strong, heavy man. Whatever she did he'd get his way in the end.

'Molly?' His hoarse whisper shattered the quiet, and then his weight sagged onto the bed. The rank smell of him, already pervading the room, grew horribly strong in her nostrils, the combined stenches of stale sweat, unwashed clothes in which he slept, and the snuff which was his solace, his addiction. Or one of them.

'Molly?' The voice was stern now. He was a hefty man, sixty-six years old, who prided himself on his youthful looks, his hair only just turning grey. Its blackness was further darkened by grease. His face, though, was lined like an old boot, the mouth curving down cruelly below a bulbous nose and eyes like cold grey stones. Molly had scarcely ever seen William Rathbone smile, and when he did it was usually at something harsh and sadistic.

'C'mon wench – let's be 'aving yer.' His hand gripped her shoulder and he was leaning over her so that she was enveloped in his stink. Molly screwed her eyes even more tightly shut. Even those times when he had done it in daylight she had tried to lock herself away in the dark, to take herself away in her own head. She had no choice but to wait until it was over, filling her heart with a dull numbness.

But even with her eyes closed she knew exactly what he was doing. It was always the same. With no further preparation he burrowed his hand roughly under the blanket until he could grope up far enough to yank down her bloomers. There was a rip – Mom would tan her for that later. With his other hand he tugged at his buttons to release his thick, purple thing, agitating it up and down, grunting as he worked at it while he jabbed his fingers hard inside her inflamed passage, for all the long time it took him to climax. Dirty words spat out between his lips. At last his fingers stilled and he gave a sputtering gasp, then let out a long, relieved breath.

Soon he was snoring on the other side of the curtain. Molly lay rigid, both hands pressed on the sore place between her legs once again to quell the burning sensation. Soon the pressure got too much and she started to sit up, dreading the loud spattering sound of her urine in the bucket. It was already too late: she couldn't hold it. A hot gush came, burning her, making her whimper with the pain. The bed was saturated.

There was nothing to do except curl up in its embracing warmth, comforting for a short while, hoping she might be asleep before the liquid cooled and she was too chilled to settle.

Pulling the blanket close round her again to keep as warm as possible, she turned onto her side and conjured up a picture of Em in Miss Lineham's class, the cane swishing down onto her hand, then Em by the railings, smiling back at her in wonder. Emma Brown, her friend.

Seven

All the Brown children's hopes of kite-flying came to nothing the next morning. The fine weather broke: they woke to a rainy day.

And Cynthia could not pretend any more.

The baby had been crying on and off in the night. Cynthia had paced the floor, taken her downstairs to hold her, feeling utterly desperate and alone in the dead of night. When daylight came she at last managed a little sleep, and Bob woke first. Muzzy with sleep, he reached for the warmth of his wife beside him and snuggled up to her.

'Umm – Sat'day,' he murmured into her neck. 'That's nice. No rush. And that'un's asleep for a change.'

Cynthia stirred and Bob leaned up on his elbow, looking down at her. Her hair curled prettily round her forehead. Often in the mornings it was quite frizzy and she cursed it and damped it down, but he could never see why. He thought it looked lovely. She was lying on her side and where the neck of her nightdress sagged forward he could see the soft, shadowy cleft between her full breasts. He longed to stroke them, fasten his lips on her milky nipples, and becoming aroused he began to stroke her back.

'There's my lovely...'

Cynthia opened her eyes. She knew he was looking at her, that his honest face would be full of desire, but she didn't move. Bob pressed on her shoulder, wanting her to roll onto her back as she would normally, reaching round to caress her breasts. She did move onto her back, but there was a deadness, her eyes fixed on the ceiling as if she was somewhere else, far away.

'Love, are you there?' He kissed her lips, then gently eased the nightdress down, exposing her swollen breasts. Gently he began to lick the nearest enlarged nipple. When he stopped for a moment, a jet of milk needled out at his cheek and he chuckled and fastened his mouth back on, tasting the milk's thin sweetness. He moved to the other breast, its dark nipple seeping in sympathy and sucked, then smiled up at Cynthia, urgently aroused now, needing to be inside her.

'Mustn't take the little'un's breakfast, must I? Let us in, Cynth – I'm burning for yer.'

He was horrified to see that she was weeping, her face contorted in anguish.

'What's up with you?' Hurt, his desire thwarted, he spoke more harshly than he meant to.

'Don't,' she begged, like a frightened child. 'Don't get angry with me...'

'It's all right, love.' He lay behind her, holding her, still longing to thrust up inside her but knowing he mustn't, not now. He summoned his patience, trying to quell his desire, and said, 'What's the matter? You still feeling poorly?'

This produced a storm of crying, her body shaking in his arms. When she could speak again, she flung out the words, 'I can't go on. I don't know what's up with me ... but I can't stand it, just can't.'

Bob was completely bewildered and flayed by her emotion. He knew things hadn't been right, but he could make no sense of this outburst, nor judge what to do.

'You're just a bit tired after the babby. It'll be all right, love. You'll be right as rain in a few days. Tell you what.' Inspiration came to him. 'Look, you have a good rest today, eh? I'll take the kids out like I was going to and you stay here, have a bit of peace. How's that?'

Cynthia turned to him, suddenly intense. 'Take the babby. Take her as well...'

'The babby? But...'

'You've got to take her!' She was wild now, as if terrified, and sat up, pulling the front of her

58

nightdress close to her in a strangely chaste gesture which made Bob feel even more shut out. 'I'm frightened of her. Don't leave me with her!'

'What d'you mean?' He was utterly lost. 'She's only a little babby! What harm can she do?'

'I'm...' Cynthia's face crumpled again. 'I'm afraid of, of ... *me*. What I might do. I'm not myself!'

'Oh, love!' He was half laughing now. 'What are you on about? You've looked after the other three with no mishaps! What's all this?'

She stared at him, knowing he didn't understand, had no idea.

'Look,' Bob climbed wearily out of bed. She averted her eyes from his aroused state. 'I'll get myself dressed and take the kiddies out, right? Now, you can have a rest like I told yer. No working round the house. We'll soon 'ave yer better, eh?'

It was far too wet to take a trip to the Lickeys. When Sid heard that they wouldn't be going he roared with disappointment and Joyce burst into tears as well. Em took the news quietly, especially as Mom had not appeared downstairs that morning. The younger ones didn't really know what was going on, but she knew something was wrong.

'Pack that in!' Bob said sharply when the bawling didn't let up. 'We'll go to the Lickeys with the kite another day. Any road, the thing'll work best if it's left to dry longer. Yer don't want it coming apart in midair, do yer, in all the wet? What we'll do – this afternoon we'll go down to the park and let your mother have a rest.'

59

'What's the matter with our mom?' Em whispered to him, solemnly.

'Oh, the babby had us up and down a lot in the night. She needs to catch up a bit, that's all.'

'I'll stay here,' Em said.

'No, Em!' Sid wailed. 'You gotta come to the park. Joycie's no good!'

'I *am* good!' Outraged, Joyce went to hit him but he dodged and she knocked her hand on the arm of the chair instead and started wailing all over again.

Em stuck her tongue out at him. 'Now look what you've done, stupid! And I'm staying to help our mom and that's that!'

'Oh for heaven's sake!' Bob shouted, already on his nerves. 'Shut it, Joycie, that's enough. You can stay behind if yer want, Em. You can mind the babby and let your mother lie down. There's a good wench. And I'll bring you back a lollipop.'

'I want a lollipop!' Joyce grizzled.

'Right, I've 'ad enough of the lot of yer!' Bob reached the end of his patience. 'Just clear out and play for a bit. I don't care if it's raining. You'll just 'ave to make the best of it!'

The children tumbled out to the wet pavement as ordered. A few minutes later Bob came out and walked through the drizzle to the corner shop for his Woodbines. Once home, he sank into his chair and lit up. He was tired out himself and his shoulders ached. He ought to get Cynthia a bite of breakfast, keep her strength up, but he'd got time for a fag, hadn't he?

Resting his feet on the fender he sucked in the smoke like a soothing balm. Cynthia being upstairs all morning felt as wrong to him as it did to the kids. The mother was the heart of the house, no doubt about it. But in another way he was relieved. What was he supposed to do or say to the woman when she was in that state? He had no idea. If he just did his best and looked after the kiddies for a bit, she'd come round, he told himself. Things'd get back to normal, and the sooner the better so far as he was concerned.

Em sat on her dad's chair by the range, feeling very grown up. They'd had a bite of dinner and the others had gone out to the park with the tall slippery slide that Sid loved to go whizzing down.

'You're going to get a wet arse,' Bob told him. 'But never mind. Come on, get moving!'

Violet had had a feed and was asleep in Em's arms. Mom had said to put her on the floor on a blanket but Em couldn't resist holding her, looking down at her face, twitching in sleep, at the tiny pink marks on her eyelids and her astonishing little ears and nostrils. Em had adored Joyce from the moment she arrived. She'd been her baby, her playmate ever since. And she felt very loving to Violet too, but she wished her new sister hadn't made Mom so poorly.

'Never mind, Violet. T'ain't your fault. I s'pect our mom'll get better soon,' she said, enjoying the milky baby smell, warm in her nostrils.

After a while her arms grew tired and she laid Violet carefully on the soft bed she had made on the floor. Now what should she do? She had her drawing, and she thought about cleaning up, the way Mom did, as she was the one grown-up and in charge today. But she couldn't seem to think how to get going on that.

Quite soon she felt lonely, and decided to go and check if her mother was asleep. If she wasn't, maybe she'd let Em cuddle up beside her on the bed, the blissful way she used to when Em was little, before the time came when there was always another babby in the way and no room for her. If Violet stayed asleep, Em thought, she could just curl up with mom until the others got back.

She tiptoed upstairs, her bare feet silent on the threadbare runner of carpet, once dark green, now an indeterminate sludge colour. Halfway up she stopped, hearing the creak of bedsprings, and realized, excited, that Cynthia was not asleep. She could go to Mom, who would smile and open her arms and say, 'Come on – you can get up here, young lady!'

The shock hit her in the pit of her stomach. Peeping round the bedroom door, she saw Cynthia sitting up in bed, head in her hands, rocking back and forth. The saddest, most desolate mewling issued from her, like an injured cat Em once saw hit by a dray on the horse road. The noise went on and on, and its inhuman strangeness made her mother seem like someone else.

Em's legs turned weak and she crept back down the stairs, trying to block out of her mind what she had seen and heard. She prayed Violet wouldn't wake up and as the baby had been on the go such a lot in the night she did settle in for a long nap. Em sat at the table with her pieces of paper, drawing all her favourite things, cats and puppies and the baby horse she once saw just after it was born in the stable over on the other side of the gas works. Horses were so hard to draw. She didn't want to go upstairs again. She wanted Dad and the others to come back. It crossed her mind to run to Dot's, or across to Mrs Button, but she didn't want to leave Violet, or wake her by moving her.

Eventually, when the others were still not back, Violet did wake. Full of dread, Em carried her upstairs, daring herself to look into the bedroom, but to her relief Cynthia was lying quietly now, though not asleep.

'I think she wants her milk, Mom,' Em suggested.

Cynthia turned on her side as if her limbs were almost too heavy to move. Her face looked puffy and strange and her nightdress fell open at the front.

'Give her here,' she commanded, in a lifeless voice.

Em perched timidly on the bed as her mother lay with the baby at her breast.

'Good girl, Em,' Cynthia said, but the words seemed to cost her a great effort.

A few moments later they heard the door open downstairs and the others come in. Normally there would be squeaks of excitement, or quarrels, but it was strangely quiet as if they had been warned not to wake their mother. She heard Bob say something, then his feet on the stairs. Somewhere in her mind she already knew something was wrong by the quiet and the way he was walking: heavily, not calling out.

And then he was standing in the doorway, pale

63

and aghast, his features sucked in tight.

'It's...' he began. For a second he seemed about to weep but caught himself. 'It's Joyce. We were down the park and I bought 'em an ice cream. They were playing and... I was only talking to John Fowler, he was passing, like, and I turned round and she weren't there – weren't nowhere. We searched high and low. We've been round and round everywhere, but ... our Joycie's disappeared.'

Eight

Within moments Cynthia was out of bed, her worry driving out all other considerations. She threw on her clothes and rushed round to Dot and the other houses nearby to ask everyone for help. She was liked in the neighbourhood and knew she could rely on them, and everyone was fond of Joyce. But at first no one else was worried. They tried to reassure her.

'Don't you go fretting, Cynth,' Dot told her. 'Young Joycie'll've just wandered off somewhere. When she's satisfied her curiosity she'll be home.'

'She'll soon come running home when she's ready for 'er tea!' someone else said.

They all wanted to believe that Joyce had just wandered off. But it wasn't like her. Sociable Joyce was like Em's shadow. She wasn't one for going off on her own.

'Was there anyone about, could've offered her

sweets?' Cynthia fired out frantic questions. 'You must've seen summat!'

'No, I never saw a thing,' Bob told her desperately. 'One minute she were there and when I turned round...' He shrugged, his face haggard with anguish.

They all rushed back to the recreation ground, Dot and some of the others as well. Cynthia, refusing to leave Violet with anyone, was pushing her in the pram, and Em and Sid had to trot to keep up. Em felt sick, sensing her mom and dad's panic. Soon after they got there the neighbours spread out around the streets. Em and Sid were still with Bob, but Cynthia had rushed off somewhere else, moving faster than the rest of them as they trawled the neighbouring area. She was rushing along, frantic, with the pram. Em followed her father's steady tread as they scanned the rec, then walked the streets, calling Joyce's name, asking people if they'd seen her. She would have been hard to pick out among a gaggle of the neighbourhood children. Em kept looking to see a blue ribbon in a little girl's hair.

'I ain't seen anything out the ordinary,' one woman said. 'No kids that looked as if they was lost... There was a little girl I ain't seen before – she had a dolly, beautiful it was – but she was with her mother, quite well-to-do looking.'

No, not Joyce. They shook their heads sadly and moved on. Most people were kind and promised they'd keep an eye out, but there was nothing else they could say.

Em held Sid's hand. He was unusually quiet and just followed and she kept thinking: We'll find her in a minute, just round the next corner. She expected to see Joycie running towards them, right as rain.

But she didn't come.

They walked and walked in the damp, grey afternoon, covering the same ground over and over again, circling back to the recreation ground as if they just couldn't believe she wasn't there, that they hadn't looked carefully enough. Now and then they met Cynthia hurtling along with the pram, her hair a wild fizz in the damp.

'I'll go this way,' she'd say, rushing off again. 'No good us all going together, is it?'

The hours passed. The neighbours had all drifted home but the family could not be persuaded to tear themselves away. How could they go home without Joycie when it was getting dark? Once again they ended up in the recreation ground, staring across at the tall slippery slide, willing Joyce to be one of the dwindling number of children queuing to go down it. They all stood in tired, defeated silence.

'Better go to the fuzz,' Bob said at last. 'If Joyce was going to turn up she'd've been here by now.'

Some of the neighbours came out to greet them in the drizzly dusk when they got back to Kenilworth Street. Em saw Katie and Molly among them. She didn't know what to say to them but was glad they were there. This was a crisis; it wasn't just a question of a child wandering off for an hour or two. Em heard the murmurs of speculation.

'D'yer think them Mormons've got her?' somebody suggested.

'What about the gyppos? They was only round with their pegs and lavender a day or two back. I wouldn't trust them as far as I could throw 'em.'

There were mutterings about sinister strangers who'd been seen in the area and about the white slave trade until Em could stand to hear no more and moved away. Sid stayed stuck to her side. He seemed younger suddenly, big-eyed and silent, clinging to her hand. Cynthia had not come back with them and Em didn't know where she was, but soon Bob appeared again, hurrying back from the police station.

'They said they'd keep an eye out,' Bob told the neighbours, bitterly. 'Fat bloody use! If you want anything done, you have to do it yer cowing self round 'ere.'

'The Land Fit for Heroes,' another old soldier, left with only one arm to fill his jacket sleeves, took up his usual complaint. 'You can be a hero if you *are* fit. The rest can go hang so far as the powers that be are concerned. No one gives a sod about us.'

'Where's your mother?' Bob asked Em.

Em shrugged. She was cold and scared. Although it was comforting having all these people out there with them, she felt overwhelmed and just wanted to go inside in the warm. Sid kept tugging on her hand saying, 'When're they going to find Joycie?'

'I dunno. Just shut yer cake'ole, will yer?' she snapped, thinking even then what a telling-off she'd have from her mom if she'd heard her using that expression.

Sid started to snivel. 'I want Mom and our

Joyce – and I want my tea!'

'Oh, Sid.' Em relented and put her arm round his shoulders, her own tears starting to well up. It was dark now, the neighbours moving like shadows between the dim street lights, talking and speculating. Everything felt serious and frightening now night had come and still there was no Joyce.

'I wish our mom'd come back,' she sobbed, as she and Sid clung together in the dark street.

Cynthia stopped in a dimly lit side street and lifted Violet out of the pram. The child had been crying for some minutes, needing a feed after the long afternoon being propelled along the streets by a mother half out of her mind with worry.

'No one'll see me here,' Cynthia panted, un-fastening the front of her dress. She crouched down on a step deep in the shadows and let the hungry infant suckle from her leaking breasts. There were patches of wet down her front that until now she had not been aware of.

It was the first time she had been still for hours. Looking round she saw that she was by the wall of the old cavalry barracks where they were planning to build the flats. Now she was still, the worry of the situation hit her even harder.

'Where are you, Joycie? For God's sake, where've you gone?' she said desperately. 'Come home, wherever you are! We just need you home.'

The tears came then, all the pent-up feelings of the afternoon tearing out of her in sobs. She wept for a time, then dashed her tears angrily away. There wasn't time for all that: she had to keep searching, to find her little girl!

All afternoon she had circled the area round the recreation ground where Bob had taken the children, entreating the heavens that in one of the streets, round one of the corners or alleys, she would spy Joyce wandering lost.

'Joycie, Joycie, where are you?' she'd muttered to herself. 'Your mom's here – come on, Joycie, come to me...'

Though she had barely eaten for days, she had been ablaze with energy, as if she could rush onwards, searching and asking everyone forever, and her strength would never run out.

She'd hurried north as far as Ashted Row, across towards the canal, winding back and forth through the narrow little streets, her whole being shrieking with need for the sight of her daughter. Once or twice she thought she saw her and tore along towards a small girl, hope pulsing in her, only to be bitterly disappointed. People looked at her strangely, a dark-eyed woman, hair scattered wildly over her shoulders, dressed only in a thin frock, tearing along with a pram as if Old Nick was after her. She stopped and asked them, over and over, and seeing their shaking heads, moved on. Hours had passed, but she scarcely noticed.

Now she had stopped, though, it was as if she had collided with a wall of weariness and despair. Sitting on the step, the child's urgent mouth on her nipple, she rubbed a hand over her wet cheeks, aching with need and worry. For a moment she closed her eyes and let out a shuddering sigh. A train was shunting in the goods yard nearby and its rhythmic chuffing seemed to

69

echo the leaden thud of her heart.

She was startled by a low, cracked voice. 'Can you spare us a penny, lady?'

Opening her eyes, she saw a small, huddled figure in the shadows, a stooped woman shrouded in rags.

'I've had not a bite since yesterday.'

'I, I've no money,' Cynthia said to the poor old dear. Normally she would have given, of course she would. The old and sick were the ones suffering the most in these hard times.

'God bless you, lovey.' The little figure shuffled away, melting into the darkness.

This brief encounter brought Cynthia back to herself. When she had given Violet a drink from each breast she snatched her nipple away and dragged herself to her feet to settle her in the pram, swaying from hunger and exhaustion. She wondered what the time was. The streets were quiet now, though the pubs were open, full of light and chatter.

Trying to summon the burning energy she had had earlier, she pushed the pram on down the street, but now she was full of chill hopelessness. How was she ever going to find Joycie? Then a new hope lit in her. Her head seemed to clear. She had no idea whether they had found Joyce already and she was at home. Perhaps it was all right after all and Joyce was already tucked up in her bed with Em while she was out here circling the streets!

Moving even faster, she propelled the pram towards home. Turning into Great Lister Street, almost running, she caught sight of a blessedly familiar figure coming her way.

'Cynth?' Her husband's voice rang along the street, sounding shrill with tension. She dashed to meet him.

'Bob! Oh what's happened? You've found her, haven't you? Tell me you've found her!' She clung to him, finding none of the reassurance she craved in the distraught lines of his face.

'No...' He shook his head brokenly. 'No, love, we ain't. I come to find *you* this time. Come home, Cynth – we'll have to carry on in the morning. It's no good now. We've looked everywhere there is to look – it's like a needle in a haystack.'

'You can't just give up and go home!' she shrieked, working herself back up into hysterics, pulling on his arm. 'We can't just leave her – she's only a babby, out in the streets without us! We've got to carry on!'

'It's no good!' Hating himself for it, he delivered a slap across her cheek and she reeled away, stunned for a moment. 'We can't just go on wandering about, wearing ourselves out! There's the others – and you'll make yerself ill. Come home with me and in the morning we'll start again.'

Commandingly, he took Cynthia's arm and all the fight suddenly went out of her. She went limp. He led her to the pram which he pushed with his other hand.

'Come on, love, let's go home.'

Em reached out her hand, but all she felt was the cold place in the bed where Joyce should be beside her. She couldn't sleep without Joyce. Princess Lucy was a tiny comfort and she cuddled her tightly, but she couldn't make up for her sister's warm, comforting little body.

She lay looking up into the dark, frightened and bewildered. Everything about the day had been wrong: Mom crying in bed, and then everything that came afterwards even worse – Joyce disappearing, the terrible worry on their faces, searching, never finding her. She didn't feel like crying now. Instead a sick feeling sat like a stone in her belly.

I should've gone with them, not stayed in with our mom!

What was Mom always saying: 'Look after our Joycie – you're the big sister.' And she always had looked after Joycie and it had been a happy, joyful part of her life. And now she'd gone and let everyone down – it was all her fault!

Unable to stand the cold, lonely bed any more she got up, taking Princess Lucy with her.

'Sid? You awake?'

There was no reply. She could hear her brother's loud, healthy breathing. Climbing in with him, she and her dolly cuddled up against his warm, solid body, and eventually Em fell into a restless sleep.

Nine

To their surprise, a policeman called at the house the next morning. Dot was already round with them, trying to give comfort when Bob let him in.

Em crouched on the peg rug by the hearth hoping no one would notice she was there, while

72

the young constable sat by the table, seeming very big. She stared at his huge black boots and his helmet, the strap tight under his fleshy chin. After a few moments he eased the helmet off, to reveal tufty brown hair.

'No sign of her, then?'

'Not a thing.' Bob stayed standing, obviously ill at ease with a copper in his house. Anguish and frustration made his tone angry.

'Please, find her for us,' Cynthia begged. She was sitting at the table with Violet in her lap and she looked sickly and exhausted. Dot was beside her.

'Our officers are searching–'

'About bloody time!' Bob exploded. He lit yet another cigarette, drawing on it in small, agitated puffs.

'Is there anywhere you can think of, anywhere she might have gone – a relative, or a friend?'

'D'you think we're stupid or summat?' Bob raged at him. 'D'yer think if there were anywhere like that we wouldn't've thought of looking ourselves? What the hell d'yer take us for, eh?'

'Just try and stay calm.' The young man stood up and put his helmet back on as if to re-establish authority. There were no more questions he could think of. 'I'm sure she'll turn up...' He edged towards the door.

'That's what they all say,' Bob said disgustedly.

Slamming the door behind the constable he shouted, 'Fat lot of sodding good to anyone!'

Dot gave Cynthia a sympathetic look and Em drew her knees up tight, curling her toes. It frightened her, hearing Bob shouting like that.

73

He was usually a mild man who deferred a lot to his wife. He even called Cynthia 'Ma' sometimes.

They were at their wits' end all that Sunday morning, not knowing what to do. The only thing they could think of was to go out and search and search again.

'We'll stick together this time,' Bob said. 'I don't want you running off, Cynth, I want you with me, me and the kids.'

'All right,' she said. 'Let's go and walk round again. What else can we do?'

She was very quiet, dull-eyed, as if all her energy and hope had been burned out yesterday, and walked beside her husband as they took it in turns to push the pram. Em and Sid trailed along behind, not thinking of doing anything else. Church bells were ringing in the distance. The rain had gone and it had dawned a mellow September day, the sun lighting up the streets full of playing children. Surely Joyce must be somewhere among all of them?

But still they were disappointed. They returned again and again to the recreation ground, as they had done yesterday, not knowing where else to begin. There were no other relatives they could turn to. Bob's brothers were far away. Cynthia's sister, Olive, lived over in Kings Heath but they were certain it would never have occurred to Joyce to try and make her way there.

So where on earth could she have gone?

'Oh God, Bob, d'yer think she's there somewhere?' Cynthia said, shuddering, as they stopped to rest on a bridge overlooking a narrow part of the cut. A sodden piece of sacking drifted by.

'Could she've fallen in?'

'No – shouldn't think so,' Bob said.

The canal's murky water gave up no clues. And neither, that afternoon, did any of the streets and alleys. People who remembered them from the day before came up and asked if they were still looking and commiserated with them, but no one had seen Joyce or had any idea where she might be. Em saw the grave looks on their faces and sensed that they were beginning to think the worst. She didn't like to imagine what the worst might mean.

The warm afternoon began to fade and none of them wanted to go home, to say that they were giving up, but then Violet began to cry again and Em and Sid were dragging their feet.

'Come on, love,' Bob said gently to Cynthia. 'We can't keep this up all night. We'll have to go home sometime.' To Em's surprise her mother didn't argue. It felt as if they'd worn out the same few streets with walking and looking and asking, then walking and looking again. They were at a loss as to what to do next.

'We need some grub inside us, that's what,' Bob said.

They went home in silence, as if no one wanted to say what they all felt: that they'd given up and left Joyce because they didn't know what else to do, or where to look, even though they would have moved heaven and earth if they'd known how.

Bob stoked up the range and Cynthia cooked eggs and fried bread and they had some leftover potatoes. Em tucked in, surprised at herself for being able to eat, but they'd been walking miles. The four of them sat round the table. Bob moved Joyce's chair out of the way, and no one could think of anything to say. It all felt wrong. They didn't put a light on, and it became hard to see as the light faded outside and the air filled inside with smoke from Bob's cigarettes.

Eventually Cynthia said, 'Best get the crocks washed, then.' She dragged herself from her seat and went to the scullery to fill the kettle. After a moment they heard her crying uncontrollably. 'Oh God. Oh God, help us! Just bring her back...'

Bob lit another Woodbine and the smell of smoke reached Em. She found it comforting. Cynthia quietened and came back into the room with the kettle. They sat listening to the whisper of it heating up.

'I don't want you kids playing out tonight.' As if they would have even thought of it. Em didn't want to play out. It seemed ages since she'd seen Katie, as if she was part of another life. She just wanted to be at home where it felt safe.

Cynthia was pouring water into a bowl on the table when there was a loud knock at the door and Dot's voice crying urgently, 'Cynth! Bob – quick!'

Em saw her mom and dad's eyes meet through the steam.

Cynthia stayed by the table, seeming unable to move as Bob went to get the door. They all heard his exclamation of surprise.

'This lady come down from Rupert Street with 'er, said they'd found 'er wandering and did I know who she was,' Dot panted. 'Said she was sure she came from Kenilworth Street but that

76

were all she knew.'

All of them were at the door now, crowding round. Em pushed past her dad.

'Joycie!' she screamed, and ran to her sister, flinging her arms round her. 'Joycie! Oh, Joycie, where've yer been?'

Sid came and joined in, shouting 'Joycie!' at the top of his voice, very excited.

Cynthia was weeping with relief and they all took it in turns to cuddle Joyce, who just looked confused and overcome, but otherwise perfectly all right.

'Oh, thanks, Dot!' Cynthia cried, the tears running down her cheeks. Dot was tearful as well. 'Oh, my little Joycie – thank God!'

Bob wiped his eyes and lit the lamp and they all stood round staring at Joyce in wonder. Cynthia peered more closely.

'What's that you're wearing? That's not your dress, is it?'

Em noticed then that Joyce was dressed in a pretty, pale pink frock with a silky pink ribbon on the front, fastened in a bow.

'Where d'you get that?' Cynthia sounded harsh in her worry. 'And where's your yellow one?'

'That lady give it me,' were Joyce's first words to them. 'I dunno where my other one is.'

'What lady?' Bob demanded. 'Where the hell've you been?'

Cynthia sat down and gently pulled her daughter to her. 'What lady? Tell us, Joycie. Where've you been? You were out all night. We've been worried to death!'

Joyce looked at her with wide eyes. She seemed

really disorientated.

'I been with the lady. She took me back to her house. And she give me a dolly only I ain't got her any more, but I kept these.'

She raised her left hand and only then did they see that she was clutching a fistful of soft, silky ribbons in different pastel shades. Joyce pulled one of the ribbons from her fist, a pale yellow one, and handed it to Em, who held it, feeling how soft it was to stroke with her fingers. She knew she would tie it in Princess Lucy's woolly hair.

Everyone stared, unable to make any sense of this.

'I had a nice bed,' Joyce volunteered. 'Big and soft. And she gave me this dress. And taters – nice taters for my tea, with butter... And she gave me these...' This time she opened her right hand, to disclose two shiny half-crowns.

Cynthia looked up at Bob, bewildered.

'Where on earth's she been?'

'God knows.' He shook his head. Already he looked more relaxed, the tightness gone from his body, and he gave a chuckle. 'We can have a feast to celebrate on that! And maybe she'll tell us in time. But she's home and none the worse for it, ain't she? That's the main thing. Eh, Em?'

He winked, and ruffled Em's hair. And Em felt she might burst with happiness.

Ten

'Where've yer been, Joycie? Go on – tell us what it was like!'

'Who was the lady? Where did she take yer?'

Everyone was full of questions the next day. Em and Joyce were running across Kenilworth Street to Mrs Button's little bakery. Cynthia had given them one and sixpence out of the two half-crowns from the mysterious 'lady' to buy cakes for everyone for tea, and told Em not to let go of Joyce's hand, as if she would have done in any case. None of them ever wanted to let Joyce out of their sight again.

Soon Katie and Molly and several others latched on, badgering Joyce with questions.

'Where did you go, Joycie?' Katie asked, outside the shop, where the smell of warm jam and buns and doughnuts beckoned them inside.

Joyce turned her puppyish face up. She liked Katie, with her long dangly plaits. Katie was always kind to her, and she looked up to her as one of the big girls.

'We went on a tram,' she announced.

Em whirled round. 'Did you? You never said!' To Katie she added, 'She just keeps saying she had a nice big bed, even though the rest of us were worried half to death...'

'And taters, with butter,' Joyce added dreamily.

'What was the lady's name?' Katie asked.

79

Joyce just stared at her and shrugged.

''Er's only four,' Molly chipped in. ''Ow's she going to know where she was or who the lady was?'

Katie gave Molly a superior look as if to say, Oh *you're* here again, are you? But it was quite a sharp remark from Molly, who usually went round with a blank, closed expression. Molly made a face back. Katie went to link arms with Em, to show Molly who was boss, but Em was too busy clinging on to her little sister.

Em led Joyce into the tiny shop while the others gathered round the door, mouths watering at the lovely smells. Mrs Button's shop consisted of her front room, and she and her husband lived in the back. The stairs were ahead and the room was blocked off by a narrow counter on which rested trays of bread and cakes. Behind it stood Mrs Button, a minute lady in height but very wide in girth. Because she was so small she had to stand on a stool to see over and serve her customers, so she appeared from behind the counter like a jack-in-a-box springing up. Her face was so chubby that her features seemed buried in it, like the currants in her buns. But she was always kind and cheerful and loved children. Now and again the Buttons' old black and white mongrel, Bullseye, would come to the door and stand looking, and Mrs Button always shooed him briskly away.

'I don't want you in here under my feet, you silly old thing. Go on, in the back!'

And Bullseye would lower his head in a disappointed way and slink back in to Mr Button and the hearth.

'I see you cheeky monkeys are back!' she greeted Em and Joyce in her high, bird-like voice, beaming down at them from atop her stool. 'Has your mother sent yer today? Ooh you did give everyone a turn running off like that, Joycie! Where did you get to, eh?'

The same vague look came over Joyce's face as every time she talked about her escapade.

'She got lost and went off with some lady,' Em said.

'Oooh,' Mrs Button said. 'Fancy. Well, you're back now, ain't yer, that's the main thing. Gave your poor mother a terrible fright, though, that you did! Now what're you going to 'ave today, then?'

Em and Joyce spent a delicious few moments choosing a bag of cakes – doughnuts and angel cakes and custard slices – Bob's favourite. Mrs Button made an approving noise with each choice they made and bundled them up. Em handed her the shilling Mom had given her and when she got her change, seeing Molly and Katie and two other girls still hanging round the door, she said, 'Let them have a cake an' all!'

She picked out four custard tarts and her friends seized on them eagerly.

'Oh, *ta,* Em!' Molly cried, eyes popping with delight at being included.

'You should thank our Joyce,' Em said.

Soon they were all tucking into the sweet, spiced custard and making noises of ecstasy.

'Ooh, they're lovely, they are, Mrs Button,' Katie said politely.

Jenny Button stood on her stool beaming down

at all this enjoyment of her wares, which meant more to her than her very meagre profits.

'You'll 'ave to come back another day for some more, then, won't yer!' she said happily.

She shooed them away from her door and Em started walking off to take the cakes home. The other girls, after the excitement of the cakes, suddenly realized that Molly Fox was still latched on to their group and that they didn't want her.

'Don't you 'ave to get 'ome or summat, Molly?' one of them said nastily.

'Yeah – home to have a wash with any luck!' Katie O'Neill said.

'Molly, Molly, washes under a brolly!' One of them thought of a new chant and soon the others were joining in.

'Molly Fox, Molly Fox, always stinks of smelly socks!'

Katie nudged Em and giggled. She couldn't stand Molly Fox and though she was not sharp about making up insults she enjoyed hearing the others tormenting Molly. Em smiled, but with mixed feelings. She didn't really want Molly hanging around her either. She didn't half stink – it put you off. But Molly had been kind to her when she got the cane, and there was something sad about Molly that made Em feel sorry for her. It couldn't be nice having everyone teasing her all the time and being the odd one out, not really knowing how to go about making friends. Em knew she was popular and that she'd hate to be like Molly Fox, trying to brazen it out and pretend she didn't care, when Em could see she was cut to the heart.

'I got to get home,' she said, glad to get away from the taunting, the thought of having to take sides. She couldn't side with Molly Fox, though, could she? Not in front of everyone else. 'Come on, Joycie! See ya!'

Cynthia had bought a joint of beef and cooked loads of roast spuds and cabbage, and they had the cakes afterwards, all on the strength of the little windfall pressed into Joyce's hand by an unknown woman.

'Well, ta very much, whoever she is,' Bob said, raising his glass of ale as they all sat round the table. 'God knows, she caused enough trouble and worry. This is very nice, Ma, very nice indeed.'

Em watched her mom and dad, saw him looking light-hearted and relaxed, Mom in her best dress the colour of cornflowers, a bit tight after the baby but she still looked lovely, and all the family round in the cosy little back room. Em had helped her mother polish up the range with black Zebo polish and it was alight and warm, the kettle gently heating on the hob. The lights were on, glinting off the jugs and a few cheap ornaments arranged along the mantel over the range. On the wall by the table there was a picture of a country scene, a field with a curving stretch of river and flowers in the grass. Things were back to normal at last, better than normal. There was Tizer for the three children and it felt like Christmas! Even baby Violet was happy and smiley as if she could sense the good mood in the room.

'Whoever she was, she had no right to any of our kids,' Cynthia said fiercely. 'God knows what happened – I don't s'pose we'll ever know now.'

They'd tried asking Joyce every question they could think of but received nothing much more in the way of answers. She didn't seem to want to talk about it, as if she'd almost forgotten about the escapade. Now she was back home and it was like a dream to her.

Em was thrumming with happiness, the memory of her mother's tears and her sister's terrible disappearance already fading as she listened to her mom and dad laughing and joking together. Now, she felt, everything was going to be all right.

Eleven

'You're not going out – I've told you. I'm not letting you out of my sight!'

'But Mom, I wanna play out with Nance!' Joyce protested. 'It's boring when Em and Sid ain't here!'

Cynthia saw the resentful expression on her little girl's face and felt as if she was going to explode with anger. She had a list of jobs to do as long as her arm and the babby was already grizzling again upstairs. But she had to keep Joyce right under her nose – had to! It was bad enough having to let Em and Sid go to school out of her sight. What if it happened again? What if next time one of them disappeared and never came back?

'You do as you're told, my girl,' she erupted furiously. Her apparent recovery had been short-lived, the fruit of Joyce's return. Now, though, every nerve in her body felt wrenched tight again, as if she might snap. 'You're staying in and that's that.'

'No I ain't!' Joyce, who was used to being shooed out of the house from under her mother's feet, wanted to get out to her friends like she usually did. She opened the door and ran out into the street.

'Don't you defy me!' Cynthia pursued her, moving to grab her out on the pavement. Joyce flung her arms up over her head to defend herself and her show of fear enraged Cynthia even more. Anyone'd think she was forever beating the child, the way she was carrying on!

'You're not going anywhere, d'you 'ear me?'

Dot appeared by her open door.

'All right, Cynth? Oh–' Her thin, good-natured face grimaced comically. 'One of them days, is it? What's up with you, Joycie? Coming out to play with Nance?'

Joyce pouted and Cynthia, too wound up even to speak, grabbed her by the arm and propelled her towards the front door, leaving Dot staring in wonder. 'Huh – like that, is it?' she muttered, going back to her work.

'You just do as I flaming well tell you and get back in the house, my girl!' Cynthia snapped, pushing Joyce indoors.

Violet's screams met them as they went inside and Cynthia's nerves tightened another notch.

'You can get up to your room and stay there till I tell you to come down!'

She saw the fear and hurt in her little girl's eyes

as Joyce resentfully stamped her way upstairs.

Cynthia sank down at the table, her heart thudding so hard that she laid her hand over it.

'God in heaven...' she whispered. What was the matter with her? Only two days ago she was running through the streets, ready to give her own life and soul if only she could see Joyce again, have her back home safe, her precious little girl. Yet now, the state she was in, she was turning on the child as if she were the devil himself! How had she come crashing down so low again in such a short time?

The baby's screams cut right through her, tearing at every nerve in her body, and she put her hands over her face, trying to find the strength to go and see to her. The tears ran out between her fingers.

'Help me...' she whispered. 'Please... Someone...'

'Cynth?'

There was a tap at the door twenty minutes later. Cynthia had dragged herself upstairs to fetch Violet and was still sitting with her, feeding by the table.

'Can I come in, bab?'

Dot pushed the door open and leaned against it, her wiry figure in a faded pale blue frock with an apron over it and stout black shoes. Her hair, long and straight and caught up in a loose bun, had once been glossy black, but was turning prematurely grey. She was smiling her toothy smile, then, seeing the state of Cynthia, her expression sobered.

'You all right, love? You look like Barney's Bull.'

Cynthia tried to say yes of course she was all right, but another wave of tearfulness choked her and her eyes filled. She looked down at Violet who was still sucking sleepily at her breast.

'Oh dear, oh dear – feeling a bit like that, are yer?' Dot said, turning to close the door, rattling its loose handle. 'I thought there was summat this morning and our Nance's been on at me, wanting Joyce out there with her. Joycie poorly an' all, is she? I'm not surprised after all that carry-on at the weekend.'

Cynthia was shaking her head. 'No, it ain't her, it's me.' The sobs broke out then and Dot came and patted her on the shoulder.

'You've 'ad a lot on yer plate, bab. I 'spect it's the blues after the babby. I always feel like drowning myself and the whole bleeding family for a week or two after!' Dot said this with such cheer that it was hard to imagine it had ever really been true. 'And you've had a shock, what with your Joyce... 'Ere–' she went over to the range – 'kettle's not been on. And the thing's almost out! Come on – I'll get it going – we could both do with a cuppa. Good job I'm still in me pinny!'

Dot stoked the range, filled the kettle in the scullery and set it on the heat. Cynthia watched her, still unable to stop crying. 'Soon 'ave yer feeling better,' Dot said, mashing the tea and flashing another smile at Cynthia, who made a weak attempt to smile back. She didn't believe she'd ever feel better.

It had all happened as if overnight. When they found Joyce again after those agonizing hours of searching, they'd all been relieved and overjoyed. Everything felt right, the low state she was in before Joyce disappeared seemed to be forgotten. They were together again as a family after the terrible threat of losing Joyce forever and nothing else mattered!

But in two days everything had changed. She could feel herself sliding down, down, like someone disappearing out of the light into a mineshaft, leaving all the others around her at the top wondering where she had gone. It was a terrible effort trying to get through even the simplest tasks. Everything felt overwhelming, as if she couldn't cope. And now there was the fear as well: it had occupied her, eating away inside like woodworm. Danger seemed to lurk everwhere, threatening her children, especially the youngest, Joyce and Violet.

'Look,' Dot said kindly as they drank their tea at the table, 'let me take Joyce and she and Nance can play out. I'll keep an eye on them.'

'No!' Cynthia protested, wild-eyed. 'I don't want her going out there again. You never know who might be about, what might happen. I'm keeping her in with me...'

Dot looked concerned. 'Cynth, you've got to get yourself together. You can't just keep her in all the time. Where is she now, upstairs? It's hardly fair on the child, is it? Not if she wants to see her pals. I know it was a bad do at the weekend but that were different – it was up the park. There's no harm'll come to her here.'

Eventually Cynthia gave in, especially when Joyce, who had crept down and was listening on the staircase, came running into the room.

'Please, Mom – let me go with Auntie Dot – please!'

She watched the ever capable Dot lead Joyce out of the house, her heart pounding, hands sweating, but she clenched her fists and said nothing. Dot was right, she could hardly keep Joyce a prisoner in the house for evermore!

When they'd gone she sat down again, staring across the room, her face a blank. She lost track of how long she stayed sitting there.

As Dot led the two little girls out of Cynthia's she almost ran slap bang into Iris Fox, who was crossing the road towards her. Dot felt her hackles rise as Iris's ignorant features formed into their usual spiteful sneer.

'Out with yer little darkie, I see?' she said, nose in the air. 'I'd've thought yer'd have more pride in yerself, *Mrs* Wiggins.'

She walked on by with a triumphant smirk. Dot's temper was boiling but she never let herself rise to Iris's taunts. She was never going to sink so low as to bandy words with that creature.

'Come on, you two,' she said tartly, ushering Joyce and Nancy through her front door. Luckily they were giggling together and hadn't even noticed Iris. The two of them were soon playing together. Dot started on some vigorous cleaning to work off her temper.

But as she cleared the floor to give it a scrub, her thoughts still dwelt furiously on Iris Fox. Iris had always been the first to come out with mouthy comments about Nancy, whoever was in earshot, and Dot especially loathed her for that. It didn't exactly take a genius to work out that Nancy wasn't Charlie's after all this time. Of course there was going to be gossip when she was first expecting and no husband in sight, but most people just accepted it and kept their traps shut, especially now Nancy was growing up. It was only Iris who would boom along the pavement so that everyone could hear, 'Huh, look at that little piccanin! Touch of the tar brush there all right! Been with a black man, 'ave yer, bab?' Her ignorant face would be screwed up with smug malice.

Dot held her head high and ignored Iris, and never said a word to anyone else either, however flaming nosy they were. Only Cynthia, her staunch friend, knew who Nancy's father was – a musician from somewhere near Naples who had been busking his way round the country, looking for somewhere to settle. He'd been staying for the time being nearby, in the Italian Quarter in Duddesdon, but Dot had met him in the Bull Ring. The mutual attraction was immediate and he walked her all the way home, carrying her bags, his squeeze box slung on a strap over one shoulder. His name was Fausto – 'Fah-oosto!' he taught her to pronounce it – and in her loneliness, her aching body and spirits had fallen easily for his flashing smile, his jaunty songs and jovial, accented conversation. Secretly he spent two nights with her before he departed for London, never knowing he had left her carrying his child.

'Fausto,' she murmured, standing the chairs on the table, trying to pronounce it the way he had. A smile played round her lips. Christ, he was a handsome bloody chancer, she thought, remembering him fondly, despite it all. Swinging into her life then swinging right out again. He'd made everything a gruelling struggle. Yet she had no regrets. If she couldn't have her Charlie back, at least she had a beautiful daughter to fill some of the loneliness. Bugger Iris Fox and her like – the silly cow was too thick even to tell a black man from an Eytie! And anyway, her Nance was the joy of her life now.

She heard the girls giggling upstairs and smiled to herself. But then the smile faded. Joycie was all right after all her adventures, that was for sure. But what about Cynth? She'd never seen her friend in such a low state. Surely she should have bucked up after the babby by now.

'I'll come and see yer again later, see you're all right,' she murmured, going to the scullery to fill a bucket of water. 'Cos I don't like the look of yer at the moment – that I don't.'

Twelve

Molly stepped out of the entry from the yard into Kenilworth Street, glad of the swathing October fog in which she could hide as she peered cautiously up and down. She shivered, having no top coat to her name and only a threadbare jersey as an outer garment. There were other children dawdling on their way to school and she could see the coalman's cart emerging out of the murk at the far end of the road. She checked instinctively for danger, this time in the shape of Katie O'Neill, and as there was no sign of her she ran across Kenilworth Street and knocked urgently on the door of number eighteen.

Her nervousness made her jiggle up and down, and for a second she was frightened she was going to wet herself. It just seemed to come over her sometimes and she was weeing without knowing it was going to happen. She stood scratching the itchy patches inside her elbows, through her clothes.

The door opened a crack and she could just make out Em's frightened face in the gloom.

'Oh – it's you.' Em opened the door a fraction wider.

'Who did yer think it was, the bogeyman?'

'Nah, stupid, the wag man.' Em came out onto the step and looked up and down even more fearfully.

'Well, ain't yer coming to school again, then?'

Retreating inside, Em shook her head. Her face was pale, her fringe needed cutting and she didn't look like the usual carefree Em. Molly wanted Em to smile and skip along the road with her. Em was being quite nice to her these days, even though she was Katie O'Neill's friend, but now she'd suddenly stopped coming to school.

'Tell 'em I'm poorly,' Em said.

'What's up with yer, then?' In her disappointment it came out harshly.

'Nothing.' Em glanced behind her, lowering her voice to a whisper. 'It's my mom. She ain't too good. I gotta stay home and help 'er.'

Molly had heard the rumours about Mrs Brown.

She'd never 'picked up' after the babby, everyone said. Wouldn't go out. The gossips said she couldn't even get down to Great Lister Street for a pound of potatoes. Dot Wiggins was doing her shopping for her and minding Joycie every day, and Em was keeping house. It was a shame. Molly found it very strange that Em was kept at home. Iris couldn't get *her* out of the door quick enough.

Out of the corner of her eye Molly suddenly saw a figure approaching who she didn't want to meet: Katie was coming, on her way to school.

'You gunna play out after?' she said, backing swiftly down the step. 'Everyone's playing tipcat.'

Em shook her head. 'I dunno.'

'Gotta go,' Molly said hurriedly. 'T'ra.'

But it was too late.

'What're you doing here, stinky?' Katie said, as Em closed the door.

'Calling for Em,' Molly said, trying to be defiant. 'Why shouldn't I?'

Katie's face screwed up and she reached out and pinched the one piece of soft, bare flesh she could find at the side of Molly's neck.

'Cos you aren't her friend, so don't think you are!' Katie sneered. 'Why'd she want to be friends with you, yeller drawers? And anyhow, she ain't coming to school, dain't yer know? Stale buns for tea!'

Katie's slim figure and long swinging hair flounced past her and along the street. Showing off to Molly, she called out to two other girls and linked arms with them and they went along chattering excitedly towards the school.

Molly watched, feeling shut out as usual. She

93

was always on the wrong side of the window pane, looking in. School was bad enough, but now Em wasn't even there either...

Trying to shrug off her loneliness, she dragged her way along the street towards the yawning doors of hell, or rather the elementary school.

'Shall I make you a cuppa tea, Mom?'

Em stood timidly at the door of the bedroom. Cynthia lay in bed on her side with Violet beside her, suckling. She raised dull eyes to her daughter. Her face was gaunt now, with dark circles under her eyes. She could not sleep properly, and she was barely eating, so the weight was dropping off her.

'All right, love,' she whispered in the flat voice with which she spoke all the time now, as if the life had been drained out of her.

'I'll put four sugars in it,' Em said. It was the only way she could think of lavishing care on her mother that might be acceptable.

'You've gotta get her to eat summat,' Bob kept urging. 'She won't take any notice of me and you're the one here all day. Try and get summat down her.'

But this was easier said than done, Em thought. You could lead a horse to water... And she wasn't used to ordering her mom around!

She went down to the silent kitchen. Sid was already at school and Dot had come and taken Joyce next door.

'I'll come back in a bit, bab, when I can find the time,' Dot had told her kindly. 'Only I'm rushed off my feet at the moment what with the girls and all the washing and that. 'Ere – I'd better help you with yours an' all.'

With her brisk, effective movements she'd got a fire going under the copper in the back kitchen, ready for the washing.

'Now, you get started and I'll see yer later. You know what to do, don't yer? You've seen your mom do it hundreds of times. If you need some help just come running round, all right? Come on, Joycie – our Nance is waiting for you.'

Joyce had trotted off happily. She and Sid were aware that their mom was poorly but they were busy getting on with their lives. The burden fell on Em. And she noticed her dad seemed to be out even more than usual these days. He had been kind and helpful for a short time but now he was running out of patience.

'You're going to have to pull yerself together, Cynth,' he'd said when he got home, tired, the night before. 'It's no good, we can't go on like this.'

His anger and her own hopelessness had reduced Cynthia to tears once again.

'For God's sake, woman is that all you can do? Sit and blart? That won't get us our dinner on the table, will it?'

Em had been shaken by her father's angry words. She'd run upstairs and hidden in her room. She knew most people's moms and dads had fights and shouting matches. Josie and Eamon Donnelly two doors away were forever at it like cats and dogs. But her mom and dad had always been different. They rubbed along without yelling and carrying-on. They'd been good pals. Hearing the hurt and fury in her father's voice had rocked Em's world. She wondered how she could make things right. If she was good, and did everything, maybe Mom would get better and they could all go back to normal.

Down in the kitchen now she tied one of her mother's pinners over her clothes. It was a faded pink thing which could have reached round her several times and she had to hitch the hem up into her drawers. Then she put the kettle on, her skinny arms shaking as she hauled its weight up onto the hob. First opening the back door to let out the steam from the hot water in the copper, as she knew Mom always did, she dragged a chair over to it to add the Hudson's soap – a bit too much, she realized, making the water froth – before climbing up and down with armfuls of washing which she shoved down into the copper with the wooden tongs which were almost as big as she was. Once the kettle boiled she mashed the tea, sweating with the effort of controlling the big kettle. When it had had its five-minute brew she poured herself and Cynthia a cup, spooning plenty of sugar into both. She loved sweet tea.

'Here y'are, Mom,' she said proudly.

Cynthia had finished feeding Violet, who was lying kicking on the bed. At six weeks old she was filling out into a pretty little thing. Cynthia barely seemed to have the strength to sit up.

'Ta, love.' She looked down, as if unable to bear the sweet sight of her daughter in the huge pinner, trying so hard to do everything right.

Em sat on the side of the bed and tickled Violet's tummy, which made her squirm and kick even more. She gave a little gurgle and Em laughed.

'She's smiling, Mom!' She looked up eagerly. 'She's ever so pretty now – you're a good girl, aren't you, Violet!' She kissed her sister's tiny cheek, then looked up, burbling eagerly, 'I've got the first lot of washing in the copper so I'll go down and get it in the maiding tub in a minute. Then I can get the next lot on and I'll have it all hung out in the yard soon.'

She wanted to please Mom, to show how much of a help she was being, but Cynthia put her hand over her eyes.

'Just go on down, will yer, Em, please. Just leave me. I can't stand it.'

Cut to the quick, and afraid Cynthia might start crying again, Em clomped down the stairs. She spent the morning washing furiously and sloshing a good deal of scummy water all over the kitchen floor and out into the little yard at the back. Hauling the wet clothes out of the copper to put them in the maiding tub, she ended up clutching them against her body. Soon she was soaked to the skin, even her boots filling with water. At first her sodden clothes were still warm as she energetically pounded the washing with the wooden dolly and rinsed it in the sink. But when she took it outside in the tin pail to mangle it and hang it out, the cold wind cut through her wet clothes, making her teeth chatter.

The mangle was a stiff old thing and Em was already exhausted. Trying to work it on her own was nigh-on impossible. She could not hold the wet garments and sheets off the ground as well as turn the handle and the ends kept dropping in the dirt so she had to rinse them all over again.

97

The third time she saw a sheet fall to the filthy ground, she sank onto her knees, buried her head in the wet cotton and burst into tears of desperate frustration.

'I'll never get it done!' she sobbed. 'I'll be here forever and ever.'

Dot's face appeared over the wall. 'Eh, bab, what's up? Oh you're not trying to do all that on your own are yer, yer silly sausage! You should've come and got me – you can't do all that without someone else. No wonder you're getting in a mess! And you're dripping wet, look at yer!'

Dot was round in a trice and soon they had her first lot of washing on the line. As it was now a sunny day, Em knew with pride that though it was cold, at least the washing would probably dry, as, eventually, would her own clothes.

She put more washing into the copper, topping up its grey contents with a bucketful of clean water, and started all over again. The morning flew by and she had no time to miss being at school or her friends, or even to think about the dreaded knock on the door from the School Board man. If he came, she told herself, she'd hide down in the coal cellar, even though it frightened her to death down there because she was afraid of the dark and of rats and roaches and anything whatsoever that might be lurking down in the sooty darkness. Even they weren't as frightening, though, as the official man who might come knocking for her.

Once the last wash was done, and Dot had come back to help her mangle it and it was all hanging out, Em's arms and shoulders were aching, her legs weak from all the effort. Dot went home, telling her to make herself and her mother a bite to eat. Before she left, she helped Em cut some slices of bread and smeared them with margarine.

'And try and see she eats some of it, eh? I must go and finish my own wash now, bab. I'll see yer later on.'

Em cut a piece of cheese and wolfed it down with the bread. Then she took a similar plateful up to her mother.

Cynthia was still lying there, staring at the ceiling. Em saw that she had used the chamber pot but apart from that it was as if she had barely moved. Half the tea remained undrunk. Em took the chamber pot downstairs to empty, then slipped back into the room.

'All the washing's on the line,' she reported, standing timidly by the bed. 'And it's a nice day.'

Cynthia turned her head, her brown eyes searching her daughter's face. As if summoning her strength, she said, 'You're golden, Em. You're a good girl. Sorry for what I said. I didn't mean to be nasty.'

'S'all right,' Em said, tears prickling in her eyes.

'Has Dot been back?'

'Yes. She gave me a hand.'

'I'm sorry, love.' Cynthia's eyes filled. Em's stomach tightened with dread. She wished Mom wouldn't keep saying sorry. 'You should be at school with yer pals. I just can't seem to help my-self.'

'Never mind, Mom, you just get a bit of rest,' Em said, feeling very grown-up. 'You going to eat summat?'

Cynthia shook her head, glancing down the bed

to where Violet was still on the go. 'Can you take her off me for a bit?'

'Yes, Mom.'

She picked up her wriggling sister from the bed and carried her downstairs and out into the yard. Next door, Dot was still hanging out her washing. She waved, seeing Em in the yard with Violet in her arms.

'You all right, bab? Washing's drying nicely! Yer a good'un!'

Em smiled and waved, feeling proud of herself. But soon a cold, sinking feeling came over her. At first it had just been the odd day she'd had to stay off school – to help on wash day, or if Mom was feeling especially bad – but now it was getting to be all the time. She hadn't been to school for a full week now and, when she stopped for long enough to think, she felt lonely and frightened. She just wanted Dot, or someone, anyone, to come and take over everything, to look after them all so she could go back to school, see her friends and stop being a mom and housekeeper at the tender age of eight.

Tipcat

Thirteen

It was late afternoon and school was out. Em answered a knock at the door, holding a grizzling Violet.

'You coming out?' Katie asked. She wrinkled her nose at the grimy state Em was in, and Violet burped up some milk which trickled over Em's wrist.

'I dunno,' Em said helplessly. She could see Sid tearing up and down the horse road and she ached to be out there with everyone. She'd got all the washing in and minded Violet all afternoon and she was fed up with the game of housekeeping. 'I'll go and ask.'

Cynthia told her she could go out so long as she kept an eye on Sid and got on with the cooking in time.

'Your dad needs his tea soon as he gets in, so don't be out too long. Dot'll help you.'

Em handed Violet back and tore downstairs and out into the street, released. It was a chilly but fine evening and there were games going on everywhere. Sid was swinging from a rope tied to the lamp post and he swung himself at her as she came along, his feet, clad in his heavy *Birmingham Daily Mail* boots, almost kicking the side of her head. The boots were issued as charity by the local paper to those considered the deserving poor.

'Gerroff, Sid!' Em said crossly.

Sid thumbed his nose at her and ran off.

'Hello, Em!' Mrs Button hailed her from the door of her shop. 'How's yer mother?'

'All right,' Em said.

'She looking any better?'

Em shrugged. She didn't understand what the matter with Mom was so it was hard to say if she was looking better. She just wanted her back, singing and cooking and bustling around downstairs.

'Wish 'er well from me,' Mrs Button said.

Further along there was one of several games of tipcat in progress. The game involved hitting a 'tipcat', a piece of wood just a few inches long and sharpened to a point at each end. With a bat the player hit the tipcat while it was on the ground to send it flying into the air, to be hit with the bat as far as possible. The next player was supposed to guess how many jumps or hops it'd take to reach the tipcat and award points accordingly. If the first player didn't think the score was high enough they would hop the distance to check the points. The player with the most points was the winner.

Em saw Molly standing by one group of players, trying, as always, to edge her way into the game.

'Why did old stinky come to your house this morning?' Katie asked.

Em was about to answer when Molly caught sight of them and came trotting over.

'You allowed out, then, Em?' she said in her plaintive way that made Em feel both sorry for her and intensely irritated at the same time. She didn't really want Molly around but couldn't bring herself to be nasty to her the way Katie could, so she just nodded.

104

She and Katie were quickly absorbed into the game, as popular members of the street groups, while Molly was still left out. Em was too desperate to play and forget all her duties at home to notice and before long she was holding the bat and whacking the tipcat as hard as she could along the street, all thoughts of cooking tea or keeping house chased from her mind. Katie, who was missing her at school, was pleased to be out playing with her and soon they were laughing and joking as usual.

Em was so taken up with the game that she didn't notice the sun sinking down, the chill fingers of smoky autumn mist reaching along the road. She was catching up on the school gossip and company.

Suddenly, though, she froze. Looking along the road she saw Bob heading towards them, on his way back from work.

'Is that the time already?' she gasped. 'I've gotta go!'

Without further explanation she tore off along the road and into the house. She looked round in utter dismay. She'd worked so hard that day and thought she had left everything in order, but what a mess it all looked now! There were piles of the clean washing she'd brought in from the line on the table and chairs, the copper was still full of scummy water, the floor was muddy and there were unwashed pots from last night that she'd completely forgotten about washing. And on top of that she hadn't even begun on the cooking!

What should she do? She was supposed to be boiling potatoes. Water – that was what was needed! She scrubbed out the biggest saucepan and filled it with water to put on the range. It was only then she realized that the worst disaster possible had happened. She had let the fire go out!

She was standing staring in horror at the lifeless range when the door juddered open and her father came in. He hung his coat and cap on the back of the door then turned to face the darkened room.

'It's dark as the grave in 'ere,' he complained, going to light the gas. 'How's yer mother?'

'In bed,' Em said carefully.

Just then Sid came bursting in through the door with Joyce.

'What's for tea?' he yelled with his usual exuberance.

Em saw her father taking in the state of the room.

'Tea nearly ready?'

Tremulously, Em said, 'The range's gone out, Dad.'

He stood very still for a minute, then suddenly hurled himself into action, grabbing the bundles of washing from the chairs into one big heap on the table.

'Get rid of this lot for a start!' he roared. 'There's nowhere even to sit down. And where's my bloody tea, eh? D'yer mean you haven't even started? I've 'ad enough of this – the whole bloody thing. Her lying about up there...' He stormed up the staircase.

Joyce and Sid stood cowering and all Em could think of doing was moving the washing out of the way. She couldn't think where to put it and in her panic decided to run upstairs and take it to her bedroom. It took her two journeys and as she passed Mom and Dad's room, where the door was slammed shut, she heard him shouting and her mother crying.

'I've had enough of this! You've got to get yerself up. Lying around here all day while the place is going to rack and ruin... It were all very well after the babby but 'er's weeks old now and yer still ain't pulled yerself together. For God's sake, what's the matter with yer, woman? Look at me when I'm talking to yer! You're no bloody good to anyone, that you're not. I'll 'ave to go out and get us some dinner – it's too late to start it now.'

As Em crept down after depositing the second load of laundry on the bed she heard, 'I want you back to normal tomorrow or there'll be trouble, that there bloody will. Call yerself a wife! I'm not sticking around to be treated like this, like I don't exist, that I'm not! And you'd better be able to hear what I'm saying, yer useless cow.'

Bob came down and said furiously, 'Fetch us a basin, Em. I'm going out to get us all some dinner.'

He returned later with a basin of steaming faggots and peas. Bob sent Sid up to his mother with some food, then they sat at the table in a strained silence. Em tucked in, realizing suddenly how hungry she was, but she could see Joyce just playing with her food, casting fearful looks at their father. He shovelled his portion down then went and put on his coat again.

'Get them to bed,' he said to Em in a horrible clipped voice that she wasn't used to. 'I'm going out. And make sure this place is cleared up by the

107

time I get back. It looks like a pigsty.'

And he was gone, slamming the door.

Bob stormed along the road towards his favourite watering hole, head down, his collar up against the cold wind. Inside he was a tangle of frightening feelings. The most immediate were anger and resentment at being so disregarded. Here he was, a working man, the breadwinner, and not a crust on the table to greet him when he arrived home! He was worried about Cynth, of course, and his worry translated into more anger. What the hell was the matter? Why couldn't she pull herself together and get on with it like other women did – like Dot, for example? Dot had always been a ball of fire, and no mistake!

A neighbour greeted Bob as he strode along Kenilworth Street but he passed without noticing, scowling into the darkness.

Nothing could happen to Cynth – for God's sake, she was his earth, sun and stars! Ever since he'd seen her that day on the tram everything had felt right. Cynth had healed the ache, the thirst in him that had lingered ever since his mother died, shortly followed by his father, both of influenza. He and his brothers had gone into the Boys' Home on the Vauxhall Road. They had each other, of course, and the company of other lads. They'd been fed and clothed, and the Home had helped them into the adult world of work so that most of them could fend for themselves. But nothing could ever fill the void of love that they'd lost. They were special to no one, nobody ever looked into their eyes with love or put their arms around them.

All the longing of Bob's scarred childhood had found fulfilment in Cynthia. His Cynth, his kids – they were his everything! Without them nothing made any sense. And now, look what was happening to her! She'd left him as surely as if she'd packed a bag and walked out of the door, slamming it behind her. When she lay with that blank expression as if something in her had died, or gone far, far away from him, he wanted to get hold of her and shake her, to make her come back to him. The feeling frightened him to death.

''Er'd better be all right tomorrow or there's no telling what I might do,' he growled to himself. 'This is no way for a wife to go on.' He stopped abruptly in the street as tears welled in his eyes. There was a tight feeling in his chest and his throat ached. For God's sake, what was the matter with him?

Dashing the tears away furiously with the back of his hand he hurried the last few steps to the Crown and pushed open the door into a refuge of light, the familiar smells of ale and smoke, sodden sawdust on the floor and the talk and laughter of other men.

Fourteen

Em sat on the second stair from the top, rocking back and forth, her fingers rammed into her ears. Her old grey skirt was spotted from crying, her vision blurred by more tears welling in her eyes.

Behind the bedroom door, Mom was crying and Violet grizzling. The sounds tore at her and she tried to plug her ears even harder. But she couldn't seem to move away.

It was a week since that terrible night when she had let the range go out so she couldn't cook Dad's tea, and in that time she had been to school only once.

Cynthia felt very bad in the mornings.

'You'll have to stay at home, Em. I can't manage, just can't...' she'd say, in the flat, hopeless tone that Em had come to dread as much as the blank look in her eyes. 'You're the eldest and you're a good girl. I need you to help.'

Staying at home spelled another lonely day of pounding at pails full of washing, black-leading the range, scrubbing and cooking. She didn't do the outside jobs like washing down and whitening the front step, or going to the shops, because she was afraid of the wag man seeing her. She stayed hidden inside. Dot popped in whenever she could but she was overstretched herself and now had Joyce to mind as well. By the afternoon Cynthia sometimes felt a bit better and could drag herself down and cook Bob's tea. She would move round the house as if in a trance, and quite often sink into a chair when in the middle of something and just leave off, forgetting what she was doing. Frequently she was so irritable that Em could do nothing right, and both of them would end up in tears. Other times she was childlike and pathetically gentle, wanting Em to do everything for her. And she was so frightened. She thought all the neighbours were watching her, talking about her.

They *were* talking about her, of course. Some were spiteful, others kind and neighbourly, but everyone knew by now that Dot was helping out because Cynthia Brown had been taken bad after the babby and wasn't herself.

Things had been looking up this week to begin with. On the Saturday, Bob had sent the three of them out to the Penny Pictures on Nechells Park Road and given them enough to get some pork scratchings before the butcher's closed on the way back. And Em was allowed to play out – until Bob sloped off to the pub again, that was. And yesterday Cynthia had a better day. Em had been downstairs bossing Sid into his little ragged shorts and shirt for school, envious of him for being able to run, carefree, out of the door. Suddenly Cynthia had appeared, already dressed and holding Violet. Em's heart had lifted. Mom was up and about – maybe she was better!

'Go on, Em,' Cynthia had said bravely. 'Get your things together and get yourself to school.'

Em's freckled face had lit up. *'Can* I, Mom? Are you sure you can manage?'

'I said so, dain't I? Go on, before I change my mind.'

Em had almost danced out of the house, running to catch up with Katie and the other girls, so excited to be allowed back to school. But the day had been a bitter disappointment.

'Is your mom better now?' Katie'd asked, turning for a second from her conversation with another girl.

'Yeah, think so!' Em had beamed, wanting it to be true. But the smile had faded from her face.

111

She had wanted Katie to be more pleased to see her. Instead she hardly seemed to care if Em was there or not.

But Miss Lineham had demanded to know why she hadn't been there.

'I've been poorly, Miss.'

'And what, *exactly*,' her tone had been heavy with sarcasm, 'has been the matter with you?'

'Had a pain in my tummy, Miss.'

'Hmph.' Miss Lineham had stared stonily, but Em was looking convincingly pale and drawn after the strain of the last days.

She'd settled thankfully at her little desk beside Katie, just wanting things to feel right and back to normal, how they'd always been. But, to her dismay, nothing had felt right. In the lessons she'd missed they'd started long multiplication. Normally good at arithmetic, she just hadn't been able to get to grips with it or keep her mind on anything and soon the rows of numbers were just a snowstorm in front of her eyes. Six more lashes with the cane left her already raw palms red and stinging. She'd walked out of school utterly miserable, her hands tucked under her arms, her head hanging. Molly had been waiting for her.

'Go away – leave me alone,' Em had said wretchedly, trying not to cry.

The sight of Molly's sad face as she slunk away towards her yard made Em feel even worse.

Today, with Mom bad again, it felt easier to stay at home.

Sitting on the stairs Em cautiously lowered her hands to her lap. Weak sobbing sounds came from the bedroom and suddenly she felt she couldn't

112

stand it any more. She got up to run into the bedroom and beg, *Mom, stop it, stop crying, will yer! Just get up and be all right, be my mom again!*

But there was a brisk knock at the door.

'Coo-ee – it's me – can I come in?'

Dot's cheerful voice rang up the stairs and Em quickly wiped her eyes and ran down to meet her. She was obviously right in the middle of her own housework, pinner on, sleeves rolled and a flowery scarf tied over her salt-and-pepper hair.

'Awright, bab?' She gave her toothy smile, but then took in the state of Em's face. 'Oh dear, like that again, is it? I'll come up and 'ave a word with her.'

Em felt much better with Dot's capable presence in the house. She followed her thin, energetic figure up the stairs and hovered, peering through the crack of the open door once Dot was inside.

'Cynth?' Her voice was gentle. 'Just thought I'd pop in. How are yer today?'

Em didn't hear a reply, other than a low moan.

'Oh dear, oh dear,' Dot said sympathetically. 'What're we going to do with you, eh? Shall I make yer a nice cuppa tea?'

'Em'll do it.' Cynthia grasped at Dot's apron. 'Stay with me a minute.'

Dot called out, 'Em! Stick the kettle on for us, will yer, bab?'

Em obeyed, and once it was safely on the range she crept upstairs to the bedroom door.

Dot was sitting on the bed, her arm round Cynthia's shoulders, stroking her hair as if she was her mother. Cynthia was crying again, just tears, no sound.

113

'I have such terrible thoughts, Dot,' she said, her face crumpling. 'I'm a wicked, wicked woman.'

'No you're not,' Dot tried to reason. '*Course* you're not, love. You're just feeling a bit any'ow after the babby. It's all got on top of you, hasn't it?' She spoke kindly, though Em could sense she was as bewildered as the rest of them by the extent of Cynthia's misery. 'She's lovely and bonny at any rate, and you'll feel better soon, you just need to hold on and get a bit of rest.'

'Bob hates me... I'm just useless. No good as a wife, as a mother. Em's such a good girl but she ought to be at school. Sometimes, I think I'd be better finishing myself off, God knows I do!'

'Cynth!' Dot was shocked. 'What's all this? You mustn't talk like that! Your Bob's devoted to yer, you know he is!'

'He hates me!' Cynthia wailed. 'He's never home now – he just goes down the boozer, filling his neck and... He's turning into a... He's horrible to me! He never used to be like that.'

'Look, love, you're seeing the black side of everything at the moment. You've just got to get your strength back and try and look on the bright side. Perk up, Cynth,' Dot said, patting her and getting up. 'Try and put a bright face on when the Old Man comes home, that's all. You can rest for now – I've got your Joycie, so don't you fret. But I'll have to get on...' She was interrupted by another abrupt hammering at the door.

'Well, who the hell can that be?'

Dot poked her head out of the window and quickly drew back with an urgent expression. 'It's the wag man with his sodding little notebook!

114

Em!' she hissed.

Abandoning all pretence that she had not been listening, Em ran to her.

'Come on, quick, into the cellar!' Dot grabbed her hand and they ran downstairs. Opening the door to the cellar, Dot urged a reluctant Em to go down the steps. 'It ain't for long,' she whispered. 'It's just in case. I'm not planning to let him in – just make sure you keep quiet as a mouse!'

Em stayed near the top of the steps, heart thumping painfully, hardly daring to breathe. She was terrified to go any deeper into the yawning maw of the cellar with its bitter soot smell and lurking horrors of her imagination. But she was just as scared that the School Board man would come and wrench the door open and find her cowering there. She seemed to be scared of everything these days – of Mom, of Dad coming home...

'Yes?' she heard Dot say boldly.

'Emma Brown,' the man said officiously. 'School says she's only been in once this week and last.'

'That's because she's unwell,' Dot said.

'You 'er mother? You're not, are yer?'

'I'm a neighbour, since you asked,' Dot replied haughtily. 'And I'm here looking after Mrs Brown as she's also unwell.'

'What's the matter with 'er?' he asked roughly.

'Problems of a female nature,' Dot said, knowing this was a good way to silence a man's questions. 'And the child has a nasty case of tonsillitis.'

Soon she was opening the coal-cellar door with a grin.

'That's got shot of him, for the moment at least! Now, Em, you're doing a good job looking after your mother and I'm sure she'll soon feel better. I've got to go and get on, but you know where I am if you need me, bab. Just say the word.'

The house seemed all too quiet without her lively presence. Em stood looking round at the mountain of work before her, at the mess of breakfast still on the table. She heaved a huge, weary sigh.

That evening Dot, who worked like a dynamo, had the stew pot on and potatoes bubbling away on the range. There was enough for both households as she'd pooled ingredients with Em, and now she was taking a short break, standing on her front step in the last of the autumn light, chatting to Mrs Donnelly at number fourteen.

'You've got a lot on your plate with her being bad,' Josie Donnelly said, leaning up against the doorframe, her arms folded over her scrawny chest.

'Poor old Cynth,' Dot mused. 'I've never seen 'er in such a bad way. She usually picks up quicker than this.'

'How's himself taking it?'

'None too well,' Dot whispered. 'Ey up, talk of the devil. Here's 'er old man now.'

The two women watched Bob come along the road, his jacket swinging open, cap on askew. For a second he swerved violently as a gaggle of lads dashed past him.

'I'll say one thing – he's a fine figure of a man,' Josie Donnelly remarked, suggestively. Both she and Dot were a few years older than Bob.

'Now, now,' Dot reprimanded her teasingly.

116

'I'd've thought you've got enough on yer plate with your Eamon, and you a good Catholic and all...' She narrowed her eyes. 'Blimey – looks as if 'e's had a skinful again tonight!'

They took in Bob's reeling gait. He was weaving along the pavement, and as he passed them, oblivious to their watching eyes, he nearly tripped over a scrawny dog that was skulking close to the houses.

'Gerr'outa my bloody way, hound!' Bob mumbled at it, indistinctly.

'Jaysus, let's hope he can get himself into the right house!'

'Well, 'e wouldn't be the first kalied bloke to climb into bed with the wrong wife!' Dot said and the two of them laughed.

'You can hardly blame 'im getting a skinful in, the way she is,' Josie Donnelly said with a sniff. 'I mean the state of her front step – hasn't been touched for days! I don't suppose she's any comfort to the poor man.'

'It ain't her fault,' Dot defended her friend, reminding herself inwardly that she must scrub the step of number eighteen. 'You wouldn't wish it on anyone, that.'

'There's a case for just getting up and getting on with what needs to be done, no matter how you're feeling,' Josie decreed. 'After all, no one's going to do it for you.' She spoke tartly, still watching Bob as he narrowly avoided bumping into someone coming along the pavement the other way.

The other passer-by glanced curiously at Bob, then continued along, staring straight ahead of her. She was a small, neatly dressed figure, black hair cut in a bob just visible under the brim of her hat, whose white band seemed to glow brightly in the half-light. Walking past Dot and Josie, she affected not to notice them, and disappeared quickly into the gloom.

'Who's that?' Dot asked. 'She looked a snooty little bit.'

'She's the one moved in round the corner,' Josie said. 'A widow, or so I've heard – with a young daughter.'

'Oh.' Dot quickly lost interest. 'Well – I'd better get on, Jose. This won't get the babby a new coat.'

Further desperate days passed. The more Em was left alone in the house with Cynthia upstairs, the more she jumped at every little sound. She was terrified of the School Board man's visits. He'd been twice and she hadn't been caught yet, but what if he came back? She'd have to tell lies, and what would he do if he saw she was all right? Would he have her thrown into prison? Was that what happened to children who played truant for too long?

Dot popped in when she could but mostly Em was left to herself, struggling to keep everything going. To save work she didn't wash her own clothes and she was too busy to notice how stained and smelly they were becoming. Her hair needed cutting and, already thin, she was becoming bony and pinched in the face. Katie had stopped bothering to call to see if she was coming to play out and now she had gone off with some of the other girls. The only person who seemed to care was Molly Fox. She appeared at the door every day asking for Em, and Em had to shake her head, sometimes feeling tears prick her eyes.

Worst of all was the fear of her father's return from work. He seldom came back in time for tea now. On the good days, which were few, he would come home, trying to do the right thing, to look after the children and his sick wife. But more often his route from the power station took him via the pub, and when he came in his mood was self-pitying and ugly. Em tried to make sure they all went up before he came back, but it was impossible to sleep, waiting for the bang of the door, his slurred, angry voice downstairs, Mom begging him to be quiet, not to shout.

Last night she and Joyce had lain clinging to one another, waiting, but as soon as they heard the shouts downstairs, Sid had appeared by their bed.

'Wanna come in with you, Em,' he'd said miserably, sounding much younger than his six years. So the three of them had squeezed in together, cuddling up and trying to block out the shouting.

'I'm not bloody having this any more! Where's my dinner, then, you skinny cow?'

Em had pressed up tight against the wall as the slamming and cursing of the mild father she had once known and her mother's weak protests and her weeping pushed their horrible way up between the floorboards. Once again she'd put her fingers in her ears and squeezed her eyes shut, trying to make it all disappear.

Fifteen

'You off 'ome now, pal?'

'I'll be off when I'm sodding well ready!' Bob's reply was a slurred snarl. He was needled by the note of concern in Stan, his workmate's voice. 'I'm having a cowing drink, if that's all right with you.' He knew they were talking about him these days, how Bob Brown had started to put away more than his ration, was making a fool of himself.

He pushed himself up, steadying himself against Stan's shoulder.

'G'night, you buggers,' he said, half affectionately.

'See yer tomorra, Bob,' Stan called after him. 'Go easy, mate.'

'Go easy ... yerself...' Bob replied vaguely, weaving his way to the door of the pub. He slid on a wet clot of sawdust and had to grab hold of the edge of a table so as not to fall. He could feel them watching him.

'I'm all right!' he insisted at full volume.

It hit him, the second he stepped outside into a bitter, mizzling evening, the ache in his heart like a black void and all the pain of loss and confusion. He stopped in the shadows and leaned against the wall of the pub for a moment, both arms braced, his spinning head slumping forward. The rain fell cold on the back of his neck. He had to go home but he felt as if he had

120

no home to go to, because she was not there. The woman he loved, his Cynthia, wife and mother of his children, was not there. Instead there was this lethargic, shrunken stranger who barely spoke, could not look at him except with the deadest of eyes, who shrank from him and would not accept his loving or his physical need of her.

'Damn and blast her!' A sob escaped him and he punched his fist against the wall, yelping with pain at the graze on his knuckles. 'What does she want? What the hell am I s'posed to do? I want my girl back!'

As he walked along in the damp, miserable night, self-pity and anger swelled inside him.

'I'm not 'aving this,' he mumbled savagely. 'She can come back and be my bloody wife or clear off – that's what!'

By the time he reached the house he was ready to explode. He slammed in through the front door, expecting her to be sitting there, passive as ever, staring at him with that deadened look which made him shrivel inside. Instead, there was no one in the front and when he strode through to the back he found Em and Sid sitting at the table hunched over a sheet of paper. The room was a dismal mess despite Em's efforts. Cynthia had taken to her bed for most of the day. There was a stench from the pail of napkins soaking by the scullery door and of stale boiled cabbage. The obvious neglect and the way his children looked up at him like terrified rabbits brought Bob's blood to boiling point.

'Where's yer mother?' he bawled.

'U-upstairs,' Em whispered.

'I s'pose 'er's been lying abed all sodding day while I'm working my guts out, swallowing bellyfuls of dust!' he roared. 'Well, the idle cow can get up and see to my tea, that she can! I'll show 'er what a wife is!'

He stumbled up the stairs, past thinking, long past being the kindly man he had been, and crashed into the bedroom. It was dark in the room as she had not even lit a candle. Bob lunged at the bed and seized hold of Cynthia's arm, even in his drunken state registering just how thin and bony she had become. She let out a shriek as he hauled her out of bed.

'Bob, stop it! What're yer doing?'

'Come out 'ere where I can see yer. I want to see yer!'

'Stop it! You'll wake Joycie and you'll scare the kiddies...'

'Scared be damned!' Bob blared. 'What've they got to be scared of? I'm their bloody father, ain't I?'

'Oh, Bob, stop it, *please!*' Cynthia was sobbing, clinging to the bedstead as he tried to drag her away.

'I'm not having any more of it... I've 'ad enough and it's time you stopped all this nonsense and started being a wife to me... Give me what I need...' He was pawing her, trying to yank her away from the bed, loathsome to himself even as he did it, but in his pain and fury he couldn't hold back, he needed her, he had to have her back or he'd go mad.

'Stop it, you're hurting me! For God's sake, Bob!' The last was a desperate scream.

Ignoring her cries he lunged at her, and in the darkness he swiped her far harder than he had intended. She crumpled to the floor and he heard a moan of pain.

'Cynth...' He grovelled round her. 'Christ!' What had he done? He felt like a small boy now, close to crying. 'Cynth, where are yer?'

'Get off me, you bastard!' Her voice was muffled. She started to weep, a weak, racking sound. 'You've hurt me. I hate you!'

With trembling hands he reached for the candle and matches, at last managing to get it alight.

'Oh Christ, Cynth–' He stumbled over to her, aghast to see blood seeping from her mouth into the blanket which she had pressed to her mouth.

'You've knocked a tooth out,' she wept.

He was too befuddled to think what to do.

'Get me some water!'

'Em!' he yelled down the stairs. 'Get some water for yer mother!'

When Em came up with a crock half full of water Bob took it from her and tried to help his wife stem the flow. Looking up after a moment Bob caught sight of Em still hovering by the door, her face white with shock.

'Get away downstairs with yer, wench! Just get out!'

His words seemed to catapult her away into the darkness with a last, terrified look.

When the bleeding gum had been staunched, Bob and Cynthia sat looking at one another warily.

'It hurts,' Cynthia said at last, plaintive as a little girl, with tears rolling down her cheeks.

Bob, all his hurt and worry plain in his face, said, *'Please*, Cynth, we can't go on like this. I can't stand it. You've shut me out and I can't get to yer. You've got to pull yerself together – or I'm going, and that's final. I can't stand any more of it. I feel as if I've lost yer...'

She gazed back at him, her eyes very wide. 'I've lost myself.'

They both fell into a restless sleep and woke to a cold, wet day. Bob groaned, sick to his stomach and his head pounding.

'Fetch us a cuppa tea, bab,' he murmured to Cynthia, half awake, forgetting how she was.

There was no reply. He rolled over and dragged his eyes open, seeing her lying there in what he thought of as her corpse state: as if lifeless, dead eyes fixed on the ceiling, a smear of blood from last night encrusted on her chin. It was as if a door had clanged shut in his face.

'I said, fetch us a cuppa tea!' he snarled.

'I can't.' Her voice was a hoarse whisper. 'I just can't move. I feel so ... terrible...'

Then the tears started up again and rage shot through him like electricity. He jumped out of bed.

'That's it, then. Summat's got to give 'ere, Cynth. You've got to get yerself sorted out cos you're neglecting your family. The place is going to rack and ruin.' He stood over her, hands on his hips, and inspiration struck him. 'I know what – you go and stay with that sister of yours for a bit. Why shouldn't she do summat to help us? We never hear a word from 'er from one year

124

to the next.'

'Olive?' Cynthia looked appalled. 'I can't just go and park myself on her! We've never been close.'

'Well, my girl...' Bob bent over and pushed his face close to hers. Cynthia winced at the stench of stale beer on his breath. 'You'd better sort it out and get yerself over there. Because if you don't get out of 'ere for a bit and try and pull yerself together it'll be me going – and for good. Got it? This is your last chance – you're no bloody good to anyone as you are!'

Sixteen

Three days later Cynthia sat squeezed into her seat in the trolleybus as it growled its way from Nechells into Birmingham. It was very crowded, but a man had given Cynthia his seat, seeing that she was carrying a small infant. She slid in gratefully beside the grimy, steamed-up window, pushing her little bag in at her feet.

She had begged and begged Bob not to send her away. Every nerve in her body was screaming that she didn't want to go, leaving home and her other children, but she knew there was no choice. Bob had made that abundantly clear. Now she was on her way to Olive's neat little terrace in Kings Heath, a suburb south of the city.

Olive's letter had come by return of post, brisk and chilly as ever, in reply to Cynthia's enquiry.

'Bob thinks I should get away for a little while.

125

I haven't been quite myself since the last child...'
Bob had hurried off to post it for her, as if he
couldn't get rid of her fast enough.

'You'd better come, then, if you must,' her
younger sister had written in her stiff, copperplate
hand. 'If that's how it is. But I'm not offering
charity, you'll have to pay your keep. Don't come
Wednesday, I won't be in. Sincerely, Olive.'

She and Olive had never seen eye to eye.
Cynthia had always far preferred their brother
Geoff, three years her senior. You could laugh
and play with Geoff, a boisterous, wholehearted
boy, whereas Olive had always been trim. Geoff
had gone to war and was killed in 1917 when
Cynthia was thirteen. She had broken her heart
over it, and still did now, whenever she thought
back to that day when they heard the news.

Beside her on the seat was a large, talkative lady
who was twisted round, holding forth to the
woman behind her. To make sure no conversation was demanded of her, Cynthia pulled the
brim of her hat down a fraction and kept her gaze
fixed on her baby, tucking the shawl round her.

'At least you're here with me,' she whispered.
'You're a good girl.' She was grateful that Violet
had been sound asleep all the way. Her shredded
nerves could not have stood a crying baby on the
journey. It was bad enough having to make her
way through Birmingham on her own. Since having her family her life had revolved round a few
streets. And she scarcely went anywhere by herself. Even when she walked to the nearest shops
in Nechells, she and Dot nearly always went together. Now here she was, surrounded by

126

strangers, all giving off a humid fog of sweat and neglect and unwashed clothing on a day so rainy it made her heart sink even further.

The tram along the Moseley Road was less crowded but, with every mile it travelled, Cynthia felt more torn apart at the thought of it carrying her further and further away from home, from the little ones and Dot and everything familiar. She had been wrenched away that morning, early, without saying goodbye to them. Bob had thought it for the best.

It won't be for long, she told herself as the tears rose once more in her eyes. I've got to get better somehow. As she sat holding Violet, though, the sight of her brass wedding ring twisted her heart even more. The day came back to her, nine years ago, when Bob slipped that ring onto her finger, his eyes alight with love and happiness. They had both felt so blessed to have found each other. How full of hope they'd been, both of them having lost their mothers so young, that they could make a family and give their children all the love and stability that had gone missing in their own childhoods. Cynthia had saved herself for her wedding night, and it had been in some ways a fumbling, shy experience, neither of them practised at love-making, but it hadn't seemed to matter. Again, it was Bob's face which was her most precious memory, the tenderness, the look of rapture as he gazed down at her once they were tucked up in bed together for the first time. Soon after, when they found out Em was on the way – how happy he'd been! Her husband was so good at appreciating life, she knew, treasuring the simple things so many other people took for granted, because of all he had lost and all those loveless years in the Boys' Home.

Her memory ran over the years of their marriage, the birth of their children. Cynthia kept her face turned to the window, her tears flowing, and it was all she could do to stop herself breaking down at the bittersweet thoughts that coursed through her mind. It had been good, her marriage, bolstered by her friendship with Dot, who had always been there like a big sister to her, the two of them helping each other through so many of the daily ups and downs, the childhood illnesses, the domestic hiccoughs.

'You got any flour to spare, Dot? I've clean run out.' Her lips turned up for a second at the memories of visiting Dot's door, so often with scrapes she had got herself into, and Dot could always help her out. Dear old Dot, always there, full of beans, keeping those kids of hers in order like no one else in the street.

She wiped her eyes on a scrap of rag and pushed it back up her sleeve, trying to calm herself, but more tears came. It felt as if everything was slipping away from her, her family, her marriage and happiness. Even her wedding ring could slide so easily from her finger now, she was so scrawny. It was all her fault! She didn't *want* to spoil anything. It was horrible the way she felt, the way she'd gone to pieces. Who was she becoming? How did it happen that she'd lost her grip on life?

'I can't help it, I can't!' she murmured desperately. Yet she had to get better for everyone's sake. She knew really that Bob was right to send her away, however much it hurt. But still his harsh words echoed in her head, words from a Bob she hardly recognized either. *This is your last chance, Cynth. Don't come back until you're better – because you're no bloody good to anyone the way you are.*

She put her hand over her face for a moment. 'God help me...'

And although it came out as a quiet whisper, it was a cry deep from the heart.

Seventeen

'You get yourself off to school today.'

Em had stared warily at her father that same morning as he came into the bedroom to wake his three drowsy children.

'Why – is our mom better?'

'Don't keep pestering me with questions,' he said. 'Just do as yer told and get yourself ready.'

Em didn't argue. She never knew what mood Dad'd be in these days. She was still smarting from the way he yelled at her the other night when Mom had blood all over her face.

He looked in at the door again. 'And you can play out tonight, there ain't no hurry to come home.'

Em frowned, her feelings a mixture of excitement and dread. Of course she wanted to go to school and to play tipcat and tag and all the other games, and no more dodging the wag man! But school was not the reliable thing it used to be.

What if none of her friends wanted to know her any more, and she couldn't keep up with any of the lessons?

Heavy-hearted, she got ready. Sid roared off out of the front door as usual, to find the other lads, but Em followed at a much more cautious pace, with butterflies in her tummy.

'Em!' Katie was coming along as Em came out of her door. 'You coming to school?'

Em's spirits lifted immediately as Katie linked her arm through hers and chatted away to her about school gossip. She was hurt that Katie had never come to see her again in all this time, but she told herself it was better that way. Mom hadn't wanted anyone else in the house and Em would have been ashamed to let her in. Em glanced at Katie's dark-eyed, pretty face as she chattered away. Katie seemed distant, as if from another world, and she never asked Em another thing about herself. But it would be all right later, Em thought, when she'd been back a while. It was just that they hadn't played together for a long time. She laughed at Katie's tales of the classroom, trying to join in.

It was lovely to be out amid the bustle of the morning street, Mrs Button's door already open and the aroma of fresh bread drifting into their nostrils, delivery boys out on their bicycles, the milk dray arriving and all the children heading for school. The sun was trying to peep out from behind the clouds and she was arm in arm with Katie, even if she couldn't join in any of the school gossip. They didn't run into Molly Fox so she didn't have to try and pretend to be nice to

130

her. As they turned the corner of Kenilworth Street and walked along towards the school Katie was telling her all about a new girl called Lily Davies who'd arrived in their form, and about Lily's older sister, Jessie, and how pretty she was.

Just before they reached the school gates, Katie interrupted herself and called out, 'Lily, over here!'

Em saw a girl with frizzy ginger hair and a pale, oval face turn round and smile shyly. Katie loosed Em's arm and ran to the girl, linking arms with her instead. Em thought she was going to bring the new girl back to meet her and that they'd all walk to school together, but instead Katie forgot all about Em and marched in through the gates still arm in arm with Lily, chattering away to her. Em watched them, cut to the quick. Dragging her feet, she followed, her hope shrinking away. Some other girls from their class came along and said, 'Hello, Em – you back, then?' They seemed happy to see her but they were all in their little world, giggling together.

Em trailed into the school in their wake. When she got to the classroom, she found that Lily Davies had been given her place in the desk beside Katie, another reason why they were becoming such bosom pals. The only spare seat, up until then, was in the desk next to Molly at the front on the left and Miss Lineham ordered her to sit there.

Molly beamed with delight and made a great show of welcoming Em into her seat and leaning close to her. Em's nose wrinkled at the smell.

'It's nice, you're sitting by me,' Molly said fawningly. 'We can play out after, can't we? And

131

I can help you if you can't do the sums.'

Em nodded, a lump in her throat. She had realized, to her surprise, that Molly was quite good at sums, better than her these days, in fact. The morning only got worse. She loathed sitting beside Molly, assailed by the smell of urine and Molly's constant fidgeting as she scratched her scaly, eczema-scarred arms under her blouse. So many of the lessons felt hard now and she was slipping right down the class. Though Em escaped a caning, Miss Lineham was mean and sarcastic to her and she felt outside everything that was going on. In the playground the people it was easiest to play with were Molly, who of course homed in on her immediately during the morning break, and a timid little girl called Doris, with a bad squint and bluish lips, who'd also been absent for a time, suffering from severe asthma.

'What shall we play?' Molly demanded aggressively, vying for Em's attention. 'We'll play pretend – you can be the mom, Em, and I'll be the dad.' Molly organized them, bossing them around. But then she changed her tone completely and became fawning again. '*You* be in charge, Em,' she said. 'You're better at everything. Tell us what to do!'

Em's heart was heavy as lead. 'Go on, then,' she shrugged, one eye watching Katie and Lily, thick as thieves over on the other side of the playground. Unshed tears sat like a lead weight in her chest. Behind them somewhere, a chant had started up:

Long-legged Italy
Kicked poor Sicily
Right in the middle of the Mediterranean Sea.

'You be the dad,' Molly was saying to Em. 'I don't wanna be the dad.'

Em thought of Molly's father, sitting there helplessly by the fire.

'Nor me, and I don't wanna be the mom neither,' Em said. 'You be the dad, Doris.'

'I ent got a dad,' Doris whispered.

'I'll tell you a secret instead,' Molly whispered, beckoning them to her. She seemed to be bursting with the news. 'I've got a little kitten. I'm keeping it in the brew house.'

Doris who also lived on a yard, looked unimpressed. 'You can't do that. Someone'll let it out.'

'No they won't,' Molly said triumphantly. 'I've hidden it.'

By the end of the school day Em was utterly dejected. The only good thing she could think was that at least maybe Mom was getting better and that's why she was at school. Dad had given them the money for school dinner so she had not been home. As soon as the last bell rang to release them in the afternoon, Katie went off with Lily Davies and she was left to walk along with Molly. She was even grateful to find Molly at her side outside the school gates. At least someone wanted to be her friend. Even Joyce spent most of her time with Nancy Wiggins these days. Molly prattled at her all the way along the road about the kitten.

'I found her, see. She's called Sooty, cos she's black, 'cept for a little white patch by her nose. Our mom wouldn't 'ave it in the 'ouse. She says

133

cats are dirty but I don't think so.' She spoke very fondly. 'D'yer wanna come and see her?'

'All right,' Em said. She might as well.

They walked along Kenilworth Street, dodging out of the way of a flying tipcat from the games already in progress along the street. As soon as they turned down the entry into the back court where Molly lived, Em wished she hadn't come. There were the slimy green walls of the entry, then the cheerless yard where the high wall of the cycle works reared up on the right, dwarfing the decrepit-looking cluster of houses. Scummy puddles lay in dips in the uneven blue bricks and the whole place was filthy.

'Come on,' Molly whispered, pulling on Em's arm. 'We don't want my mom seeing us.'

Ducking past the windows of number four, they dashed to the brew house at the end of the yard, next to the row of toilets.

'Phwoor,' Em said, before she could help herself.

'Yeah, they'm stink, don't they?' Molly agreed matter-of-factly. Cautiously she tried the handle of the brew house, opening the door a crack. Immediately Em heard a pitiful mewing.

'Where is it?' She waited for her eyes to adjust to the gloomy interior. Little bits of coal crunched under their feet and the place smelled of a mixture of smoke and soap.

'In the copper!' Molly announced excitedly. 'I knew no one'd use it today! But I'm gunna put her in a box for tomorrow.'

She lifted the heavy wooden lid off the copper and the mewing grew louder. Upturning a pail, Molly stood on it and reached down inside.

'There yer go, no don't wriggle. I can't pick yer up if yer carry on like that!'

The cat was panicking and Molly just managed to hold on to it. She got down off the bucket, hugging the scrawny little scrap to her chest.

'See – ain't she lovely? She's my little poppet.' Molly kissed the cat's head, squeezing her tightly until she mewed even more pitifully. 'I'm gunna dress 'er up and look after her...'

'You can't just keep her in there, though, can yer,' Em objected. 'It ain't nice for her, and anyway, someone'll find her.'

'I've got an orange box,' Molly said dreamily. She obviously hadn't thought this through, she was just besotted with the cat. 'She can 'ave scraps from my dinner and from the miskins, and most of the time I'll–'

'Molly!'

Both of them froze as a rough, blaring voice interrupted from outside. Em went cold with fright at the sound of Iris Fox's bullying tone. Molly went to fling the cat back into the copper but it was too late. Iris was already opening the door, blocking out the light with her ample body.

'I saw yer go ducking past the winder! What're yer playing at, yer sneaky little cow? And who's that with yer?' Iris's eyesight wasn't the best even in full daylight when she was sober. 'Get out 'ere where I can see yer!'

Em went out, followed by Molly. Iris was a massive, big-boned woman. She was wearing a tight black dress which hugged her rolls of fat and accentuated a vast, aggressively jutting bosom. On her feet were sloppy old black shoes, collapsed at

135

the back, and her tar-coloured hair was scraped up, as usual, into a little topknot. From her puffy, narrowed-eyed face her gaze bored down into her daughter.

'What're yer doing? You're up to no good if yer creeping about...' It was then she noticed the cat. 'WHAT'S THAT THING?' she roared. Most of her communications were at full volume.

Em had been surprised at Iris noticing anything Molly was doing. Mostly she didn't seem to care. But she could smell the fumes of alcohol coming to her from Iris and realized she was spoiling for a fight, even if she had to box her own shadow.

'What're yer doing with that filthy bloody vermin?' Iris shouted. Em saw another woman come and stand at her doorway, watching.

'It's not filthy,' Molly said, hugging the poor cat even more tightly. 'It's my little cat. Oh, can I keep 'er, Mom, please? I won't bring 'er in the house. 'Er can stay out 'ere and I won't give 'er any of our food...'

'NO, YER WON'T!' Iris bawled. 'Cos it ain't gunna be anywhere near the place.' She advanced on Molly, who was cowering, and whipped the cat away from her by the scruff of its neck.

'Don't, Mom!' Molly started to sob. 'Don't hurt her!'

'Don't hurt her!' Iris mocked her daughter, her face creased with malice in a way that made Em's blood turn cold.

'No – don't, *don't*, Mom!' Molly shrieked as her mother strode over to the wall where the yard tap was dripping into a fetid puddle. Iris turned the tap on and thrust the limp little body underneath until it was a pitiful soaked rag of fur, mewling in terror.

'Right – let's see the back of yer, yer little rat!' Iris swung her arm back and lobbed the pathetic, bony body over the wall.

Molly and Em were both sobbing helplessly by now. Iris turned to them in contempt.

'What the 'ell's the matter with you whining little buggers?' And she stormed away like a great battleship, into her house. A few seconds later she opened the door and shouted, 'And don't you go next door looking for the ruddy thing. I'll drown it next time.'

Molly was crying pitifully. 'My little cat,' she wept. 'My poor little Sooty...What d'yer 'ave to go and do that for?' she yelled in her mother's direction. 'Why d'yer do that? I hate yer...' Her hands went over her face. 'I hate yer,' she cried brokenly, her voice shrinking to a despairing whimper. 'I *hate* yer so much, I just hate yer.'

Em didn't know what to say or do. She squeezed Molly's arm for a moment, then fled out of the yard.

'Mom?' She ran into number eighteen, just wanting her own kind, sweet mother, forgetting she was poorly, forgetting everything about the rest of the day. Iris Fox's cruel brutality drove everything out of her mind.

Neither Sid nor Joyce was there. She ran up the stairs to look for Cynthia in her bedroom and burst through the door. The bed was empty.

She ran halfway down the stairs. 'Mom?'

There was no reply. No one was in the house. Sinking down onto the staircase in the silent house, she could hear the distant voices of the other children playing outside. She was shaking all over.

'Your mother's gone away for a few days.'

The three children stood looking up at their father, round-eyed with shock.

'Where?' Em asked. 'Why's she done that? Where's Violet?'

'Her sister, your aunt Olive, said she could stop there for a bit, with the babby,' Bob said brusquely. 'Until she's feeling better.'

'Is Mom coming back tonight?' Joyce asked, her lower lip beginning to wobble. This had never, ever happened before, Mom not being at home.

'No – I've just told yer,' Bob snapped. 'I don't know how long she'll be away. Till she gets better, that's what I told her.'

Joyce burst into tears and Sid was beginning to snivel as well.

'I want Mom and the babby!' Joyce cried. 'I don't want our mom to be poorly.' She sank down on the floor, rubbing her knuckles in her eyes.

'Neither do any of us,' Bob said, trying to cheer them along. 'We'll just 'ave to make the best of it. You've got me.'

'I don't want *you*,' Joyce said mutinously. 'I want our mom.'

Em could feel a lump rising in her own throat but she could see her father's temper was on a knife edge and she swallowed hard and went to kneel next to Joyce.

'Come on, dry your tears, Joycie. We've all got to be brave, and our mom'll soon be back.'

Then Sid came to her and she put her arm round his solid little body. Sid rested his tired head on her shoulder.

'Want our mom,' he sobbed.

'For God's sake, pack in that racket!' Bob erupted, his nerves fraying even further. 'None of us like it – we're all just going to have to make the best of it and help out. Em – you're going to have to keep house. Mrs Wiggins'll help and she'll mind Joyce. But you'll 'ave to stop home till your mother gets back – school'll have to wait.'

He glanced wearily at the clock on the mantelpiece. 'It's too late to start cooking tea now – we'll have chips tonight. I'll go out and get 'em if you set the table. But from now on you'll have to do the cooking again, Em. You're the woman of the house now.'

Eighteen

Em opened the front door a crack, wide enough to look warily up and down the street, then ran across to Mrs Button's shop and waited for the woman in front of her to be served.

Mrs Button surveyed the scene from atop her stool behind the counter, on which lay a lovely fresh array of buns and doughnuts. Em looked up at her kindly face with a wan smile and nodded. It was nice to come out to Mrs Button's shop and get away from the house where she felt as if she had become almost a prisoner. She

139

could have gone out more when there was time, but she was in such a state of nerves she was constantly afraid of forgetting to do something. And she felt distant from the other children now, as if she was not quite one of them.

Once the other customer had gone, for a few moments Em was the only one in the shop and Mrs Button turned her full attention on her.

'Hello there, Em. How're you getting on today, then? How's little Joycie, and that cheeky Sid? I ain't seen them in here in a while. And how's yer mother getting on? And your dad?'

Not sure exactly which question most required an answer, Em said shyly, 'All right.'

'She getting better, then, is she? I gather she's gone for a little rest at her sister's.'

Em nodded, feeling her face go red. More people were coming into the shop now and queuing behind her in the little passage, listening to every word. She realized Josie Donnelly was behind her, and a couple of other sharp-tongued gossips. Sweat broke out on Em's palms and she rubbed them on her skirt. Why had Mom being poorly become something shameful? But that was how it felt. And she could hardly tell the truth about the huge, stormy tantrums Joyce had starting throwing, about Sid wetting the bed every night now, or about Dad's drinking.

'Your poor father,' Mrs Button lowered her voice just a fraction. 'You can't help feeling sorry for him, but I s'pose it's for the best. I don't know what my Stan would've done... He'd've gone to pieces without me. But I s'pose your mother'll be back soon.'

'Can I have a tin loaf, please,' Em said, aware of all the ears flapping behind her. As Mrs Button at last got round to handing her a loaf, Em saw another customer join the back of the queue, dressed in a black coat, her dark hair tucked under her hat. Last time Em had come to Mrs Button's this lady had queued just in front of her. She was a neat, curvaceous person and, close up to her, Em had noticed that she had a nice clean smell, and a scent of flowers about her. Em had seen that pinned to the lapel of her coat was a sparkling diamanté brooch shaped like a small rosette. She had not been able to stop staring at it, it was so pretty.

The lady had asked for her purchases in a quiet voice and paid with a faint smile, not quite looking anyone in the eye though nodding politely enough at the others who were waiting as she left. Mrs Button had watched her go.

'Well, she's a dark horse that one.'

'That's Flossie Dawson, ain't it?' the woman behind Em had said. 'She's moved in round the corner from me. There's a daughter, but I don't know where the husband is.'

'They say she's a widow,' Mrs Button had said. 'Though she ain't one for letting on much herself so far as I can tell.' She'd spoken in a slightly affronted way, as if she thought Flossie Dawson was putting on airs.

Em had seen the lady go up and down the road a few times, but never talking to anyone. She seemed to keep herself to herself. Em noticed her, though, because she always looked so pretty and nicely dressed.

'There yer go, bab.' Mrs Button handed Em

141

her loaf. 'Don't go eating it all at once! 'Ere–' she reached to the side where there was a plate of leftover cakes from the day before – 'I'll throw in a couple of doughnuts. You share them with yer brother and sister, eh?'

Em departed gratefully from the shop and Mrs Button stared after her.

'Poor little thing, look at her. Thin as a pin, and the state of 'er clothes!'

'Well, what would you expect, with the mother taking off the way she has,' Josie Donnelly said. 'Leaving the poor child to keep house. That front step hasn't seen a scrubbing brush for days – and Dot Wiggins is in and out of there having to take it on, as if she hasn't got enough on her plate! It's disgraceful, carrying on like that.'

Josie, with her eight children and a work-shy gambler of a husband, had always felt inferior to Cynthia, so now she welcomed an opportunity to crow.

'Well, it's that little 'un I feel sorry for,' Mrs Button said. 'She were always a nice little thing, sunny somehow and happy-looking. The state of 'er now you'd hardly know she was the same child. Even her freckles have gone pale.'

Em carried the loaf and cakes home and as soon as she was inside the door she pulled one of the stale doughnuts out of the bag, perched on the back step and bit into it ravenously. She always seemed to be hungry these days. Sid and Joyce would have to share the other one. The doughnut was delicious and she finished it in seconds, enjoying the sugar and jam tastes lingering in her mouth.

Nursing her sore hands under her armpits, she stared dully at the bits of washing she'd hung out earlier. Her hands were red raw and cracked from water and harsh soap and constant drudgery. She had to wash out Sid's sheet every morning since Mom had gone. And her brother was so subdued. He didn't go out hanging about with Bert Fox and the other toughs any more and at night he kept wanting to come into bed with her and Joyce. Em had taken to getting in with him and waiting until he was asleep before going back to Joyce. She didn't want to wake up and find all three of them soaking wet.

Mom had left ten days ago and already it seemed as if she'd been gone for months. Em didn't go to school; she stayed at home and did her best to keep house, with Dot popping in as often as she could and Joyce running between the two houses. She struggled with the heavy load of washing on Monday, heating up the copper as Mom had done. Bob helped with that before he went to work. She never managed it without getting most of the water all over the floor. She tried to keep the house clean, getting down on her hands and knees and taking the scrubbing brush to the floor, sweeping, dusting, wiping. Then there was the food. Quite often Dot cooked for all of them, or she gave Em advice about how to cook things and Bob would help when he got home. If he came home in time. He was still frequenting the pub quite often but, under constant vigilance from Dot, he did try to get home early most nights.

When he was there, though, he was so unhappy, so silent and angry that Em and the others were frightened of him. Even Joyce, the apple of his eye, could not get through to him.

Em tried and tried to do her best, to be good like Mom always said she was, but even when she struggled hard all day everything seemed to go wrong and get in a mess. Sid's mattress was never dry and it stank, the house was becoming infested with bugs and silver fish and she knew they should stove it to get rid of them. She would have to ask Dot to help. Sid and Joyce didn't seem to understand or want to lend a hand with anything.

'Come out and play,' Joyce kept on every night, but Em always had to say, 'But I've got to get the dinner.'

She knew Bob would be furious if she was out when he came in.

That afternoon she sat day-dreaming on her lonely step, eyes closed, leaning her head back against the door frame. Her one dream was always of having her mother home, well and happy the way she used to be. One day soon, Mom would just walk in, back to her old self after her stay with Auntie Olive. She'd call out 'Coo-ee!' the way she and Dot always did when they popped into each other's houses, Violet would be in her arms, and she'd come and cuddle Em and tell her what a good girl she'd been and how well she'd done. Mom and Dad would be happy like they used to be when they had laughed and joked together, Mom would never go away again and Em would go back to school, everyone would be pleased to see her and she'd be top of the class. It would happen soon, any day now, Em was sure it would, if she was good and did her best. All she had to do was make sure everything was right for Mom when she came home. She opened her eyes again and smiled out from under her fringe, gazing across the brick yard with the sheet flapping in the breeze.

Her dream was pierced by a tap at the door. She got up stiffly from the back step, and went to the front to find Katie outside. Her heart leapt. Katie had come to see her, at last! Maybe she'd fallen out with Lily Davies and wanted to say sorry and make friends!

But Katie's expression froze the smile on Em's face.

'I've come to pass on a message from my mom.' Katie didn't sound her normal self. Her voice was stiff and formal as if she was talking to a teacher and someone had told her what to say.

'Thing is,' she went on, staring down at the doorstep, which Em saw to her shame was covered in soot and dirt, 'I can't play with you no more. Mom says she doesn't...' Here, Katie at least had the decency to stumble over her words. 'She doesn't want me having anything to do with you. She says it ain't right, the way your mom's gone and left you. She says your mom's not right – you know, in the head – and that I'm not to be friends with you.'

A burning flame of hurt and rage flashed through Em. She clenched her fists. How dare snooty Mrs O'Neill say things like that about her mom! All her hurt feelings boiled over.

'Why d'you think I care?' she yelled. 'You're a

rotten, stuck-up little cow, and I don't wunna play
out with you anyhow!' And she slammed the door
in Katie's face before crumpling to her knees,
curling up until her forehead rested on the floor
and bursting into tears of exhaustion and fury.

Nineteen

'Coo-ee – Em?'

Dot's face appeared round the front door on a
wet, windy November Monday when Em was
alone, having waved Sid off to school and Joyce
next door only just a few minutes ago. But Dot
came bringing a sulky-looking Joyce back again.

'You'd better keep her at home today, bab. I've
got our Nance down with the measles. I don't
know if it's too late.' She eyed Joyce. 'She might
already be brewing with it. But she'd best stop at
home to be on the safe side.'

Joyce flung herself mutinously into a chair and
sat scowling.

'You all right, love?' Dot asked Em, her dark eyes
full of concern. It wrung her heart to see these
children left without their mom, and poor little
Em trying to cope. She missed Cynthia enough
herself. 'I'll look in when I can.' She lowered her
voice slightly. 'You heard from yer mother?'

Em nodded. She went to the mantelpiece and
brought a flimsy piece of lined blue paper, with
Cynthia's careful writing on it.

Dear family,

Just a line to say I hope you are all well and looking arter one another and helping your father. I am doing well and hope I can come home soon. Am missing you all.

From

Your loving Mother

'Oh – that's nice, then!' Dot cried, her thin face lighting up with relief. 'When did that come?'

'Sat'dy,' Em said, with slight upturn of her lips. The little note had lifted her spirits no end and had brought a smile to her father's face.

'There yer go, I told yer a bit of a rest would sort her out,' he'd said. It was the first time she had seen him look light-hearted in many weeks.

'I've got a bit of leftover stew you two can have for your dinner,' Dot offered as she headed out of the door. 'I'll bring it in later. Must go now, though – but you know to come and knock if you want any help, don't yer, bab?'

Em nodded, strengthened by Dot's kindness. She knew they'd never have survived without Dot. The sight of Joyce's sulky face could have brought her close to losing her temper, but she took a deep breath and said, 'Come on, Joycie. We've all got to be big and brave for our mom. Come and help me – there's work to do.'

'When's our mom coming 'ome?' Joyce asked, for the umpteenth time.

'Soon, I s'pect,' Em told her. She was suddenly filled with energy. 'Now come on – you can be a good girl and help me sweep out the bedrooms.'

'I'm not emptying the po'!' Joyce said in horror.

147

'No,' Em sighed. The brimming po' under her father's bed was one of the day's tasks she dreaded the most. Now he was drinking more, she was forced to deal with the consequences.

The two girls set to, Em getting Joyce to help her make the beds and soak the middle patch of Sid's sheet once again, before hanging it by the range. It was too wet outside for it to dry in the stinging wind. Em swept the dust into little piles for Joyce to pick up with the old tin dustpan. When they'd finished, Joyce said, 'I'm hungry. I want my dinner.'

'It's only half past ten!' Em said. 'Come on, you can have a drink of milk and a crust off the loaf to fill you up.'

Both of them had some milk and shared the crust off the loaf with a scraping of margarine. Em made Joycie sit at the table to eat it and afterwards they started playing one of their old games, 'Mrs Maud Mayberry and her maid'.

Neither of them knew where the name Mayberry had come from, or Maud for that matter. Em had probably made it up, but Mrs Maud Mayberry was a very, very rich and fine lady who wore exquisite dresses and spoke in a quavering, cut-glass voice, which was the way the girls imagined very rich ladies must speak. Em always played Mrs Maud Mayberry, preening and walking back and forth across the room swishing her imaginary silken skirts and sticking her nose in the air as befitted a lady. Her maid was called Miss Susan and Joyce nearly always had to play her. But she was a very clever and beautifully dressed maid who wore a starched uniform and always brought every item requested by Mrs Maud Mayberry on a silver platter.

'Ay think ay'd lake may brush and comb, please, Miss Susan,' Mrs Maud Mayberry pronounced, stretching her face and bringing out the best upper-class vowels she could muster because that was how grown-ups talked when they were taking off posh people. She extended her arm to take the comb in the languid manner Em imagined true to all rich ladies of leisure. 'May hair is looking truly fraytful...'

'Yes, Mrs Maud Mayberry, Your Royal Highness,' Joycie said with an unctuous bow.

'I ain't Queen Mary, silly!' Em said, falling out of role for a second. 'Yer don't just say '"Your Royal Highness" to any old person, yer know.'

'Well, I dain't know,' Joyce protested, stamping her foot. 'Why can't I be Mrs Maud Mayberry for once? I always have to be Miss Susan and it ain't fair...'

'Oh, all right, then,' Em said grumpily, trying to keep the peace. 'And don't say "ain't".'

They exchanged roles, Joyce strutting back and forth across the back room as if to the manner born and Em being a spirited Miss Susan. The hours disappeared into the game, the other chores forgotten, until Dot knocked on the door again.

'All right, you two? 'Ere's a bit of dinner for yer – we had it left over. I'd've 'ad you come round and eat at ours only you should see the state of Nance – she's all spots!'

She sat the two little girls down at the table and lifted the lid off a delicious-smelling portion of stew.

149

'There yer go – I've shoved a few taters in to make it go further so that should keep you going. Eat it all up – I'll see yer later.'

And off she went again. They wolfed down the stew. Em liked having Joyce at home. It stopped the long hours of the day being so lonely. Today she had almost forgotten about Mom and about trying to do everything right to make her come back. She and Joyce had been lost in the game, like old times.

She spilled some gravy in her lap as she was eating, and as she scraped it up she saw with dismay just how dirty her frock was.

'I'd better wash it,' she told Joyce. 'And Sid's sheet should be dry by now.'

All the mundane realities were coming back now the game was over.

They left their dirty plates on the table and Em went down to the coal cellar which the coalman had newly stocked two days ago, the coal rattling down through the opening outside. Always glad to get out of there again she hurried up with the heavy scuttle and stoked the range. Then she filled another bucket of water, added some warm from the kettle and stripped off her dress.

'I might as well wash yours while I'm at it, Joycie...'

The two girls stood in their bloomers and vests and *Daily Mail* boots, plunging the dresses down into the soapy water. It quickly became a game and they giggled, dotting soap bubbles on each other's noses and yanking the dresses up and down in the pail, wringing them into soaking wet snakes. Soon there was water splashed all across the linoleum in the back room and they were getting wet themselves as well.

They were so caught up in the washing game that they didn't hear the front-door opening.

It was Em, raising her head from dipping her frock in the bucket, who gasped at the sight of the figure standing by the door of the back room. She stood stock still for a second, as if afraid to believe her eyes, then the cry burst pitifully from her throat.

'Mom! Oh, Mom!'

Cynthia, with Violet in her arms, sank to her knees, regardless of the wet floor, and her two little girls ran to her. She held out her spare arm and wrapped it round Joyce, and Em clung round her neck and shoulders, drinking in the warmth of her body, the reality that she was with them again.

'Oh, my babbies, my little ones...' Cynthia broke down and wept heartbrokenly at the sight of her daughters, all the more sweet and vulnerable for being clad only in their shabby underclothes. Frantically she stroked their hair, their cheeks, ravenous for the feel of them. She looked wildly into their faces. 'Are you all right? Has Dot been coming in?'

They nodded, too excited to see her to take in just how gaunt her face was, the dark, sleepless rings under her eyes. They cuddled Violet and exclaimed that she was bigger, and then Em stood back and said, very grown-up, 'I'll put the kettle on, shall I, Mom?'

More tears ran down Cynthia's face as she said, 'Yes please, bab. I'm dying for a cuppa. That's my girl.'

Twenty

There was great excitement that afternoon. Dot came in, delighted to see her friend back home, and Em and Joyce scurried down to the school together to fetch Sid and tell him the news.

'Mom's home!' they cried as soon as they saw him. He looked uncertainly at them, as if he couldn't dare to believe it, before tearing home as fast as his little legs would carry him. Cynthia had been away for three weeks, but to the children it seemed like an eternity. They all clung round her.

'You better now, Mom?' Sid was the only one of the children to inherit Cynthia's brown eyes, and now they gazed at her full of longing.

'Course I am,' she said bravely, hugging him to her. 'I'm not going away again.' To Dot she added in a whisper, 'Not to that hard-faced bitch over there, I can tell yer.'

Dot rolled her eyes. 'Like that, is it?'

'I can't tell you, Dot.' Cynthia's eyes started to fill and she shooed the children away. 'Go on, all of you – go and play out for a bit while Dot and me have a chinwag.'

The children did as they were told, though obviously reluctant to leave her.

'You all right now, Cynth?' Dot asked carefully.

'Oh, Dot.' Cynthia broke down then. 'Olive's so mean and spiteful. She's not got an ounce of

152

kindness in her! I was grieving all the time I was there and she was horrible to me, making me feel in the way. I didn't know where to put myself. She made me hide upstairs when she had visitors round! She's always been hard-faced, but I never knew she was that bad.'

'Never mind, bab, you're back home now,' Dot comforted her. 'Your kiddies need you here. Your Em's been ever such a good girl, trying to look after everyone the way she has. You should be proud of her.'

'I know,' Cynthia nodded. 'And I'll try and make it up to her.'

'I'd best be off now, our Nance is all spots,' Dot said. 'I hope we ain't all spreading it about.'

'Yes you'd better,' Cynthia urged. 'And thanks, Dot. You're the best friend anyone could have.'

'T'ain't been the same without you around, Mrs Brown,' Dot said with a lopsided smile which meant she was close to tears. 'T'ra for now.'

It seemed so quiet once Dot had gone. Violet was asleep and Cynthia sat, soaking in the feeling of being at home again. It wasn't much, their house, but today it seemed to her like a palace. She looked round her simple room, with its poor furniture, the old range with the battered kettle resting on top, the big saucepan with mendits screwed through the bottom to keep the water in, the mantelshelf with its cover of threadbare red velvet and their few ornaments on it. Their precious photographs graced the mantel in the front room: their wedding portrait and the faded face of Bob's mother looking out across the bare room. Cynthia had often wondered what she was

153

like: she had a kindly face. Perhaps she'd change things round, she thought, and bring the pictures in here where they could see them all the time instead of saving them for best. They were family and what could be more important?

'I've got to make it up to Bob,' she said to herself. 'I've got to be better – for his sake, and the kids.'

But she thought about the days before she left home, the hurt and anger in his face, and fear rose up to choke her. What if he couldn't forgive her? And what if she couldn't be the wife he needed her to be?

Putting her hands over her face she rocked back and forth, deep racking sobs working their way out of her.

She was home at last, but everything still felt impossible and overwhelming. How on earth was she going to manage?

Em helped her make the tea. She was in the habit now and Cynthia seemed almost to have forgotten how. She had wanted to come home and take up the reins, be in charge as a mother, but she found herself standing helplessly, as if she couldn't remember what to do.

'I feel all mithered,' she said, as Em turned from peeling potatoes in a bowl at the table, to see her mother just gazing at her in bewilderment. She was so thin, even Em could see her clothes were hanging on her. Her eyes had a stretched, staring look which had not been there before.

'Why don't you go and sit down, Mom?' Em said cautiously. 'You don't want to go getting tired.'

'No!' She was shouting suddenly, but seeing the look of terror on Em's face she tried to quieten herself. 'No, I must help, I've got to. I'm your mother!'

Em stood back, offering her the old knife, talking cautiously to her. 'You do the taters. I'll get the cabbage done, shall I?'

'All right,' Cynthia said quietly, and Em had a terrible feeling suddenly, more frightening than all that had gone before. It was as if a big black pit was opening in front of her, because she was utterly alone: out of the two of them it was Mom who was the child, and there was no one above her to rely on. Together, they cooked liver and potatoes and cabbage, Em reminding Cynthia what to do at every step.

By the time it was ready Bob had not come home. Em had set the table and was ready to feed everyone, but Cynthia hovered expectantly by the front window.

'Tea's ready, Mom,' Em called to her.

'But your dad's not here. We'd best not start without him.'

Em exchanged looks with Sid and Joyce. 'I s'pect he'll be late,' Em said. 'He is sometimes.'

Cynthia came in frowning. 'Why? 'E's never late normally. Always home by half past five.'

Em didn't like to tell her that it was sometimes another three hours before Bob rolled in these days.

'Well, let's have ours and he'll soon be here,' she said.

By the time they had eaten and washed up, still there was no sign of him. His dinner congealed on his plate at the table. It was an awful evening, with Cynthia on pins asking again and again where her husband was and why he was late. In the end Em had had to say, 'I s'pect he's gone down the boozer. 'E does sometimes. 'E dain't know you was coming home, Mom.'

'He doesn't, not "'e dain't",' Cynthia corrected automatically. 'Don't drop your aitches, it's common.' Then she remembered what they were talking about. 'You mean, he's left you, every night like this? Oh, I should never've gone away. I shouldn't've listened to him! I thought it'd be for the best, the way I was feeling, but I never should've.'

'It's all right, Mom. We've not come to any harm,' Em said.

'No but it's not right!' She was working herself up into a terrible state. 'What's come over 'im? And what the neighbours must've been saying...'

As time passed she was almost on the point of marching along to the pub and dragging him out, but Em stopped her.

It was past Em's bedtime and she was already lying beside Sid, trying to soothe him to sleep, when she heard the front door open. She pulled the blanket and Bob's old army coat up over her ears and screwed her eyes tightly shut.

Bob came round the door, and saw her waiting there. He was well oiled but not blind drunk, though he stopped and blinked a time or two to check he wasn't seeing things.

'Cynth?'

'Where've you been?' Her pent-up emotion

156

came out in a shrewish wail. 'It's a fine thing, me coming home and you're not here, and Em says you've been out every night! Why weren't you here?'

She wanted him to come to her, to be sweet and reassuring and glad to see her, but her anger and misery had the opposite effect.

'So, you're back, are yer?' He stuck his cap angrily on the hook at the back of the door. 'Well, I hope you've pulled yourself together, cos if you ain't you can pack your bag and go back there until yer have.'

'Yes, of course I'm better.' She wiped her eyes hurriedly at this threat and spoke appeasingly. 'I was just worried, that's all, love. It's not like you to be out every evening and I was looking forward to seeing you. I didn't know where you were, that's all.'

'I just went out for a drink, if that's all right with you,' he said sarcastically. 'Since there weren't no company at 'ome. What d'yer want, me sitting in by the fire waiting for you every night?'

'No, I...'

'Just cos you'd gone off on a little holiday...'

But he softened then and came to her, putting his hands on her shoulders, and her heart leapt with relief as he looked into her eyes.

'So – you better, then, wench?' His voice was gentler.

'I th-think so.' She ached for it to be true, though she still so strange, so lost and shut away from everyone. But she must make him believe she was better.

'Glad to 'ear it.'

157

He took her in his arms and was immediately full of desire for her, fumbling to unbutton her blouse.

'Bob, no...'

'Come upstairs,' he cajoled, tugging on her hand. 'Come on – the kids are in bed, ain't they? What's to stop us?'

'But I–'

'But be dammed!' he roared. 'I said, get upstairs!'

Terrified, she could hardly recognize him. She begged him to be quiet but he dragged her up to the bedroom, kicked the door shut and forced her up against it, pushing himself against her, his beery tongue in her mouth. She felt his fingers digging into her arms as he pulled her to the bed, starting to tug her clothes off her, bruising her.

'No...' she wept. 'Don't ... don't...'

'Oh, for Christ's sake, you miserable bitch, what's the matter with yer now?' The stinging slap he delivered across her face made her whimper.

'Just stop yer blarting,' he panted.

His need and arousal were so great that he forced her legs apart and pushed himself into her, thrusting and muttering until he came, quickly, with a sob of release. Cynthia turned her head aside, her eyes clenched shut. She could smell him, a mixture of sweat, coal dust and beer.

He withdrew from her abruptly and lit the candle. Seeing her there, limp on the bed, he was full of remorse and came and lay beside her, stroking her hair.

'God, Cynth ... I'm sorry. It's been so long, so bloody miserable – I just had to... I dain't mean to hurt yer...'

With a sob she snuggled up to him. She didn't want to be angry with him, she needed to feel the comfort of his arms round her. Into his chest she murmured, 'I don't know what to do. I don't know what's the matter with me.'

Gentler now, and close to sleep, he held her. 'Never mind, love. It's been awful without yer. But we can make it better, can't we, my bab? It'll be all right.'

Twenty-One

For the first few days Em thought it was going to be all right.

She went back to school, trying to resign herself to Katie's rejection of her and hanging about with anyone who was prepared to be her friend, which of course Molly always was. She tried to push from her mind what had happened with Molly's mom and the cat. Everything about Molly and her family horrified her. Cynthia had always said the Foxes were a dirty family, but it wasn't just the dirt which made her stomach turn with dread. It was the feeling of chaos and cruelty which she saw in Bert and which had been so horribly demonstrated by Iris Fox that day with Molly's kitten. So she looked upon Molly with mixed pity and dread.

A few days went past but even though they all tried to pretend everything was back to normal, Cynthia was anything but recovered. She seemed

159

to exist on a knife edge, barely able to cope but trying too hard and flying into hysterics over the slightest thing.

There was no lying in bed now. Instead she got up each morning and flung herself into a fever of activity, cleaning and washing the neglected house. Soon her energy would run out. She was already very thin and had no appetite, and feeding Violet took a lot from her. Her face was white and her jaw seemed permanently clenched. At the slightest thing she dissolved into tears.

'Hey – you're s'posed to be getting a bit of rest, ain't yer?' Dot upbraided her when she dropped in for a cup of tea during a lull one afternoon. She found Cynthia ironing frantically, a blanket spread over the table. 'Come and sit down for a bit and drink your tea.'

Cynthia snatched up the iron which had been heating on the range, a square of worn leather in her hand to prevent her from burning herself on the handle.

'I can't stop, Dot – I've got so much to do.' She gave her strained, intense look. 'What with me being away, the place is squalid! I've got to clean up – get everything put right...'

Dot got up from her chair with a determined expression, firmly took the iron out of Cynthia's hand and replaced it on the range.

'Cynth–' she put her arm round her friend's shoulders and looked into her eyes – 'come and sit down. The house can wait. It never ruddy well ends whatever you do, does it? You look all in.'

Cynthia protested, but allowed herself to be seated on one of the chairs. Dot drew hers closer and looked at her very seriously.

'Look, bab, what's ailing yer? You're not right, you're thin as a railing and you've got a look on yer face all the time now as if the devil's behind yer. You want to go careful or you're going to have a breakdown. You're driving yourself too hard!'

'I'm not,' Cynthia said earnestly, knitting her bony fingers together. She blinked and rolled her eyes in the strange way that she did now. 'I'm all right, Dot, really I am. But I've let Bob down, and the kids, and I'm just trying to make everything right again. He gets so angry with me.' She trailed off, looking sad and bewildered.

'He's worried about yer. We all are!' Dot leaned forward and gripped her hand. 'For God's sake, take it easy, love. I'll come and help if there's that much to do...'

'No!' Cynthia protested. 'You've got your Nance down with the measles.'

'Oh, she's on the mend – they're all tough little buggers, my lot,' Dot said fondly. 'I just don't want to see my pal in this state. If you go on like this–' She bit her words back. 'Look, everything's all right - your husband, kids, you've got a nice healthy bab there – you've no need to be in such a state.'

She patted Cynthia's hand and sat back, smiling. But Cynthia suddenly put her hands over her face.

'I feel so bad sometimes, Dot. I can't tell yer how bad. I feel ... *evil*. I'm making everything worse for everyone, but I don't know how to help myself.' She moved her hands away, her face screwed up in revulsion. 'I'm an evil woman. I don't deserve to live.'

'Cynth, what are you *on* about?' Dot was really concerned but as a coper herself she was at a loss. 'You'll perk up soon. It's just the babby, and what with the shock you had over Joycie and that. Come on, you need to get enough rest and try and look on the bright side.'

She sat chatting, trying to make Cynthia laugh and tell her jokes and bits of gossip. Her son Terry, she said, had a new girlfriend – quite a looker. 'And I reckon Old Man Donnelly's playing away again,' she said in her comical way. 'And with that hatchet face of hers you can hardly blame him!'

Before she left she managed to get a wan smile out of Cynthia. It was the last any of them were to see for a very long time.

Her mood of frantic energy began to slip away. The withdrawn, glassy-eyed mother reappeared, who seemed barely able to move a limb of her body without enormous effort.

Em noticed that suddenly Cynthia seemed not to want to take care of Violet. Em was allowed to struggle on at school. She caught up with her lessons quite easily, but still felt terribly hurt by Katie O'Neill's abandonment of her. Katie was inseparable from Lily. Em pretended she didn't care and went out to play with anyone who'd have her. When she got home she would often find Cynthia in bed or sitting in a chair, staring, taking no notice of her baby. If she was upstairs, as often as not she left Violet down in the back room, shutting out the sound of her cries.

'I got Dot to get me some formula,' Cynthia said

to Em one day, her hollow-eyed face looking up at her from the pillow. 'You just mix it with water in one of them bottles. I'm not going to feed her myself any more. It's making me too tired. And I don't want them to see me with her anyway.'

'Who?' Em asked, bewildered.

'Oh—' Cynthia waved a bony hand, scornfully – 'the people from the Welfare. They spy on people like me, you know. You never know when they might be watching you. So you take her and sort her out, will you, love?'

Em couldn't make any sense of this, but she liked looking after Violet who, despite everything, was a round-faced, rather placid child whose smiles revealed a deep dimple in her left cheek. Em was sure her baby sister recognized her and began to wave her arms about when she appeared. She enjoyed sitting with the warm, milky weight of Violet in her lap, watching her suck out of a bottle. Violet was cross at first and spat the formula milk out, asking for the familiar warm nipple, but she was soon hungry enough to get used to it. Em and Joyce took turns.

Em wondered what Mom had been talking about. Did the Welfare people really watch you if you had a baby? And were they watching her as she fed Violet? She shrugged the thought away. They could only be looking through the window and she couldn't see anyone. Besides, she wasn't doing anything wrong, was she?

Things came quickly to a head. Bob came straight home that Friday evening, not going to the pub, trying to do his best for his family. The night was cold, he had a cough and was exhausted, and was as black as a chimney sweep as ever. He came in to find the downstairs rooms full of blue smoke and rank with the smell of burned fat. Sid and Joyce were squabbling and Em was jiggling a wailing Violet in her arms while the sausages she was cooking were charring on the stove.

He ran and snatched the pan off the heat, slamming it down at the back of the range.

'For Christ's sake!' he exploded. 'What the hell's going on – where's yer mother?' Without waiting for Em to answer he tore off his coat and hat, flinging them onto a chair and stormed up the stairs. Sid and Joyce had stopped fighting and the three children all stood still, listening in dread.

The bedroom door was flung open, followed by the sound of terrifying screams.

Cynthia, who had been lying in bed like a rag, leapt up, electrified by terror at the sight of someone coming through the door.

'No!' she screamed. 'Get away from me! Get out of my room – no, don't touch me! AAAAAA-AAAAAAGH!'

Bob, startled and horribly disturbed by the hysteria in her voice, dealt her a stinging slap across the face.

'Don't take me away!' Cynthia was crying, begging. 'Don't... I'll be better, I will. I don't want to be bad... Oh, help me, help me, for God's sake!'

'Cynth! CYNTHIA!' Bob knelt on the bed and grasped her hands, shaking her, forcing her to sit still. 'It's me, for Christ's sake. Stop screaming, woman, I can't stand it.'

'I thought they were coming to take me away.' She was stunned and trembling, her hair wild, eyes full of fear.

Bob looked at her, the alien, strange woman beside him, and cautiously released her hands. He was beyond trying to comfort her. He was deeply afraid.

'It's no good.' His voice was low and grave. 'I can't live with you no more, not carrying on like this. I don't know what's going on with you, Cynth, but you can get your things packed. You're going back to your sister till you can pull yerself together, or not bother coming back at all!'

'No, Bob – no, don't make me go back there!' Cynthia begged, weeping heartbrokenly. 'I don't want to go back there. She's horrible to me, Olive is, and it's all worse there. They'll be watching me and I can't stand it. I can't stand them watching me... Their eyes...'

'For God's sake, woman!' He was yelling now, completely distraught. 'You carry on like this and you'll end up in the asylum, that you will. You're going off yer head and I can't stand it! I can't live with yer when you're like this. I want my bloody wife back, that's what I want – not some sodding loony who talks a load of bloody rubbish all the time!'

There was a momentary lull. Em stared at the floor, hugging Violet. She couldn't look at Sid or Joyce, because upstairs something was happening that they'd never known before. Both their parents were weeping. Bob's sobs came to them in raw, jerking sounds. It seemed shameful, hear-

165

ing a grown man cry, and frightening because it was their dad. Over it came desperate weeping from Cynthia.

'I'm not giving in to you no more,' they heard, more quietly then. 'You've got to go, Cynth. I can't stand it and you're no good to me or the kids in this state. I don't want to do it, but it's for the best. I can't stand living with you as you are. Come back and be my wife, for God's sake, love. But for now you've got to go – first thing in the morning. And that's final.'

The night seemed to go on forever. None of them slept much. All night Em kept falling into a doze only to be woken by Violet crying, or her mother weeping and begging incoherently in the next room.

Sid got into bed with the girls, top to toe with them, so that rest was made all the more difficult by all being cramped in together. Em was afraid he'd wet the bed, but she was quite glad of the comfort of having her brother and sister close when her heart felt cold and full of dread. None of them had heard their father's exact words; they just knew something awful and frightening was happening, that the sunny, secure life they had known before seemed to be being swept away forever.

In the grey light of dawn, Em woke, wet and clammy, enveloped in the pungent smell of Sid's urine, and she clambered from the bed, her vest and pants clinging to her. Sid woke immediately and sat bolt upright, saying, 'Where's Mom?'

'I dunno,' Em said. 'In bed, I s'pose.'

She woke Joyce and tugged the sodden sheet off the bed once more. They were growing used to the stinging ammonia smell, and the mattress was ringed with stains and this new damp patch. She went to take the sheet down to soak it, and the others followed her as if they didn't dare let her out of their sight.

As their bare feet progressed down the stairs, there was a wail from the front room.

'Oh God, Bob – they're awake!'

Cynthia was standing by the front door in her hat and coat. Her little brown bag was up against the door and Violet was resting on a blanket in the seat of the chair. To Em, her mother seemed like a scrawny stranger. Her real mom, the old Cynthia, had gone away somewhere already.

Bob came from the back. He looked very annoyed to see the children standing at the foot of the stairs.

'Right, well, you'd best say goodbye to your mother,' he said brusquely. ''Er's going away again, just for a few days, to your auntie Olive's.'

'Oh, Mom, I don't want you to go away, you said you'd never!' Sid ran to her, as did Joyce, both sobbing, holding out their arms to be picked up. Em, swept by the most terrible sense of dread, felt sobs forcing up in her chest. She wanted to be the big sister, who could control herself, but it was too frightening and difficult.

'Don't go, Mom!' A wail of anguish tore out of her. 'Please don't go away again!'

'Oh my Lord,' Cynthia cried, holding out her pitifully thin arms to embrace all her children. Em felt her boniness as she was pressed to her and she

167

clung to her mother, never wanting to let go.

'I don't want to go,' Cynthia wept, her cheeks brushed by her children's soft hair as they clung to her, all crying desperately. 'I don't want to leave you. It won't be for long. I'll come back as soon as I can.'

'Come on now – let's get it over.' Jaw set, his own suffering locked within him, Bob pulled his wife to her feet. 'You've got to go, Cynth, it's no good.'

Em tore herself away from her mother but the two younger children were not so easy to shift. Sid roared in protest and in the end Bob hauled both him and Joyce roughly away, knocking Joyce's leg painfully on the chair as he did so, making her cry even louder. He plonked the two of them on the rag rug, as Cynthia wept uncontrollably.

'Now you stay there and stop yer blarting!' he shouted at his distressed children. 'I'm going to put your mother on the bus and I'll be back.'

He picked up Violet in one arm and the bag in the other.

'Open the door,' he ordered.

Cynthia did so, gazing back at her children.

'Go on – out, woman!'

Her distraught eyes drank in their tear-stained faces. 'I'll be back soon, little'uns. Take care of each other!'

With tears rolling down her cheeks, Cynthia was urged out through the front door by her husband, the children's cries following her leaden steps along the freezing street.

Jack Stones

Twenty-Two

'Em – oi, Em! You coming to play?'

Em had just come out of the house when she was hailed by a group of girls from school. They were squatting on the pavement playing jack stones, the latest craze to hit the neighbourhood.

Em pretended she didn't hear, immediately wishing she could escape indoors again. Katie O'Neill was among the girls, though she had not been the one who shouted. Of course not, Em thought sourly. Katie wouldn't have anything to do with her now. It was a long time since Em had been out to the Girls' Brigade or anything like that.

'Em?'

She shook her head, hurrying past. 'Can't – I got to go somewhere.'

'Be like that, then,' the girl said, but not nastily. Katie didn't even look up. She kept her head down so low that the ends of her plaits were dragging on the pavement. The girls went back to their game, throwing a stone in the air and trying to pick up another of the five before it hit the ground.

The street was humming with life and most of the neighbourhood children were outside, shooed from under their mothers' heels. The sun was sinking low, though well disguised with a pall of grey cloud, and a mean wind was blowing the smoke from the chimneys to one side. Em put her

171

head down, hugging herself in her thin jersey as she hurried to Mrs Button's shop. As she got to the door, Mrs Button was standing there about to close up. Bullseye the dog was peering out from behind her skirts.

'Ah – so you've come, 'ave yer?' she said, her chins wobbling cheerfully. She led Em into the little house. 'I was about to shut up for the night. In fact I'd just said to my Stanley, "I think I'll shut up shop," so you've come just in time – don't mind the dog, 'e'll only sniff at yer – not that I wouldn't open the door to yer, but Stanley ain't too keen on callers after hours. 'E says 'e wants me all to 'imself then!'

'Quite right!' Stanley Button's jovial voice called from out the back somewhere. 'Who is it, Jen?'

'It's little Em Brown – you know, from over the road.'

'Oh ar,' Stanley said. 'Well, I'm sure you've got summat for the wench, ain't yer, Jen?'

Everyone knew there was something badly wrong with her mother by now, Em realized, or they thought they knew and made up the rest. Some were very kind. Others were not and seized on the opportunity to look down on someone else's misfortunes. Em's heart warmed at the sound of Stanley Burton's kindness. Bullseye kept gently pushing his wet nose into her hand and she patted him, enjoying the feel of his wiry coat. There was a smell of bleach in the room.

'Oh, you ain't come in vain, bab. I've a couple of things for yer.' With a grunt Jenny Button bent down to retrieve a small paper package from under the counter.

'There ain't no bread left today but there's a couple of cakes for you and yer dad. What d'yer say?'

'Thank you,' Em said politely, as her mother had taught her. 'It's very nice of you.'

'Well, there ain't much I can do but a bit of cake always helps to cheer you up, that's what I say.'

Em bought the family's bread from Mrs Button as usual in the morning, but for a week now she had been telling Em to come back at the end of the day to see if she had any leftovers. It was her way of helping.

'Any news of your mother?'

Miserably, Em shook her head. She was back to her burden of care in the house, though she had managed to get to school three times. Bob had told her to go.

'We'll 'ave that nosy bugger from the Corporation round, else...' They didn't think the School Board man would take notice if she stayed at home for wash day and another day in the week, so long as she was there most of the time.

'And how're you managing?' Mrs Button asked. 'It's hard on yer, bab, that it is. You're a poor skinny little waif as it is. You need feeding up.'

Em hung her head. She couldn't explain to Mrs Burton just how alone she felt, trying to be housekeeper and mother to her brother and sister when all she ached for herself was her mom back, taking care of them.

'Poor little things,' Mrs Button said. Then, as if on impulse, she suddenly added, "Ere, now you come through here with me a minute. I've got summat to show yer'll lift your spirits.'

173

To her surprise, Mrs Button led her though to the back room. Em had never been in there before, and she looked round curiously. A large part of the room was taken up with a big double bed, pushed into the corner by the window. Stanley Burton, a pink, plump little man, was sitting in a chair which was squeezed in between the bed and the hearth, and he was reading his paper. His wheelchair was in front of him, between him and another easy chair, and it was acting as a table, with an empty cup and saucer resting in the seat. Right in the corner, behind him, was a small table with a cage on it, in which were perched two chattering green budgerigars.

'I know it's a bit of a squeeze,' Jenny Button explained, seeing Em's surprise. 'We have to stop down here, see, cos my Stanley can't do stairs. I've got my little bakehouse out the back, see? And I keep my stores and suchlike up there. But down here it's the menagerie!' She shook with laughter at this.

Em nodded and smiled at Stanley Button, who had looked up in surprise. His blue eyes were friendly.

'Well, you're a sight for sore eyes,' he said amiably. 'All right, are yer, bab? See my little pals? Peter and Poll, I call them. Don't know if they're boys or girls or what!' He gave a wheezing laugh. Em gazed fascinated at the birds and their beady eyes seemed to stare back at her.

'Thought I'd show it her,' Mrs Button said with a significant nod towards the back door. 'I shan't be long, Stanley.'

'That's all right.' He smiled and winked at Em.

174

He reminded her of a baby because he was so round and chubby and had only a thin fluff of hair. She felt sorry for him because his legs didn't work.

With Bullseye shadowing their steps, Mrs Button led Em out into a tiny yard at the back, with the little brewhouse where she baked at one side. Apart from a strip across the middle, above which hung a sagging clothes line, there was no space to move, as the place was absolutely crammed on all sides with pots full of plants. Em's eyes widened in amazement.

'See, I like my flowers,' Jenny Button said, taking Em round them as if introducing her to friends of hers. Bullseye wandered into a corner and cocked his leg. 'Dirty boy,' Mrs Button tutted. 'See, here I've got my herbs – rosemary, mint, sage...Then here's my pretty flowers for the summer. But this is my favourite – look at her.'

In the corner stood a wide pot containing a shrub with glossy green leaves and tight buds, at the tip of which peeped the tips of crimson flowers.

'You wait – come back after Christmas and she'll be a beauty, all blooms,' Mrs Button said. She spoke about her flowers so lovingly as if they were children.

'It's lovely,' Em said shyly.

'She's called a camellia,' she was told. 'My little camellia. You come back and see her when she's in flower.'

'I will,' Em said.

She left, holding her packet of cake, feeling a little comforted. As she was going back along the road she saw there were people standing outside her house. Narrowing her eyes she peered to try and see who it was. Her father was one side of the conversation. She noticed then, with a tiny part of her mind, that he looked different. It was the way he was standing – upright, attentive, handsome again, not like the weary, wilting man they mostly saw these days. He had just come back from work and he was talking to the widow lady from round the corner, Flossie Dawson. As Em crossed the road and came closer she saw that there was also a girl with them. The girl saw Em coming and Em felt herself being stared at. She was older than Em, with a pale oval face and straight brown hair, not black like her mother's, and red-rimmed eyes that made Em think of a rabbit. Em also saw that the dark red coat she was wearing was lovely and warm and soft-looking so that she almost wanted to stroke it. But perched on her hair was a knitted hat in a bright, vicious green. Bogey-coloured, Em thought. Why did she wear that with that nice coat?

They all noticed Em's arrival.

''Ere's one of mine,' Bob said. 'Awright, love? This is Em – 'er's seven.'

'Eight. Nearly nine,' Em corrected him crossly.

'Oh ar – so you are!' Bob laughed. He sounded more jovial and relaxed than he had in ages. 'I lost count!'

'Oh, I'm sure you haven't really!' Mrs Dawson gave a laugh that gurgled like a stream. She obviously thought it impossible that anyone could forget their child's age. Em found herself being observed.

Close up she realized that Flossie Dawson was shorter in stature than she seemed, as if the strength of her personality somehow added to her height. Her black hair was, as ever, tucked under the black cloche hat with its white band and narrow brim, from under which her eyes took in Em with a teasing expression. She had a healthy, pink complexion and prominent cheekbones, the left one of which was marked by a mole. Em noticed the shine on her black button-up boots, and her own scuffed, charity *Mail* boots suddenly felt dreadfully tatty in comparison.

'Nice to meet you, Em,' Mrs Dawson said, in a tinkling voice. 'Aren't you a pretty little girl? I've seen you in the baker's shop, haven't I?'

Overwhelmed by the woman's vivacious attention, and her genteel accent, Em just nodded shyly.

'Say summat, Em,' her father urged. Em could feel the girl staring at her. It wasn't a very nice stare. It matched her nasty hat.

'Yes,' Em murmured.

'Well, this is my daughter, Daisy,' Mrs Dawson said, her hand on her daughter's back to propel her forward. 'Daisy's a bit older than you, dear, she's thirteen. Say hello, Daisy.'

'Hello,' Daisy said sulkily, as if speaking to Em was completely beneath her.

Em said hello back with as little enthusiasm. 'Goodness me!' The woman laughed. 'They're not very forthcoming at this age, are they? Anyway, I mustn't stand here idling all day. It's been very nice to meet you, Mr Brown. No doubt we'll meet again.'

177

'Yes,' Bob said, rather gushingly. 'Well, yes – I hope so.'

Em stood beside him as they watched the mother and daughter walk down the street. Em looked up at her father, a question that she had never asked before forming in her mind.

'Dad – are we poor?'

He barely seemed to hear her. 'What?' he asked vaguely, still staring after the shapely Mrs Dawson. Em tugged on his hand and repeated the question.

He looked down at her, trying to make sense of what she was asking.

'Well, we ain't living in a palace, that's for sure.' He stroked a hand over his stubbly chin.

'No, but are we?' It had felt as if Mrs Dawson was above them in some way and she wanted to know why.

'We ain't the poorest – not like them's on the Parish, like, with all them Means Test meddlers coming in their 'ouses... I s'pose you'd 'ave to say we're middling.'

His face, quite lit up during the conversation, clouded again and his body seemed to sag as he came back to the sorrow and worry of his daily reality.

'You got the tea on?' he asked.

Twenty-Three

Somehow they'd got through the next weekend. Em found herself on her own with Joyce and Sid and they went and played outside. Bob took himself off, unshaven, to the pub both days, came home and slept away the afternoon. His wife's absence had floored him. He seemed scarcely capable of being a father to the three of them, let alone trying to be a mother as well.

On the Monday Em stayed at home for wash day. It was a cold, miserable morning and the water heating in the copper gave off clouds of steam which wafted out through the open back door. Sid was at school, and Joyce had gone grizzling round to Dot's.

'Don't wanna go!' she cried. 'Don't like Nance, she's nasty to me!'

'Don't be so silly,' Em said, trying to sound grown-up and in command. 'You and Nance are best friends.'

'No!' Joycie wailed. 'She's nasty – she keeps pinching me!'

Em dragged her round there all the same. These days Joyce was not the sunny little sister she remembered. Her face often wore a woeful, sulky expression and Em found more and more she was having to tell Joyce off and put up with her tantrums. What with that and Sid's bed-wetting and bad dreams, her own nerves were

179

badly frayed. All she could think of was trying to do everything she knew Mom would want her to do, to try and keep her bereft family together.

She gathered up the clothes for washing, dragged the bedding down from upstairs. Each day now she exchanged the threadbare sheet from Sid's bed with that of hers and Joyce's as Sid had taken up permanent residence in bed with them anyway. Every morning they were all drenched in his urine and Joyce would scream and cry and say she didn't want her 'smelly brother' in bed with them. Em bore it all quietly. There wasn't anyone she could appeal to anyway. Her father was numb with his own misery. But the sheets badly needed a proper wash and a constant aroma of urine hung over the bedroom. Sometimes Em felt like giving up, but Mom was proud that they slept in beds with sheets on.

She sorted the dark clothes from the white ones. She was just about to plunge the whites into the hot water when she heard a timid knock at the door. On her hands and knees in the scullery she hesitated, her heart heating faster. It wasn't Dot's knock – she always came straight in, 'cooee-ing' as she did so. And it didn't sound like the School Board man either; he knocked as if he had a right to come in.

She crept to the front and peered out. Molly was on the doorstep. Em breathed out with relief and opened up.

'What're you doing here?'

Molly was looking nervously up and down the street. 'Can I come in?'

Em stood back to let Molly in and quickly shut

the door. 'Why ain't you at school?'

Molly's face so often wore a blank, self-protecting expression, but now she looked hunted. 'Our mom doesn't know I'm 'ere... I didn't want to go to school.' Now she looked upset. 'Can I stop 'ere instead?'

'Won't your mom find out?' The thought of Iris Fox in a rage was something Em found terrifying. But she found she wanted Molly to stay. She was glad of the company.

Molly shrugged. 'Not if you don't tell 'er. You doing the washing? I'll help yer.'

Suddenly the thought of the long, lonely day didn't seem so bad. The girls rolled up their sleeves. Molly was wearing a thick brown skirt that was too long for her and got in the way so she tucked it up pushing the hem up inside her bloomers, and the two of them got to work with the dolly and maiding tub and mangle. Em found that Molly was surprisingly strong and they managed to get the washing done without flooding the place as much as Em did on her own. Some of the time they laughed and joked or sang snatches of songs. They played a guessing game, 'Guess what I'm thinking of: is it animal, vegetable or mineral?'

'When's yer mom coming back?' Molly asked while they were pegging out clothes across the yard in the cold wind.

'Dunno. Soon.' Em tried to sound nonchalant, reaching up to peg out Bob's shirt. 'She's gone to stay with her sister for a bit, for a rest.'

'Our mom says your mom's a loony and 'er's never coming back.'

Blood rushed to Em's cheeks. 'No, she's not!'

she shouted, on the point of hurling the rest of the pegs in Molly's face. 'Don't you say nasty things about my mom! You say that again and I'll slap yer!'

Molly looked genuinely taken aback. 'I dain't mean to be nasty – that's what Mom said, that's all.'

'She doesn't know anything. She's a fat COW!'

'Don't call my mom a cow!'

'Well, she is – she's a fat, soppy, ruddy cow!' Em felt a strange exaltation at the language she was using. If Mom could have heard her she'd have been for it all right! 'And you can bugger off home – I don't want your help. I never asked you to come, did I?'

Molly threw to the ground the pegs she was holding and disappeared inside. Em stared after her, close to tears, her chest heaving. How *dare* Molly say that – and her horrible bullying mother? She wanted to roar and shout and hit something. But the anger quickly passed; and now that Molly had gone and she was alone, the tears washed down her cheeks. She dropped the peg bag and went and slid down against the rough brick wall, curled up so that her arms were clutched round her legs, head leaning on her bony knees.

'I hate her!' she raged against Molly's mother. 'She's a cow, a fat stupid *cow!*'

The sobs were wrenched out of her and for once she gave in to them. She seldom cried, because most of the time she was trying so hard, doing everything, trying to be a mom to Sid and Joycie and look after her dad, who was not the big strong man she had always thought he was,

182

but fragile as a paper flower. That was as frightening as all the rest of it.

At last she raised her head, coming back out of her darkness with her face pink and stained. Startled, she realized that Molly was squatting beside her, looking at her with sad, bewildered eyes.

'You thought I'd gone home, but I can't,' she said. 'I can't go now – Mom'd beat me. What's up, Em? I've never seen you cry before.'

Em could hardly trust herself to speak, but Molly had seen her crying already and the truth poured out. 'I j-just w-want everything back how it was. I want my mom...' More tears ran down her cheeks though she tried to stop them.

Molly moved closer and sat right up close. Even with her blocked nose, Em caught a whiff of her, like the smell of Sid's sheet. But it was comforting, her sitting there like that.

'I'll stay with yer,' was all Molly said. 'I'll be your friend.'

Em looked at her and solemnly nodded.

Molly fumbled in the pocket of her once-white blouse.

'D'yer wanna play?'

On her hand lay five stones. Em nodded again.

Molly stayed all day while the washing dried slowly in the cold. Sid came back from school, quiet now, not roaring in through the door shouting 'Mom – what's to eat? Can I have a piece?' Normally he could be sure that Cynthia would send him out again with a 'piece' – a slice off the loaf with a scraping of margarine and, if it really

183

was his lucky day, a sparse sprinkling of sugar as well.

But today he came in quietly and said sullenly, 'I'm hungry.'

'Have these,' Em said, giving him some broken biscuits Dot had bought for them from the Bull Ring. 'Say ta!' she said crossly as he snatched them from her and crammed them into his mouth, disappearing through the door again to the playground of the street.

Dot had taught her how to make stew and she had it all ready by the time Bob was due home. Molly had slunk off home to pretend she had been at school all day. 'I'll come another day,' she said.

While she was frying up an onion, Em caught her right index finger on the scalding side of the pan and a blister came up which she wrapped in a piece of rag, feeling sorry for herself. Once the stew was bubbling on the range she went to the window, still nursing her throbbing finger. It was time Joycie came home, and Dad.

Pushing aside the greying net curtain she looked out. Her attention was drawn immediately by a smiling couple just along the street. It took her seconds to realize that the man, looking vivacious in a way he never did at any other time now, was her father and the lady was Mrs Dawson. This time there was no sign of snotty-faced Daisy. Bob and the woman seemed to be deep in conversation. Mrs Dawson was smiling. Raising a hand she fiddled with the band on her hat. Em saw that her lips were painted red, not glaringly, but you could see there was lipstick. Em noticed she had nice even teeth. She watched her father's face. He was transformed by the woman's company. His smiles made Em go cold inside, though she couldn't have said why. Grown-up ways were hard to understand. But there was too much in Mrs Dawson's manner and in his smile for polite conversation.

A few moments later they parted, Bob raising his cap and nodding. Flossie Dawson fiddled coquettishly with her hat again and turned back along Kenilworth Street with her brisk, graceful walk.

'Got the dinner on?' Bob greeted Em as he came in, humming a tune and hanging up his cap. The smiles had gone but something of his cheerfulness lasted for a time. 'Smells a bit of all right, wench. Is it ready? I'll get that down me – then I'm off to the Crown.'

Twenty-Four

All that week, Em kept asking Bob when their mom was coming home, when they could go and see her. In the end he said wearily, 'Look, I'll go and see your mother Sat'dy. Now stop keeping on.'

On Saturday after dinner he made the journey over to Kings Heath. Em was hardly able to wait until he came back. Maybe Mom would come as well? She'd be better, she and Dad would come in laughing through the door with Violet, and everything would be all right.

Bob came back just as the light was beginning to fade. Sid was outside but Em and Joyce heard the door open and ran into the front room.

'Dad!' Joycie cried, rushing to him as he limped into the house, his whole body sagging with dejection, and pulled at his coat, wanting his attention. Only Em knew that he had been to see their mother.

Em's leaping heart at the sound of the door plummeted into disappointment. No Mom, no Violet. And her father's demeanour prevented her from going to him. She stood in the doorway, shivering at the cold air which gusted into the room with him, and sick at heart at the way he pushed Joyce aside with a curse.

'Leave us, will yer!' He sent Joyce flying back into Em and tore off his coat, flinging it over the back of a chair. Joyce started to cry.

Em felt herself flare with rage. 'What did you push her for?' She put her arms round her little sister. 'You're nasty, you are! You don't care about us!' She was amazed at herself. She'd *never* have said that to Dad before!

'And you can button yer lip an' all!' Bob yelled at her, striding through to the back room. 'Sodding kids, keeping on. You're a bloody nuisance, the lot of yer! You'd better not've let the fire go out or I'll tan yer backsides for you an' all!'

Realizing that the range was still burning well he quietened down and flung himself into his chair.

'Em, make us a cuppa tea.'

Em obeyed mutinously, while Joyce crouched in the hearth, sniffing dejectedly. Bob lit a Woodbine and sat silently smoking it. Em was biding her time. She brewed her father's tea and stirred in his three spoonfuls of sugar, quietly handing it to him.

'Ta,' he muttered.

'Dad...'

'*What now*, wench?' He still sounded ready to explode.

'Is Mom better now?'

He made a sudden movement and Em flinched, expecting him to shout again, but instead he bent down to rest his cup and saucer on the floor. Leaning forward, he rubbed his hands over his face, gave a long, ragged sigh and without looking up, said, 'I don't know what to say. I wish I could tell yer she was, love. God knows, I do.'

The next Monday, a dismal, rainy day, Em started on the weekly wash, half hoping that she might hear a knock at the door and Molly would come instead of going to school. But Molly didn't come, and Em toiled all morning at the washing as the rain tippled down outside, and she saw no one except Dot.

The rain had let up when school was over and the puddle-dotted streets filled with children. Em, arms and shoulders aching, her hands raw and cracked, had festooned the chairs and the range with drying washing. When Sid came in he was after food as usual, but he said, 'Bert says Molly wants to see yer.'

'Bert? What d'you mean?'

''Er's in bed, summat the matter with her. Bert says you've gotta go and see 'er.'

Em wasn't at all pleased about being ordered around by Bert Fox, but she felt badly about Molly. She found it hard to admit that she and Molly were really friends, not the way she and Katie had been – or she thought they had. What would Mom say if she knew Em was knocking about with Molly Fox? Molly grated on Em with her constant chatter and rough ways, but she was the only one who had been kind and really proved to be not just a fair-weather friend.

'All right, then,' Em said grudgingly. 'I'll go. Tell Dot where I've gone, will yer?'

Taking off her mom's apron, which dangled to her ankles, Em ran across the wet street and into Molly's yard before anyone could stop her. Coming in through the entry she found the way almost completely blocked by a huge, scummy puddle. Em made a face and slid round the edge of it, trying not to wipe her back on the slimy wall.

The door of number four was open a crack and he could hear voices and Iris's distinctive bleating tone. When she knocked, Iris shouted, 'Oooh's that?'

Trying to stop her voice trembling, Em said, 'It's me, Emma Brown. I've come to see Molly.'

'Can't hear yer. Open the door, for Christ's sake, or bugger off!'

Going in, Em saw Iris turn and look blearily at her with her narrow eyes. There was a flushed red patch on her left cheek and she was dressed in her usual black, her clothes straining over her voluptuous bulges. She was squatting on a stool between the two men, Molly's vacant, bewildered-looking father and the whiskery old grandfather, in their chairs by the grate. Apart from a table there was no other furniture in the room. Fumes of drink filled the air, mixed with smells of sweat and other things, none of them nice. The scene filled Em with dread.

'What d'yer want?' Iris said, her voice slurred and over-loud with drink.

'I've come to see Molly. They said she was poorly.'

Iris waved the white cup she was holding, in a convivial way. 'You can go up – go on, bab. Up the stairs – at the top!'

Em had to steel herself to scuttle across the room, feeling the old man leering at her. He had whiskers the colour of gun-metal, a big nose and deep-engraved features which reminded her of a Mr Punch which had once frightened her in a pavement puppet show. She wasn't frightened of Joe Fox, Molly's father, but it was peculiar the way he just sat staring and she was relieved to get to the winding staircase. She climbed, trying not to breathe in the smells of the house. The stairs to the attic were like a corkscrew, with very little light. She had to feel her way up, and sliding her hand up the wall she felt the throb from the factory next door. As she reached the top the pungent stench of urine which pervaded the house grew stronger.

'Molly?' she whispered into the dark room. There came a moaning sound in reply. As Em's eyes got more used to the dark she detected a faint square of light in front of her from where the sound had come, and as she groped her way past the iron bedstead which took up a lot of the space, she realized Molly was lying behind a curtain which divided the room, blocking what little light was seeping through the threadbare window curtains from the grey day outside. Stepping round the dividing curtain, Em saw Molly's fair hair in the gloomy light, as her head moved restlessly

189

from side to side.

'Molly, it's me – Em.'

Molly groaned and managed to open her eyes. Close to her, Em could feel that she was burning up with heat and that she was very unwell. Her big eyes looked up at Em in bewilderment.

'I don't want them to come,' she muttered, still moving her head back and forth. 'Don't let them come, please don't. Let me stay by myself...'

Em jiggled her hand on Molly's shoulder. 'It's me – Em! Molly, you're having a dream.'

Molly seemed to surface then, and Em was touched to see her try to smile.

'You came to see me.' Her hand appeared from under the blanket, as if reaching for something.

'Bert said you was feeling bad.'

'Bert?' She sounded surprised. 'I need a drink, Em. Get me some water, will yer?'

Em braved the downstairs again. Iris was obviously past caring whether her daughter was burning up with a fever upstairs. When Em asked for a cup, Iris hitched to her feet and slopped over to the side to fetch a chipped white teacup. 'Tap's in the yard.'

Molly gulped down the water as if she hadn't drunk for days, and seemed to revive a bit.

'Who sleeps in the other bed?' Em asked.

'My grandad, and Bert,' Molly said

Em took this in. There was one other bedroom where Mr and Mrs Fox must sleep.

'Where does Tom sleep, then?' she said. Tom, who was now sixteen, was out at work.

'With Mom.' Molly lay down again, shivering now and pulling the blanket over her. 'Dad stops

190

downstairs all the time.'

'Oh,' Em said, her heart sinking even further at the strangeness of the household. 'Does your mom look after you?'

Molly stared at her. 'What d'yer mean?'

'Well, when you're poorly?' Cynthia had always been so kind when any of them were ill. She came up with drinks and fussed around them. 'I think I should have been a nurse,' she joked sometimes. 'Seems to be the only thing I'm good at!'

But Molly barely seemed to understand what being looked after could mean.

'You going to school tomorrow?' Em asked.

'Dunno. Depends if she makes me.'

There was a silence. Em thought about the house. She was longing to get away from it, it was so cold up here and cheerless.

'You ain't got much furniture, have yer?'

'No. Anyway, they took the rest away. The piano and that.'

'Who did?' Em frowned.

'Those men – from the Parish.'

Everyone was talking about the cruel Means Test which the government had brought in. Even the most meagre amount of assistance depended on houses being inspected, and anything that could be sold had to be disposed of before help would be given.

'It was our dad's piano. Mom said he used to play it lovely before the war did for 'im.' Molly tried to raise herself up on one elbow but sank down giddily. 'I don't half feel bad.'

'You'll be better soon, I expect.' She laid her hand on Molly's head for a moment, the way

Cynthia did when they were poorly in bed.

Molly's lids were closing and she soon drifted back to sleep. Em crept downstairs and the others barely seemed to notice as she slunk out of the house. She would have liked to take Molly up some more water but she didn't dare go back and forth through that room too much. Once out in the street she took in a big breath, as if set free.

The same evening, after they'd finished tea and Em was washing up in a bowl of water on the table, there was a tap at the door.

'Come in!' Bob shouted from the back room, expecting it to be Dot. The door opened and there was a pause, before a soft, feminine voice said, 'Is anybody there?'

Bob Brown leapt to his feet as if he'd been shocked. Em saw him throw his waistcoat on and frantically smooth back his hair. 'Just a minute!' he called.

Em knew it was Mrs Dawson; she could tell by the voice and the way her father came to life. There was a conflab in the front room.

'Who's that?' Joyce said loudly and Em shushed her so they could hear what was being said.

'...So sorry... Got myself into difficulties... Wouldn't dream of disturbing you but I don't know where to turn...'

They heard him assuring her that it was no trouble at all, yes of course he'd see what he could do. Without a word to the children he left the house with Flossie Dawson.

Em got Sid and Joyce to bed and he was still not back. She sat with Princess Lucy on her lap for company, and with a pencil and paper she tried to do some of the sums they were doing at school. Her attention soon drifted, however, and she drew pictures of pretty ladies with fine, curling hair. The drawings never turned out quite how she wanted, the beauty of the ladies seeming to get lost between the lead pencil and the old scrap of paper, but she liked to see them in her mind's eye and try to capture them in a drawing. Then she tried to draw a picture of her mother but found she couldn't remember what she looked like. She dug the pencil angrily into the paper and dragged it across, spoiling all the other sketches.

She didn't hear Bob come back from his errand at Flossie Dawson's house. She was already in bed, tired out from another day of drudgery.

Twenty-Five

Another week went by and Em did the very best she could, working herself to exhaustion in the house and trying to keep going to school. Every day, her spirits sank lower and Bob was too wrapped-up in his own preoccupations to notice. From the night that Mrs Dawson had called round, he was out more and more. He gave no explanation, and when he came home he was not reeling from drink as he had been before. He seemed to expect Em to take over doing everything, running the house and looking after the others. Dot helped out as much as she could. She did not know, then, quite how things were, but she was soon to find out.

On Sunday night the three of them were left alone again. Bob had eaten his tea and gone straight out. Sunday night had always been bath night, ready for the week, and Em decided she must stick to it. Besides, she felt like a nice warm dip in the tub by the fire. She didn't want to go next door and ask Dot for help again. She would show she could do it!

'C'mon,' she ordered Sid. 'Give us a hand getting the bath in.'

The two of them managed to hulk the tin bath down off its rusty nail in the yard and bring it in beside the range where Em had started pans and kettles of water heating to fill it. She waited until they were nearly boiling, as she had seen Mom do. She had filled the pans very full and it took all her strength to lift the big kettle down off the hob and tip it into the bath.

'Now don't touch that – it's too hot for you!' she barked at Joycie, who came and looked into it, squeaking with excitement as the clouds of steam billowed up to fill the chilly room. She and Sid were already undressed and shivering, wrapped in the old blankets from their bed.

It was when she came to tip in the first big saucepanful that things went badly wrong. Where it was standing on the heat was too high for her skinny arms to control it properly. Em eased it down, one hand on the handle and the other in a cloth holding the side. Her muscles were shaking with the effort it took to control the pan's weight, and she tipped it, some of the scalding water going over her hand and splashing her legs. Screaming at Sid to get out of the way, she rushed it to the bath, but only some of the water went in. The rest slopped onto the floor and Sid's feet.

He shrieked in agony, running to try and get away from the hot water, which followed him across the room. Joyce, who was further away, leapt onto a chair before it could reach her.

Em, her scalded left hand stinging horribly, ran to her brother whose yells of agony filled the room.

'My feet – oo-o-w, you've burned my feet!' he cried.

Em dragged him into the scullery and tipped a half bucket of cold water, which had been there to cool the bath, over his pink, scalded feet. She ran her smarting hand under the tap, tears of pain and desperation rising in her eyes. Sid was crying pitifully, stepping from one foot to the other, not knowing where to put himself. She wet an old rag and sat him in the back room, wrapping it round his feet. Joyce, stark naked because she had dropped the blanket when she jumped onto the chair, was crying as well, in fear at what had happened.

Em looked round the room, pools of water all over the floor, the bath still steaming, and her injured brother and frightened little sister both sobbing their hearts out, and something broke in her. Something had to be done: she couldn't stand any more.

Quietly, with a deadly calm, she went into the scullery and refilled the bucket of cold water. A couple of buckets later, the bath was cooled sufficiently.

'Come on, Joycie,' she said, taking her sister's hand. 'You can have yer bath. It's all right now – it ain't too hot for you.'

Joyce followed her like a lamb and climbed in the tub, settling her pink, chubby body into the soothing water, and she soon stopped crying.

'I don't want a bath,' Sid snivelled. He wasn't putting his feet anywhere near any water after that.

'I'll just give yer a little wash outside the bath,' Em said. She rinsed the cool cloth for his feet again, and with another rag went to wash her brother's face. She went into the scullery to look for the bar of Lifebuoy that was usually there. Then she remembered: Bob had used the final wafer-thin remnant of it earlier on in the week, the last of it melting away into the water as he cleaned himself up after work. No one had thought to buy any more. Em searched the scullery and found a little knob of green washing soap and took it into Joyce. It was hard and gritty, like a stone.

'What're yer washing me with that for?' Joyce whined. 'It's not nice, that.'

'It's all there is,' Em said wearily, trying to work up any sort of lather with the rotten old green soap. It wasn't much in itself, but the absence of soap made her spirits sink to rock bottom. They'd never run out of soap when Mom was there. Mom, who used to be their mother, here, caring for them. She had to swallow hard to stop the tears coming again.

By the time she had got Joyce ready for bed and had a quick bath herself, Sid was still grizzling, saying his feet hurt, and when she peeled back

196

the damp rag his pink skin had come up in blisters. Em's stomach clenched at the sight of it.

'I don't know what to do,' she said tearfully. If only Dad would come home – where was he? She felt so hopeless and foolish that she'd made such a mess of everything. 'I'll have to go and ask Mrs Wiggins.'

After putting her clothes back on, she ran next door to Dot's house.

'What's up, bab? Anything wrong? I thought I heard a bit of noise earlier, only I was up with Nance. She ain't feeling too well again. And Terry was making enough racket himself.'

In the state she was in, Em did not notice Dot's own tear-stained eyes. Dot bore her burdens with great bravery but sometimes her own loneliness overtook her, and she was missing Cynthia no end.

'It's Sid.' Em had a job not crying again herself. 'I dropped some water on his feet and they're all blisters...'

'You scalded him? Oh, my word...' Dot was round to the house immediately.

Squatting down, she took one look at Sid's feet and said, 'You poor little feller... Oh, Em, why didn't you ask me to help, bab? Why's yer dad not here?'

Em shrugged helplessly, nursing her own smarting hand.

'What's up? Have you burnt your hand an' all?'

'No – it's all right,' Em said bravely. Dot turned her attention back to Sid.

'That's a nasty burn, that is. You got an egg?'

Em shook her head. There wasn't much in the

197

larder at all.

'How about a bit of flour? Here – I'll find it.' Dot sprinkled some flour over Sid's feet and the light tickling of it seemed to soothe him momentarily. Dot sat down and took the little boy on her lap and he leaned into her gratefully. His face screwed up with pain every few moments, but he seemed soothed as much by Dot's kindly, maternal presence in the house as by anything she was putting on his feet.

'That's going to be sore for a bit, bab,' she said. 'But it will get better. Now – shall I put you into bed?'

'Want to stay here,' Sid said, snuggling up to her.

Dot laughed, but her eyes filled again, full of pity and sadness. She stroked Sid's dark head.

'We all miss your mother, don't we? Poor little mites. But I can't sit here all evening, Sid. Come on, up the wooden hill – and you, Joycie. You wait here a tick, Em.'

She carried Sid and Joyce followed, both happy to be put to bed by a mom even if it wasn't their own. When Dot came back down, her face was sober, though kindly. She sat down for a moment, looking solemnly at Em.

'So – where's yer father?'

Em shrugged, shaking her head.

'Down the boozer?'

'I dunno. Don't think so.'

'Well, where? Is he out a lot of an evening?'

Em nodded. She felt a bit bad, as though she was sneaking on him, but it was the truth.

'I see,' Dot said grimly. She stood up. 'Well, this's got to stop. I can't do anything tonight, bab.

198

You'd best go up to bed. Don't worry about Sid. You're doing your best, love. He'll be all right.'

Em went up and got in beside Joyce. Her hand was stinging, but it was not scalded as badly as Sid's feet. He, for once, was in his own bed and both of them were already almost asleep, though Sid was still snuffling. Em lay looking up into the darkness. She hadn't wanted to say anything tonight. But she knew what she had to do in the morning.

Twenty-Six

The fog had a yellowish tinge the next morning, the sun struggling to break through when Em knocked at Dot's front door.

'Who is it? Come in!'

The door was open a crack anyway and Em pushed her way in and went through the almost empty front room, to find Dot sitting at the table. It was still strewn with breakfast things, bowls with a layer of gluey porridge residue, the teapot and crocks. There was no sign of Joyce and Nancy: they must have been out the back. Dot looked sad, Em thought.

'What is it, bab?' She spoke kindly but Em could hear the strain in her voice.

Em had meant to come straight out with it, to ask politely and with no fuss, but to her dismay her own emotion welled up and the tears came. She had woken with a sore throat and thumping head and her tears came more easily than usual. 'I want to see my mom.' She swallowed, looking up at Dot with welling eyes. 'Please, Mrs Wiggins, will yer take me, on the bus?'

Dot looked taken aback, and to Em's surprise she began to laugh.

'What – you mean me go with yer to Kings Heath – this morning?'

Em shrunk inside with disappointment. She had pinned all her hopes on being able to go and see her mom! If she could just set eyes on her she knew she'd feel stronger. But of course Dot wouldn't just drop everything and go to Kings Heath on a busy wash day! How could she have been so stupid?

Dot was still laughing and shaking her head. 'I've heard it all now. Well, bab – all right, why not? The cowing washing can wait, that it can. The whole bloody house can wait so far as I'm concerned. I miss your mother rotten, I do. I've not wanted to poke my nose in where it's not wanted, but it's high time I went to see how she is.'

'You mean you will?' Em gasped. 'I can pay my fare ... I'll fetch it.'

Before Dot could argue she ran back next door, to the old jug where Cynthia had put her odd bits of change, and Em had continued to do the same when she remembered. There were a few odd coppers in there. Em twisted them into the corner of an old paper bag and put her coat on.

When she went back to Dot's, she met her coming back across the street from taking Joyce and Nancy to a Mrs Hill, who had two small children herself. Em was relieved to see that Dot was looking more cheerful.

'I'll just stoke the fire and then we'll be off,' she said. Em showed her the twist of money and Dot smiled. 'We'll be all right, then.'

They took the trolleybus into Birmingham and as they rode along, the sun started to shine.

'Well, that's a good omen,' Dot said. Em found it strange sitting beside her, the coarse weave of her dark green coat brushing against her arm, and looking up to see Dot's thin face and greying hair instead of Mom's thick brown curls. Dot caught her looking and turned and winked at her. 'You all right, bab? You look a bit flushed.'

Em nodded, although every time she swallowed it hurt and her head was bumping. But she wasn't going to let that stop her seeing Mom! She was very excited, yet also full of nervous dread. Surely she could persuade Mom to come back home with them? Even having her at home and feeling poorly was better than the bereft awfulness of her not being there at all. And surely Dad would feel the same? In any case, Mom must be feeling better by now, mustn't she?

Dot led her between the tall buildings of Birmingham to the tram stop. Em liked the smells, the whiff of men's pipe tobacco, or of perfume worn by the posh ladies with their expensive clothes and shining shoes with thin, delicate heels, women who wore lipstick every day and carried leather handbags. And she liked the delicious whiffs from the hot potato and chestnut stalls and wondered if they might have enough pennies left to buy some on the way home. It was a rare treat to come into town, but she knew today there was no time to mooch round the Bull Ring and the Rag Market. They had more serious things to do. The tram came along, sparking from its wires, and they glided their way to Kings Heath. Dot seemed to know where Auntie Olive lived, because she didn't have to ask.

It was a side road called Bank Street, off the Alcester Road. Em saw a little curving road of terraced houses, their red bricks dusted with soot, like face powder, and soon they were knocking on the door of a house down on the left. They stepped back, looking up at the windows. After several attempts to get an answer, the door still didn't open.

'Well, that's odd,' Dot said, sounding put out. Here, in this unfamiliar street, she seemed diminished to Em, not like when she was Queen Bee in her own house. Em saw how thin and fragile she was, despite the impression she gave of wiriness. Her rather protruding teeth and angular way of holding herself seemed to stand out more here. At home, she was just Dot. 'I wonder if Cynthia's in and not answering. I s'pect Olive's gone down the shops.'

She knocked once again, calling up at the windows. 'Cynth? Cynthia – it's Dot. I've got Em with me! Are you in there? Open up, will yer?'

Em saw the nets twitching in the next house and a woman's face peering out, but she didn't open her door. The house stayed silent and no one came.

Dot frowned, chewing on the end of her thumb. 'Where the hell can she be?' She looked at Em kindly. 'P'rhaps your mother's feeling better and they've gone out somewhere. Tell yer what – it's a nice day. Let's go for a walk round the block and see if we meet them. Or she might be in when we get back. I flaming hope so – I could do with a cuppa off her, I can tell yer!'

Cheered by Dot's optimism, Em walked beside her up along Kings Heath High Street, peering in the shop windows, and along as far as the park. There was a cool wind but the sun stayed out, with moments of deep shade as clouds passed over it. Em kept going hot and cold but she was too interested in being in a new place to take much notice.

'It'd be nice to live out 'ere, wouldn't it?' Dot said wistfully as they passed the side streets of neat terraces. Everything looked much cleaner and more respectable than in their district. 'Fat chance of that ever happening, though,' she added, sounding more bitter than Em had ever heard her before. Em looked up at her, round-eyed.

'Don't get me wrong,' Dot said hastily. 'I'm content with my lot, me. I'll be glad when your mother's back, though.'

They took their time, strolling along the Alcester Road, which was busy with cycles, horses and carts and jostling shoppers, until they were back at Bank Street. Dot tried knocking on the door again and once more there was no reply, but then she saw a figure turn in at the end of the street.

'Ah, now who's this?' She narrowed her eyes. 'Is this her?'

Her heart picking up speed, Em turned, thinking to see her mother. Instead, a tall, gaunt woman was coming towards them pushing a pram. Em had never seen the pram before and she had only seen her auntie Olive on a very few occasions, but she felt sure this was her.

'I think so,' she said. Violet must be in the pram and she longed to see her and kiss her warm cheeks. But where was Mom?

As the woman drew closer and saw the two of them waiting outside her house, her bony face pulled into a frown.

'Yes, what d'you want?' she demanded. She had dark eyes like Cynthia, but did not resemble her in any other way.

'Are you Olive Harker?' Em could see Dot wondering how this severe beanpole of a woman could be her friend's sister.

'Mrs Harker to you. Yes. Who're you?'

Dot indicated Em beside her. 'This is Em, your niece. Don't you recognize her? I'm Dorothy Wiggins – a friend of Cynthia's. I've brought Em to see her.'

Em had nipped round to look in the pram. It was a much smarter one than the old pram at home. She smiled, reassured at seeing her baby sister's round face above the covers. Her eyes were closed and she looked pink and well and had grown quite a lot bigger.

'Well, she's not here, I'm afraid,' Olive said dismissively. 'You've come on the wrong day.' She went to open the door of her house, but Dot, who was not going to stand any nonsense, stood in her way.

'Excuse me!' Olive exclaimed, scandalized. 'Get out of my way, if you please, and let me go into my own house.'

Em straightened up, startled. She had not expected a quarrel.

'I'd like to see my friend,' Dot said, still maintaining a veneer of politeness, but Em could hear that her patience was wearing out fast. 'So could you tell me where she is, please? Last time I saw her she wasn't very well and in no state to be out. So I wonder where it is, exactly, she's gone.'

'That,' Olive said unpleasantly, 'is none of your business. Now get out of my way!'

Em found her hands gripping the handle of the pram. She wasn't going to let Violet go back any too easily.

'Just tell me where Cynthia is,' Dot said. 'If she's inside I'd like to see her. I ain't traipsed all the way over 'ere to be fobbed off by the likes of you, yer know.'

'The likes of me!' Olive's face creased into a sneer. 'I'm not dealing with some slum dweller like you. You get back to where you belong and let me get into my house.'

'Look, love,' Dot said, all pretence of politeness vanishing. Em watched, at once excited and scared. She knew Dot was not someone to tangle with when she was in a temper! 'We can stay out 'ere all morning, if yer like. But I want to know where Cynthia is and how she is, and until you tell me what's going on I ain't moving from 'ere.'

'I'll call the police!'

'You can do what the hell you like, love.' Dot folded her arms. 'You call 'em and I'll ask them to persuade you to tell us what we want to know, if yer want. It'd be a hell of a lot easier if you just let us in to see her. You don't want to deprive a young child of her mother, now do yer?'

A few seconds passed as the two women stood

205

locked in each other's loathing gaze. Olive looked away, glancing at the pram. She could obviously see that it was going to be impossible to get both herself and the baby in through the door while Dot was camped there and there were eyes watching from the nearby houses. With her face soured with anger and distaste she snapped, 'Very well – you'd better come in for a minute.'

Resentment in every line of her body, she opened the front door and led them into the front room, pulling the pram in furiously behind them. Em looked round in astonishment. It was like she imagined living in a doll's house would be – all flouncy curtains with pelmets and carpet on the floor, a little table with a lacy cloth and rows of dolls in strange costumes and other ornaments all along the shelves of the dresser. The back room into which she led them was less ornamental but still a great deal more fancy and expensively furnished than her sister's poor Nechells house.

'I'm not going to ask you to sit down,' Olive said. For a moment they all just stood there.

'Well?' Dot said. 'Where is she, then?'

'Not here. She's gone.'

Em felt her chest tighten. What did Auntie Olive mean? Surely Mom wasn't gone forever, wasn't dead? Was that what she meant?

'Where?' Dot demanded, her patience gone. 'Come on, spit it out.'

'I couldn't–' Olive put a hand over her face for a moment, and her sour, closed face seemed about to crack. 'I couldn't have her here any more. She was too far gone. I can't tell you what it was like.'

Dot's face had gone pale. 'Where is she?' she whispered.

Defiantly, Olive squared her chin. 'In the only place fit for her in that state. I had to put her in the ... in the hospital. The asylum.'

Dot gasped as if she'd been slapped. 'You bitch! You mean you–? When? Does Bob know?'

Shamed, Olive looked down at the grey linoleum. 'No. It was only three days ago. I was at my wits' end.' She looked up again, angrily. 'I had to. They came for her and took her to Hollymoor. *They* could see I was in the right. I was frightened of what she'd do. I thought she was going to–' Her sentence trailed off as her gaze fell on Violet. 'I didn't know what she might do.'

Twenty-Seven

Em wept all the way home. Her bitter disappointment at not being able to see her mother and her bewilderment at what her aunt had done spilled out and she couldn't stop. What *was* the asylum? Mom had been sent away to a place that Em didn't understand anything about, except that everyone talked about it in hushed, fearful tones. She knew Dot was upset and outraged as well, and Em was heartbroken at parting from Violet again. She had pleaded and pleaded with both of them to let her bring the baby back home, but she had had to leave her little sister behind after holding her just once.

'She misses me,' Em had insisted, cuddling her close in her arms. Violet was heavier than she remembered. 'She wants me, I know she does!'

'Don't be ridiculous; she can't go back to *that*,' Olive had decreed, condemning everything about her sister's household out of hand. 'I'm not letting you take the child when she's well settled here. She's not going anywhere! My sister entrusted her to me and that's how it's going to stay.'

Dot had to agree, reluctantly. She was quite surprised that Olive Harker was so eager to keep the child, with all the work and effort looking after her would entail. Dot would have fought her tooth and nail if she could not see for herself how impossible it would be to bring a baby back into the Brown household, the way things were. And surely, tart and mean as she seemed, as Cynthia's sister, the woman must be trustworthy? Violet seemed very well on it so far.

'Think how it'd be,' Dot had pointed out gently to Em. 'You'd have to look after the babby as well as the others, and you'd never be able to go to school.' She'd looked defiantly at Mrs Harker. 'She's been a marvel the way she's looked after things while Cynthia's been bad. But Em, love – you'd never manage with a babby as well.'

Em had looked up at her in anguish, but in her heart she'd known Dot was right. Everything was such a struggle as it was. Sid had howled with pain that morning when he had to force his scalded feet into socks and boots for school. How could she manage a baby as well? She'd had to be almost torn away from Violet, though, as if the child's warmth was the closest thing she could find to her mother and she could hardly bear to let go.

'Don't fret, your little Violet'll be all right,' Dot said, when they were back sitting side by side on the tram. Then she looked more carefully at Em, realizing that the child's flushed face was not just because of her tears. 'Eh, bab – you're burning up, ain't yer?'

Em nodded miserably, more tears coming at the sight of Dot's kind eyes. 'I've got a sore throat,' she said huskily. She had felt more and more unwell as the day went by and now her neck felt thicker than usual, her head was throbbing and the blood banging in her ears. The feverishness magnified all her feelings. The whole day had come to feel like a nightmare.

'I thought there was summat.' Suddenly Dot reached out and put her arm round Em as if she was one of her own and cuddled her close. Em, so hungry for a mother's love, leaned against her, comforted.

'When we get back, you can have a lie-down,' Dot promised. 'And later, when yer dad gets home, I'll tell 'im everything that's happened. All right?'

Em nodded her head against Dot's scratchy sleeve, before her eyes closed and she fell into a feverish sleep.

She sat on the chair in the front room, her cheeks burning and everything seeming to swim around her, distant and unreal. Sid and Joyce were standing in the doorway through to the back because no one had thought to tell them not to listen. Bob was leaning on the mantelshelf, his back to everyone.

Dot stood just inside the front door, her face very grave.

Bob turned to face her, after the shocked silence while the news sank in. 'You mean that woman's just packed her off, without asking me, or anyone? Just like that?'

'That's what she told me,' Dot said grimly. 'Cynth weren't there, only the babby. She'd got that bad, summat had to be done. That's what she said.'

'But for Christ's sake!' His voice rose, clamouring against Em's ears. 'Not a word to anyone! How could she just–?' He made a helpless gesture. 'You'd think that'd be the last thing... Her own sister! The cruel bitch, she was s'posed to be looking after her!' He sank down into his chair in shock and put his head in his hands. For a moment he looked as if he was going to weep. Even in his distress, he knew he had not been able to manage Cynthia either. 'My poor girl, in one of them places.' He looked up, distraught, at Dot. 'I can't stand the thought of it. I don't know what to do. Why can't she just be 'ere and be all right?'

Dot looked down, trying to hide the tears in her own eyes. 'I dunno, Bob,' she said, shaking her head. She controlled herself, and looked up. 'But that woman should never've done it – not without coming to you. It weren't up to her. She seems a scheming sort, I'd say.'

'There was never any love lost.' Bob got to his feet, anger rising in him. 'I'm not going to stand for it. That ruddy heartless cow – interfering in my family...' He went to the door, but Dot was standing in the way, arms folded.

210

'And where d'yer think you're going, Bob?'

'I dunno – anywhere.' He paced back and forth. 'I've got to get my head straight.' He clutched it as if he was physically hurting. 'I need a drink...'

'So yer off down the boozer again. And does drowning yer sorrows make any difference? Does it bring her back? And what about them?' She nodded at the three children, all waiting silent and scared. 'You've got kids, in case you ain't noticed. They ain't mine to bring up, yer know. When're you going to stop piling it all on Em's shoulders? It's a disgrace the way you treat her, that it is. They need their mom but you're all they've got, and what're you going to do about it, eh?'

Cowed by Dot's fierceness, Bob swayed in front of her as if he already had several pints inside him.

'What do I do?' he asked, and his voice cut through Em because he sounded so lost, as if he was only a child himself.

'Be a man. Look after your family,' Dot said, more gently now. 'I know what it's like doing it on your own, remember? And I know it's punishing hard, but it has to be done. Look, you've been good to me over the years, you and Cynth. You've been real neighbours to me. I'm only saying this for your own good.'

'I will, Dot. Soon as I can, I will. But–' He looked round despairingly at his children. 'Please, Dot ... I can't – not tonight. You have 'em...'

'Tonight, and what about all the other nights?' Dot flared again, her chin jutting. 'And when're you going to hand over some money for all the times I've fed 'em and looked after 'em?'

To Em, Dot looked magnificent in her anger,

and awesome, but Bob found her provoking.

'Just get out of my way, woman!' He went to push past her. 'You can stop ordering me about in my own house – I've had enough. I'm going out and that's that – I've got to clear my head!'

He seized Dot's arm and pulled her aside, slamming out through the front door. Enraged, she opened it again.

'That's it – just run away again, yer useless bugger!' she screamed after him along the street. 'You're all the bloody same!'

Banging the door shut, Dot stood furious and panting in the middle of the room before taking in the three desperate little faces in front of her. She went to Bob's chair and beckoned them to her, sitting Joyce on her lap. Em stood giddily. Her throat felt as if it had been scraped with broken glass.

'Where's our mom gone?' Sid asked with a dreadfully solemn face. He was old enough to have understood some of what had been said.

'She's gone to a place where they want to try and make her feel better,' Dot said, suppressing a shudder at the thought of the dark asylum walls.

'When's 'er coming back?' he asked, wide-eyed.

'I can't tell yer, bab, and that's the truth,' Dot said, tears welling in her eyes again at the sight of the bereft children. 'But I hope it's soon, that's all I can say.'

As she spoke, Em toppled to the floor. Her illness and the strain of the day had all been too much and she lay in a dead faint.

Twenty-Eight

The next Saturday afternoon, Bob Brown, a small parcel tucked under his arm, stepped in through the gates onto the long drive of Hollymoor Hospital.

The journey had seemed endless. The asylum had been built on farmland to the south of the city, to give its inmates space and fresh air and the farm to provide much of their food. To Bob, who had always lived in the cramped streets of the city's heart, it already felt as if he was in a foreign land. His nerves were all a-jangle, the more so at his first sight of the forbidding hospital buildings, and he drew in a deep breath and let it out raggedly. A strange sense of familiarity and safety was mixed with a dread so strong that he nearly turned round and ran back out to the road. The building aroused dark memories of the Boys' Home. He was grateful to them for the start they'd given him, but the hospital brought back all the feelings of being shut in, trapped inside an institution, of being completely in the control of others. He thought he had left all that behind. His wife was in here, his sweet Cynthia. No, it couldn't be. Panic rose up and almost suffocated him.

'*Christ.*' Next to what he realized must be the chapel, he had to stoop over for a moment to regain his breath, along with a scrap of composure. He couldn't go in like this – he was

213

shaking like a leaf!

Someone else was coming along the path and he straightened up, feeling foolish, and turned to see a middle-aged woman with a tired face. Seeing him hesitate she said, 'This your first time? It's not so bad when you get used to it, you know. We see them in the big hall. I'll show you if you like.'

Stepping inside the dark, imposing entrance was a terrible moment, as if the building was engulfing him and he might drown. In the big hall he saw a short queue of other visitors lining up in front of two stiffly dressed nurses who sat at small tables positioned in the far corners of the room on each side of a curtained-off stage, beyond a scattering of chairs. Younger nurses were hurrying to and fro.

'Yes, what name is it?'

Intimidated by the nurse in her stiff veil, he managed to cough out, 'Brown, Cynthia.'

'And that is for her?' She held her hands out for the newspaper wrapped parcel. Bob hesitated; he had wanted to give it to Cynthia himself. After all, it was the only thing he could offer. Left to himself, though, it would never have occurred to him to bring anything with him. He was in too much of a state to think. It was Dot who suggested the sweets and plums. In fact he knew that if it wasn't for Dot, he wouldn't be here at all. He would have chickened out.

'We'll see that she gets it. Now, you wait on that side.'

One of the scurrying nurses was dispatched to find Cynthia. Bob sat watching as other patients arrived, though he had an impulse to avert his eyes

214

at the pity of it. Most were men, shuffling down to the other side of the hall. A few women came in, in shapeless gowns. Bob thought at first that this was the reason they somehow all looked the same, apart from the shuffling, depressed gait. Then he realized it was their hair. Almost all of them had the same look, their hair chopped round their ears and in a stern fringe. Patients. Inmates. He couldn't marry it up in his mind, not with his Cynth.

Because of that he didn't see her coming at first, as if she was just another one. She was walking slowly, led by the young nurse. Her head was down and her hands clasped. He saw at once that she had a long plaster on her left wrist and she was nursing her hand, her overall appearance that of a supplicant who has come to apologize for some terrible misdeed. She seemed to cringe as if the very light hurt her.

'Here you are, Mrs Brown,' the nurse announced. 'Here's your visitor.'

She waited until her charge was safely sitting before moving away to receive fresh orders.

There was a long silence. Bob was not quite sure she had even seen him. Cynthia kept her head down and clutched her hands together in her lap so tightly that her knuckles strained at the flesh. Bob stared at her in shock. She was clad in a strange smock of tough material, almost like canvas, which neutered all her womanly curves, and her hair, those lovely curls, had been subjected to the same institutional hacking. Even her fringe was too short and had convulsed into a frizz. He was so appalled he could hardly stand to

215

look at her. His throat tightened and he found himself fighting tears.

'Cynth?' he dared to say. He didn't think she had heard, amid the murmur of the other patients and their guests, so he repeated it, almost breaking down. 'Look at us, will yer?'

She moved her head at a slant, squinting at him for a second as painfully as if he were the summer sun, then looked back in her lap. She picked restlessly at the dressing on her arm now, rocking slightly back and forth.

'What've yer done?' He leaned forward, longing to be close, yet repelled by her. 'Did you hurt yourself?' He found himself speaking as if she was a child.

There was a faint, indifferent nod in reply. And suddenly he couldn't stand it. He felt as if his chest was going to rip open.

'Cynth – love. For God's sake! Speak to me! You're my wife. When're yer going to get better? When're you coming home?'

Her rocking increased and she was obviously in terrible distress. Aghast, he saw her fling herself abruptly from the chair, face down, and start to bang her head on the floor.

'Don't!' he cried, leaping to stop her. He was joined immediately by two nurses, who pulled her now feather-light body from the floor as Cynthia cried and struggled, flinging her head from side to side. Her mouth widened in a grimace and to his horror he saw that she was missing a good number of her teeth at the back and sides.

'God!' Bob cried. 'Don't, Cynth – stop it, for God's sake!'

216

'She'll have to go back,' one of the nurses told him. 'She's in no state.'

'Wait!' Bob moved closer. 'Cynth...' Restrained on each side by the nurses, she turned wild eyes on him as if he was dangerous and terrifying, holding her head at an odd angle. Then, abruptly, she went limp and the nurses loosened their hold.

'Leave us – just for a minute, will yer?' Bob pleaded.

Cynthia was compliant now. She sank back down onto the chair and the nurses retreated a little.

'What've they done?' he nodded at her. 'Your teeth?'

She put her hand vaguely to her mouth. 'They said my teeth was bad. That it might help.' Leaning forward, eyes stretched very wide, she whispered, 'What about the little 'uns? Tell me!'

'They're all right,' he assured her. 'Em's been a bit poorly. Dot's looking after her and Joycie. They saw Violet – Olive's got her and she's thriving.'

'Sid? Joycie?' She spoke with great hunger to know.

'They're all right, love.' Relief coursed through him. She was talking – only a whisper, mind, but talking properly. He was dangerously close to weeping. 'They miss yer though. We all miss yer, terrible, like.'

He could have bitten his tongue off for the distress this provoked in her. She was trembling, tears filling her brown eyes. Staring at her lap again, she whispered, 'I want to die. That's the only thing. I'm no good... No good.'

'Oh, love...' He was breaking down, her despair

sinking through him, as if he was in a black pit with her. 'Don't... Don't say that...'

Seeing them both weeping, the nurses came forward again. 'She must go back now,' they said. 'We don't want you getting worked up again, do we?'

And without a glance, a farewell or the touch of a hand, she was gone, in a tough guided shuffle across the hall and into the dark corridor.

Oh Christ... Oh Christ... The words banged in his head as he sat on the tram. He didn't know why those words. He'd never been religious, except for the bits forced on him in the Home. It was more like that Indian habit someone once told him about, sitting quietly and saying a word over and over. Made you calm, they said. It gave him something to hold on to because there was that tight, bursting feeling in his chest again and he'd be terrified to let it out. He might cry and not be able to stop, or find he was unravelling like the end of a frayed rope.

He kept his head turned to the window as the leaf-sogged afternoon glided by outside, and took deep, convulsive breaths. Thank Christ there was no one in the seat beside him. Too grim a time of year for trippers out to the Lickeys for walks.

Again and again he kept seeing it: Cynthia flinging herself to the floor, the red mark on her forehead as they dragged her up, that stretch-eyed look she had – not her, not her at all. It *wasn't* her. He hadn't been to see his wife, but some stranger, possessed by a demon. Something that looked at him out of her eyes, which had swallowed her and taken her from him, encasing her in a shell of despair. His wife, his love – the only woman he had ever loved and he'd never wanted anyone else. She was just his Cynth, that was all. But over the months his Cynth had shrunk and shrunk until she was a tiny dot of light inside the desperate woman he had just seen, the dot of light he had glimpsed just in those seconds when she asked about the kids. Next time – if there ever was a next time – he visited, would that minute flame have been doused as well?

He put his head in his hands, his breathing fast and desperate. He had lost her. His Cynthia was gone, forever it seemed.

As the tram neared the middle of Birmingham, his thoughts moved back to what he had to go home to. A house bereft of wife and mother to his children, no comfort, sick kids... Em had been very poorly all week and Sid seemed to be going down with it as well and his feet had got infected after Em scalded him. Dot had given him a roasting over that, over his being out so much.

He decided to walk out to Nechells. It'd save some coppers and give him time. The thought of home dragged his feelings even further down. No – he couldn't face it. Not yet. A few pints and he'd be set up. He'd find the first pub that sold his favourite ale.

Then another temptation arose in his mind, one which as the days passed he had kept trying to push away. Flossie Dawson. Try as he might, she was seldom far from his thoughts. He wanted sympathy, comfort: where better to find that than with Flossie? He corrected himself. Mrs Dawson. Could he call in on a Saturday afternoon? It

219

wouldn't hurt – his visit to Cynthia had been so short after all that he was early. And Mrs Dawson seemed to be pleased to see him at any time. Gratifyingly so, for a woman as classy as that.

A tremor of excitement went through him, lightening his despair over Cynthia. After all, what was the harm? She was a lonely widow and he, well, the way things were looking, he was more like a widower himself. It was all above board, they were just giving each other a bit of company. There'd be no repetition of what happened last time, when the girl was up in bed. He'd apologized for that. It was when she'd brushed past him that time, and he hadn't been able to help but reach out for her. Course, Cynthia being the way she was, he was deprived in that department. He hadn't been able to help it. It wouldn't happen again, not with a respectable lady like that.

But the memory of Flossie Dawson's full lips meeting his, that stolen kiss which had so filled her with blushes and him with startling desire, made him walk even faster in the direction of her house.

Twenty-Nine

Late on, that grey Saturday afternoon, Dot made up the fire and sank down into a chair for a much-needed rest. On the rug at her feet, Em, Joyce and Nancy were playing a game – amiably for the moment – with some bits and pieces and a large helping of imagination: old cotton reels, a wooden spoon, little rag doll, broken clock and a small wooden box all figured in an elaborate game of 'pretend'. Sid was out with the other boys, still walking gingerly as his sore feet gradually healed.

Leaning back exhaustedly in her chair, Dot smiled down at the three absorbed little faces in the firelight. Having only her brothers, so much older, Nance loved having the Brown girls there, and they were like sisters to her. Dot experienced a pang looking at them, though. Nance, with her swarthy complexion and bouncy coils of black hair round her chubby cheeks, looked so much more robust now than the others. Joyce was more subdued, but it was in Em that the strain showed worst. Of course, she had just been very poorly, although she was on the mend now, but the days of fever had left her even thinner and paler than before. Dot thought of the freckly, open-faced Em before Cynthia's troubles began, and the child's grief brought tears to her own eyes. Em was a shadow of what she had been before – more withdrawn, all the strain and loss of the past weeks showing in her pinched face. It felt as if Cynthia was dead and, Dot thought, she might just as well be so far as the children were concerned.

Em looked up and caught Dot watching her with tears in her eyes. Em's own eyes, in her hollow face, wore a hunted look.

'All right, bab?' Dot said gently. 'D'yer need to 'ave another lie-down now?'

Em shook her head determinedly.

'You just go easy, then.'

The merest shadow of a smile touched Em's

221

lips and she went back to her game.

Dot's mind wandered to the hospital. How was Bob getting on with his visit to Cynthia? She would go next time, she resolved. She missed her friend dreadfully. Of course, someone had to have the kids again for the afternoon and who else was going to offer but her, even though she'd looked after Em all week – and the others a lot of the time. She couldn't just leave the poor little mite alone and poorly while Bob was at work – or out getting tanked up, which he seemed to be most of the time.

And the Browns' troubles took her mind off her own loneliness, which came looming up whenever she stopped rushing about for long enough to let it. Then she allowed herself to imagine how things might have been if Charlie had not been killed. He'd been called up before they were married, even though they knew already they were made for each other. The twins had been well on the way before they tied the knot. She smiled wistfully at the thought of them as babies, one dark, one fairer like Charlie from the start. She and Charlie had married when he was on leave in 1916, a few months before the big push on the Somme. He'd survived it, not like the thousands of others. There was to be one more leave, when David and Terry were seven months old. Dot closed her eyes and let herself embrace the memory. They had been such sweet days, so few, and the last of her married life as it turned out, with her husband home and her two healthy sons, but with the war forever hanging over them like a louring cliff waiting to fall on their heads. It made every moment intense, poignant. Her mind strained to see Charlie's face as he gazed down at her while they were making love, his laughter, bouncing David and Terry in his lap in turn, his eyes meeting hers, smiles of love and happiness, walking together so proudly with the old double perambulator Charlie's mom had given them, she pushing the boys, Charlie's arm warm around her waist. And the goodbye at the station, she holding up first David then Terry to be kissed, waving as Charlie disappeared, getting smaller and smaller, the smoke whirling past the carriage smudging him until he was gone. Gone. The pain stabbed through her, raw and agonizing, when she let it in.

'Mom?' Nance's voice cut through her memories. 'I'm 'ungry!'

Dot jerked back to the present and forced a smile to her lips. 'You can't be, Nance – you only 'ad yer dinner a little while ago. Oh–' she looked at, the clock – 'blimey, where does the time go? It's later than I thought!'

'Can us 'ave a penny?' Nancy wheedled. 'To go down to Missus Price's.' Nancy always talked about the Miss Prices as if they were one person.

'You're a one, ain't yer,' Dot said. 'You don't want to go down there – it's cold! And Em ain't up to going out yet.'

'Yes I am!' Em said, the thought of a few sweets producing a remarkable acceleration in her recovery.

'Well...' Dot softened. After all, it'd be nice to have a few minutes' peace. 'Tell yer what, you can have tuppence. Get yer coat on, Em. And you could ask Molly to come with yer, get her

223

some rocks?'

'Molly Fox?' Nancy wrinkled her nose.

'It won't hurt yer for once. Molly's been ever so good to Em.'

Em said nothing but Dot could see from her eyes that she agreed. Dot had a soft spot for waifs and strays. And Molly, to her surprise, had turned up on the doorstep every day that week while Em was poorly and came and sat with her. Her fingers itched to get hold of the child and sort her out. There was something not right with her, Dot could sense, but she didn't like to say anything and couldn't quite put her finger on it. It was the way Molly always seemed to be dolled up in something a bit too old for her which made her look both waif and trollop at the same time. There was always that aroma of wee about her, and several times when she thought no one was looking, Dot had seen Molly press her hand to her privates as if they were sore. Dot longed to strip her off and give her a good scrub down and dress her in something else. But what could you expect with a mother like Iris Fox and that vile old father of hers? Dot, with her ready intelligence, could see that Iris was a slow-witted, vicious woman who had been a handsome looker when young and lured a good man into marriage. If the war hadn't done for Joe Fox the way it had he might have been able to keep Iris in line. But she'd been landed with the care of him and her father as well. You could almost feel sorry for Iris, but as it was she was such a foul-mouthed harridan without an ounce of kindness in her that Dot avoided her as much as she possibly could.

'Go on, then – a joey's all I've got and I want the penny back!' She handed Em a threepenny bit from the old tea caddy and the girls made eagerly for the door. Dot watched them head across in the direction of the court where Molly lived.

'Time for a cuppa,' she said aloud.

By the time she'd drunk her tea the girls were back, mouths busily working. They seemed to have picked up Sid on the way as well and he had something pink and chewy trailing from the corner of his mouth.

'There yer go – come on in. Get warm by the fire. I expect your dad'll be in any minute,' she said to the Brown children.

Em turned, shaking her head, a hurt expression on her face. 'We've just seen him,' she said quietly, as the others chattered, holding their hands out to the fire's warmth. 'But he weren't going home – he was going up the other way.'

It was more than a couple of hours before Bob Brown came home. Dot kept an eye out, growing more and more enraged. What the *hell* did he think be was playing at, taking off again, tonight of all nights, when he'd been to see Cynthia? Not to mention taking it for granted that she'd give them all some tea, she cursed to herself. Typical bloody man. Thought meals just fell from the sky. She was also on pins herself, wanting to hear how Cynthia was, but she tried to keep her agitation under control for the children's sake. Every so often she popped out to see whether there was any light in the house.

'Right – yer dad's back,' she said when at last

he appeared.

She led the three of them next door.

'I see you finally managed to get yourself home,' she said so frostily that he could hardly fail to notice. 'Forget where you lived, did yer?'

Bob had taken his coat off but seemed to be standing there at a loss. 'Yeah – sorry. 'Bout the time, I mean.'

She wasn't going to ask where he'd been with the three sets of wide, longing eyes all looking up at them.

More gently she said, 'So how did yer find her?'

He looked down, avoiding all their desperate looks. 'Well,' he said, then drew in a long breath and looked at Dot. She saw him begin lying, or at least finding something good to tell them, something to hold on to. 'Yer mom's looking ... quite well,' he said, trying to smile.

Dot's anger melted away and her heart went out to him. The old Bob she was fond of re-appeared suddenly, the good, stumbling man trying to do his best. He was here struggling in front of her.

'She sent her love to you all and said she misses yer – a lot.' He roved round in his imagination for something else to say. ''Er's in a nice room, with ... with a comfortable bed and she can see out of the window–'

'Is our mom coming 'ome?' Joyce cut through his attempts at story-telling to ask the one thing they all really wanted to know. Her little face seemed almost to pulsate with need.

Bob looked down again. 'Well – perhaps not quite yet.' He cast a desperate glance at Dot. 'But

226

soon, we hope, eh?'

'It'll be all right,' Dot said reassuringly. 'These things take time. Now – you all run upstairs and get undressed, all of yer, like your mom'd want yer to!'

Dragging their feet, unsure whether the news was good or not, the children went off upstairs. Dot didn't have to say anything. Bob put his hand over his face, all pretence gone. She realized he was weeping.

'It's bad,' he said hoarsely at last. 'I've never seen 'er that bad. She started trying to hurt herself, banging her head...' He took his hand away, his cheeks wet with tears. 'She won't be coming home – not the state she's in. She's best off where she is. I've never seen anything like it, I can tell yer, Dot. It were horrible.' His face contorting again, he cried, 'I think I've lost my Cynth – lost 'er for good!'

Hoops

Thirty

Em sat in her desk beside Molly, a bright beam of winter sunshine slicing in through the classroom windows and lighting up their ink-stained desk. She was used to sitting next to Molly now, and tried not to look in Katie's direction. In any case, once again this morning her thoughts were far away from school.

'Now,' Miss Lineham turned from writing on the blackboard, pulling her cardigan more tightly round her rather plump frame, 'can anyone tell me what new season has just begun?'

Hands went up. 'Winter, miss?'

'Yes – but I meant another, *Christian* season.' Miss Lineham was obsessively religious.

No hands went up. Miss Lineham's eyes roved round the room. Em felt a sudden sharp jab in her side from Molly's elbow and a warning glance. Jarred, but grateful, Em tried to pay attention. Fortunately Miss Lineham had stopped picking on her for the moment and mostly ignored her.

'Can *no one* tell me?' Their silence seemed to be a personal disappointment. 'Well, it's *Advent*, because last Sunday was the fourth Sunday before Christmas.'

Em drifted off again as Miss Lineham droned on about waiting for Jesus and coloured candles. Religion always seemed to mean waiting for something. In her head the teacher's grating tones

231

were drowned by the echo of Dot's words, over-heard on Sunday when Dot hadn't known she was within earshot.

After Sunday dinner the children had all been playing out as it was dry. A group of them, Em and Joyce, Nancy, Molly and some others were out at the front. Sid had his go-cart and they were taking it in turns to whiz each other along the street. Em had suddenly needed to go to the toilet, so she ran down the entry to the privy in the yard, pushing the rusty bolt across to secure her privacy.

While she was on the toilet she could hear raised voices. She knew it was her dad and Dot, in the house, though she couldn't make out their words. She flushed the toilet and crept to the back door; pushing it open she stood just inside, shoving her hands down into the pockets of her old brown coat. It was too short for her now and barely reached her knees. The two of them were in the front room. Dot had caught Bob before he disappeared out, as usual.

'Just leave us alone – I'll sort it out,' Bob kept saying, very irritably, like someone batting away a fly.

'What d'you *mean* you'll sort it out?' Dot's temper was already getting well out of hand. 'It's no good saying you'll "sort it out" and then bug-gering off out again while I look after your kids. You never cowing well *do* sort anything out – that's your trouble!'

'I gave yer some money, dain't I?' Bob said indignantly.

There was an outraged silence. 'Money,' Dot said quietly, then, with her voice rising, 'Yes – you gave me a pay-off. Bloody decent of yer, I must say, when I'm bringing up your family! D'you think that's it – you can just pay me a pittance and then swan off and do what you like? What d'yer think you're doing, carrying on with that woman?' For a moment her voice sounded tearful. 'You should be ashamed of yourself with poor Cynth in that place. And d'you think no one's noticed?'

'Oh, leave off, yer bloody interfering nag! Get out of my way!' Em heard a chair scrape on the floor as if he was trying to get out past her.

'You're not going nowhere, matey – not till I've had my say. What's come over you, Bob? You used to be a decent man, not carrying on like this with that painted-up slut...'

'Don't you call Mrs Dawson that – she's a respectable widow and she gets lonely, that's all,' Bob flared up. A door opened and, thinking they were coming out to the back, Em got ready to run away, but then they carried on.

'Huh, won't she let you 'ave any of what you're after, then, Bob?' Dot said disgustedly.

'You're a bloody fine one to talk, you ain't always been so good at keeping yer legs together, 'ave yer?'

'Don't you dare start on me!' Dot's voice sank to a venomous hiss for a moment. 'Whatever I've done I've paid the price and faced up to things. Not like you, running scared at the first hint of trouble. What about Cynthia? Your wife, remember her? You going to just leave her in there to rot?

233

I'm going to go and see her, Bob – this Sat'dy...'

'You won't say anything?' She had punctured his anger.

'No, Bob. I won't say anything. D'you think she needs to know what a spineless bastard you are the minute she's poorly and can't help herself? And what about your kids?'

'What about 'em? They're all right, ain't they, for now – it won't hurt.' His voice was uncertain now, then desperate. 'I don't know what it is, Dot, it's summat about the woman. I just can't seem to help myself.'

'Bob.' Dot's voice lowered and she spoke carefully, as if trying to hammer some sense into him. 'Listen to me. You've got to help yourself. It ain't my job to bring up two families. The only thing that keeps me from going to the Welfare people and saying they're being neglected is that I couldn't do it to 'em – I love the poor little buggers like my own. And Cynth is my best friend. I don't want to do it to any of 'em, but they're your job, not mine. I swear to God, this can't go on. If you don't start facing up to things and looking after them, I'll report you. And they'll come and take 'em away and put them in a home...'

The words clanged in Em's head like the clapper of a doom-laden bell. She didn't stay to hear any more. Tearing out again along the entry she wanted to scream out what she had heard to Sid and Joyce, to anyone, to burst the bubble of terror that was building up inside her. But her feet slowed. She couldn't say anything – not about Dad, or about the men who'd come to take them away to the home. She couldn't. It was all locked

234

up inside her and she couldn't go scaring the little ones. Talking about it might make it happen!

She straightened her coat and went out into the street again as if she hadn't a care in the world.

'Come on, Em, your turn!' Molly, shouted. 'We was waiting for you!'

She hardly slept that night. She was disturbed by dreams of men with giant hands coming and dragging her off and locking her away, and Dot's voice echoing, echoing in her mind.

After playtime it was PT. Playing at the back of Em's mind was the fact that as she came into school that morning, she had crossed paths with Katie O'Neill. Katie didn't seem quite so thick with Lily Davies as she had been, and as they passed each other earlier, Em thought she had seen Katie smile at her, a quick, darting smile, but at least Katie had been looking in her direction. In her sad, frightened state, it had raised a little glow of hope. Perhaps she could have her friend back again? Katie might regret what she'd said before, might miss her and really want to be friends again. And in any case, Lily Davies was absent today.

Their breath blew out in white clouds as they stood shivering in the school yard, but the sun was out, shining so brilliantly that they had to screw up their eyes. Miss Lineham strode out, a thick, moss-coloured coat belted tightly round her solid form, carrying a stack of wooden hoops. She put them down, grunting with the exertion, and clapped her hands.

'Right, children! Line up in twos, please. I said twos, Maggie Minchin, not sixes! That's better,

235

come along. We're going to work with hoops today. One between two! You must share nicely.'

As the children scrimmaged to find a partner, Em knew Molly would make straight for her and, though she was ashamed to do it, she edged away, trying to separate herself from her. In those seconds, her little pilot light of hope that Katie might want to be her partner again burst into a bright flame as Katie seemed to be heading towards her. In those seconds there came a glimpse of past happiness, Katie's pretty, dark-featured face and swinging plaits making for her and her only, the whispered secrets, the games – everything from before, when things were good. Em found a smile of welcome rising on her lips, but then Katie, with a kind of half smile, half smirk, passed her by and paired up with Gladys Day, who looked as pleased with herself as anything and went smugly to Miss Lineham to collect her hoop.

'You gunna be my partner?' Molly was beside Em again immediately, always there, always willing, like a puppy that wants its tummy tickled.

'All right,' Em said crossly, stinging with hurt. She felt bad about Molly. She *ought* to like her. Molly was kind. Once, Em had woken from the nightmare delirium of the fever and she had been glad to see Molly beside her then. Now, though Em was grateful, Molly still had her irritating effect on her and she wished someone else was so keen to be her friend. She'd have to make the most of it.

The next half-hour passed busily. To keep them warm, Miss Lineham got the children running up and down the yard pushing the hoops. They had to get in a big circle and roll them to each other, and the ones who had no hoops were expected to run round the edge of the yard to keep warm. She got them standing in the hoops, circling them round their hips, trying to keep them twirling off the ground as long as possible.

'The girls will probably find this easier,' Miss Lineham said, giving one of her very rare smiles. This immediately sent the boys into a fever of competition, furiously snaking their bodies in their long shorts and shirts to keep the hoops spinning.

Em enjoyed rolling and catching the hoop but she was soon exhausted. Even now she still felt weak after her illness. Running round the yard made her feel hot and shaky, but she kept forcing one foot in front of the other so as not to attract Miss Lineham's attention.

At last the bell rang to end the lesson and the children gathered up the hoops and went to the door in a knot. Em found herself towards the back of the crowd, and seeing Katie O'Neill even further behind, she hung back. Even pride couldn't prevent her. She so longed for things to be right, back how they were before when she and Katie were friends and cock of the walk at school. Surely Katie couldn't really have meant what she said before about them not playing together?

The two of them were at the back, in their little gymslips. Katie looked lovely in hers, of course. She was the sort who looked nice wearing anything. Em seized all her courage.

'Hello, Katie,' she said, blushing and her heart pounding with fear but determined to take her chance. 'Will you come and play out later? I

237

haven't seen you for ages.'

Katie looked down for a second, biting her lip. When she looked up there was a hard, impatient expression in her eyes.

'I *told* you, didn't I? How many more times? My mom says I shouldn't have anything to do with you, with your mother being funny in the head and in the asylum. And cos you play with Molly Fox. Mom says I should keep away from both of you. We thought you were from a nice family – but you're not. Sorry, Em.' And she moved away.

Em stood as if glued to the spot. The children in front of them had heard every word of Katie's clear tones and had turned round to stare. None of the sharp retorts she thought of later came to her mind then. Instead she simply froze under this icy blast of cruelty. The others went on inside, leaving her behind.

'Come along, girl!' Miss Lineham was shouting angrily at her. 'Move! Whatever's the matter with you?'

Somehow she unstuck her feet from the surface of the yard and followed them inside, moving dazed, like a sleepwalker.

Snowballs

Thirty-One

The next Saturday afternoon, a knock at the door made Em jump violently. She started at the slightest thing since she'd heard Dot saying they might all be taken away to the Home.

Bob hurried through to the front to open up. Em stood by the stairs and saw Dot on the doorstep in her hat and coat, ushering Nancy inside for Bob to look after her.

'Right – I'm off now,' Dot said. Her face wore a grim, challenging expression. 'You are staying in with 'em, ain't yer? You'd better be. If I hear different...'

Bob held his hands up as if Dot was brandishing a gun. 'I'm staying in. I told yer,' He lowered his hands. 'Send her my love,' he said, very quietly. 'If you can get through to her.'

Dot gave a nod, backing away. 'See yer later.'

Bob closed the door, pausing next to it for a few seconds, his head bowed. Unaware that Em was watching, he moved to the window and peered out, leaning first to one side, then the other as if he was looking for something along the street. Whatever it was failed to appear and he sighed.

'Where's Dot going?' Em asked. Bob didn't turn to look at her.

'To visit your mother.'

She felt a glimmer of excitement. 'Is Mom coming home?'

Bob made a bitter sound. 'Don't think so, love.'

'Are you looking for Mrs Dawson?'

He swung round then, moving from the window.

'Course not. Don't talk daft.'

It started snowing as Dot made her way to Hollymoor Hospital. There had been a sudden slight warming of the air and the expectant stillness which precedes a fall of snow. As she walked to the tram stop in the middle of Birmingham, the first dry flakes were beginning to drift down from an iron-coloured sky, frosting hats and shoulders. By the time she reached Hollymoor the flakes were larger. The long drive was dark and silent, but suddenly she met her first view of the imposing hospital buildings with their lights on early in the gloom, looking something like a palace in a fairy story. Except, of course, it was not a palace.

'God Almighty,' Dot murmured under her breath. 'Are you really in there, Cynth?' It gave her the creeps just looking at the place. All the associations and fears connected with the asylum rose up in her mind and she had to keep a tight grip on herself not to turn round and run. After giving herself a stern talking-to she took in a few breaths of the sharp air, stamped the snow from her boots and stepped inside, out of the darkening afternoon.

During the wait in the main hall, she sat with her hat in her lap, her hands clenched into fists underneath it. It felt wrong to her to keep the hat on indoors, though some of the other visitors did, as if they were in church. The high electric lights made the sky outside the long windows look even blacker, making her feel shut in, as if she might not be allowed to leave, and she had to keep taking deep breaths to calm her nerves. The sight of the inmates shuffling in on the arms of the young nurses did nothing to reassure her. What was Cynthia going to be like? From what Bob had said, she had been in a very bad way when he visited. So much so that he had not been able to face coming back since.

She recognized Cynthia immediately, yet part of her mind was telling her no, it couldn't be! It was the chopped hair, the slow, laborious gait and deadened expression. Her eyes focused on the face. Surely not? Yes – it was her... Dot forced her legs to stand, her lips to attempt a welcoming smile.

'Here we are,' the nurse said brightly. To Cynthia she added with loud optimism, 'You sit down there and you can both have a nice chat.'

Cynthia obeyed, head bowed, taking an age to settle her scrawny frame on the chair as if it was a puzzling, even painful activity. Once the nurse had moved away she looked up in a dazed way. It was only then that Dot was completely sure they had brought her the right patient. She felt tears prickle her eyes at the wretched sight of her friend, but she made herself smile.

'Hello, Cynth,' she said, leaning towards her.

'Hello, Dot,' Cynthia whispered. Her lips tried to smile but the attempt quickly faded. She seemed to have shrunk right into herself, helpless and like a very small child. What on earth could they talk about, Dot thought, panic rising in her.

Then she admonished herself. This is Cynth, silly, your old pal – just talk like you normally would!

'How are you?' she asked gently.

'All right.' Cynthia shrugged. It seemed hopeless to say anything further. Her eyes were stretched wide, as if in constant appeal.

'Are they taking care of you all right?'

'Yes. All right.'

There was no sign of the distress Bob had described, the need to harm herself. Not at this moment anyway. It felt more as if she was a candle with a faulty wick, guttering and struggling to burn. Dot longed suddenly to reach out and hold her, as if by embracing her she could pour her own warmth and vitality into her friend.

'Bob sent his love to yer,' she said.

'The kids... How are they?' The eyes wider, wilder now.

'They're all right, love. Em was a bit poorly a few weeks ago, but she's back to normal now. We had a little tea party on her birthday. Joyce and Sid are well...' She wasn't going to mention about Sid's feet, which had only just healed, or the big gash Joyce had on her chin from falling off the back wall in the week. Certainly not that their father spent every daily moment he could manage – and, for all she knew, some of the nightly ones too – at the house of a certain Mrs Flossie Dawson. None of this would help Cynthia now. 'They all sent their love and they hope you'll soon be feeling better.'

'My babby – how's my little Violet?' She never spoke above a whisper, those eyes wide and apprehensive as if she expected someone to tell

244

her off at any moment.

'Oh, doing well. She's still with your sister.' Dot thought guiltily that she should go and see, check how Violet was. Whatever else she thought of Olive, she did appear to be caring well for the baby.

'I miss them so much.' Cynthia looked up towards the windows for a moment, as if trying to see their faces. Her eyes began to stream and she looked down. Dot reached out and took her hands, unable now to stop her own tears.

'They miss you too, bab. But they're all right. They're looking forward to you coming home.'

Cynthia was shaking her head hopelessly. 'No. I shan't go home.' She gazed across at the dark windows again. 'No, I can't do that.'

'You will – of *course* you will!' Dot squeezed her hands more tightly, trying to pacify her as if she were a child. Where had her bubbly, loving, best pal gone, leaving only this whispering shell?

'It's all right, Cynth. Look, you're just feeling a bit low at the moment and everything seems bad. But you'll get better, course you will! You'll come home and be with them all again.'

Cynthia raised her tearful face, clutching at Dot's words. 'Will I? No.' More head shaking. 'I can't. I *won't*. I can't even make a cup of tea for myself any more. I can't do anything... I don't know what's happened to me. I feel so lost, so *bad...*'

Dot leaned close and took Cynthia in her arms, feeling the coarse material of the dress which was draped over her bones. The material seemed indestructible, as it was no doubt intended to be.

245

A sour, sweaty smell came from her friend and made Dot's spirits sink further, but she felt overwhelmingly that she must hold Cynthia like one of her own children, while her friend sobbed in her arms.

'Just hang on.' She had no reference or authority for her words, apart from a desperate hope that Cynthia's sickness was like any other – something that could, in the end, heal. 'If you hang on, and rest, and let yourself get better, it'll all be all right. It *will*, love! I'm helping your Bob look after the kids – they're all right – and my Nance loves it. It's like having more brothers and sisters for her! We all love you and we're waiting to have you back. But you just take your time, Cynth. You'll get better – you *will*. One day the sun'll come out and you'll be able to see it proper, like.'

'Oh God!' Cynthia fell into sudden sobbing and, to Dot's astonishment, she burst out, 'I want, oh, I want my mom! I want her, I want her... She shouldn't have died... I just wish she'd been here sometimes!'

'There, oh, poor little lovey, there, there...' Dot held her, rocking her gently. There seemed nothing else to do except hold her and help her grasp on to some kind of hope.

By the time Dot walked out of the hospital into the whitening world beyond, she felt sad and drained beyond belief.

Thirty-Two

Em waited all the afternoon on tenterhooks for Dot to come back. Whatever Dad said, surely she might return with the news they all longed to hear, even bring Mom home with her?

At last, her footfalls silenced by the snow, she arrived with a tapping on the window.

'Coo-ee – it's me.'

Em flung the door open expectantly and saw Dot's brave smile, but her hopes slid right down. No Mom. There was to be no miracle.

'Make us a cuppa tea, will yer, bab. I'm dying for one.' Exhaustedly Dot laid her hat on the table in the back room, after shaking the melting flakes from it. Em scurried to reheat the kettle, then hovered round Dot with the others. Nancy climbed onto her lap, glad her mom was back.

'So – how did yer find 'er?' Bob asked.

'Not too bad,' Dot spoke cautiously in front of the children, sinking onto one of the chairs by the table. 'By crikey, it's cold out there now...'

'Is that all?' He stood over her as if to drag the words out of her.

Dot's face puckered with anger. 'If you want to know that bad, why don't you get yerself over there?'

'I will... I mean... But how did you find 'er today?'

Dot looked round at the eager faces all waiting

247

for her reply and she spoke chiefly to the children.

'Your mom's not too bad,' she told them, reaching out to stroke Joyce's head. 'There's no need to worry. She's still feeling a little bit poorly, but she sends her love and says she'll be back with yer as soon as she can, all right? Now – you run along a minute and let me have a word with your dad.'

Sid and Joyce disappeared to the front room where the fire was lit. Nancy followed reluctantly and Em went back into the scullery.

'So?' Bob said.

'Well – what d'yer think? Not herself. Down in the dumps. Hardly able to drag herself about. Can't even think how to make a cup of tea – that was what she said.' Dot recited. The strain of the day was telling on her and her voice rose harshly. 'Sad, cried a lot. Misses the kids.' She glared at Bob. 'Misses you. Not the woman I know as Cynthia Brown, if you really want to know.'

Em, carrying the teapot in, saw Dot put her hands over her face and burst into tears. 'It's so sad to see 'er like that. It's terrible...'

Bob turned away, as if he couldn't face her tears. Dot looked up and saw Em's desolate expression.

'Oh, come 'ere, love – I'm sorry.' She held her arms out and cuddled Em close to her, speaking as cheerfully as she could, trying to offer a glimmer of hope. 'I dain't mean to upset you, bab. It's just a bit sad that she can't be here with you all. She just needs a bit more time to rest.'

'Why can't she rest here?' Em asked, looking up wide-eyed at Dot. 'I could look after her.'

Bob interrupted suddenly, getting up from his

248

chair. 'I'm off out for a bit.'

'Bob – for Christ's sake!' Dot erupted, jumping to her feet. 'You're not going anywhere. I've only just got 'ere – what am I s'posed to do? Your kids need you. You're not dumping everything on me again!'

But he was flinging his coat on. 'I'm not – I'll be back. But I've got to go.' They heard the front door slam.

'I s'pect he's gone to see Mrs Dawson,' Em said. 'That's where he always goes.'

'What?' Dot couldn't keep the horrified tone out of her voice; she was shocked that Em was so aware of this. 'Oh, I don't s'pose so, love! I s'pect he's gone down the Crown the way 'e usually does.'

Dot was breathing heavily, trying to bite back all the things she would have liked to scream after Bob: *Useless, heartless bugger!* But she controlled herself and patted Em's shoulder. 'That tea must be ready to pour, eh? You're such a good girl, that you are.'

Em poured the tea, frowning with sadness and confusion after all she had overheard from the scullery. And everyone kept telling her how good she was when she did everything they wanted. 'Good girl, Em – you'll run an errand for me, won't you? What a good girl...' Like Dad, every time he went off to that Mrs Dawson and left her in charge: 'You'll look after the others won't you, Em? You're a good wench.'

Her frown deepened. Why was it always her who had to try so hard when Dad kept going off and leaving them? She wasn't so sure she wanted

249

to be a good girl any more.

Half an hour later, tanked up with a quick pint for courage, Bob was standing on Flossie Dawson's front step, which was now cushioned with half an inch of snow. He leaned his head back, took in a long breath of the freezing air and expelled it in a rush, trying to calm himself. He had got here, the place he had dreamed of being all day, and now he was so nervous his legs were fit to give way.

'Christ, man – get a grip!' he urged himself. It had got so that the thought of the woman almost unhinged him. All day long she floated before his eyes, her sweet, vulnerable face against her black widow's weeds, the soft, well-spoken Staffordshire accent, that look in her eyes when she opened the door to him. She was like no one he had ever known before, and she possessed him. He had to see her, had to...

He steadied himself and rapped twice on the door. In a moment she would come, he would be with her.

He heard a slight movement inside – her step – and thought his heart would burst out of his chest. Then her shape in the dimly lit little hall, and her face behind the patterned glass, uncertain as a cloud-obscured moon, so that he could not read whether she was pleased to see him.

'Oh, Bob – it's you,' her soft voice greeted him. She was always polite, proper, but her tone held that hint of seductiveness which had hooked him in the first place. She did sound a little flustered, though, and he took this as a good sign.

'Evening,' he said gruffly. 'Just thought I'd pop

round, see if you was both all right. If you need any help with anything, like.'

He felt rough and awkward beside her, with her genteel manner, but something in the way she appealed to him, sweetly grateful for his small acts of help, made him feel strong and manly and heroic. She needed the help of a man, now she was left alone. She said so often. And she'd fixed on him.

'Oh, that's very kind of you,' Flossie said, sounding surprised, though his visits to offer help had become so very frequent. But they both kept up the pretence that his coming here was rare and surprising. She gave a little laugh, seeming breathless. 'Well, I think I'm all right at the moment, thank you. But as you've taken the trouble, perhaps you'd like to come in for a cup of tea?'

'Well, thank you! That's good of you.' He played surprised as well, stepping inside with a glow of triumph, his snow-flecked cap in his hand. Once she had closed the door behind them he felt safe. He was here, here at last, close to her, this neat, curvaceous woman, a scent of flowers always about her, a cut above this neighbourhood, he thought. She had class. Her clothes were better than anything Cynthia had ever had. And something about her, the direct yet shy way she looked at him, her demure manners, her vulnerability and seeming need of him, drew him like a drug.

Of course they weren't alone. That made it all above board. The girl was there. The times Bob had wished her gone, anywhere else but here, that she would disappear in a puff of smoke by some magician's trick! He had learned that on Sunday afternoons she visited an aunt somewhere. Flossie had let him know this, casually, signalling that this would be a good time to visit. But she was here now, perched on a leather pouffe by the fire, looking up at him in that insolent way of hers which got right under his skin.

'Hello, Daisy,' he said, in a false, jolly voice.

Daisy stared. Her face was very pale amid the tumbling dark hair, her eyes hooded.

'Manners, Daisy,' Flossie reprimanded sharply. 'Say hello to Mr Brown.'

'Hello, Mr Brown,' Daisy said, with barely veiled sarcasm. 'How're your children?'

'They're all right, ta,' Bob said lightly.

'Go and put on some tea, please, Daisy,' Flossie said. To Bob's surprise there were already teacups on a tray, resting on the side table. Had they had company before? But it seemed nosy to ask.

'Oh, but you've already had your tea...' he protested.

'No – it's quite all right. I should like another,' Flossie said firmly. 'And you've been out in the cold. Go along, Daisy.'

Daisy got up and sulkily picked up the tray, and Bob's heart bucked at the thought that she would be out of the room, at least for a few minutes! What difference this made he was not sure, except that in his acute state of unsatisfied longing he could imagine that there might be some possibility. A quick kiss, perhaps. Something.

He knew really that there was not much hope. Since that one time when Flossie had turned, standing close to him with that look in her eyes, since that one kiss, touching his mouth with her sweet, soft lips, which keyed him up with desire

252

every time he thought of it, she had withdrawn as if afraid. Of course she was afraid! He tried to get a grip on himself. Here she was, a respectable though lonely widow, and he a married man. He mustn't do anything to worry her. She wasn't the sort.

But whatever his head said, he was hooked on her, his thoughts possessed by her, by all that he'd like to do with her, for her, and he didn't mean just fixing door hinges. Over and over again he played the dream of undoing the buttons of her white blouse, revealing the lacy garments underneath, unpeeling them, her rounded, feminine body naked before his eyes, him laying her down, her eyes beckoning him.

'How is your wife? Did your neighbour go to see her? And do sit down, please.' She was talking to him – Bob jerked his thoughts back to reality. Flossie sat on the worn old pouffe by the fire which Daisy had just vacated. There was an attractive rug woven in warm colours, partially covering the bare boards. He couldn't help noticing that while Flossie pleaded poverty, what possessions she did have were of fine quality, some quite exotic. Bob sat on the chair opposite her, only noticing then that her cheeks were flushed pink. She seemed to be nervous, as if trying to collect herself.

'Yes, ta, er, thank you,' he said. 'Dot – our neighbour – saw her. Said she's a bit better, but still not right. My turn to go next, of course.' He looked down, his cheeks reddening, and fiddled with his cap. She might think he was neglecting Cynthia and that wouldn't do! And he was, of course, but he was filled with dread of that place, of having to go back there.

Flossie's big grey eyes took on a look of deep concern.

'The poor, *poor* thing,' she said. 'How terrible. And for you, having to try and do everything for the children. My late husband's sister was very bad after one of her babies and I must say she was never quite the same again. It happens that way with some women. Of course, I'm sure your wife will make a full recovery, but it must be ever so upsetting for you.'

For a moment Bob had the awful feeling he was going to cry. Bathed in her sympathy, his chest tightened and a lump came into his throat. What he wanted most at that moment was to surrender himself into her soft arms, to be held and to weep like a baby himself. Instead he looked up and said gruffly, 'Well, we manage the best we can. My girl Em, she's a good'un.'

'The poor little thing.' Again, the head held on one side, the sweet sympathy. 'My Daisy was only nine when her father passed away.' She said the last two words in a pained whisper. 'It's so very difficult for children but they can be very brave, can't they? I do have some idea what it must be like, you see.'

Her words chimed in with his sense of despair that he had lost Cynthia for good, as if she was actually dead. He found he could not stand the conversation any more because he was choking back the urge to weep.

'That door all right?' he managed to bark out. 'The one I had a go at?'

One hinge to the scullery door had been snapped off and he had mended it for her.

'Oh yes, thank you, it's working perfectly now.' Her face clouded. 'I am a bit concerned that there's a hole in the roof. I suppose I'd better find someone who can get up and look at the tiles.'

Bob wanted to say he could do it, that he could in fact fly: anything to please her.

'I might be able to look at it,' he offered, though he had little idea about roofs or tiles.

She clasped her hands in wonder. 'Bob, could you? Oh, to have a strong capable man about – I can't tell you! It'd put my mind at rest no end. I'd be so grateful.'

'I'll 'ave a look tomorrow,' he promised. Now he had an excuse to come the next day! A firm, harmless reason! He glowed inside.

Soon Daisy came back with the tea and stubbornly planted herself on a stool between the two of them, slurping her tea loudly until Flossie asked her to find better manners. So they continued to make stilted conversation with the girl there, until Bob had finished his tea. They had so little to talk about, not sharing day-to-day life. He could see there was no chance of being with Flossie on her own that night and his conscience was beginning to itch about what might be going on at home.

'I'll come in tomorrow afternoon,' he said as he went out to the hall to get his coat. 'My pal's got a ladder I could borrow.'

'Oh, Bob, you really are marvellous,' Flossie said softly. It was a bedroom voice, full of promise. And at least the girl hadn't followed them out there.

Christ, how he wanted to take hold of her and kiss her, however wrong it was. He couldn't give a fig how wrong anything was, the way he felt. He gave her a long look in the shadowy hall, but she simply returned a gentle smile.

'Thanks for the tea, then.'

'See you tomorrow, Bob.' Then once he was safely out on the step she added, 'I'm so glad.' Three words said in such a way that he was shaken again at the force of his desire for her.

'Cheerio, then,' he said breezily, putting on his hat.

'Goodbye, Bob.'

The door closed and he was alone on the snow-muffled pavement, his breath whirling out of him in the light of the street lamp.

He gave a groan, bending over for a moment in an agony. All the feeling she brought out in him seemed to overwhelm him: need, clumsiness, unworthiness, awe. And desire, that above all.

'*Christ*,' he muttered. 'What a woman!'

Thirty-Three

Em woke from a dream the next morning. She was cradling Violet close to her in the bed, feeling the soft fuzz of baby hair against her cheek. She woke, bereft when she discovered it wasn't true. When she opened her eyes, a hard, unusual light was seeping round the curtain.

'There's lots more snow!' Joycie came back into

256

the room a minute later, bouncing with excitement. 'It's everywhere, let's go out and play. Come on, Em, Sid!'

Sid and Joyce threw on their clothes and belted off downstairs, but Em was slower, lingering in the yearning of her dream. She cuddled Princess Lucy to her, snuggling against her embroidered cotton face, but it had nothing of the roundness and warmth of Violet's.

She got out of bed, suddenly determined, and went to her father's room, peering through the door, which had been left open an inch. He was in bed, his eyes closed, and the bedclothes were moving. She watched, frowning, puzzled. His hand seemed to be pumping furiously up and down under the bedclothes.

'Dad?' She pushed the door open.

'What?' he shouted, flying into a rage as his eyes snapped open. 'Don't come barging in 'ere like that!'

'Sorry...'

The sight of her standing in her little nightdress, trailing her doll from one hand, seemed to shame him.

'Didn't mean to shout, love,' he said, sitting up wearily. 'I just didn't hear yer coming, that's all.'

'Can we go and see Violet today?'

'Violet?' For a second it was as though he couldn't think who she meant. 'Oh – no, bab. Can't go anywhere today. I've got things to do.'

'Oh.' He always seemed to have things to do these days. No time for any of them.

She went and dressed, sadly. Downstairs she stoked the range and put on a big pan of porridge.

Sid and Joyce came in to eat it, with pink cheeks and noses and bright eyes.

'Ooh, my fingers're freezing!' Sid cried, hopping from one foot to the other and wincing as he tried to warm them by the range.

Joyce eyed the steaming pan of porridge, wrinkling her nose.

'Can us have sugar on it, Em?'

'No,' Em said grumpily. 'Ain't got none.'

'Don't say "ain't!"' She heard Cynthia's voice in her head.

Joyce pouted but was hungry enough to eat it anyway.

Bob came to join them. 'Good wench,' he said absent-mindedly.

'Dad–' Sid was still jiggling with excitement – 'will yer take us down the park this afternoon? Or out to the country so we can play in the snow?'

Bob shook his head. 'Can't, son. Got things to do.'

'What things?' Sid's face fell.

'Promised someone some help.'

Em knew instinctively that the person he had promised help to was Mrs Dawson, but she didn't dare say anything. Joyce was less hesitant, though.

'You never do anything for us,' she said, with a smouldering expression. 'You're not like our dad any more.'

Horrified, Em waited for his wrath to fall on Joyce. Surely she'd get a belting for that? But all Bob said was, 'That's enough. Eat yer porridge,' as if he'd barely heard. As if he was somewhere else in his head. And that felt worse than him getting angry.

Joyce slid down from the table. 'I *hate* you,' she said, running off upstairs. Em was shocked to the core. She never dared use words like that.

Bob disappeared soon after breakfast, letting in the distant sound of church bells and the glaring white light as the front door swung open and shut. He didn't stop to say goodbye or tell them where he was going. Em stood hunched over the sink in the scullery, scraping out the porridge pan with her fingernails. The porridge was caked on and slimy to the touch. Tears ran down her cheeks and dropped into the water.

'I *hate you...*' Joyce's words rang in her head. What had happened to her loving family?

She pushed her hair off of her face with her forearm. Her fringe was constantly in her eyes. Dot kept saying she must cut it for her and then forgetting. Almost immediately the hair slipped down across her eyes again and she slammed her hands down in the water suddenly, sending out a great splash.

'Bugger it. I'm not bloody well doing it!'

Misery enveloped her then and she sank down on a chair by the table, picking up Princess Lucy as she went. She put her head down on the milk-splashed table and, in the dark ring of her arms, wept lonely, angry tears.

A soft tapping brought her out of it. Quickly wiping her eyes she opened the door to find Molly, and gasped at the sight of her face, its right side swollen and her eye puffed up with a great big shiner.

'Blimey – who did that?'

Molly shrugged as if she hardly knew what Em was talking about. 'You crying? What's up?'

'Nothing.'

'Coming out to play?'

Em only took in then that the street was full of life, shrieks of fun and snowballs flying. 'All right, then.'

She pulled on her coat and went out. The day was turning bright, the snow powdery, creaking slightly underfoot. Up and down the street all the children were out, balling up the snow, dragging one another along on trays or home-made sleds cobbled together from bits of wood. Several wonky snowmen with coal eyes and parsnip noses graced the pavement and there was a huge one under construction right in the middle of the road.

Some older boys were out, chasing and shouting, and doors were open along the street as the adults watched the party. She saw Bullseye, the Buttons' black and white dog, snuffing in the road, then noticed Mrs Button standing by her door, with Stanley watching from just inside in his wheelchair, bundled up to his chin with blankets. Mrs Button had on her Sunday best under her cherry-red coat and black hat and she smiled and waved at Em and so did Stanley. Em waved back, cheered by Mrs Button's kindness. She could not know that behind Jenny Button's smile that morning was the longing that almost overwhelmed her sometimes, for a man who was able-bodied and could still make love to her. But she loved her Stanley and continued to smile even though she ached inside.

Em and Molly joined the crowd, pressing

gathered snow in their fists and throwing it. Soon they were laughing, running, pink-cheeked, their necks wet and cold from snowballs flung at them. It was all fun until Bert Fox came out as well and then there was too much force and nastiness behind the throwing. Em shrank back, seeing Bert hurl a ball of snow at a boy much smaller than him. He had put a stone in the middle of it and it cut the boy's head and made him cry, his blood vivid against all the white.

'You're a vicious little bugger, you are, Bert Fox. You should be locked up!' Jenny Button reprimanded him, waddling over to assist the young boy. But Bert ran away laughing, his thin, stoat face twisted with defiance.

'Sorry about my brother,' Molly said shamefully.

'T'ain't your fault, bab,' Jenny Button said. She looked closely at Molly. 'You been in the wars as well? Did he do that?'

Molly shook her head and Mrs Button didn't like to ask any more. She took the boy with the cut off to her house to clean him up.

'I'm going in,' Em said, noticing how cold it was, how her bare hands were now agony.

'Can I come with yer?' Molly said. 'I don't want to go 'ome.'

Em nodded and the two of them went into the house. They ate some broken biscuits and sat by the fire, wincing as their hands came back to life.

Who did your face?' Em asked.

Molly looked down at her lap. 'Mom,' she said very quietly.

'Why – what did you do?'

261

'Dunno. Nothing.'

Em shuddered. The thought of having Iris Fox as your mom was terrible.

There was a long silence. Molly picked at the hole in the chair where the stuffing was coming through. Eventually she said, 'I'm not going home again.'

'What d'you mean?'

'I don't want to live with them no more.' She looked at Em. 'Can I come and live with you? I'd help and everything...' Her face was so bright and eager.

Em stared at her. What would Dad say? 'I ... I dunno. I don't think my dad would let you.'

'He's round at Mrs Dawson's again, ain't 'e?'

'How d'you know?'

'Saw 'im. I don't like that girl, Daisy. She's a stuck-up cow, she is.'

'Yes, she is,' Em agreed enthusiastically.

'And her hat's like bogeys.'

Em giggled, delighted that she had had just the same thought about Daisy's green hat.

'Is 'e carrying on with her?'

'Carrying on? What d'yer mean?' Em didn't know anything except that Dad was never here and even when he was, he was somewhere else in his head.

'You *know*. Getting up to more than he should be. That's what everyone's saying. Cos of your mom being away and that.'

Em didn't know. She had hardly the remotest idea what Molly was talking about, except that she did know Bob was forever at Mrs Dawson's, even when he pretended he wasn't.

'I hate her,' she said. Joyce's words had released her. She poked the fire. 'Hate her, *hate* her.'

'Eh–' Molly leaned forward – 'why don't you get back at her?'

Em felt a wicked tingle of excitement. 'How d'yer mean?'

'Oh,' Molly said triumphantly. 'There's all sorts of things we can do. Now, what shall we start with?'

Thirty-Four

'You'd never believe it – the cheek of some of them ruddy kids!'

Bob came ranting into the house as Em was stirring the stew-pot at the back. Molly was still there, adamant that she wasn't going home, and she was playing with Sid and Joyce.

They all stared at Bob with innocent expressions – genuinely innocent in Sid's and Joyce's case, since they had no idea what had happened.

'What, Dad?' Sid said.

'I was round at...' He hesitated, suddenly realizing he was going to have to own up to where he'd been all afternoon. 'Any road, those kids, one of 'em chucked a brick. It came right through the flaming window, smashed the pane.' He jammed his coat onto the hook. 'If I find out–' He turned to Molly with a nasty expression. 'Sort of thing that bloody brother of yours'd do.'

'Yes,' Molly said angelically. 'It is. Maybe it *was*

263

him. He cut a lad's head this morning.'

There was no love lost between Molly and Bert, who was about the most unpopular boy in the district.

'Oh dear,' Em said, her face furrowed with mock concern. Inside, the giggles were straining to get out. 'So did they break Mrs Dawson's window?'

'Yes, they cowing well did! I've been boarding it up for 'er until they can fix it proper tomorrow. So, is dinner ready?'

He sat down and picked up yesterday's paper. Behind him, Em and Molly exchanged looks. They'd been so careful, waiting until after dark, choosing a moment when the street was quiet. It was Molly who had thrown the half brick, aiming with all her strength, and they heard the magnificent smash of glass. Em tore off along the street feeling as if electricity was pumping along her limbs with the power of what they had done. Going the back way, she and Molly were home in a twinkling, bursting into the house and laughing until the tears ran down their faces.

'That'll show 'er!' Em gasped, thrilled and aghast at what they had done. 'D'you think they saw us?'

'No. Course not!' They roared and snorted for ages.

Reminded of this now, as they looked at each other, they could barely stop themselves laughing all over again.

Bob suddenly swivelled round. 'What're you still doing here?' he said to Molly.

'Can she stop over?' Em asked. She felt bold

now, as if she could do or say anything.

'No, she bloody can't!' Bob erupted. 'As if I ain't got enough on my plate without half the neighbours' kids 'ere as well. You get off now,' he ordered Molly.

Molly cast a reluctant look at Em, but she had to go. Once the door had closed behind her, Bob said, 'What's one of them Foxes doing 'ere any road? We don't want 'er sort about.'

'I think she's nice,' Joyce contradicted. Joyce seemed to be able to get away with anything.

'Oh, yer do, do yer?' Bob said sarcastically, before going back to his paper.

Em and Molly were taken aback by their own daring. After their first bold assault on Flossie Dawson they were rather stumped as to what to do next. It was as if they had done the most outrageous thing they could think of already. They whispered in the playground at school, plotting and hatching plans. It made Em feel much more cheerful, as if she had a secret magic power.

As they filed inside after playtime in the slushy playground one day that week, Em found that by chance she was next to Katie. At one time Em might have been excited, and hopeful. Now, though, she couldn't care less. She felt stronger; Katie was spiteful and disloyal. Why should she want to suck up to her and be her friend?

'You're very chummy with Molly Fox these days,' Katie remarked. Her tone was friendly, but Em knew she was being nosy. Maybe she was miffed that Em was not running after *her* for a change!

Em looked stonily at her. 'What's it got to do with you?'

'There's no need to be like that. I was just saying,' Katie said huffily.

Em watched her walk away, and poked out her tongue at Katie's departing rear.

Their next assaults on Flossie Dawson were small and mostly harmless, but they also made Em feel better, because at least they were doing something. They left broken glass on the doorstep for her to tread on, and dog muck in her path right outside. They smeared greasy soot on the door, hoping that either Flossie or Daisy would rub up against it and soil their clothes. Every day after school they met, scheming about what they might do next, and hung about near the house after dark, spying and whispering. Em knew that quite often her father was in there too. There was no point in trying to hide the fact from Molly. Everyone seemed to know their business anyway.

One afternoon, in the week before Christmas, Molly came along in high excitement. The snow had almost gone and the girls were in the street near the timber yard. Molly pulled Em into the entry to the courtyard of houses opposite. It was a double knack – a yard with two entrances, so any mischief-maker could speed out at the other side if necessary.

'I know what we can do!' Molly went importantly to the end of the entry and peered out to check no one was coming. Returning, she pulled out something that was tucked in the waist of her skirt: a new white candle, quite a fat one.

'Where d'yer get that?' Em asked, bemused.

'Never you mind.' Molly had a light-fingered way of getting hold of things. 'D'you know what we're gunna do with it?'

She gave a dramatic pause for Em to shake her head.

'Voodoo! See – we melt it down, make a statue of Mrs Dawson and then anything we do to it, it'll happen to her, see?'

'But–'

'It's *magic*,' Molly insisted. 'She'll be screaming in pain and she'll never know who's done it.'

'Oh,' Em said doubtfully. Even to her, to have Flossie Dawson screaming in pain seemed a bit extreme, but it was an interesting idea.

'Come on, then. Not round mine. Let's do it at yours, out the back.'

When they tried the melting-down procedure in the yard behind Em's house the wind kept on blowing out the matches so they retreated into the scullery, melting the candle down into a bowl until they had a handful of soft wax.

'How does the magic know it's Mrs Dawson?' Em wondered, looking at the pale dolly they had shaped with one thin leg and one fat one, Molly breathing heavily in concentration.

'It just does,' Molly insisted.

'Shouldn't we put her name on it or summat?'

'No. We just have to say.' Molly was loving being the one to lead the way. The bruising on her face had faded to a swirl of green and yellow and her eyes were bright and excited. 'Now – get a pin!'

They started by sticking pins into the manikin, howling with Mrs Dawson's imagined pain with each prick. At first they chose a spot carefully

267

and aimed the pin. After a while they were jabbing it in all over, giggling uncontrollably.

'I know,' Em said after a while. She picked up a knife. 'I'm going to cut her!'

Unfortunately she cut so vigorously into the dolly's thin leg that the end of it snapped right off. They held up the bits, appalled for a moment, then burst into hysterical fits of laughter.

'Look what you've done!' Molly cried, convulsed.

'D'you think she can feel it?' Em was awed by the thought that the magic might be working, before being overtaken by giggles again.

'Course she can,' Molly said importantly.

'We'd better try and fix it on again before it's too late!' Em spluttered.

They struck a match and heated the wax so that they could fix the leg haphazardly back on.

'We'd best stop now, I think,' Molly said solemnly. 'We've done enough to her.'

After laying the wax doll back in the little bowl, both quiet suddenly, they looked at each other, wondering.

Thirty-Five

'Now, come and sit down, all of you. Here's a bit of paper each. You can write a little message to your mom and I'll take it to her tomorrow.'

Dot stood over the three Brown children who were seated at the table in her house. Each of them had a sheet from a pad of cheap paper and were taking it in turns with a pencil. Bob wouldn't think of it, she was certain. But the prospect of being in a place like that at Christmas was too much for Dot. She had to do anything she could for her friend.

'What do I have to write?' Sid asked, squirming at the difficulty of the task. The girls were looking to her for an answer as well. Although they ached for nothing more than to have their mother back, the person who was absent in this unimaginable place called the 'asylum' seemed to be someone else altogether. What might anyone say to her?

'Well.' Dot sat at the table with them. Nancy was standing next to Joyce, who was in possession of the pencil, watching quietly as if aware that this was a solemn moment. 'You could tell her a few things you've been doing.'

'Playing in the snow!' Joyce beamed as inspiration came to her.

'Yes!' Dot said. 'She'd like to know that. I bet she was thinking of you playing out when she saw the snow from her window. You can tell her all about your games.'

'I can tell her Miss Jenkins gave me the cane,' Sid said uncertainly.

'Perhaps not that, bab. She might worry. Try and tell her nice things.'

He thought hard, frowning. 'I was milk monitor?'

'Yes – now that's a good thing. And you can tell her you miss her and hope she feels better.'

One by one she helped the younger children shape their letters. Joyce covered the page in big, painstaking letters.

Dear Mom,
I am well. I hav been makeing snowballs. I hav ben a good girl. I want to see you.
Love
Joyce Brown
xxx

'That's lovely, Joycie,' Dot said, having helped her with 'snowballs'. 'She'll like seeing that.'

Sid seemed to find a sudden flow of words as well, accompanied by much sniffing. His tongue slid out as he wrote, spit and snot mingling on his upper lip.

'Let's give your nose a wipe, shall we?' Dot suggested.

Dear Mom,
I hope you are wel. I am wel. I have been a very good boy at school no trubble. I went on a tray in the snow and threw snowballs at Wally and Gordon.

We are all here. Dad is looking after us and Mrs Wiggins is. We want you back. Happy Christmas where you are.
Your son,
Sid X

Sid and Joyce ran out to play, but Em sat for a long time chewing the end of her pencil and looking round Dot's room. Though she always struggled for money, Dot had the place looking as cheerful as possible. They had all helped make paper streamers which were crisscrossing the

270

room, and Dot had made sure they put some up next door as well. There was a cherry-red cloth hanging over the mantelshelf with a few knick-knacks arranged on it and a mirror hanging over it, which helped add light to the room. On the wall opposite the table hung a picture, painted in bright colours, of two young girls in pretty, old-fashioned dresses and plentiful hair, looking at each other as if they were both about to burst out laughing. They looked like friends or sisters and Em had always liked the picture. She especially liked the girl on the left, who had a dimple in her cheek and a pale blue ribbon tied in her hair. She wished the girl was her best friend. Somehow Em knew that the girl would be kind and sweet and never behave like Katie O'Neill. She tried to imagine the girl in Kenilworth Street, playing out with them all. She looked older than Em but she would be like a big sister and look after her...

'How're you getting on, Em?' Dot dragged her back to the present.

'All right,' she whispered. But the truth was she could not think of a single thing to say to her mother.

'What's up?' Dot said gently.

Em shrugged. Her cheeks burned and she suddenly felt like crying.

'Oh, bab, I know it's hard!' Dot put her arm round her and squeezed her. 'You don't have to say much. Your mom'll just be pleased to have a little note from yer. Or you could do her one of your drawings?'

Em shook her head emphatically. She turned her eyes up to Dot. 'When are we going to see

271

Mom? Can we see her at Christmas?'

'Oh no, love, I don't think so.' Even if children were allowed in that place, she felt sure Bob would not take them. She wouldn't want them to see in there either. 'I expect your dad'll go, though.'

'Can we come to see you on Christmas Day?' Em asked.

Dot's face broke into a weary smile. 'I wish you could, love. But I always go to my brother and his wife – it's the one day of the year when someone cooks a meal for me. But I'll see you're all right before I go.'

Em turned back to her unwritten letter. Dot's smile changed to a look of sad worry. What sort of Christmas were they going to have, with no Cynthia and Bob besotted with that woman? She'd have to give him a good talking-to about it. And how much did Em know? Dot had a terrible misgiving, from the pained look so often in Em's eyes, that she understood a lot more about everything than they all realized. She watched, her heart aching, as Em hurriedly wrote the following stilted note:

Dear Mom,

How are you? We are all well. I am doing well at school. Sid and Joyce are being good. We hope you have a nice Xmas.

From

Em

Visitors were allowed at Hollymoor Hospital on a Wednesday as well as a Saturday afternoon. Dot travelled with a heavy heart to see Cynthia, carry-

272

ing a few treats for her, as well as the little notes from her children and Bob's verbal message – 'Just, er, say I hope she's feeling better. I'll be along to see her soon. Got a lot on my plate, like. Send her my love.'

Dot swelled with anger inside, thinking about it. It was so obvious now that Bob was sniffing round that scheming Mrs Dawson. Though she barely knew the woman, Dot thoroughly mistrusted her. There she was, playing the wide-eyed, helpless widow, too smooth for words, preying on a man who already had a wife – yet whatever Dot said, Bob was deaf to her warnings. He seemed to have lost all sense.

'Whatever she says about how hard up she is, she's dressed up like a fourpenny rabbit,' Dot pointed out to him. 'Don't that make you wonder? If she's so flaming poor, why's she got them clothes? I wish *I* had a coat like that, I can tell yer! And if she ain't hard up, what's she doing living round 'ere with the likes of us?'

'For God's sake, woman!' Bob leapt to Flossie Dawson's defence. 'Keep your bloody nose out of it! Mrs Dawson's fallen on hard times since her husband died. I'm just giving 'er a bit of help from time to time, that's all.'

'I bet that's not the only thing you wish you was giving her an' all,' Dot said bluntly. 'I know a schemer when I see one and there's summat about her that ain't right. You wait and see. But don't forget you've got a wife, Bob – one that's stuck with you through thick and thin. You ain't showing much sign of standing by her, are yer?'

Whatever she said to Bob, he shrugged it off. It

was as if he was locked in a world of his own making. And here she was, carting over to see his wife when he never bothered! And she'd find herself making excuses for him because she didn't want to see Cynthia in any more pain than she was in already.

She came away from her visit that day not sure whether to be hopeful or even more worried. Cynthia looked much the same as on her last visits, if noticeably thinner. She said she didn't like the food in the hospital and had no appetite. When Dot handed her the children's letters and invented loving excuses and messages from Bob, Cynthia filled up and hugged the little letters to her chest, crying with longing for her children. But instead of distress and agitation, there was more calmness about her this time. She asked after Dot's family, wanted to know more about the children, the neighbours. She had also been able to make three little knitted figures, a soldier with a tall black hat for Sid and two tiny girl dolls for Em and Joyce.

'D'you feel any better?' Dot dared ask at last.

Cynthia's dark eyes turned to her but there was something drifty in her expression, almost as if the question had no meaning.

'Yes, a bit,' she whispered.

When Dot left to go she said, 'Thanks, Dot. You're a real friend.'

Thinking about it on the way home Dot tried to make out what it was she had seen. That still, quiet air Cynthia had worn – was it a sign of her settling, of real improvement, or was it the calm before another storm whose dark clouds were massing in the distance? It was impossible to tell.

But she went home and told the little ones that their mom was feeling better and sent her love to all of them. She handed each of them the tiny dolls their mother had made. She saw Em hug it against her and give the faintest of smiles.

Later that week, Bob dropped his bombshell. They were all sitting down for tea one evening.

'I've had a very kind offer.' He seemed excited. 'It's about Christmas.'

Their eyes were all fixed on him.

'One of our neighbours has said we can go to her – for Christmas dinner, like.'

'We're going to Auntie Dot's!' Joyce cried happily.

'Ain't our mom coming home for Christmas?' Sid asked. Em thought she saw his bottom lip quiver.

'No, she ain't,' Bob said brusquely. 'And it ain't Dot who's asked us. I reckon Dot's seen quite enough of you all as it is. No, we've been asked by Mrs Dawson.'

'Who's Mrs Dawson?' Joyce asked sulkily. She knew perfectly well who Mrs Dawson was by now. 'I want to go to Mrs Wiggins.'

'Mrs Dawson lives round the corner,' Bob explained. 'I've got to know 'er a bit and she's on her own, with her daughter, like, and we thought it'd be a good idea to get together.'

'Is Mrs Dawson all right?' Em asked innocently.

'Why? Yes, course she is,' he said. 'What's got

into you?'

'I don't want to go to Mrs Dawson,' Joyce said, pouting.

'Well, we're going.' Bob roared at them. 'And that's that!'

The subject was closed. The children all looked at each other in silence.

Christmas Day dawned grey and very cold. It was a poor Christmas for many, the Depression biting deep into the household pockets of the neighbourhood. Dot had badgered Bob into making sure the children had a few small presents to open and he managed to get up and come into their bedroom to watch as they peeled off the pages of the *Sports Argus* he'd wrapped them in.

Sid was especially delighted with a red tin engine Bob had bought for him and spent the morning vrooming it round the floor and getting under everyone's feet. Joyce had a little rag doll and Em some coloured pencils and paper for more of her drawings.

Mrs Button came across to wish everyone a happy Christmas and handed Em some mince pies she'd made.

'Just a little something,' she said, wrapped up in her cheerful red coat. She smiled with delight when they all thanked her, and was obviously enjoying being among the children. She didn't seem any too eager to go home again.

Bob got very irritable with them all, trying to get them ready to go for their dinner at Mrs Dawson's. None of their clothes looked very clean and Sid's socks seemed to have disappeared without trace, only to be found finally under his mattress.

'You'll just have to go without any!' Bob said, exasperated. 'Come on – we need to get going. Get your coats!'

'I don't want to go.' Joyce, as ever, was able to put into words what no one else dared. 'I don't like Mrs Dawson and I don't like Daisy, she's nasty. And she wears an ugly hat.'

'What's her hat got to do with it?' Bob was finally losing his temper. 'We're going and that's that. And you'd all bloody well better behave yourselves when you get there!'

They all trooped along the quiet street and round the corner to Flossie Dawson's house. Sid was grizzling because Bob had not let him bring his engine with him. Em held the tiny doll Mom had given in her fist, clutched inside her pocket. She saw that Bob had on his Sunday best and looked as smart as she ever saw him. He must have got it out of Mrs Larkin's pawn shop himself. He looked bright-eyed, expectant and handsome.

'Right – pack that in!' he hissed fiercely at Sid once they were outside the house. Sid, seeing that it was no use, did as he was told.

There was a pause after he knocked on the door, before it swung open on this mutinous little family. A delicious smell of roasting meat greeted them.

'Ah hello, Mrs Dawson, this is very kind–' Bob began, gushingly, then stopped as he took in what Em also noticed at the same time.

'Oh, my word,' Bob said.

Em's eyes widened in horror. Mrs Dawson had come limping to the door on sticks, and on her

277

leg was a big white plaster cast. It was the same leg – Em knew straight away – that she had lopped off the candle-wax dolly with the knife!

'It's all right.' Flossie Dawson was the picture of heroic bravery. 'It happened yesterday evening. I slipped on a patch of ice. But everything's all right. Your piece of beef is in the oven, Bob, er ... Mr Brown. Happy Christmas to all of you!'

Daisy was standing in the narrow hall and as they all squeezed inside she stood behind her mother, wrinkling her nose and sticking her tongue out at each of them in turn.

Marbles

Thirty-Six

Cynthia sat looking out through one of the long windows at the side of the ward. They were called 'sun balconies', constructed especially so that inmates could benefit in mood from the touch of any available rays.

These days of February had been some of the darkest, dead-seeming of the year, with no sign of the sun and no breeze. Hardly a crack had appeared in the clouds, which spread themselves like a brooding lid between horizons. It was as if they were doubly shut in, by the weather and by the high walls and long drive curving out towards that distant world outside the hospital.

Today, though, the leaden cover suddenly crumpled apart and spears of sunlight pierced through. Cynthia, reclining in a chair, tilted her drawn, pasty face to drink in the light. The warmth seemed to stroke her closed eyelids like gentle fingers.

She breathed in deeply, her hands relaxing their grip on the arms of the chair. For some moments it felt as if she was floating; she was aware of a light, neutral sensation, as if there was no feeling, no mood inside her, like the moment of day-break, neither dark nor light. She breathed in deeply and let out an 'O-o-o-o-h' sigh. Startled, she opened her eyes, realizing that what she felt was new and strange, like the first glimmering of

281

dawn. She was experiencing pleasure.

'Why don't you put those away for a bit, dear –
you'll wear them out looking at them.'

One of the nurses came up to Cynthia later that
day while she was gazing, for the thousandth
time, at her little Christmas letters sent by Em,
Sid and Joyce. In two months the folds of the
cheap paper had become so worn that they were
almost falling apart, but they were Cynthia's most
precious possessions.

Without a word, she clutched the flimsy pages
defensively to her chest.

'It's all right, I only asked!' the nurse said. 'If it
matters that much to you I s'pose they can't do
you any harm.'

Cynthia watched her move right away in her
white uniform before she felt she could relax
again. Nothing was your own here. They were
always watching and interfering.

'Dear Mom...' She read again and again, trying
to picture each of their faces.

At first, when Olive made her come here, she
was in the most terrible distress after being torn
away from Violet. She craved her baby with a
wildness that several times resulted in her being
dragged into the padded room to beat herself to
exhaustion against the walls. In those early days
her body was hot and feverish. At night, waking
from uneasy pools of sleep she found the bed
drenched in sweat and was convinced that Violet
was there with her, but when she felt round in the
dark she would meet only nothingness and the
rough hospital covers, no warm baby form beside

her. Each time she was overwhelmed by grief and hopelessness.

But she didn't blame Olive for putting her in here. Nor did she blame Bob for not visiting. Christmas had hurt terribly. He had not come to join the relatives' party on Christmas Day – no one had. She didn't like to think back to that day – no husband or children, abandoned by everyone. She told herself it was all she deserved. She knew her man Bob could not stand her being weak or ill. What he needed, had always needed, was for her to be strong and steady, to mother him as well as be his wife, and in all these she had failed. It was all her fault. She had let everyone down. Somewhere in her she knew she had never been good enough and everyone would always leave her in the end because she was a bad daughter, wife and mother.

In the early days, her agony was so overwhelming that she found it better to bite into the dwindling flesh of her arms until her teeth left deep pink grooves, and sometimes drew blood. Or she would bang her head against the wall, the floor, anything to let out the volcanic pulses of pain and loathing inside her.

Those first weeks, her whole being had craved Violet, but over time she found that she longed for her other children just as much: their voices, those cheeky smiles, their soft skin, the feel of them, the life in them. They were the only spark left in her, she decided, when she had none of her own.

At the same time she was so frightened of them coming anywhere near her because she could not trust herself. The thought of going home, to the house which had been her cosy haven, was utterly terrifying. Sometimes she imagined walking in through the green front door in Kenilworth Street, seeing all her familiar things, but with everyone watching for her, expecting, needing... All she could imagine doing was crawling into the tiny space under the stairs for safety, curling up tight in the gloom, from where her presence would seep, like a black, evil stink, through the house. She was bad, and lost to life: there was no possibility of going back. That was for other people, but not her.

At the darkest times, early in her stay, the other women in her ward did not affect her, by either their shrieking rages, the draggings away into padded rooms, their stony despair or their paraldehyde stupors. She was locked into a stupor of her own, a tight, sealed place where no one else's happiness or misery could reach her.

They had taken out six of her teeth, four at the back and her two bottom incisors.

'You're harbouring infection in your teeth,' the doctor told her. 'You'd be surprised how much that can poison the whole of your system and make you ill – we often find that.' Gently, he added, 'Childbirth exacts a high price from women's teeth.'

Afterwards, her tongue searched the strange, bloodied gaps that had appeared between the remaining teeth, but now she had grown used to them and the gums were smoother and felt part of her. The diet of porridge and overcooked stew presented no problem to chewing.

As the days passed she started to notice the

women on either side of her. One was an old lady called Alice Gregory, who seemed truly but quietly deranged, the other a woman in her fifties called Connie Spall. She was big and moved slowly but sometimes she looked at Cynthia and something like a smile seemed to flash over her face.

Now Cynthia had become calmer they put her to work in the kitchens, cooking. Every morning they made huge pots of porridge and Cynthia found the rhythmic stirring and smell of hot milk comforting, as if they were beginning to break through her pain and numbness and connect her back into life.

Next time Dot came, on one of the dark, lid-of-cloud days, she said, 'Well, the weather's enough to get you down. But you seem different somehow, Cynth. Is it me, or are you feeling a bit better?'

And Cynthia dared to look her in the eyes. 'I think… Oh God, I can hardly say it. A bit. Maybe.'

Thirty-Seven

'Hurry up, will yer! You'll be late again and then there'll be hell to pay!'

Dot stood wearily at the door of number eighteen, shooing Em and Sid off to school, as she had done for so many mornings now. When David and Terry set off for work she took Nance next door and did all that needed doing. She stood watching the poor little scruffs scuttling along the road together, ragged-arsed Sid staggering along with his pockets bulging full of marbles, and Em, a skinny stick, her hair tousled as a bird's nest. Dot had had Nancy up sick in the night and overslept herself so there'd been no time to search for the comb, which always seemed to be missing.

Em turned briefly and waved at her and Dot raised her own arm, touched, despite her tiredness and resentment that she had been put in this position. Em's foal-like sweetness, her silent suffering could always melt Dot's heart.

It was no good even pretending that their father was looking after them, and many said how could he be expected to, a man on his own and holding down an exhausting job and with Cynth being the way she was? Dot felt for him, of course, some of the time. The poor sod was like a lost soul, just as lost as his kids, truth to tell – more like a kid himself.

That was where her sympathy ended. Bob wasn't even trying to look after his family. All he could think about these days was that bloody woman, Flossie Dawson. In Dot's mind now she was always *That Woman*. Of course everyone knew about their carry-on by now – Bob was up and down the road to her like a fiddler's elbow. Every so often someone'd take him to task about it, even some of the other blokes. But it was like talking to the wall. Whatever Dot said to him, however many ding-dongs they had over the children, the old, dutiful, biddable Bob had vanished.

'They're all right, ain't they?' That was all he ever said. 'They've food in their bellies and they've got you looking after them.'

'But I ain't their mom!' Dot would explode at him. 'It ain't my job – they're your kids, not mine. Don't you think I've got enough on my plate without bringing up your family as well?'

'Oh, don't keep on, woman,' he'd said during their last set-to. 'I've handed you my wages. What more d'yer want?'

'Oh yes!' Dot's voice was harsh with sarcasm. 'What's left of 'em after *she's* helped herself.'

'Well, that's my bloody business.'

He was deaf to any other voice but Flossie Dawson's. The fact that he had not, in the end, gone to see Cynthia on Christmas Day as he'd said he would, but stayed at Flossie's instead, still made Dot burn with hurt and outrage for her friend. So the woman had broken her leg – so what? That wasn't the end of the world, was it?

However deaf to all pleading Bob was, in the meantime someone had to keep things together for the children, and Dot knew the lot had fallen to her. In the name of friendship, as well as her great fondness for Cynthia's kids, she knew she had no choice but to carry on doing whatever she could. God alone knew what would become of them if she didn't, the way things were going. The burden on her shoulders felt a sad and heavy one.

'Oh, Cynth,' she murmured, watching the two children disappear along the road. 'It'd break your heart to see 'em, that it would. You'd better get yourself well soon, love... You've just got to.'

Her thoughts were broken into by a little hand sliding into hers. She looked down and saw Joycie, still in her vest and pants from bed and a thumb in her mouth, looking up sleepily at her.

'What's up, bab? I was just seeing Em and Sid off.'

Without a word, Joyce held her arms up to the woman who had become like a mother to her.

'Oh, you want a bit of a love, is that it?' Dot said fondly, bending her aching back to pick the child up. 'Come on, then. Let's get this door shut or you'll catch yer death.'

She carried the little girl inside, feeling some comfort herself in the little warm body pressed close to hers.

'Now,' she said kindly, 'our Nance's been up poorly all night so she'll stay asleep for a bit. When you've had yer breakfast, d'you want to come and help me do a few bits of shopping?'

Joyce nodded, wide-eyed.

Dot rumpled her hair. 'Right, bab – you can finish off the porridge, and then yer can go up and get yerself dressed.'

Since Christmas, Em and Molly had called off their campaign against Mrs Dawson. The shock of seeing Flossie come to the door that afternoon with the cast on her leg had been almost too much for Em and she couldn't stop staring at it, wondering what they'd done. What if it'd been the head that came off the wax dolly instead? It was too frightening to imagine!

After dinner, during which Bob and Flossie struggled with bright, difficult conversation, and Daisy made hideous faces at them over the potatoes, the children squirmed with boredom in the yawning, endless afternoon.

Em looked round curiously at Mrs Dawson's

knick-knacks. Her eye was caught by a red Chinese dragon with a long tail that sat on the mantlepiece. It fascinated her but she didn't dare ask to look at it.

'Can us go out and play?' Sid asked eventually, from the prison of Mrs Dawson's back room.

'Yeah – go on, off yer go,' Bob said. His face wore an ardent, desperate look and they knew he wanted them gone.

'Yes of course you can,' Mrs Dawson said in her sweet-honey voice, as if she was bestowing a great favour on them instead of her obvious relief to get them out of her hair. 'Why don't you go and play as well, Daisy?'

'Don't want to.' Daisy pouted.

Em, Sid and Joyce didn't wait for Daisy to change her mind. They bolted out through the front door fast as blinking. Em dashed round to Kenilworth Street, thinking she'd go off pop if she didn't tell Molly the news. To her relief she didn't have to go into the yard as Molly was already out with Bert and some others.

'Molly!' Em tore along so her. Molly's face broke into a grin at the sight of Em, who pulled her urgently to one side and they both turned their faces to the wall. 'Mrs Dawson – she's broken her leg!' Em gabbled. 'She's got a thing on it, a plaster, and *it's the same leg we cut off the wax one!* We must've done it, we must've voodoo'd her! D'yer think we did?'

Molly's face took on an expression of great self-importance. 'I knew it – I knew it'd work,' she said, awed. 'Was it really 'er left leg? Like with the dolly?'

'Yes!' Em was nodding until her own head practically fell off.

'Well,' Molly said very solemnly, 'we'd better stop there, then. If we do anything else,' and here she lowered her voice even more, 'it'll be the end of her. The magic gets stronger and stronger each time you use it!'

'Does it?' Em shuddered in horror at what else they might be the cause of. 'Have you still got the dolly?'

Molly nodded. 'I hid it in the brew house.'

'Hadn't we better get rid of it?'

'We can't burn it,' Molly said. 'What would that make happen? And if we throw it out, we don't know who else might get hold of it.'

They stared at each other, overcome by the awesome and dreadful thing they had started.

'P'raps we'd better just leave it where it is and not touch it,' Em whispered, wide-eyed.

'What're you two swuss-swussing about?' The voice made them both jump violently. It was Bert, Molly's mean-eyed brother.

'Nothing,' Molly snapped. 'Go away.'

'*Nothing*,' he mocked in a silly voice. He aimed an idle kick at them. '*Your* mom's locked up in the loony bin,' he sneered at Em then ambled off as if he couldn't be bothered. They were only stupid *girls*.

Molly's face burned with shame. 'Don't take no notice of *him*.'

'I won't,' Em said, but the cruel words still stabbed right through her.

In the six weeks since Christmas, life had otherwise gone on much the same By the end of January, when Molly peeped into her hiding place in the yard brew house, the wax dolly had disappeared and a small coop had appeared with three chickens in it. Someone must have found the wax and either used or disposed of it, and there had been no bad effects on Mrs Dawson that they could see. In fact soon after that she had had her cast removed and other than needing support from a stick, she was now walking normally, so Em relaxed over it. And she and Molly liked going and talking to the hens, with their darting heads.

But during this time, Bob's preoccupation with Flossie Dawson had turned into an obsession which the children were even beginning to get used to. Once she'd broken her leg – slipping on a patch of ice, she said – she needed every help that Bob could give her.

'She's a woman on her own,' he said repeatedly when Dot kept on at him. 'She needs help to manage.'

'*I'm* a woman on my own an' all!' Dot retorted furiously. 'Or haven't you noticed? I don't see you coming round to give *me* any help!'

'But I *have* helped yer at times,' Bob argued – which was true. Bob and Cynthia had done Dot a lot of favours in the past. 'And it's all new to Floss … to Mrs Dawson. She only buried her old man less than two years ago. She ain't got anyone else. I've got to do what I can for her – she's delicate, like.'

'Oh yes – about as delicate as a bloody sledgehammer, that one,' Dot muttered.

But there was no getting through to him.

Thirty-Eight

Bob stood on Flossie Dawson's step, holding a bunch of daffodils. It was a Sunday afternoon, he was all spruced up and in a state of high excitement which he was trying to keep under control, but when he heard her limping to the door to open it he was trembling with anticipation. Today was the day he was going to lay his cards on the table – so long as the girl wasn't in. She had to be out – just *had* to be!

'Ah, Bob!' Flossie's pretty face, and the sound of her soft Staffordshire accent, made his innards do a somersault. 'How nice to see you!' She spoke with polite formality.

'Here, I brought you these,' he said before he'd even got over the threshold. 'It's St Valentine's Day. I thought you'd like 'em...'

He tried to thrust them into her hands but of course she was holding the stick.

'Oh, how nice. You'll bring them in for me, will you?'

'Yes, course. Silly of me, sorry.'

'No, it's very nice of you.' Once inside the door the intimate, seductive tone of her voice returned. Its effect on him was, as usual, electric. Even the rise and fall of her voice now could arouse him in seconds, he was at such a pitch.

'Would you like a cup of tea?'

'Oh – tea? Yes. Yes, please!' God, it wasn't tea he

wanted. He wanted *her*, right now. He wanted to lift her off her feet in those dainty boots, carry her upstairs, lay her back over what would of course be a whopping great bed and...

'I think it's getting a bit warmer at last,' she remarked from the back. He heard the sound of water.

'Yes!' he agreed, peeping into the front room to check. Surely to God the girl wasn't in there, not this time, watching him slyly and silently the way she always did. No! He almost punched the air. No sign of her. He hung up his cap, then went and sat on one of the green chairs, expectantly, his foot tapping.

'There.' Flossie came in. She was wearing a black dress that fitted her curves precisely. It was his favourite. He fought the desire to stand up and draw her to him. Her blue eyes looked at him – laughingly, did he imagine that? – and she said, 'Kettle's on. Won't be long.'

'Where's young Daisy today?' he asked, innocently. 'At auntie's?'

'Yes – it's her weekend away. I expect they'll go out together somewhere. They usually do.'

As if he cared, so long as the girl wasn't going to walk in any moment. He'd waited so long, telling himself at first that Flossie was too good for him, more of a lady who he could admire from afar. Then of course she broke her leg and any suggestion of things going further seemed impossibly inconsiderate. Most of the time he wanted her so badly that he wouldn't have cared if she had every limb in plaster. But to suggest it would have been wrong. All those signs she gave, the eyes, the way she spoke and moved herself seductively in front of him. God, yes, she wanted him, he knew. She was just too genteel to ask. And of course normally the girl was here...

They drank tea but his sense of decency could only last so long. Once he'd downed his to the dregs, sitting the other side of the fire from her, he could bear it no longer.

'Flossie...' He stumbled into words, then helplessly out of them again, and sat in an agonized silence.

'Yes?' she said encouragingly.

'I ... I can't help the feeling... I mean, I've noticed you...' He stood up, burning, frustrated to the point of madness. 'Christ, woman, I need you. Let's go up to bed!'

He'd said it – bloody hell, did he really say that? It was out now!

Flossie stared up at him, her cheeks blushing gratifyingly as if she was struggling with the idea, but as she didn't seem about to reject him, Bob flung himself to his knees in front of her. 'I can't think of anything but you, woman. I'm beside myself with it.'

'Bob,' she said archly. 'D'you mean what you're saying? You're a married man, you know.'

'Married! Yes, I'm married,' he cried passionately. 'But where is she? I ain't had a wife for months! It's not that I'm not sorry for her, but what do I do? And what about me? I'm a healthy man – and then you come along and as soon as I saw yer... Well, I can't help myself – I just can't.'

He looked down at the bright reds and blues of the Turkey rug on which he was kneeling. It was his turn to blush. He'd laid himself right in her hands now.

'Bob–' she put two fingers under his chin and gently drew his face up – 'that's so sweet. You're a very lovely man. I'm quite overcome.'

He stared back like a little boy. 'Are yer?' He could hardly believe it all.

Flossie nodded. He began to lean towards her, to kiss her lovely pink cheek, but she held back.

'The thing is, Bob, I'm not that sort of woman. I never have been. Before Arthur passed away...' She looked down, seeming grief-stricken. 'Well, there's only been him, my husband. You do have an effect on me, dear, I can't say you don't.'

'Well, then!' he cried. 'Look, I'm not messing with yer. I'll come and be with yer, give you everything. I'm not married any more, that's how it feels. You know that's how it is. I want to be 'ere – be your feller.'

'Oh!' She gave a smile that melted his already besotted heart even further. 'That's so sweet, deary. You see I've been so worried. My nerves are shattered all the time worrying about things. About how I'm going to cope. Money's such a problem.'

'You mustn't worry. I'll help – I earn a wage, don't I! It's not princely of course but it's summat. And I'll give it all to yer, Flossie love. I'll look after you!' He hardly knew what he was saying. Wages were low and there was never a week when they didn't have to hock something to get by, but he couldn't think of that now.

'Oh, Bob,' she sat back yieldingly in the chair, 'that would be such a weight off my mind. If perhaps you could let me have a little something this week? It would make all the difference in the world.'

'Yes, of course!' He promised her every bit of his money he could find, anything. He was hot and aching with desire. 'I'll help you, only kiss me, you lovely girl. Please do that for me.'

Flossie looked at his desperate condition. 'We must be careful, dear. I shouldn't want another child. It happens so easily...'

'No...' He hardly knew what he was saying. 'Of course not.'

She stood up and, taking him by the hand, pulled him to his feet. 'You must withdraw. D'you think you can?'

'Yes!' He was in a trance, ready to agree to anything.

Flossie pulled him to her and pressed herself against his urgent body.

'You won't forget about the money, will you, dear? You promise?'

Bob promised, anything, everything, as she led him to the stairs.

'Let me undress you,' he gasped. 'I've thought of it that many times.'

In her bedroom, with its not-so-big bed, though he barely noticed this, she slowly unfastened the top button of her dress, then, fixing him with her eyes, took his shaking hand and guided him to do the rest.

Later that afternoon he slipped out of Flossie's house, sated, confused, and almost unable to believe what had happened. All this time and finally he'd been able to have her, to lie with her all the afternoon. She'd blown his mind, the way she'd taken charge of him, making him withdraw when he was at his most excited, then leaning down to take him in her mouth. This was something Cynthia had never done – she was quite prim in her way – and even the sensation made him lose control immediately so that he had no choice but to let go between her lips, gasping with gratitude and amazement that she would do such a thing.

She smiled down at him afterwards, still caressing him. 'Well, you're a powerful boy, aren't you?'

And he had lain spent and in a haze of relieved fulfilment, 'God, Floss, oh God...'

Afterwards he found his feet heading automatically towards the Crown, even though he knew be should go home. He needed to drown out the other niggling feelings that crowded in to spoil his triumph. His guilt as a husband, which over the weeks he had kept pushing away, finding reasons to justify himself. But as well as that, something worse played round the edges of his mind, so uncomfortable that he needed to blank it out. It was that as he lay with Florrie Dawson, even at the peak of their union, he knew she was not loving him, but acting. She did not desire him and much of the time her eyes, cold and separate, would hardly meet his. Even, her smile held triumph, a kind of control. Bob knew what intimate love was like, the way he and Cynth were before, when she would turn to him, her brown eyes full of love and longing warmth. Flossie Dawson's eyes had not opened her heart to him, they had held a blue blankness which chilled him. And yet

297

what she had done for him, had made him feel! He knew the woman was like a drug for him: he'd have to keep coming back and back to her.

Hurrying over the sawdust-scattered floor to the bar, he ordered a pint. 'And make it quick,' he said grumpily. Drinking deeply, froth covering his upper lip, he downed the pint and slammed the glass on the bar.

'Give us another.'

Thirty-Nine

'Sid – get down here. We've got to go!' Em shouted grumpily up the stairs. It was a day when she could go to school.

Bob had got up and gone off to work, leaving them to get themselves ready, as usual. Though only nine years old, Em felt like a bad-tempered mom already.

'You don't have to do anything 'cept get your clothes on. Why does it take you twice as long as me?'

'I'm *coming*,' Sid yelled, from the top of the stairs, pulling on his jacket. There was a bang, then another and another in a growing clatter as his marble collection began to empty itself down the staircase from his torn pockets.

'Oh, Sid!' Joyce giggled, hand over her mouth.

'*It's not funny*,' Em raged at them. 'We're gunna be late again. Come on, Joycie – you get along to Dot's. And I'm going without you, Sid – I've had

298

enough of you!'

Leaving Sid scrabbling to pick up his marbles, which seemed to have to accompany him every-where now marbles were all the rage, Em pulled Joyce through to the front, to tie a ribbon in her hair as Mom had always done. It was only then she noticed the piece of paper which must have been pushed under the door then blown to one side when Bob opened it to go to work. It was torn from a piece of brown parcel paper, folded over. Picking it up she saw writing scrawled on it, obviously in a hurry:

I WILL COME BACK AND SEE YOU I
PROMISS. YOURE FRIEND MOLLY

'What's that?' Joyce was pushing at her to see.

'Dunno.' Em frowned. 'Just Molly being silly. Come on.'

But Molly was not at school that day and soon the word got around that the Fox family had vanished in the night, lock, stock and barrel.

'Trust that bloody shower to do a moonlight,' was Dot's comment that afternoon. 'Never done an honest day's work between the lot of 'em, that they haven't. Well, good riddance, I say. Although Molly's not all bad, considering, I'll say that for 'er, poor kid.'

Em *had* missed Molly at school. She was surprised how much she had come to rely on her now everything had changed, as if she and Molly were bound together by troubles that neither of them could speak of.

'Where d'you think they went?' she asked Dot

later, a lump in her throat.

Dot shrugged. Rather harshly she said, 'Could be anywhere by now. The likes of them won't be going far, though, I don't s'pose, not with a handcart in the small hours.' Then she noticed the tears welling in Em's eyes. 'Ahh – you and Molly were pals a bit, like, weren't yer? Never mind, eh. Look, I made a few tarts today. They were for later really, but I'll let you taste one as a treat to cheer you up. Come and sit at the table and have it.'

Em eagerly swallowed down Dot's raspberry jam tart and it made her feel better for a little while, but it didn't take away the sad, tight feeling she had inside.

Dot watched her wolfing down the pastry, touched by the way Em's feet didn't even reach the floor when she was on a chair. Poor little mite, she thought. Trying to be so grown-up when she's only a babby really. She was about to tell Em that she was planning to visit her mother at the week-end, but she kept quiet. She'd see what state Cynthia was in first before she said anything. No point in causing more upset. Instead, she said, 'Shall I give your hair a cut later? It's getting in your eyes.'

Em nodded, scrambling up from the table. 'Ta, Mrs Wiggins,' she said. 'But I'd better go now – I've got to go to Mrs Button's.' She ran out into the overcast afternoon.

'Hello, little'un,' Jenny Button greeted her as usual, as she, appeared in her shop. 'I've kept your bread for you. I've no cakes today, though, I'm a bit short. My Stanley's a bit under the weather, see, so I've not had the time. Never mind, bab, there'll be some tomorrow, I s'pect.'

Em smiled shyly and waited for the bread.

''Ere.' Jenny Button leaned over the counter, and almost lost her balance for a second. 'Ooh my – I'll 'ave to watch myself. I nearly fell off! Made my heart go, that did!' She peered towards the door to check they were really alone. 'I 'aven't seen *her* in here in a while.'

Em stared back at her, knowing she didn't need to say anything. Mrs Button never spoke of Flossie Dawson by name these days, nor anything else about her because anything she might have mentioned was not right to be spoken in the world of children. But it seemed to be her way of letting Em know she was on her side.

'Ooh – now, I've got summat to show you,' Jenny Button said, getting down wheezily from her stool. 'Come through a minute.'

Em hesitated.

'It's all right – Stanley won't mind. Come on – we won't bite yer.'

Em followed Mrs Button's panting progress through the back room. It was very stuffy and all she saw of Stanley was a mound of bedclothes. He must have been asleep. Mrs Button flung the door to the back yard open and said, 'There you are – there's my little lovely, just like I said.'

For a moment Em couldn't think what she was talking about, but then, among all the chaotic array of pots taking up most of the yard, her eye was caught by the biggest plant which she remembered in the corner. The camellia's tight green buds had opened out into the most beautiful crimson blooms and their deep red glowed in the winter light. The flowers were at their most

301

perfect and Em gasped.

'It's lovely!' she said. The gorgeous thing seemed to give off life and colour and joy, just when it was most needed, in the dead depths of winter.

'Makes yer feel better to look at it, doesn't it, bab?' Jenny Button said, all smiles. 'She's my little love, she is – just look at her!'

Em was surprised to find she did feel a bit more cheerful as she came out of Mrs Button's shop. Then she remembered Molly and her spirits sank again. She decided she'd creep into the yard where the Foxes lived and see. Had they really gone? In some ways she didn't want to know the truth but she made herself walk up the entry of Seven Court, relieved to see that there was no one about in the yard.

The door of number four was ajar. Heart pounding at the thought of finding Iris Fox sitting inside staring at her, she pushed against it. She was ready to jump at the slightest thing but the room was dark in the gloomy afternoon light, and empty. It looked very squalid, and was icy cold. The dull throb came through the wall from the factory. All that remained of the Fox family's existence there was the old greasy range, scattered with grey ash, and, lurching on the top of it, a battered old kettle with its handle missing. There was a stale odour of smoke mixed with alcohol and the damp mustiness of the place. Altogether, the sight of it sapped Em's spirits. It was so depressing. She didn't go in further

A slurred voice called to her from out of another of the windows as she left. 'There ain't no one there, they've all gone, and good riddance. And

302

you can clear off an' all!'

Em fled. She loathed Molly's yard. They're a rough lot in there, Cynthia always used to say. None of them seemed to have a kind word for anyone.

Going back into her own empty house, her spirits sank even lower. The tight feeling came back and she sat down at the table, kicking her legs against the chair. She kicked harder and harder. There was liver to cook – Dot had shown her how and she'd done it before. And she ought to be peeling the potatoes, which had nasty black bits in and always took her a long time in the cold, gritty water. But something stopped her. Harder and harder she kicked at the chair legs until she caught her ankle bone by accident and yelped with pain, her eyes filling.

'*Bugger it!*' she shouted, nursing her smarting ankle.

She got up and filled the enamel bowl to peel the spuds, kneeling on a chair so she could reach the table, still bursting with mutinous feelings. Sid ran in and out and she snapped at him, and after a while Bob came back from work. He was covered in coal dust as ever, and tired. As he came in, taking off his coat, he called out, 'Em?'

'What?'

'What's for tea? You got it ready?'

She didn't answer. The tight feeling seemed to rise up into her chest.

'I'm talking to yer.' He appeared in the doorway. 'That as far as you've got?'

When she didn't answer and kept her face mulishly turned down, he came and stood at the other side of the table.

'What's the hold-up? It ought to be ready by now. I've got to get out tonight, after tea.'

Something snapped in her then, the tight feeling bursting like a boil. Picking up a muddy potato she threw it straight at his face, then violently overturned the bowl of peelings so the water splashed down his front.

'I hate you!' she yelled at him. 'And I hate doing all the work all the time. I'm not Mom! Make your own tea and stop bossing me about. All you care about is that bloody woman!'

There was a moment of sunned silence, both of them aghast.

'Christ – you little bugger,' Bob started on her, his voice rising as he wiped the dirty water from his face. 'I'll put you over my cowing knee…'

'I don't care!' She stamped upstairs and fell onto her bed, curling up tight, her arms round Princess Lucy, sobbing so hard she could scarcely breathe as weeks of pent-up grief and despair flooded out of her. Her tears rested like tiny jewels on Princess Lucy's embroidered face and on the old grey blanket before sinking in, forming little wet patches. She didn't hear Bob coming up the stairs but she did feel the bed sink down as he sat beside her. She curled up tighter, afraid he'd punish her. The old dad wouldn't have, but the new, faithless dad – you never knew what he might do.

'Em?'

He spoke roughly as he had no other way of speaking, but she could tell he wasn't angry. She listened in silence.

'I know yer doing her best, wench. I shouldn't've

304

been so hard on yer.'

She was too far gone now to hold back. Jerking up onto one elbow she cried, 'What about Mom? You said you'd bring her home. You *promised*, and you never even go and see her. And what about Mrs Dawson? She ain't your wife. You're no good for us, Dad.' She fixed him with a heartbroken stare, not caring if he punished her. Nothing could feel any worse now. 'You're just no good.'

She saw his face twitch, ripples of conflicting emotions passing though: anger, sorrow, pain. Mostly pain. He raised his head towards the dusky light seeping through the window and took a big, shuddering breath. He looked as if he was about to say something, but he choked it back.

'I don't know what to say to yer,' was what came out eventually. 'I want to give yer a clout for talking to me like that, but I know I'm in the wrong. I dunno what's happened ... to all of us... It didn't ought to be like this...' He sat for a few moments longer, then roughly patted her shoulder. 'Look, love, I'll go and do the spuds.

Forty

Dot knocked and walked straight into number eighteen the next Saturday evening, full of urgent news.

'Bob – you there?'

There was a smell of frying onions from the back and Sid and Joyce were wildly rolling marbles to and fro across the front-room floor in a game that was already getting out of hand.

'What're yer doing that in 'ere for?' Dot snapped at them. 'You can't walk down the road without nearly breaking yer neck on marbles and now you're throwing 'em! You'll break the winder! Go on get outside.'

'It's dark, nearly,' Sid pointed out.

'Well, put them away then, and do summat else. Where's yer dad?'

She addressed the question to Em, who had appeared from the back in her giant pinner.

Em shrugged.

'Is he...?' Dot made an enquiring movement of her neck, raising her eyebrows. They both knew what she meant but she wasn't going to say anything in front of the little ones. Em nodded sullenly.

'Right – that's it,' Dot said, with steely intent.

She stormed along the road and round the corner. After a thunderous rap with her fist she didn't wait to be invited in, but pushed the door open. In the front room she found a very startled Bob with Flossie Dawson, whose hair looked unusually dishevelled. It was abundantly obvious what had been going on.

'Dot!' Bob protested. 'What the hell–?'

'How dare you come barging into my house–' Flossie started up.

'Don't you what-the-hell me!' Dot erupted at the two of them. 'You know perfectly well where I've been this afternoon while *you*–' she thrust her finger at Bob's face like a pistol – 'were supposed to be minding your kids.'

She gave Flossie a look of searing contempt. 'And you're a fine one to accuse *me* of barging in. I'm Dorothy Wiggins, by the way. I don't think we've ever been introduced. I'm Cynthia's best friend – Cynthia, Bob's *wife*, that is. Or didn't he mention that he's got a wife?'

As Flossie began to protest, Dot leaned towards her, hissing threateningly, 'Don't think I can't see through you. I've seen your sort before and there's summat about you that doesn't add up, for all your talk and your airs and graces...'

'Get out of my house!' Flossie shrieked. 'How dare you come in here shouting at me in that common way. Bob, tell her to leave.'

'Oh-ho!' Dot laughed triumphantly, hands on her hips. 'You're a fish wife with the best of 'em, ain't yer, in spite of yer hoity-toity ways! Bob,' she commanded, 'you'd better get home. Now. I've got summat to say to yer.'

'Don't let her order you about!' Flossie tried to say but Dot turned on her again.

'*You* – just keep out of it! Come on, Bob.'

'I'd better go,' Bob said. 'I'll see yer later, Floss.'

Dot strode along the road ahead of him.

'Right,' she said once they were inside. 'Sit down. Kids – upstairs – now.'

She paused while they heard the sound of clattering feet on the stairs. Looking at Bob she wondered why she felt like his mother even though she was younger than him.

'What's happened?' he asked fearfully.

Angry replies sprang to her lips. *What do you care? You never go and see her... It was me there today instead of you, again* ... She swallowed them down,

307

sinking onto the chair at the other side of the table.

'They want her to come home. Not for always, not at first. On a visit, like. You need to go and say it's all right.'

Bob stared at her. He wiped his hand over his face.

She thought he was about to cry but he looked up again, seeming stunned.

'Cynth, coming home?'

'Just for a day, to start with.'

'I thought, I dunno. I thought she'd never...' He shook his head. 'Christ, Dot. I thought it was all over, and that's the truth. When I saw her, the way she was... She was, well, it weren't Cynth. Is she...?'

'She's better. They said she could come next weekend. It's going to take time, Bob. And you're going to have to look after her, stop all this nonsense with *that* one.' She couldn't even sound angry any more, just matter-of-fact and sad.

'God...' He put his head in his hands for a moment, then looked at her again with frightened eyes. 'I don't know what to do. I don't even know whether...'

'What, whether you want her back?'

He couldn't look at her. 'I don't know if she's my Cynth any more. I don't know what to do for her.'

'Let her come home a few times and settle down. She does seem better.'

He grasped onto her words. 'Does she? D'you think so?'

Tears rose in Dot's eyes as she nodded. 'I think

we might get her back. But you've got to get rid of that woman. And you've got to be kind to her, Bob – and patient.'

Em saw her first. The children were all waiting by the window, in a state of almost unbearable excitement, knowing Mom was coming home – if only for a visit.

'You'll have to be very good and quiet with her,' Dot told them. She had misgivings about them all being there, whether Cynthia would be overwhelmed by it all, but they'd been deprived of their mother for so long, how could she stop them? And Cynthia was aching to see them.

Even Sid was quiet, seeming awed by the occasion. They could all just fit by the window, squeezed in shoulder to shoulder with Joycie raised up on a stool, their breath misting up the glass. They didn't even start drawing on the misted-up window as they would have done normally. They watched, every fibre of them alert, waiting for Mom to arrive.

Bob, Dot and little Nance were waiting outside. Eleven o'clock, they'd said. Until three. A short visit to start with. At two minutes after eleven the lumbering hospital transport pulled up just along the road and the children craned their necks to see. Then the four of them came along Kenilworth Street, Cynthia in the middle with Bob and Dot on each side, Nancy trailing along behind them. They walked slowly, guiding her carefully, almost as if she was blind.

'There's our mom!' Sid's voice, normally so raucous, sank to a whisper. Joyce stood there without a word, her eyes huge, as if she couldn't believe what she was seeing.

At the first sight of her mother Em felt an enormous, aching lump come up in her throat. She blinked hard, drinking in the sight of Cynthia's face, hardly able to believe it was really her. Mom, their Mom, home again, in her same old coat and on Dad's arm – instead of Flossie Dawson. Mom and Dad together, as things should be. They'd been told not to rush out and startle her, but they all felt suddenly shy and rooted to the spot in any case. The ache spread to Em's chest.

They stopped at the gate in the weak winter sunshine. Cynthia gazed up at the house, seeming to stall, ready to turn back and run away again. She shrank behind the others, as if frightened. Bob said something to her, and Dot put one arm round her friend's shoulders and pointed with the other towards the window, talking gently all the while. Em saw her mom take in the shadowy little figures behind the glass and a look came over her face that was both fearful and full of yearning. She forced a smile onto her face and waved, and then they led her into the house.

The sound of the latch was like a spell being broken.

'Mom!' Sid cried.

Em held back as the younger ones ran forward. It was so strange seeing her there now, in the room.

'There, they've been waiting for yer,' Dot said. She and Bob released Cynthia's arms and Sid and Joyce went and buried themselves in her skirts, clinging like monkeys.

'Oh!' Cynthia gasped. Her voice came out quietly, as if she wasn't used to talking. 'Oh, babbies!' Bending over, she was already weeping, holding them tightly to her. 'Em, come here. Oh, my little Em!'

And Em was taken into the embrace as well and she sank into her mother's body, a button of her coat pressed against her face. She smelled more or less like Mom, though there was an odd, hospital smell too. Em closed her eyes. She could hear crying, feel her mother's body convulsing but all she wanted was to rest there and be held, and nothing else. Mom... Mom...

After a few moments Dot said tearfully, 'Let's let your mother sit down, eh?'

The children peeled themselves off Cynthia. They were all still in the front room. Bob had gone out to put the kettle on and hide his own emotion.

'Come on, love – sit down. Let's take your coat for yer.' Cynthia was wearing the clothes she had had on when she went in, though they hung even looser on her. Dot led her to a chair. 'Nance, you go and carry some of the cups in for Bob.'

'Are you all right now, Mom?' Sid asked, edging onto her lap immediately. Joyce wiggled her way on as well and Em perched on the arm so that her shoulder rubbed up against her mother's.

'I'm getting better, I think,' Cynthia said, wiping her eyes then putting her arms round Sid and Joyce and holding them close. 'I hope I'll soon be better. Oh, it's so lovely to see you all!'

As she talked, Em saw the gaps in her mouth where they'd taken out her teeth.

Bob brought in tea and biscuits. He didn't

seem to know what else to do, or say. It was Dot who gave orders to the children and kept things going, who understood that Cynthia just needed to see her children, to hold them; and after they had talked for a little while over cups of tea, it was Dot who saw that Cynthia was soon feeling tired and beginning to look overwhelmed.

'Now, your mother's only here for a short time today,' she told the children. 'Just so let her have a little taste of being at home and get her used to it. We'll have a bit of dinner together, but she'll have to go back this afternoon.'

'Oh, Mom, you're not going away again, are yer?' Sid said. He had a little snip of her dove-grey cardigan between his finger and thumb, rubbing on the soft wool for comfort. 'Can't you stay now?'

'I don't think they'd let me,' Cynthia said, stroking her hand fondly over his head. 'I'm still a bit tired all the time, bab. I don't want to go back to being poorly again. I need to be better to look after you, see. But I'll come home soon.'

Em just sat drinking and drinking in the sight of her face, her being here. All of them wanted to tell her things about school and their games and friends. But after they'd had some sausages and mash and the day was rushing by, Dot said, 'Now, kids – you come next door with me for a few minutes. I've got some nice sweets for yer. We'll let your mom and dad have a little chat together by themselves, all right?'

'Mom'll stay till we get back, won't she?' Joycie asked anxiously.

'Course she will. Come on. And you, Nance,

I've got sherbet lemons – special treat for yer.'

Bob's heart was pounding, his hands breaking out in a sweat. He felt very small, like a child, with no idea how to break the silence that began as soon as Dot had taken the others next door. They were each side of the fire and Cynthia couldn't seem to look at him. She sat staring at her bony hands clenched together in her lap.

Seeing her there, seeing her the moment she had arrived in the house, thinner but herself, had been like a bubble bursting for him. His real life had arrived again, as if he had been let out of something which he'd run to for escape. Now he was full of shame. She must know, must sense all the wrong things he had done. He had not been to see her, not once since that first time, as if she was nothing to him and could be just disposed of. And the way he had carried on, falling into the arms of another woman so fast and so easily! He could hardly believe now that he was the same man. He wanted to groan with shame at the thought, seeing her here, so thin and distant-looking after all her suffering. Why had he not been able to look after her better? Be more of a man?

He was trying to find the courage to speak, to say something about the way he hadn't come to the hospital, to find excuses, but she spoke first, in barely more than a whisper.

'I'm sorry, Bob.' Her thin, pale face creased painfully and she looked up, wide-eyed, longing for his forgiveness. 'I'm ever so sorry. I've let you all down so bad...'

He leaned forward, barely still on his chair.

'No, Cynth – you haven't. You couldn't help it. It were the babby – it's like that sometimes. They explained it to me...'

'Yes, but I should've...' Her tears began to fall. They still seemed to come so easily. 'It shouldn't've happened. I've been no good to anyone, leaving you all...'

'It's all right, love.' He meant it, felt full of forgiveness and shame and sorrow. Hopefully, not knowing what else to say, he asked, 'D'you think you'll be better now?'

Again she looked very pained. She seemed to shrink into herself. 'I don't know. I feel so frightened.' And she was shaking, he could see. He shrank inside, afraid himself, not knowing what to do. He sat staring at her.

'Bob?' Her voice was tiny. 'Would you put your arms round me? That's all I want.'

He leapt up at her request, his throat blocked with tears, and pulled her gently to her feet.

'Come 'ere, love,' he said roughly, and held her lovely familiar shape, so thin and trembling, in his arms.

'That's my little love.' Putting his hand gently on the back of her head with its cropped, institutional bob, he leaned his forehead against hers and closed his eyes.

Forty-One

A few days later, Em went to Dot's after school as she usually did, for a drink of milk and a slice of bread, before going back to cook the tea.

'I've done yer some scrag end,' Dot said. 'Look, I'll bring it round and all you need to do is put the spuds on.'

It was a gloomy evening and Joyce had come straight home as well, instead of playing out for a while.

'Now you stay out of my way in the back, Joycie,' Em bossed her, but amiably, as they went inside number eighteen. 'You can play by the fire but you've got to let me get the tea on.'

Joyce took advantage of Em's good mood and said, 'Can I play with Princess Lucy?'

'Yes, all right, so long as you're careful with her,' Em said.

Things were more relaxed. There had been tearful goodbyes when it was time for Cynthia to return to the hospital on the Saturday. Dot had almost had to wrestle Sid away from his mother's arms, where he was clinging as if he would never let go.

'It's all right, son,' she'd tried to reassure him as Bob led Cynthia out of the house, away from the sound of the children's crying. 'Your mom'll be back. She just needs a bit more of a rest, that's all.'

Cynthia had said goodbye bravely. 'They'll let

315

me come again,' she told them hesitantly. 'I don't know when exactly, but I'll see you all soon.' By the time she left she had gone very pale and seemed so drained that she could hardly speak, but she did manage a wan smile for Jenny Button, who waved across the road at her and called out, 'Nice to see you home, bab!'

She also left the children with hope that the separation would now be temporary.

The visit made all the difference to Em. It was terrible seeing Mom walking away from them again, but now they had hope. Soon she'd be coming home! Em no longer minded all the drudgery of the house, and she vowed that when Mom came home she would always be a help to her and not let her get overtired. Sid and Joyce were much happier as well and the days passed in much lighter spirits. Even school did not seem so bad. She had settled into being one of the mousier members of the class, playing with anyone who would let her join in. All she wanted was a quiet life.

Em put the scrag end on the heat and started peeling potatoes. Joyce had run upstairs for the doll and settled herself on the mucky rug near the range as it was the warmest spot. She was soon lost in her game. Em saw that as well as Princess Lucy she had brought down some socks and gathered together several empty cotton reels and clothes pegs and an old magnifying glass with a cracked handle. She held the glass to one eye so that it looked enormous and distorted.

'Now,' Joycie said to the rows of cotton reels, 'you've all got to do as you're told cos your mom's 'ad a babby and she's feeling poorly. And you–' Princess Lucy was scooped up by the hair, 'you're the mom and you're in the hospital but you're coming back soon.' She got up and placed Princess Lucy in a far corner of the room, still with the magnifying glass pressed to one eye.

Em giggled at the sight of her. 'Your eye's all big – like a giant's!'

Joyce came right up close to her and the girls stared at each other through the bulging glass, pressing their noses together. They were giggling so much that at first they didn't hear the tapping at the back window.

'Who's that?' Em said at last.

'Sid,' Joyce said. 'Being silly. He's always silly.' But the thought that entered Em's head was: Maybe it's Mom? Maybe she'd run away from the hospital to be with them and crept round the back so they wouldn't see her?

Cautiously she opened the back door. It was pitch black out in the yard and for a moment she couldn't see, only hear the husky voice that whispered out of the darkness.

'Em? Em – it's me.'

'Molly?'

'Quick – let me in, will yer? It's freezing out 'ere.'

The smiles dropped from Em's and Joyce's faces as Molly stepped into the light. They stared at her in horror. Molly looked down, seeming ashamed. Her face was a mess of bruises and swelling. The skin round her right eye was so swollen that the eye was a shrunken slit. Her face showed signs of other bruising and there was a

317

bloody wound on her lower lip.

'Who's hit yer?' Joyce asked.

'Can I stay here?' Molly said. She didn't cry but there was a bleak desperation in her voice. 'I've run away. I ain't never going back there...'

Em's instincts told her not to go and get Dot, or anyone yet, until they'd had time to think. They must find out what had happened and deal with it themselves. She closed the back door, thinking of what the grown-ups did whenever there was trouble.

'You come in by the fire, Moll,' she said. 'I'll make yer a cuppa tea. Our dad won't be in for a bit yet.'

Molly meekly did as she was told and sat at the table.

'Who did that to yer?' Joyce persisted. 'Was it your mom?'

Molly nodded, dabbing her weeping eye cautiously on her sleeve.

'What did her do that for?'

Molly shrugged. Normally, things seemed to wash over her, but this time Em had never seen her so subdued and defeated-looking.

'Where've yer been?' she asked. 'Why did you go away?'

'We've got another house, in Aston.' All the expression seemed to have drained from Molly's voice. 'But the landlord's been round carrying on already. Mom says we'll 'ave to move on. I didn't want to go to the school there but she made me, so I ran off. I want to come back 'ere.'

Em and Joyce stared at her, full of sympathy and worry. Em cut Molly a slice of bread. Thanks

318

to Mrs Button they didn't go short of it.

'Ta.' Molly took it and started eating ravenously. Through a bulging mouth, she said, 'I ain't going back. Never.'

She didn't need to explain any more. Even the thought of Molly's mom scared the wits out of Em and Joyce.

'You can come and sleep in with us,' Joyce said stricken at the sight of her. 'We won't tell no one.'

Molly's swollen face puckered into something like a smile. 'Ta, Joycie. You're my best friends.'

The children agreed that Molly should hide in their bedroom for tonight while they thought what to do. Bob scarcely ever went in there.

'You go up now,' Em said. 'Dad'll be home soon and I'll bring you up a plate of tea when he's not looking. We'll have to think what to do after that. And you go out and find Sid, Joycie. He won't be far away but we'll have to tell him and get him to keep his mouth shut.'

The girls spent a cramped night together on the same bed. Joyce refused to be turfed out to sleep with Sid.

'He wees in the bed, I'm not going with him!'

In the night, Em woke several times to find Molly getting up and sitting on the po'. She wondered sleepily why Molly needed to go so many times.

'What's the matter?' she asked the third time.

'Nothing. I just need to go. You go back to sleep.'

But Em lay worrying about what they were going to do. It was no good telling Dad, he'd just order Molly to go home, and she didn't like to

319

trouble Dot. Dot had done so much for them, and she didn't want to get her into any trouble. But how could they just hide Molly here? They'd be found out sooner or later, and what if Iris Fox came looking for her? It chilled Em's blood just to think about it.

She had an argument with Molly the next morning because Molly wanted to go to school.

'You can't!' Em, objected. They were having a whispered argument because Bob had not yet left for work. 'They think you've left and everyone'll see you. What're we going to say?'

'I dunno,' Molly said sulkily. 'I just want to go back to normal.'

'Well, you can't. You've got to stay here for today.'

Em racked her brains all day long and still couldn't think what to do. In her desperation she almost thought about asking Miss Lineham, but she didn't think she'd get any sympathy there. It was only when she stopped off to pick up the bread on the way home from school that she had a stroke of luck.

Jenny Button was her usual cheerful self and greeted Em kindly.

'How's Mr Button?' Em asked politely. 'Is he feeling better?'

'Oh yes, he is, ta,' Jenny Button said. 'He did have a bit of a temperature and he doesn't throw anything off easily, you know. But he's up again now, tucked up by the fire with his paper.' She gave a brave smile. 'Now, bab, here's your bread and I'll see if I've got anything else for you.'

'I've got an extra mouth to feed tonight,' Em

320

blurted out.

'Oh?' Jenny Button grunted, her head invisible behind the counter. 'Who's that, then?'

'Molly Fox.' It was a relief when the story came tumbling out. 'She's run away from home and she says she ain't going back and she wants to stay with us. Her mom keeps hitting her and her face is all swollen up and it looks bad, but I don't know what to do in case our dad finds out.'

Jenny Button's head popped up again and she stared in consternation at the anxious child before her, fully aware of the fragile state of the Brown family.

'You mean that mother of hers doesn't know where she is? Well, I can't say I blame the child, the state of that woman. I shouldn't want to get on the wrong side of her even when she hasn't had a skinful.' Mrs Button's eyes narrowed. 'So where is she? Iris Fox, I mean?'

'Aston, Molly says.'

'And she doesn't want to go back?'

Em shook her head. Jenny Button's mind seemed to be going through a process that Em didn't understand at all. She was surprised that she had not told Em to send Molly home straight away. She thought that was what any grown-up would do. Instead she stood balanced on the stool, hands on hips, scratched her head, then said, 'Well, now, what're we going to do?'

'I don't know.' Em poured out all the worries that had kept her awake half the night. 'She can't stay on with us cos our dad won't have it, and I don't like to ask Mrs Wiggins...'

'Well.' Jenny Button decisively wiped her floury

hands on her apron. 'You can tell Molly to come over here. There's only the two of us and there's plenty of room upstairs, so she can stay here, that she can, and welcome. And if I get any trouble...' she finished darkly.

Em gaped at her. 'You mean Molly can live with you?'

'Send her over here and we'll see how it goes. But I could do with some young life about the place and she needs a place to go – so, Bob's yer uncle.' She grinned, realizing what she'd said. 'Well, yer dad in your case, bab!'

Forty-Two

For a few days there were questions.

'What's that Fox girl doing here?'

'Isn't that Molly Fox? Where's the rest of 'em, then?'

Some of the neighbours recognized Molly and wanted to know what was what. Others didn't particularly care, and very few had any time for Iris Fox.

'She's just stopping here for a bit,' was all Jenny Button said in explanation.

'Well, I shouldn't blame her for running away,' one customer observed. 'How anyone could live with that harridan Iris is a mystery. Poor old Joe Fox ain't nothing but a wreck. I dunno what done 'im in worst – the war, or living with her!'

Quite soon everyone got used to Molly living

with Jenny and Stanley Button. She went back to school, played out in the street and soon the ripples of gossip settled down.

Jenny Button was in her element

'We'll have to get you some clothes sorted out,' she told Molly. As soon as she had time she was off down the Rag Market, selecting a few things to alter for Molly. Her old treadle sewing machine click-clicked away in an upstairs room while Stan watched her with eagerness, both amiable and sad. He had never been able to give his energetic wife a child and he saw the passion with which she turned to looking after Molly.

'Poor little wench,' she confided in Stan one morning when Molly had gone to school. "'Er bed's wet every night, soaked through, and at her age! There's summat not right there.'

'Living on her nerves,' Stan commented kindly.

'Hmm,' Jenny said grimly. 'Well, whatever's been going on, at least we can feed her proper and teach her some manners.'

Molly, shy and awkward at first, began to blossom in the peace and kindness of the Buttons' home. It was rough and ready, but compared to what she was used to it felt like the lap of luxury. Jenny Button had even stitched her a couple of cotton slips to go to bed in – something Molly had never known before. She was so ashamed of the fact that each morning they were almost always drenched in urine. She would try and wake herself and get up onto the po', but as often as not she was fast asleep and when she woke it was too late. Jenny Button didn't comment or ask questions. If it went on, she thought, she'd take

323

Molly to the doctor, but for now she saw to it that the sheets were washed through and a clean one put on the bed every day.

'D'you miss your mom and dad?' Jenny asked her after a few days.

Molly thought about it. 'A bit, I s'pose. But it's quieter here and I like it.' So far she'd been as good as gold, going off to school and coming back after playing out with the others and eating her tea. Apart from the sheets and having to get her to hold her knife and fork properly, not to wipe her nose on her sleeve and to say 'please' and 'thank you', Jenny and Stan Button had no major complaints. The three of them even sat and played cards of an evening sometimes and Stan was teaching Molly to play dominoes as well and was glad of the company in his slow life. Molly had settled in miraculously well. But there was always a nagging worry in her mind, and now her round face creased with anxiety. 'What'm I going to do if our mam comes?'

Jenny Button's curranty eyes looked kindly at her. 'Well, bab, we'll 'ave to cross that bridge when we come to it.'

'Our mom's coming home for a visit tomorrow,' Em said excitedly to Molly, ten days after Molly's arrival. The two of them were walking home from school together.

'That's nice,' Molly said as they turned the corner into Kenilworth Street, dodging round the lamp post which was being used as a swing by two boys.

'Watch it!' they yelled.

324

'You watch it yerselves!' Em shouted back. She realized she wouldn't have done that before. Even Molly looked surprised.

Em was in really good spirits. Molly's coming back had cheered her up, the weather was becoming more spring-like now February had turned to March and there were daffodils and crocuses in the parks. Best of all, it looked as if Mom would be back at home for good. Em had a spring in her step now.

''Ere, let's have a game,' Molly said, producing a frayed, grey piece of string from her pocket. The marbles craze had given way to a rash of hand-clap games and cat's cradles for the girls, while the boys were tearing round with whatever they had in the way of footballs, even if they were made of newspapers tied with string.

The two of them were soon involved in their cat's cradle game, with furrowed brows, hands burrowing into the twists of string, groaning when it didn't come tight. Em was absorbed with her fingers nipping the string when she felt Molly jump violently.

'Oi, don't!' Em protested, but Molly was pulling the string off her hands in a desperate panic.

'That's Mom coming, I heard her!' Her face was white with fear.

Another shout from the end of the road confirmed it.

'Quick, she ain't seen me yet!' Molly tore off along the street and disappeared into the Buttons' house almost before Em had turned round. She squinted, then made out the looming shape of Iris Fox in her big black coat. Everyone was turning

325

to stare. Her voice, slurred with drink, boomed unmistakably along the street. Iris was tanked up and raging furious.

Em's legs went weak but she managed to dash along the street to her own house, grabbing Sid along the way.

'Get inside, quick!'

'Ouch, Em, you're hurting! What're yer doing?'

'Just do as I say,' Em hissed urgently, pushing home the rusty bolt which was hardly ever used. 'That's Molly's mom carrying on down there.'

Sid's eyes widened. 'No one'd better tell 'er!' He and Joyce had been sworn to secrecy about where Molly was living.

The two of them waited, trembling, kneeling on the floor behind the front door as they heard Iris bawl and curse her way up the road. There was a brief quiet when, by the sound of things, she had disappeared into the old yard to look into the house, which soon led to an outburst of shouting between her and her old neighbours, then Iris erupted out of there again in full voice.

'You – stinking heap of – bastards...!' More curses followed as she wove her way across the road.

Sid's eyes bulged. 'Is she coming here?'

'Sssh, I dunno, do I?' Em snapped, frantically. The two of them curled up into frightened little balls on the floor, covering their heads as if Iris was an imminent explosion.

But the hammering on the door came anyway.

'Open this – door! Come on – open it, you...' Her voice fell to a mumble for a moment. 'Molly! Molly, come out! I know yer in there! I'll knock this cowing door down if I 'ave to.'

She gave up shouting then and just banged and kicked at the door like a crazed bull, grunting and muttering.

'What the bleeding hell d'yer think *you're* doing?' They heard Dot's voice outside. Dot wasn't afraid of anyone. 'Just pack it in! You'll knock the door down going on like that.'

'They've got my Molly,' Iris whined. 'I know she's in there. She's got to come home with me. Don't want her living with no bloody loonies like 'er.'

'She ain't in there – I can tell you that for nothing,' Dot said, holding on tight to her temper.

'Yes she is!' Iris started hammering again.

'All right,' Dot said, 'I'll show yer. Em, Sid – open the door!'

Em scrambled up and wrestled with the bolt again. Quivering, she opened the door to Iris's mountainous figure topped by her swollen, angry face and bloodshot eyes. She was like a walking volcano in full eruption.

'Molly!' Iris barged in, knocking Em against the wall. 'I know yer 'ere – it's no good hiding from me. You got to come 'ome with me.' She wheezed her way up the stairs. 'I'm 'er bloody mother,' they heard. 'Taking people's kids from them. I'll 'ave the rozzers on yer...'

'Best if she looks for herself,' Dot said, rolling her eyes. 'There's no reasoning with her.'

They heard Iris lumbering about upstairs, cursing and searching under beds and in the cupboard in Bob and Cynthia's room. There was a crash as something fell to the floor, but eventually she had to admit defeat and came roaring down the stairs again.

'Where is she?' Em thought for a moment she was going to punch Dot but instead she stood swaying and the whining tone came back. 'You'd better tell me. In your 'ouse, ain't she, you smug cow you, stealing people's kids...'

'You can look in my house if you want,' Dot said. 'But you won't find anything. You ought to take better care of yer own daughter, that's all I can say.'

This produced another outburst of language from Iris. She stormed her way through Dot's house, then out into the street where she marched up and down for some time shouting and demanding that Molly come out and be handed to her. An audience gathered to watch the performance, some shouting back at her, telling her to clear off. Of the people who knew where Iris's daughter was staying, not one gave Molly away, not even meddling Josie Donnelly.

'She's a bloody disgrace,' Josie said to Dot as Iris raged up and down. 'I wouldn't hand a dog over to her, so I wouldn't.'

Eventually Iris's rage blew itself out and she had to give up, finally leaving with threats that she'd be back with the police.

'I should think there's a few questions they'd like to ask that shower,' Dot said.

Em and Sid finally dared to come out of the house as Iris departed

'It's all right,' Dot said. 'She ain't found her little skivvy – not yet.'

Forty-Three

It was a Monday and as had become their habit, Em and Dot were doing the washing together at number eighteen. Joyce and Nancy were in the house, and every so often the sound of them squabbling floated out to the yard and Dot tutted.

'Pass me over that sheet of Sid's, bab, and then we're done,' Dot said, waiting by the mangle in the yard.

Em pulled the sheet out of the maiding tub, twisting water out of it and passing one end to Dot, and holding the other off the ground.

'Ta, love.' Dot wearily pushed her hair out of her eyes and fed the sheet between the rollers of the mangle. They'd both been working hard, almost in silence, doing the main body of the work, but now Dot looked across at her.

'Your mom was looking better, wasn't she?' Em didn't notice the cautious tone in Dot's voice. She was still feeling excited after Mom's visit on Saturday. It had been the third time, and now they were talking about her coming home soon – to stay!

Em nodded, smiling happily, pulling on the sheet as it emerged from the mangle.

'Mom's all right now – she's better, isn't she? When will she come home?'

'Soon, bab. They didn't say. In a week or two, I

think. They want to make sure she's really properly better.'

Dot had as usual helped the family through the day visit, but seeing Cynthia's still frail state she couldn't help fretting about how it was all going to be if she was allowed to come and live at home. And what was Bob up to? He was all right with her when she came – quite gentle and helpful, the way he could be when he put his mind to it. But Dot knew he wasn't seeing any less of Flossie Dawson than he ever had. When was he going to face up to things, she wondered angrily. A moment later, as they were pegging out the sheet across the yard, she said, 'Where does that Daisy Dawson go off to – you know, when you see her mooching off on a Sunday?'

Em removed a clothes peg from her mouth. 'To her auntie, I think. So she says.'

'Oh, I see. Well, that's nice that she's got some other family about. You'd think her mother'd get her a nicer hat, though, the way she dresses herself up.'

Em's face clouded. 'I *hate* Daisy,' she said.

The afternoon of the previous day had been drizzly. Bob and Flossie lay side by side in her bed after making love, or what passed for it, Bob thought bitterly. Despite Flossie's inventiveness, getting himself all worked up and then having to withdraw for the crowning glory of it was not his idea of proper love-making. He lay there feeling sticky and somehow humiliated. It would be different if they were together properly, he thought, instead of all this creeping about, having to be so

330

careful, in bed and out of it. He turned towards Flossie. She was lying on her back with her eyes closed, the sheet arranged so that he could see tantalizing glimpses of the soft cleft between her breasts. He looked at her profile, the dark hair and crescent of her lashes, the sweet, upturned nose, her strong neck leading down to her sturdy, pale body. He loved it when she was like this, hair in disarray, naked, *loose* somehow, when normally she was a neat, prim-looking person. And it was for him, he who saw her like that. God knows why; she could have done better, surely? He moved his lips close to her ear.

'If we was living together, regular like, we wouldn't have all this, would we? We could do things properly.' He dared himself to say the words, almost playing with them.

Sleepily she opened her eyes, turning her head slightly.

'What are you saying, you naughty boy?' He loved this archness. It made him feel young and daring. And he could tell she liked to portray herself as wicked. It was another of the things that made her so desirable. 'Are you asking me to marry you, or live in sin with you? Just remember–' she tapped his nose playfully with her finger – 'you're a married man. You'd have to get a divorce first.'

He drew back. Her words punctured his fantasy like pins. This was how it was. He lived in two separate worlds, as if there were two paths possible for him all the time. When he was with Flossie he imagined his future with her, the two of them living in his house, making a life with

331

her, untouched by anything outside. When his mind followed this path his real life, home, wife, children, ceased to exist. Daisy was also conveniently removed from it. It was a new beginning which left him free. Her words forced him back to reality. Flossie was not living a fantasy. There were things she wanted.

Real life bludgeoned him again. Cynthia had been home yesterday. The thought of her, back in their house where she belonged, flooded him with a sense of longing, and of terrible guilt and fear. Her being there felt right, yet so painful and difficult. It knifed him with feelings, tore him apart. Here, things were simpler. He was besotted with Flossie, enslaved by her, flattered by her attention. The fact that he had still not wholly possessed her drove him on. He knew it had to end, that he had to tell her so – but he could not bear the fact or let it go.

'Bob?'

'Umm?' This time it was he lying with his eyes closed.

'You didn't answer my question.' She was half playful, half serious.

Tell her. You've got to tell her...

He opened his eyes, and saw her raising herself onto her elbow. He caught a whiff of her body, the juices of love-making mixed with sweet talcum powder. Flossie looked down at him, and her teasing expression contained a calculating edge which he both saw and chose not to see.

'I thought you were serious, you naughty, handsome boy.' She traced her finger round his face, along the length of his nose, over his prominent cheekbones and the two bridges of his eyebrows. The tickling sensation irritated him. 'Coming and taking advantage of a poor widow woman, running away with her feelings. That's not very nice, is it?'

'Divorcing my wife wouldn't be very nice either, would it?' He spoke more harshly than he intended, as his two worlds collided.

Her finger stopped moving over his face. 'I thought she was... Well, she's not right, is she? That's what everyone says.'

'Oh, *do* they?' He found himself coming hotly to Cynthia's defence. These days he never knew what he was going to say next. 'There's always bloody wagging tongues ready to say the worst. It was just after the babby, that was all. It can happen sometimes.'

'Ah well,' she withdrew, coldly, lying back down, 'that's right, defend her now. A bit late, though, don't you think? I might have known you were only using me, goodness knows...' She was working herself up now, with tears in her voice. 'It's been like that ever since my Arthur died. My hopes raised, hopes of safety and security and love – then dashed again, cast away like a piece of rubbish...'

She turned her back on him, her shoulders shaking with sobs.

'Floss!' He tried to get her to turn to him again. 'Don't say that! It ain't like that, you know I'm yours. I wouldn't carry on like that!'

'Are you?' She turned her head, eyes welling with tears. 'How can I ever know you're really mine when I'm struggling on here, trying to make

333

ends meet and I never know if I'll see you again or not? You just pick me up and put me down like a toy.'

The sight of her tears wrung him out. He felt sorry and protective and guilty all at once. And once again, aching with arousal.

'Don't, Floss! I know it's hard for yer. I'm doing my best. I'll see if I can find yer a bit more money but it ain't easy with four mouths to feed. You know I'm yours and I won't leave yer. I just need a bit of time. Cynthia's – well, she's not at her best and if I tell her right away... You'll have to give me a bit of time.'

'But can I trust you?' She turned to him, big-eyed. 'You really mean I matter to you as much as she does?'

Once again she had him so that he would say anything, promise her anything, he was so over-powered by her. His other life faded away as if it had all been a dream and he was here in Flossie's arms, kissing her, wanting her all over again, and making promises, helplessly.

Cat's Cradle

Forty-Four

'For Christ's sake, woman, let a man get into his own house!'

'So, when're you going to go and get her?' Dot demanded, her feet planted firmly on the doorstep as he came in from work.

They'd all been told Cynthia was coming home soon, but so far nothing definite had been done. Dot was torn between worrying for Cynthia's health when she returned and anger with Bob. She thought he was putting it off because he was still tangled up with *that woman*. Her guess was pretty accurate and, for the children's sake, she couldn't let it go on. Every day Em's eager little face looked up at her saying, 'D'you think Mom's coming home soon?' And all Dot could say in reply was, 'I expect so, love. We'll have to wait and see.'

Bob made as if so get past her but Dot dodged and stood stubbornly in his path.

'I asked you a question. When're you going to go and get your wife?'

'Arrangements are being made.'

'Oh yes? What, by you? Listen, Bob, if anything's happening you'd better tell your kids. They're on pins waiting. And as for me, I'd quite like to know too since I'm ruddy well bringing them up for yer.'

Bob turned. 'Next Sat'dy,' he said avoiding her eyes.

'*What?*' Dot landed a punch against his shoulder in her exasperation. 'You mean Cynth's coming home on Sat'dy and you ain't said a word to any of us?'

'That's what I said.'

Dot stood back and let Bob open the front door, which he tried to shut in her face but she pushed her way in. Knowing that the girls were safely out of the way in her house she didn't hold back.

'Look, I don't know what you think you're playing at, Bob. You're not living in the real world. You're a bloody disgrace! Cynthia's coming home and you're in and out of that floozie's house day in, day out.'

'Don't call her that!' he flared up.

Dot's temper frayed quickly as well. She gave him a bawling-out with the fluency born of bottled-up anger.

'I'll call her what I bloody like, and what suits her! She's a scheming trollop, and if you can't see it you're a bigger fool than I thought. Now either you tell her it's all over or I'll do it for yer, and I wouldn't want to be in her shoes if it's me does the job. You may not care a fig about your wife and kids, but Cynthia happens to be my best friend and I'm bloody well going to see she's all right and not let you drag her any further down. And don't you forget it. When I think what she's been through while you're just ... just *playing around*. You're not the only one who misses her, yer know.' To Dot's consternation her voice cracked as she spoke and she was fighting back her tears. 'You're better than this, Bob.' She was struggling to speak and not start blarting. 'I don't know what's happened to yer.'

Bob stared at her, not seeming to have it in him to fight back. He looked confused and miserable. Dot softened a little. She'd always been fond of Bob, the handsome so-and-so, however much of a fool he was.

'You're a stupid bugger,' she said gruffly, turning away to wipe her eyes. 'For the love of God, get yourself sorted out. Do us all a favour.'

Later that evening, Bob went out again. Dot watched him hurrying along the street, weaving between the gaggles of children,

I hope I've managed to drum some sense into him, she thought, and he's gone to tell *her* where to go. She had promised Bob she'd tell the children their mother was coming home. He even seemed reluctant to do that.

She walked into number eighteen and beckoned the children, sitting Joyce on her lap while the other two stood by her.

'I've got summat to tell yer,' she said gently, a smile on her lips.

'Is it about Mom?' Em asked eagerly. They were ready to drink in her every word.

'Yes, your dad's going to bring her home on Saturday,' Dot announced, to their gasps of excitement. 'So before then we'll have to make the place sparkling as a new pin for her won't we?'

Em's face was aglow with happiness. 'We'll clean everything from top to bottom!' she cried. 'Let's start now!'

Dot smiled fondly. It was lovely to see the

child's little face lit up, bless her.

'It's only Tuesday, bab,' she said. 'And it's too late tonight. There's plenty of time.'

'Oh, I want it to be Saturday *now*,' Joyce said.

'Tell yer what,' Dot said, pushing Joyce's fringe out of her eyes, 'I'll give you all a haircut for the occasion as well!'

'Oh no!' Sid protested.

'And make sure you've got clean necks and ears,' she went on, making Sid groan even more. 'You've got to look your best for yer mom, haven't you? Now, I think it's time for you to go up the wooden hill and get some sleep.'

'I'll *never* sleep,' Sid said. 'I'm not going to sleep till our mom comes home!'

Dot smiled and led him upstairs to tuck him in, seeing his eyelids growing heavy as soon as his head touched the pillow. She leaned down and stroked his hair.

'Goodnight, son.'

Going to the girls' bed, where Em and Joyce were cuddled up together, she smiled down at them.

'Hope the bugs don't bite.'

And she went downstairs, the smile giving way to a more pensive expression.

God, Cynth, she thought. I hope you're going to be all right. For everyone's sake.

The children were in a state of high excitement all week. The news that Mom was coming home, at last, was all Em could think about. As soon as she got home from school on Wednesday she spent the afternoon scrubbing and cleaning and

Molly stayed in to help her.

'Mrs B says she's going to make your mom a coming-home cake,' Molly said as she swept the bare floorboards in the children's bedroom. Molly had soon been allowed to call Jenny Button 'Mrs B' and she announced the news proudly, as if Mrs Button was her real mother – of whom mercifully there had been no sign for over a week.

'That's nice,' Em said smiling. She felt bubbly inside with excitement. Everyone was being so kind! It was even fun cleaning the house when she and Molly did it together. Life was looking so much better at last!

But the next afternoon, something upsetting and frightening happened.

The bell clanged at the end of school and soon the children of Cromwell Street School were pouring out along the streets towards their houses. Em and Molly got ready to go together. Katie O'Neill stuck her nose in the air as if there was a smell when they passed her and they both completely ignored her. Molly still had her problems, but Mrs Button kept her spotlessly clean and in clothes which let her be the young girl she was instead of appearing prematurely grown-up.

The two girls headed out into the spring sunshine, their heads close together, chatting away.

'I'm gunna do the downstairs today, clean out the scullery and everything,' Em said. 'I want it all to look perfect for our mom so she never has to do anything!'

'We could sweep the yard as well,' Molly suggested. 'Mrs B's got a big hard broom and she'd

341

lend it to yer.'

'And I'll clear out the cupboard...'

Neither of them noticed anything until the long shadow fell over them and Molly shrieked as her arm was grabbed and bent back brutally behind her.

'Got yer!'

Em screamed in shock seeing Iris Fox looming above them, teeth bared in angry determination.

'You're coming with me, yer little rat!'

'No I'm not!' Molly cried, starting to fight her off. Em was in shock and couldn't move. 'I'm not coming with yer. I hate yer. Gerroff me!'

Iris bent until her face was level with Molly's, at the same time taking a handful of Molly's hair and jerking her head back.

'Just you listen to me, yer little vermin. Think you're bloody clever, don't yer, running off like that. Where've yer been? Which of this bloody interfering lot've been hiding yer, eh?' She gave a savage tug on Molly's hair, making her cry out. 'Go on – tell me and I'll go and have a little word with 'em.' These last words were spoken with a savage sneer.

'No!' Molly twisted this way and that, trying to escape. But the pain and the vicious rage of her mother seemed to be draining away her will.

Other children were staring but no one dared stop or challenge Iris Fox. Most of them knew of her bullying ways, and if they didn't, the sight of her heavily built frame would have put them off.

'Let her go!' Em shouted, amazed at her own daring. 'She doesn't want to come home with you. She's stopping here!'

342

'Oh-ho – who asked you?' Iris gave a big, nasty laugh. 'Whoever said anything about 'er coming home with me, eh? I'll put her in the bloody home for orphans and criminals, that's what she needs! Any more trouble from *you*–' once more she yanked on Molly's hair – 'and that's where yer going. Now come on.'

'I don't want to go with you, I want to stop 'ere!' Molly wailed, all her courage breaking down. She burst into sobs as her mother dragged her off down the street by her hair. 'Em, help me!'

'Shut it!' Iris slapped her. 'And you can all stop bloody gawping an' all!' she bawled at the appalled faces watching her. 'Ain't yer got anything better to do, yer nosy buggers?'

Em had no idea what to do. She followed for a short time, but she knew there was nothing she could do to rescue Molly. Molly gave up struggling as well and trailed along with her mother. She even gave up looking back and they disappeared in among the clusters of other people along Bloomsbury Street. Em stopped. Her legs were shaking. There was only one thing to do.

She hurried back and burst in through the door of Jenny Button's bakery.

'Goodness, what's got into you?' Mrs Button said, before seeing the horror in her face. 'Oh my Lord, what's happened, bab?'

As Em poured out what she'd just witnessed, Jenny Button sank onto the stool behind the counter. Her face, which lately had been blooming with a new happiness, tightened, and a light in it died.

'Oh dear, oh dear,' she said, shaking her head. Any hope Em had had that she could do something also died then. 'Well, I don't know if we'll see her again. I can't snatch her away from her own mother, can I? Even if I knew where they were. Just as she was beginning to calm down in herself a bit too...' Half to herself, she added, 'I'm frightened for that child, that I am.'

Forty-Five

Saturday came, of course, and the moment they had all dreamed of – Mom home!

'So, here she is!'

Bob ushered Cynthia in through the front door, both their hats beaded with raindrops, and the three children stood together in the front room, well scrubbed up with their hair trimmed into abrupt fringes by Dot, all suddenly overcome with shyness. Bob put Cynthia's little bag down behind the door.

'Well, ain't yer going to come and say hello?'

Cynthia's eyes drank them in, shining in her thin face. She held out her arms, and it was Joycie who ran forward first, as ever, to be cuddled. When it was Em's turn she pressed her face against her mother's wet coat and stood there quietly for a moment, her eyes closed.

'Let yer mother sit down, then,' Bob said gruffly. 'I expect she's tired, coming all the way over here.'

They went through to the back and he put the kettle on. Cynthia did as she was told and sat at the table. The habit of obedience, of trying to

344

please, had grown in her in the hospital. Once she was feeling a little better it had seemed the best route out. She looked around her.

'Everything looks very nice.'

'We've been getting everything ready for you all week,' Em said proudly. 'And Dot came today and helped again – she's always helping, and Mrs Button gave us the flowers for you.'

On the table was a jar of some of the last narcissi of the season from the pots in Jenny Button's yard. Cynthia smiled. 'That's nice of her. I've got a lot of people to thank.'

Em thought Mom seemed a bit slower in herself, but at least she was smiling now, not crying all the time, and that felt a lot better.

They sat and drank their tea and then there was a tap at the door.

'Coo-ee, can I come in?'

'Course yer can, Dot,' Bob said, jumping up. He was all smiles and suddenly couldn't seem to do enough to please.

'I thought I should let you all be by yourselves, but I couldn't keep away any longer.' Emotionally, she flung her arms round Cynthia. 'Welcome home, love, we've all missed yer like anything.'

'Thanks, Dot,' Cynthia said, watery-eyed. 'It's good to be back.'

'How d'you feel?' Dot stood with her hand protectively on Cynthia's shoulder, looking down at her.

'All right. I'm perfectly all right,' Cynthia said cheerily. Then added, 'Well, I feel a bit funny, I s'pose, but there we are. Early days.'

'Yes – early days!' Bob agreed. 'Cuppa tea, Dot?'

'Yes, ta.'

'I need to pop out – just for a few minutes.' His voice came from the scullery. Em saw Dot's gaze burning into him as he came out, but she scarcely paid any attention, so caught up was she in being near her mother now she was here.

Bob left the gaggle of women and children gathered round the table and slipped out. Cynthia didn't question where he had gone.

'These kids of yours have been marvellous,' Dot said. 'Specially Em here – she's a little gem – a real good'un. Grown up no end, she has.'

Em squirmed, blushing with pleasure. Although it was nice to be approved of, she knew she'd learned to stand up more for herself now as well.

'It's going to be funny, getting back into harness.' Cynthia spoke lightly, but there was an edge of panic to her voice.

'Take it slow,' Dot said. 'And don't you worry, bab, we'll all help you, won't we, Em?'

Em nodded. 'I'm used to doing everything, Mom, washing and cooking and cleaning. All of it! I'll help you!'

Cynthia's eyes filled with tears at the sweet eagerness of her daughter. 'That's lovely, bab. Only you shouldn't've been left with so much.'

'Dot helped me.'

'You're golden, Dot.'

Dot was watching her anxiously. 'You going to be all right, Cynth?'

'Oh yes,' Cynthia said shakily. 'Course. I'll have to be, won't I?'

Bob couldn't stay in the house, not like this, not

until he'd done it. Seeing Cynth there like that, home for good – well, he'd known it was coming, of course, but it was a shock. It was what he most wanted, deep inside, but he was terrified all the same. What was she going to be like? Had he got his wife back, or the stranger who had left for Hollymoor, who had been lost to him in her misery? He hadn't been able to let go of Flossie, not yet. He had felt he would drown without her. Every night he'd slipped out and gone to her in a fever of need. Even now as he hurried down the road to her house to do the thing that had to be done, the right thing, there was something pulling him back, saying no, don't let her go, you could go to her and be happy with her...

But the sight of Cynthia and Dot at the table, and all the tension inside him, sent him out to do it now, while he had the courage.

On Flossie's doorstep he was panting with nerves, as if he had been running. His whole body jumped as the door opened. Flossie's usual wary expression shifted quickly to surprise, then seductive pleasure.

'Bob, I didn't expect to see you!'

'Let me in, Floss. There's summat I've got to say to yer.'

It was no good mincing his words. He didn't know if the kid was listening somewhere nearby but it was too bad. If he slowed down now, let other things slip in between, he'd lose his nerve.

'My wife's come home, Floss. It's no good. I've got to give this up. We've got to stop.'

'Stop, Bob? How d'you mean?'

He wrung his cap between his hands. 'Don't

make it any harder, Floss! This is bloody awful. But I've got to stop calling on yer, being with yer. You know what I mean. I'm a married man. I've got to go home and try and look after my wife.'

He didn't know what he expected. At least for her to protest, for there to be tears, or anger and spite. But he had to hand it to her, she was a woman who could remain in full command. Her manner was calm. She took in a deep breath and looked at him very directly, saying, 'Well, Bob, I'm very sorry to hear what you've got to say. I always knew you had a wife, of course, but you did lead me to believe that she might not be coming home again. You obviously misled me there. Especially after, well, after this week.'

She raised her eyes to him, blushing. Heat rose in him. God, yes – things had got out of hand the last few days.

'I won't hold it against you, though. I don't want to come between man and wife. I shall miss you, of course, but you must do what you think is right.'

'Oh ... well, I'm...' he stuttered, astonished, even a little wounded by her chilly calm. 'That's very...'

'Just do one thing before you go – just give me a kiss to remember you by.'

She leaned forward so that he could kiss her cheek. The sweet lily smell of her made him catch his breath, but before he knew it he was on the step again, the door closing behind him.

He had done it! He shoved his hands in his pockets and made his way back, his gaze fixed on the ground. He could hardly believe it. It had been far easier than he'd imagined! His chest heaved, as if he might start crying and he pushed the feeling away, horrified. Flossie had been his lifeline and he had just cut it loose. He had to go home now and face whatever came – and he hardly knew whether he had the strength.

Forty-Six

'How's your mother?' Jenny Button asked a few days later when Em went over to collect the bread. 'She settling back home all right?'

'Yes, ta,' Em said. So far as she could see that was the truth of the matter. Except for what had happened over Violet, but she didn't want to tell Mrs Button about that. Dot said it would all get sorted out and they mustn't worry.

There were a couple of other people just coming into the shop, so Jenny Button leaned over the counter so far that she almost toppled off her stool. Em could see from her eyes how upset she was.

'You heard anything?'

Em shook her head sadly. There had been no word from Molly, and no sign of any of the Foxes. They all wondered if Molly would run away again, but Em's hope of this was fading. Knowing Iris, she'd got Molly tightly under her thumb.

Jenny Button tutted. All the glow that had come over her while she was looking after Molly had faded away and she looked pasty-faced and sad.

'It's a scandal, that's what,' she said. 'That poor little girl.'

Em missed Molly too. It wasn't the same without her around, and she felt so sorry for Mrs Button. She had seen how happy it had made her having Molly live with them. But at the moment Em was too happy to give it more thought than that. All that mattered was having Mom home and feeling as if things could go back to normal.

Dot had gone with Cynthia to fetch Violet. Cynthia was very nervous of facing her sister. She felt weak and vulnerable in front of her after what had happened. Olive was already bossy enough. Now she owed her for looking after her baby when she hadn't been able to do it herself. As well as aching to have Violet back, Cynthia also hoped it would make things right with Bob again. He was so distant from her still, wary, as if he was afraid of her, and she knew he *was* frightened – she knew he could not trust her yet to be well, to come back to him and be his wife. She was afraid too, that she might slip away again into the black cave of her depression, yet she was very determined. Once they were all together and could get back onto a normal footing, she would make things right. She *had* to.

They went one morning, once the kids were off to school, Dot leaving Nancy with a neighbour. It was a happy morning for Dot, being able to walk out with her old pal again, even if their errand was a difficult one. Cynthia was still very thin, but her hair was already beginning to grow back and curl more at the edges. Soon she'd look more like her old self.

'You excited?' Dot asked, as they sat side by side on the tram.

'Yes, but I'm scared stiff!' Cynthia said. 'I mean I've missed such a lot of her already – she's getting on for seven months old. I might not even recognize her!'

'Don't be daft, course you will.'

'But she's only really known Olive as her mother,' Cynthia was close to tears suddenly. 'What if she doesn't want to know me?'

'Look, you're her mom. She'll soon get used to you again.'

'I'm so glad you're here, Dot,' Cynthia said tremulously. 'I feel sick just at the thought of having to deal with Olive.'

'Yes, she ain't exactly all sweetness and light, your sister.'

'You can say that again.' Cynthia managed a quick twitch of the lips, almost a smile. 'She thinks I'm no good to anyone, I s'pose.'

'Let her think. Don't you fret, Cynth. I'll deal with her.'

Dot expected Olive to be disgruntled and sarcastic, to demand money for her pains in looking after Violet. She certainly didn't expect anything like what happened when they arrived.

Standing outside the house, both of them thought they could hear a baby crying inside.

'That must be her!' Cynthia gasped, a hand going to her throat. 'Oh my word, Dot, I do feel queer.'

Dot saw her stagger and lean an arm against the wall, and she hurried to help steady her friend.

351

'Ooh, there were lights dancing in my eyes then,' Cynthia said, closing them for a moment. 'I'm all right now, though.'

'Oh dear, you are in a state, aren't you?' Dot said, taking her arm. 'Come on, love, you'll be all right. Let's get it over with, shall we?'

She rapped on the door and they waited. Eventually it opened and Olive's sharp-featured face peered out. She looked mightily put out when she saw who was there.

'Oh, it's you. Let you out, did they? Huh – don't suppose that'll last. What d'you want?'

'I–' Cynthia began faintly.

'We've come to collect the babby,' Dot said, trying to sound patient and reasonable. 'You've been very kind looking after her but Cynthia's back home now and the little'un needs to be back with her family,'

'Huh!' Olive said again, folding her arms aggressively. 'Family! That's a good one. You don't think I'm going to hand a child over to *her*, do you? The way she goes on she's not fit to look after a dog let alone a baby like our little Margaret. D'you really think she'd want to come and live with you in that slum when she can be here having a proper upbringing?' She gave a mocking laugh.

'She's not called Margaret, she's my Violet!' Cynthia cried, quickly growing distraught. 'You can't just take her away and change her name!'

A nasty, sly expression came over Olive's face. 'What makes you think she is yours anyway? And who's going to believe you any more – you're nothing but a mental case. You might say anything!'

352

Even Dot was silenced for a few seconds by the sheer wickedness of this.

'You evil scheming cow!' she erupted as Cynthia began weeping weakly beside her. 'You can't keep her. She ain't yours. They've got the birth certificate and everything – we'll have the law on yer!'

Olive smirked. 'You do that, then. Let's see yer.' And she slammed the door shut.

Dot turned to Cynthia. She was prepared for her to be falling to pieces, since she was vulnerable even before this, but though Cynthia had tears rolling down her cheeks she was staring at the hostile black front door with a suddenly steely expression.

'I always knew she was vile,' she said, 'but I never thought she'd do summat like this. She can't just keep her, can she?' Her eyes widened in terrible appeal.

'No, course not,' Dot said.

It was as if something hardened in Cynthia in that moment. Dot could see it happening. Even her face changed, losing its lost look in a thunderous frown.

'She can't do that to me, to us. She *can't*.'

'No,' Dot said grimly. 'She can't, but short of breaking the bloody door down there's not much we can do now. We'll have to go home and think what we're going to do.'

All the way home Cynthia grew more and more angry and when Dot asked what she was going to say to the kids, who were all expecting Violet home, she launched into a speech, not caring who heard her.

'I'll bloody tell 'em what sort of an auntie they've got, that's what I'll do!' she burst out. 'Why should I pretend she's some kind soul when she's anything but, the evil bitch? She always pretended to be such a goody two-shoes after Mom died, with our stepmother and that. Always sucking up and getting me into trouble.' Her voice did sink then, to an emphatic hiss. 'They beat me because of her sneaking and snitching when things weren't my fault. Years of misery I had off her. It was bad enough that we'd lost our mom but she made it a hundred times worse. I *hated* her for it and she hasn't changed at all. She wasn't looking after Violet out of kindness, she just wanted her for herself because she's barren as a dead twig in winter. You wait till we tell Bob...'

Dot, startled by the strongest outburst of rancour she'd ever heard from Cynthia, said doubtfully, 'Well, yes, Bob won't be pleased.'

'Ha – pleased! You just wait and see!' Cynthia gave a wild laugh and Dot feared for her sanity for a moment, yet at the same time she could see something was being released in her friend and that she was suddenly full of spirit. 'Bob can't stand the woman. Never could. He'll soon go and get Violet out of there, you just wait and see.'

He was calm at first. Truth to tell, Bob had not given a lot of thought to Violet over these months. Other than a deep-down, barely acknowledged discomfort that his family was scattered and everything was wrong, he had had too much on his plate to miss another mouth to feed.

When he came in from work, Cynthia and the

children were all waiting expectantly. Cynthia sat him down, gave him a cup of tea and told him what had happened.

'She slammed the door in your face?' he was incredulous at first. What really got through to him was that this woman, this bossy, sour-faced, snooty, sister-in-law, had renamed *his* child. He didn't hesitate.

'Right.' He downed his tea, put his hat and coat back on and went to the door. 'I'm not having this,' was all he said, before disappearing into the fading light.

The family all looked at each other.

'Is Dad going to give her a good hiding?' Sid asked hopefully.

'I don't know what he's going to do,' Cynthia said with relish. 'We'll just have to wait and see, won't we?'

Bob was away for what seemed an eternity. It was a long way there and back. Cynthia tried to behave calmly, even though she was almost beside herself wondering what was going on. Would Bob even make the last tram back, with or without the baby? As the evening wore on she insisted that the children got ready for bed.

'But I want to see Violet!' Em wailed. Of all of them she seemed to remember Violet the best and had missed her.

'Well, it won't make any difference to Violet whether you've got yer day clothes on, will it? Now go and get ready, like I told yer.'

'Can we stay up?'

'Well, it depends...'

'You've *got* to let us!' Em insisted. *'I'm* not

going to bed without Violet.'

Cynthia was taken aback by the urgency in her voice. Her shy, biddable little girl had been developing an iron will of her own in the last months.

'You can stay up for a bit,' she agreed.

Their eyelids were beginning to droop as they sat by the fire waiting, undressed for bed, with their jumpers over the top. As soon as the door latch lifted they were all on their feet.

'Bob?' Cynthia's voice held a note of hysteria, then rose in amazement as he came into the room. 'Oh my God! You've got her! Is that...?' She hardly dared believe it. 'Is that her?'

He was grinning. 'Course it's her, d'yer think I'd run off with someone else's babby by mistake?'

'Oh, let me hold her!'

Tears of joy coursed down Cynthia's cheeks as she cradled her baby, after so many months. 'Oh, ain't she bonny! I'd hardly know her, but it is her – there's that little pink mark on her forehead. Oh, she's lovely! Come and say hello to your brother and sisters, Violet.'

They all crowded round. Em kissed and kissed her baby sister's cheeks, laughing with delight.

It was only when the first hubbub had died down that Cynthia said, 'What did you do? How did you get her?'

'I kicked the door in,' Bob said matter-of-factly, as if he kicked a door in every day. 'I ain't having that dried-up bitch telling me what to do. She tried turning me away and I wasn't having it.'

Cynthia was laughing, hardly believing it. 'You mean you actually...'

'She shut it in my face an' all, so I booted the bloody thing open.'

He sat down with the dignified air of a man who's done a good day's work.

'Can I have my tea now, d'yer think?'

That night was the first time he dared turn to her properly, to ask her to be his wife again. The first nights he had lain beside her, cautious as if she were porcelain. He was afraid of her, and it felt so strange after lying with Flossie. In his confusion and guilt he had urged her to sleep, told her she needed to get well properly. Once, he had half woken in the night to find her cuddled up against his back and he ached with longing. It was a sexual ache, but not just that – it was a longing for her, for the rightness of what he had once taken for granted. He knew he had spoiled it and hardly deserved to have it back again.

Tonight, Violet was back in their room, seeming quite undisturbed by the changes around her. Careful not to wake her they tiptoed their way to bed in the candlelight. On every other night Cynthia had turned away and closed her eyes, as if exhausted, her thin body curled away from him, and he had taken it that she did not want him. This time she lay on her back looking upwards and let out a long, apparently contented breath.

'All home,' was all she said.

Bob lay with his head on the pillow looking at her. Compared with Flossie he realized Cynthia was beautiful – more homely, and especially before, when she had been more rounded – but real and herself. He looked as if for the first time at her profile, the strong, high cheekbones, her nose more rounded, not like Flossie's upward tilting one, her full lips with those square, widely spaced teeth, which somehow made her laughter more infectious.

Very gently he lifted his hand and laid it on her stomach, feeling the yielding warmth of the place where each of their four children had pushed her out into tight roundness. She turned her head and they looked each other in the eye, fully, for the first time in many weeks. Then he thought of Flossie and couldn't hold her gaze.

'Are you back, love?' he asked shamefully, looking down at the pillow close to her head.

'I hope so,' she whispered.

'Can I – you know?' The very words made him erect. His hand moved over her breast.

And slowly, tentatively, she inched across the bed towards him.

Forty-Seven

Now Easter was over it really felt as if spring had begun, mild enough for doors to be left open all along the street. The warm, still air was thick with the sulphurous smells from the gas works and chemicals from factories as Em sat on the front step one afternoon, idly playing with her old cat's cradle string and looking dreamily about her. It was still the school holidays but she wasn't in the mood for playing out, like Joyce, Nance and Sid.

Joyce and Nancy, both with March birthdays, had just turned five and were making the most of their freedom before starting school. They were all too young for Em. She missed Molly and just felt like staying quiet where she was. Cynthia was sitting feeding Violet from a bottle in the back room and Em could hear a wonderful, miraculous sound: her mother softly humming a lullaby that she had sung to all of them as babies. Em sat drinking in the familiar notes and suddenly found she couldn't see the string wound round her hands for tears.

'All right, bab? Nothing the matter is there?'

She hadn't seen Dot coming, checking that Cynthia was all right as she so often did. Em shook her head, smiling despite her watery eyes. Dot patted her head.

'Good girl. Thought I'd pop in and see your mom.' She stepped in past Em. 'Coo-ee, Cynth! It's me again! You don't get rid of me that easily!'

Soon the two women were talking in low voices in the back room and Em heard the sounds of the kettle being put on the stove and cups clinking. She drank in the feeling of life returning to normal. She heard Violet gurgling cheerfully after her feed which made her smile, but then a cold, hard feeling grew inside her because Mom was crying. She did cry sometimes when Dot came and Em hated it. It terrified her.

'It's all right, love,' she heard Dot saying soothingly. 'It's not like that. Just give her a chance to settle in again. She knows you're her mother...'

There was more muffled talk, then Em heard Cynthia saying, 'I'm scared Dot,' in a high, frightened voice. 'Sometimes, the way Bob looks at me, I know he's waiting for me to do or say summat that'll make him think I'm... I don't want to go back there again.'

'You're not going back there, Cynth. You're doing ever so well.'

'But it's Bob...' She lowered her voice a little. 'It's not the same. It's not that he's unkind – he's falling over himself to help and that. But he's not right, as if he's keeping summat from me and I can't get through to him properly. Not like it used to be.'

'Give him a bit of time,' Dot advised. 'It's been hard for 'im. I expect he's scared you'll get bad again. You need a bit of time and you'll feel more yourself again. I know it ain't easy for you.'

'Now I've got this little one back, I'm never giving *her* up again, or the others. I never want to leave my kids again.' Her voice sounded stronger suddenly. 'D'you know, when I was in the asylum, once I could think about anything I kept thinking about our mom. I don't know why, it was as if it all came back to me again after all these years, how it was when she died and everything. It was a terrible time, Dot, and I'd never given it a thought since, never wanted to go back over it, I s'pose. It all came flooding back and I kept having a weep about it. I couldn't seem to stop for a bit. Funny really, isn't it?'

'Maybe it'll help,' Dot said. 'They say having a babby brings things back.'

'But it wasn't as if she was my first!'

'No, well, there you are. But you seem stronger, Cynth.'

'I can keep cheerful with the kids, that's the main thing. But I do get frightened sometimes. It all just wells up.'

Em listened, wanting and half not wanting to hear what was being said. Clouds drifted across the sun, sending diaphanous shadows chasing along the street. The pavement was busy with children, and with housewives coming in and out with shopping bags, chatting by their front steps before going back to the daily grind.

Someone came skipping along the road on the other side, past the pawn shop. Em sat up straight, narrowing her eyes. It couldn't be, could it?

Then she was sure, and scrambled excitedly to her feet.

'Molly!'

Molly waved, a grin spreading across her face as she saw Em, and she came running along exuberantly. Em jumped up and down with excitement as well.

'What're you doing here? Have you run away again?'

'No, I just wanted to come and see yer! I got me grandad to give me the bus fare. Mom'd kill me if she knew I was 'ere!' Molly chattered excitedly. She looked thinner, and there was a shadow round her left eye, the ghost of a bruise. 'Any road, our mom says she wants to come and live back over this way. She don't like it up Aston but they've got to find somewhere away from this landlord so he don't find out they're here.'

'So you're coming back?'

'Might be. I ain't going to that school over there neither. I went once and I dain't like it so after

361

that I pretended to go and then I just hung about up the park. They never caught me. I want to come back and go to school with you.'

Em beamed. Seeing Molly felt like another thing returning to normal. Even the familiar aroma that hung around her didn't matter at all. Molly had shown herself to be a friend, not like some of the others, and that was all that counted.

She thrust her hands towards Molly, the string wrapped round them ready. 'Here, give us a game!'

In a moment they were lost in playing, their troubles forgotten.

Within a fortnight, the Fox family had moved back to Nechells, this time to a house in a yard off Lupin Street.

'At least they're not too close,' Bob said when Em told him the news. 'We don't need that bloody lot round the corner from us.'

'Molly's all right,' Em said. 'There's no need to be nasty about her.'

'Don't talk back at me like that!'

'Why not?' Em wasn't going to be silenced. 'She's my friend.'

'You're a cheeky so-and-so these days,' Bob said. He was riddling the grate as he talked. 'Well, she may be your friend, but as for the rest of 'em – that old man Rathbone, Iris's father, he's a filthy old bugger.' Bob stopped, as if he'd said too much. 'It's Joe I feel sorry for. He used to be a decent bloke before the war did for 'im.' He wiped his arm over his face. 'Course, he's got a few years on me, but I can remember Joe Fox when he was a young'un with the arse hanging out of his trousers.' He shook his head sorrowfully.

'Was that before you went to the Home, Dad?' Em asked. It was so seldom that he ever said anything about his past that she jumped at the opportunity.

'Yes.' He turned away, picking up the coal scuttle. 'Many moons ago.'

The other person who was delighted to see Molly was Jenny Button.

'You come and see us whenever you like,' she told her. 'Stanley and me've missed your company. And any trouble, bab – you know where to come.'

'All right – ta,' Molly said, beaming at this warm welcome.

Em and Molly often popped in to the Buttons' now, to collect bread and see the flowers in the back yard which Jenny tended devotedly, and to say hello to Stanley and Bullseye and the budgies. It was a bit further to get to Molly's, across the other side of Great Lister Street, but Molly ran up to Kenilworth Street to meet Em on the way to school.

Things got back into a routine, much like they used to be. Cynthia was still fragile but she put on a brave face in front of the children, and Em and the others would hardly ever have known if she was having a difficult day, or was in one of her panics. Now they were all back at school, Em had not heard her crying for a long time. She was always there when they came in from school, just like before. Day by day, inch by inch, the family

363

was coming together again, getting back to something like normal, and trying to heal the scars of the past terrible months.

Then, that Sunday evening in April, a month after Cynthia came home, they were all sitting round the table having tea. Bob was standing, carving slices off a little joint of beef, and the room was full of the delicious smells of roast meat and potatoes.

'There yer go, son, you can get that down yer, give yer muscles of iron!' Bob put a plate down in front of Sid, who received it eagerly, licking his lips. Cynthia spooned potatoes onto his plate.

'Roast!' Sid said in raptures. 'All Em ever does is nasty boiled ones.'

'Now, now, Em was doing the best she could, weren't you, love?' Cynthia said, seeing Em stick her tongue out at Sid. 'And I don't s'pose you gave her much help, young man.'

'I'm a man,' Sid said loftily. 'Men don't do cooking.'

They were all laughing at this when there came a knocking on the front door. Bob tutted, laying down the carving knife.

'What a flaming ridiculous time to call. I'll get rid of 'em. Don't want anything to spoil our tea, do we?'

A moment later there was a commotion in the front room.

'I'm coming in, Bob, and you're not stopping me.' It was Flossie's voice, shrill in defiance. The children looked at each other, knowing this was trouble.

'Who's that?' Cynthia frowned. 'Whatever's going on?'

Flossie erupted into the room with Bob behind, trying to pull her back.

'It's no good, Bob,' Flossie announced. 'It's all got to come out.' She spoke in a pert, triumphant way. Cynthia, still sitting at the table, stared at her in total bewilderment. 'You must be Bob's wife. I'm very sorry to say I've got some bad news for you.' She cast a look at Bob.

'While you've been, er, *away*,' she began spitefully, 'I'm afraid you may not have realized that your husband has not been all he seems. You see, Bob and I are in love and he's been living discreetly with me whenever he could, and he wants to marry me. The fact is, *Mrs Brown*–' and here she paused for effect – 'I'm expecting a child, and it's Bob's.'

'No!' Bob cried, looking as if he wanted to stuff the words back into Flossie's mouth. 'That's not right, it can't be! You know that, Floss – I mean, I never...'

'Oh you did, Bob.' She dropped her voice into the seductive tone she had used with him so often. 'That last week. Surely you haven't forgotten?'

There was a look of dawning horror on Bob's face. God, it was true, of course he hadn't forgotten, but it was just that couple of times when he hadn't been able to hold back and pull out when he was at the height of his excitement. She hadn't done anything to put him off – she'd wanted it too. And she'd said it would be all right! He squeezed his eyes tightly closed, then opened them again to look at Flossie, his face etched with shame and utter defeat.

Everyone was silent. Em watched her mother, barely understanding, but so afraid of the feeling that something bad was about to happen.

Then Cynthia stood up. She seemed ominously calm.

'Cynth,' Bob said in warning.

Pushing the chair in under the table, but still holding on to it as if she might at any moment pick it up and throw it, Cynthia faced Flossie Dawson.

'Now you've come and spread your poison,' she said quietly, 'you can get out of my house. *Our house*. Go on!' Her voice began to rise. 'Just clear off out of here!'

'You'd best go,' Bob urged Flossie, who had dropped her ladylike air and looked as if she was spoiling for a fight.

'I'm not going anywhere!' she began, but Bob took her by the shoulders and steered her forcibly out of the room, still screeching. 'You've got to see me right. You haven't heard the end of this! I'm having your baby, I tell you!'

'Look,' they heard Bob pleading, 'this is my family. You didn't have to come in like this. Why did yer have to do it like this?'

'Oh, that's right, have your fun and clear off, leaving me all alone with a child to bring up! And think you can keep it all secret! I thought you were a man, Bob Brown.'

'Keep yer voice down, Floss, for Christ's sake!' Bob's voice was low and urgent. 'Look, what d'you want off me? I don't know what to do.'

'You'll have to pay for its upbringing, that's

what, if you're not going to keep your promises and marry me. You needn't think you can get away with it. You men are all the same – sow your oats and think you can turn your back on the issue. Well, I'm not standing for being treated like some street whore!'

'Look, I'll come and see yer.' He was speaking very low, hoping they couldn't hear him, but of course they could. 'Just leave now, Floss, for God's sake.'

'I'm going,' she declared loudly. 'But you needn't think you're going to worm your way out of this. I want every penny I deserve for the way you've treated me – and don't you forget it.'

The door slammed. Having stood still as a statue while all this was going on, Cynthia suddenly released the back of the chair and strode across the room. The children heard her disappear upstairs. After a few moments, Bob followed her.

Joyce gazed in confusion at Em and Sid. 'What was Mrs Dawson saying?' she asked. 'Is she going to do summat bad to our dad?'

Em, shaking all over, tried to gather her shattered wits to comfort her little sister. 'No, I don't suppose so. She's just in a temper about summat. Don't worry, Joycie. Let's let Mom and Dad sort it out. We'll do the washing-up, shall we?'

'Is it true?'

Cynthia was sitting on the bed, her back to Bob when he came into their room. He stood by the door, afraid to go in any further. He was astonished, and frightened by her icy calm.

'What, that she's having a babby?'

367

'That it could be yours. That you want to marry her.'

The answer did not come for some time. The sound of the children clattering the plates came through the floorboards. At last he said, 'It could be. She says it is.'

There was silence. Bob was in a torment.

'And *her*, d'you want *her?*' Her voice cut him like a blade.

'No...' But he didn't quite mean it, even after what he had just seen: her cold, calculating spite. Still she had the old hold on him which would not release him. Still he longed to protect her.

'I just...' He shrugged helplessly, an impossible tension within him.

'Because if you do, you'd better go...'

'*What?* Cynth, no, I dain't mean... All that happened was...'

Cynthia twisted round to look at him. 'Don't tell me about it!' she cried fiercely. 'I don't want to know. There was me feeling that bad for letting you all down, when all the time...' She turned away again, her voice quiet and sad. 'But I did let you down, so maybe it's no more than I deserve. If you're not going to stand by us, don't want us – if you love her – then go. I don't want you here.'

'No! It ain't that! None of that was your fault, Cynth!' He hurried round the bed towards her but she held out her hand to keep him away. She was not emotional. She seemed detached and iron hard.

'Do you love her?'

He put a hand to his head. 'No, but...'

'You do,' she stated.

'*No!*' He was breathing hard, almost sobbing. 'But she's got a grip on me, like. I was lonely – *scared*. I dain't know if you was ever coming back. And now I've gone and got myself into this. I can't just leave her.'

Cynthia watched him with her frigid, terrible calm, then turned away. 'Then go. I don't want you in my bed.'

'But Cynth!'

'I said *go.*' She waved a hand, her devastating hurt bursting out in a snarl. 'Take your things and bugger off. You've got another family now. We'll manage without you.'

Forty-Eight

'Did you know, Dot?'

Cynthia was in such a state, she didn't even wait for Dot to clear the twins and Nancy out of the room. The four of them were sitting round the table finishing their tea when she erupted into the house, trembling with emotion. The children all stared. Dot stood up, holding a white rag that had been in her lap.

'Know what, Cynth?' she asked carefully. But her eyes held a mixture of fear and sorrow.

'You knew about her, didn't you?'

Without turning her head, Dot ordered, 'Boys, Nance – out.'

'But Mom, I haven't–' Terry began.

'I said out!'

369

In seconds they were alone. Dot looked down, wringing the rag between her hands. 'It's hard not to know things round here.' She had not seen Flossie's coming and going next door this evening, but Cynthia had obviously found out somehow.

'You were helping him, looking after the kids all the time – so he could be with *her!*'

'No!' Dot's eyes flashed now and she flung the cloth on the table. 'That's not how it was, Cynth! I ended up minding your kids all the time cos he was never bloody well here! He spent every moment he could with the sodding woman and–' She stopped, realizing she'd said too much. More gently, she went on, 'Thing was, Cynth – Em was left doing everything and she couldn't manage, not at her age. The poor kid was in a right state, wearing herself to a wafer. Joycie spent most of her time round here with Nance. What else could I do? In the end I was getting them to school – and to bed most nights. They needed a mom and I was the nearest thing. It wasn't to help him play about. I just tried to do my best for 'em when it was you they wanted. I felt for the little mites.'

Cynthia sank shakily onto a chair. 'God, Dot, I don't half owe yer,' she said, tears welling in her eyes. 'I didn't really come round 'ere to have a go. I just don't know which way to turn. I s'pose you didn't really have a choice, keeping quiet about it, not wanting to upset me. I'd've done the same.' She gave a deep sigh, wiping her hands over her face. 'While I was in that place I was too wrapped up in myself. I mean, I worried about the kids, course I did, but it was like another world over there: nothing else was real. And I couldn't do anything about it all so I sort of shut it out of my mind, the day-to-day stuff and how they were managing. I just hoped they were. But I owe it all to you, Dot.'

'How did you find out about her?'

'She came. Just now while we were having tea.'

'What, just turned up?'

Cynthia nodded bleakly.

'I s'pose she came to spread her spite and make trouble,' Dot said bitterly. 'I always knew she was a nasty piece of work. I tried to get through to Bob, please believe me, Cynth.' Dot came and sat beside her, talking earnestly. 'We had some right old ding-dongs. But he wouldn't listen. It was as if that woman had bewitched him!'

'Did the kids know about it?' Cynthia looked directly at her. She was still trembling, but her eyes were clear of tears.

Dot hesitated, then nodded. She was surprised by her friend's new strength.

'Is that where he was, Christmas Day?'

'I only knew when Em said after. I wasn't here on the day cos I went to Jean and David's. I thought he was coming to see you. But he didn't, did he?'

Cynthia shook her head wanly. She was shaking even harder, her teeth chattering as if all the shock was coming out. 'But I was glad in a way. I felt so bad.'

'Oh, love, look at the state of yer. Where is 'e now? Down the boozer, I s'pose, drowning his sorrows?'

'He's gone. To her. I threw him out.'

'*What?*' Dot cried. 'You never!'

Cynthia's shoulders began to heave with sobs. 'That's what he wants. I could see. And with a babby on the way, what's the use in me being a millstone round his neck? He's always going to be wishing he was somewhere else, or sneaking off to her. I couldn't stand that.'

'A *babby*? You mean she's...? God, Cynth...' It began to sink in. 'And he just went? But you can't let him get away just like that! How're you going to manage? I mean, four kids...'

'Well, you've managed,' Cynthia wept. 'I dunno, I haven't had time. I'll have to get out to work.' She clutched her head in confusion. 'I can't even think straight.'

'Oh, love.' Dot leaned forward and put her arms round her distraught friend. 'That's it, you have a bit of a blart, make yer feel better. Oh dear, after all you've been through an' all... I'd give you a drop of hard stuff to buck you up if I had any – but I don't!'

'It doesn't suit me anyhow!' Cynthia sniffed. 'Makes me sick...' She wiped her eyes, looking stunned.

'I can't believe Bob'd just take off and desert you all,' Dot said, in shock herself. 'He's no good with her anyway.'

'What d'you mean? She looks pretty and... Well, better than me.'

'No,' Dot said emphatically. 'Oh no. She's a looker all right, but that one's a smooth operator if ever I saw one! She hung about getting her claws into Bob. Course he's handsome and strong, but he ain't no Rockefeller. Why not go for someone better off?' She frowned. 'There's summat fishy about her in my opinion. Summat doesn't add up.'

'What d'you mean?' Cynthia seemed dazed.

Dot shook her head. 'I can't put my finger on it but she's just queer – the way she talks and puts on airs, and she's not as poor as you'd expect, not for a widow bringing up a girl on her own. I mean, she ain't rich but she seems to be comfortable. Summat just doesn't fit right about her.'

Cynthia looked despairing. 'But whatever it is, he'd rather be with her than me.'

'No – I don't think that's it. You've got to fight for him, bab, not just let that strumpet walk all over the pair of yer. Bob's a weak man in some ways, but you and the kids are his sun and stars, you know that. He's always been a family man! He'll soon miss you all like hell and come running back. I don't know what the hold she has on him is, but somehow she's pulled him right off the rails.' Dot was looking thoughtful. 'Tell you what, bide your time, give 'im a chance to get sick of her and let's see if we can find out a bit about her. We could talk to Em, see what she knows. I know they've been in her house.'

Cynthia looked reluctant. 'I don't want the kids dragged into this. They've had enough to put up with.'

'They're in it anyway,' Dot said. 'What with her turning up and carrying on the way she did. And you're going to have to say he's gone with her for the moment. What choice have you got? Look, Em's quite grown-up for her age now, she's had to be. We'll talk to her. But you'll have to tell them. You don't want them finding out from someone else, do yer?'

Later that evening, Cynthia gathered the children round her before they went to bed. She had been surprised none of them had asked where Bob was, until Sid remarked, 'I s'pose Dad's down the Crown again?'

Things had obviously been even worse than she realized while she was away, but once they were all round her, scrubbed and ready, Violet in her arms, she said, 'I've got summat to tell you that's not easy to explain. You know that lady who came round this evening?'

'Mrs Dawson?' Joyce said earnestly.

'Yes. Well, as you've no doubt noticed, your dad's got rather...' She had to hold on to herself very tightly so as not to cry. 'He's rather fond of her. Anyway, for the moment, he's going to be staying with her in her house.'

'Why?' Sid asked, frowning furiously. 'I don't like her. Why's he stopping with her?'

'To – help her out a little bit,' Cynthia said, groping desperately for reasons that would make any sense to the children.

'Is that because of the babby?' Em asked.

'Yes,' Cynthia said faintly. The children had obviously not missed any of the shouted exchange when Flossie turned up. 'That's right. She just ... she just needs a bit of help.'

'Well, when's he coming back? Tomorrow?' Sid demanded.

'I don't know,' Cynthia had to say. 'I'm sorry, love.'

Sid and Joyce asked more questions, but Em

stood silent, her face very solemn, her eyes like two despairing pools.

Em sat biting her nails through her lessons the next day and got told off by Miss Lineham. She felt sick and couldn't keep her mind on anything after what had happened with Flossie Dawson, and seeing Mom and Dad both looking so upset and frightened, then Dad going. Mom had been trying to act as if everything was normal that morning as they got ready for school, but Em could see how pale and upset she was. Just when things had been getting better, they were all falling apart again.

Out in the playground she saw Sid and Joyce. Sid was running round in the gang of footballers, but Joyce came up to her looking upset.

'I hurt my finger,' she said, tears rolling down her cheeks as she showed Em her bruised right middle finger. She had got it caught in one of the doors as someone closed it and it was already purple and swollen.

Em gave her a cuddle and tried to distract her, but she could see that her little sister was feeling as unsettled as she was.

'Can I come round and play at yours?' Molly said afterwards and Em nodded gladly. If they played out she could forget everything that was happening at home.

When their got to the house, Dot and Cynthia were both waiting for them. Both the women had pegged out their washing after a hard morning's work and it was swinging gently on the lines in their back yards under a threatening sky.

'Here, there's a piece for you,' Cynthia greeted them as they came in, trying to sound calm. The plate of bread with a scraping of dripping was on the table. 'Oh hello, Molly. I didn't know you were coming as well.' She made herself speak kindly, even though her nerves were screaming that she didn't want anyone else there, just family and Dot.

''Ello, Mrs Brown,' Molly said.

'Can Molly have a piece?' Em asked.

'Go on, then,' Cynthia said. She was surprised at the bond that had formed between Em and Molly Fox, and she found Molly quite a likeable girl, once you got past the scruffy, smelly state of her. Jenny Button's instruction in the manners department had also been a great improvement.

'Thing is, we want to have a word with you, Em,' she said, once Sid, Joyce and Nance had taken their bread and run off outside. 'Nothing to worry about, you ain't in trouble. Only maybe Molly'd better go on home.'

Em's face fell. 'But we wanted to play!'

'Why don't you let Molly stay?' Dot suggested, topping up the teacups. 'It'll be all right.' To Cynthia she added in a whisper, 'You never know, she might know summat. She hears a lot and she's no fool, that one.'

Cynthia was none too keen to discuss her business in front of Molly Fox, but she had to realize that a lot of things had changed in the months she'd been away. None of her business was going to be private now, that was one thing for certain.

'What d'you want to know?' Em said warily,

through a thick mouthful of bread. When adults said they wanted to talk to you it usually meant bad news and trouble. She looked poised to run away.

'Well,' Cynthia began gently. She was determined to keep herself under control and not cry. 'You know that lady who came round last night?'

Em's lip curled in contempt. 'Flossie the Floozy.'

'What? Where did you hear that?' Cynthia and Dot couldn't help laughing.

'Dunno,' Em said evasively. 'It's just what some people call her.'

'You've been to her house, haven't you? What's it like?'

Em swallowed her last mouthful, shrugging. 'S'all right. Quite nice.'

'Has she got some nice things?' Dot asked.

Em looked a bit blank. 'She's got a dragon – a red one.'

The two women exchanged glances, but this didn't seem to be getting them anywhere.

'What about her daughter?' Cynthia asked.

'She's called Daisy and she's horrible. She was always nasty to us. She isn't always there. She goes out and they argue about it.'

'Where does she go?'

'She's got an auntie, I think...' Em didn't seem quite sure.

'I saw her,' Molly put in, but no one took any notice.

'Did she say anything about her auntie?'

Em shook her head. 'She goes for tea or summat – Sundays.'

'She was outside this house...' Molly spoke

more loudly and at last they all looked at her.

'Go on, bab,' Dot said. 'Tell us what you were going to say.'

'I saw Daisy – weeks back, when we was living up Aston. She was going along the road – you couldn't miss her in that hat she wears. I followed her cos I dain't have anything else to do and I wanted to see where she'd go. It were only for a couple of minutes because she went and knocked on the door of this house, and then someone let her in.'

She had Cynthia's and Dot's full attention now. 'D'you know where the house was?' Dot asked.

Molly's eye wandered. 'I dunno the name of the road – but I know where it is. I could show yer if you want to know that bad.'

Skipping

Forty-Nine

Gradually the news spread throughout the neighbourhood and gossiping voices looked at the situation from every angle.

Em dreaded going out, knowing that everyone was tattling about her and her family. All the months she had hung on while Mom was in the hospital, wishing and praying for her family to be together again, and now this – Dad was gone instead, and living with that woman and horrible Daisy Dawson.

Sid took it very badly as well and played up. His bedwetting had got better since Mom came home but now it started again with a vengeance.

They saw their father coming back from work on the Wednesday and all left the rope they'd been skipping with and ran to him as he came down the road.

'Dad, Dad!'

Bob tried to smile but his eyes showed the tension in them as they swarmed round him.

'All right, kids, all right. Hey, don't push me over, lad! How's yer mother?'

'She keeps crying,' Joyce said. 'When're you going to come home, Dad?'

He straightened up, pushing them away. 'I'm not sure. Can't tell yer.'

And he was gone.

'Yer dirty bastard!' they heard a woman's voice

shout from one of the houses along the street.

The words made Em curl up inside, hearing her dad being called names like that! It made her feel sick with shame. But *why* was he living with Mrs Dawson, just when Mom had finally come home? Why was Mrs Dawson going on about a baby? What did that have to do with them and why did Dad have to look after her? She didn't understand any of it. She lay awake that night, burning inside at the injustice of it all and with rage at her father. All the struggling she'd done, all the work and drudgery, missing school, trying to keep things going while Mom was away, and he'd gone and spoiled it all just like that, thrown it all away without a care! She turned to the wall and sobbed with hurt, anger and helplessness. Beneath all her rage was the longing for him to come home, to be her daddy, and for things to be right. Spent with sobbing, she rolled onto her back, staring up into the darkness. And that was when she decided it was up to her. Mom and Dad couldn't seem to sort themselves out.

Next day, still fit to explode, she waited until she knew Bob would be back from work, then marched round to Flossie's house. She didn't even tell Molly where she was going. Molly had joined in one of the skipping games which had taken over the street and Em ran off, leaving her to it.

Her courage high, she hammered her fists on Flossie's door.

Daisy opened it.

'Oh, what *d'you* want?' she asked sneeringly.

'I want me dad.'

'Well, you're flaming well welcome to him – *I* don't want him here!' Daisy snarled.

She disappeared and Em heard low voices inside. A smell of stew and cabbage wafted out to her along the hall. She stood with her fists clenched. From the back room she heard Mrs Dawson say harshly, 'You just button your lip, Daisy, or else.' Then Bob appeared.

'Em?' He sounded worried. 'What's up, love?'

'You've got to come home, Dad!' she erupted at him. It all started pouring out and tears came as well. 'It's horrible you living here and everyone saying dirty things about you. We want you at home! So what if Mrs Dawson's having a babby, our mom's got a babby as well and the rest of us. It's stupid and it's not *fair!* You're our dad and you used to be nice and you ain't any more. You're nasty and *stupid!*' In enraged frustration she stamped her foot, shrieking and sobbing like a tiny child.

'Hey, Em!' Bob tried to sound appeasing. His voice was wretched. 'Don't go on like that now. You'll get everyone upset. It'll all be all right...'

'No, it *won't!*' She was beside herself now at this hopeless response. 'Why won't you listen? Mom's not well and we're all on our own and you've got to come home! Why're you living here with this silly woman?'

'Oh now, bab...' He sank down onto the step, squatting so he could look into her face. 'Come on, Em – c'm'ere.' He held his arms out.

'NO!' she shouted, backing away.

'All right. But come here while I talk to yer. To try and explain...'

383

'Bob, what's going on?' Em heard Flossie's voice from inside.

'Nothing much. I'll be in in a minute.' He sounded almost fearful. Em froze inside. Her tears stopped. *Nothing much.*

'You're *stupid!*' she cried, taking off down the road. 'I hate you!'

Bob turned up on the Friday evening of that miserable week and shamefacedly handed Cynthia most of the contents of his wage packet. The sight of him on the doorstep, knocking like a visitor, felt worse to Cynthia than anything else.

'Didn't expect to see yer,' she said coldly, facing him with her arms folded, fighting to remain proud and hostile when all she wanted to do was weep and beg him to come home.

'Don't want you to go short,' he said.

'Oh, and what about *poor* Mrs Dawson?' she said savagely. 'Won't she go short if you give us your wages?'

Bob hung his head. 'We'll manage.' He dared to look up at her for a moment. 'I could come and help you do a few things.'

'Oh no you don't!' Her anger flared out at him. 'You don't have it both ways. You've shown where you want to be so you can bloody stay there, with your floozy and her sodding brat. You made your bed and you lie on it, and good luck to the two of yer!'

She slammed the door in his face. Leaning against it, her face contorted in anguish and she slid down, shaking with sobs.

During that week she and Dot had helped each other out as usual, and talked endlessly over what had happened and more on finding out about Flossie Dawson.

'I can't see what good all this is going to do,' Cynthia said sometimes, in a desperate voice.

'You just wait and see,' Dot told her. 'We're gunna get that bitch – one way or another.'

No one in the neighbourhood seemed to know a thing about her, though she was not greatly liked. People found her stand-offish, as if she thought she was better than anyone else. Now she had made off with the father of a popular family in the street when his wife hadn't been well, no one had a good word to say about her.

They resolved to do something at the weekend when Molly could help them. In the meantime, though, Molly was in more trouble.

She turned up at school one morning that week with her face badly bruised again, her left cheek-bone very shiny and swollen. She was obviously in pain, and after struggling through school that day, with everyone's comments and questions, she paid her usual visit to Mrs Button's.

'My house can be your home from home,' Jenny Button had told her. And Molly loved going there, where she was received with the kindness and affection that had been so lacking in her life, and often cake or other treats as well.

But that day Jenny Button took one look at her and climbed soberly off her stool. She lifted the counter and beckoned Molly through to the back.

'Look at this, Stanley.' Her voice was clipped

with rage as she pushed Molly before her husband.

'Oh my,' Stanley said, seeing Molly's injured face.

'Who did that to you, love?' Jenny asked, already certain of the answer.

Molly squatted down, taking refuge in stroking Bullseye's wiry coat.

'Was it your mom?'

Molly nodded shamefully. 'It was only cos she'd had a bit to drink...'

'Right.' Jenny Button unfastened her pinner and flung it on the chair. 'Come on – I'm taking you home.'

'No!' Molly's head jerked up. 'I'll go on my own!' she cried, horrified. 'You mustn't come!'

'And why not?' Jenny Button asked.

'Cos she gets so angry. I don't want no trouble. You don't know what she might do.'

'Oh, I wouldn't worry about that,' Jenny Button said. 'Don't worry, Molly. I've just got a few things to say to her. Now you lead the way.'

'Please don't!' Molly was almost in tears. She wanted sympathy, but not trouble.

'Don't you worry,' Jenny Button said firmly. 'All I want is a quick word with her.'

Molly fearfully led Jenny Button's determined, waddling figure along to Lupin Street and into the latest poverty-stricken yard where the Foxes had taken up residence. In fact it was not quite as dismal as the one in Kenilworth Street, being a little wider and open to more sunlight. But Jenny Button, a clean, fastidious woman, wrinkled her nose in dismay at the sight of the piles of rubbish up at the far end and the doors of the shared privies swinging open on their hinges.

She had reason to recoil further. There was already a whiff outside the door of the Foxes' house, and when Molly pushed it open the smell that hit her from that small downstairs room was ferocious. Jenny had time just to take in the two men in their chairs, who seemed to be taking up most of the space, the older one with grizzled mutton-chop whiskers, the other pale and prematurely aged. Molly disappeared inside and Iris Fox loomed from behind the door. As usual she was dressed all in black, and her eyes were glazed and senseless with drink. She leaned voluptuously against one side of the door frame.

'Who're you?' she demanded, trying to focus her gaze. 'Oh, it's you – what d'you want? Come to interfere in other people's business, 'ave yer?'

Jenny Button was barely four feet ten inches in height, but she pulled herself to the full extent of it and looked forbiddingly at Iris, without the slightest hint of fear.

'You don't deserve to have a child,' she began. 'You're a bloody disgrace and you only want her as your little skivvy.'

'It weren't me!' Iris said petulantly. 'I never lay a finger on 'er – do I, Molly?'

There was no reply. Molly seemed to have disappeared into the house.

'It's 'er Dad 'its 'er,' Iris confided, in a self-pitying whine. ''E's not right in the 'ead – the war done 'im. I'm as good as widowed...'

Barely able to control her temper, Jenny Button moved closer to Iris's bulky figure. 'You aren't the only one with a ruined husband, you know – only some of us work for a living instead of drowning our sorrows. Now, you lay your finger on Molly again, and I'll report you for child cruelty.'

'Oh, will yer?' Iris's foul temper soon surfaced. 'Yer sodding nosy cow! What's it got to do with you? Who're you gunna report me to any road? There ain't no one knows us.'

'Oh, make no mistake,' Jenny came back at her. 'There's the Welfare people, the police, the NSPCC – they come and take children away when the family ain't fit. And I'll tell you something, you filthy slattern – you do anything to hurt this young wench and I'll take her away myself. Oh,' she added. 'And I expect your old landlord'd like to know where you are an' all...'

'Don't you bloody dare tell 'im, the bastard!' Iris roared, bunching her fist.

'You gunna hit me an' all, then?' Jenny turned away with a disgusted look. 'You'd better remember what I've said.'

'That's right, you get out of 'ere before I punch yer lights out!' Iris bawled after her. 'Yer nosy, meddling bitch!'

Jenny picked her way with dignity back down the entry and out into Lupin Street. Lord, if she could only get that child away from that house! The vile stench of the place seemed to be burned into her nostrils, almost making her gag. There was something horribly familiar about it and it was only as she was walking back across Great Lister Street that it came to her what it was. Old Reggie, a friend of Stan's, had died shortly after the war, of a wound that never healed. His house had also been filled with that ghastly, suppurating smell, which she now recognized as the deathly odour of gangrene.

Fifty

On Saturday afternoon, Cynthia and Dot set off for Aston with Molly and Em in tow. They had been discussing it all week. Molly was to show them the way.

'Why does your mom want to go and see Mrs Floozy's sister anyway?' Molly asked Em. They always called Flossie Mrs Floozy now.

Em shrugged angrily. 'Dunno.' She didn't care. She just wanted Flossie Dawson to disappear in a puff of smoke and have everything back as it should be.

'There's no point in all of us going,' Cynthia had argued to Dot. 'Molly can show me where the house is...'

'No – I'm not having you going off on your own, the state you're in. You don't know how you might be treated by that trollop's sister! And if Molly's got to come, Em can keep her company.'

'It'll cost us in tram fares...' Cynthia was all nerves.

'Don't be daft – we'll walk,' Dot said. 'That's if you're up to it.'

It was a couple of miles away, but Saturday dawned dry and quite warm and the four of them set off, leaving the younger children to be minded by a neighbour. They even took bread and butter, some cake and bottles of tea.

'Might as well make an outing of it,' Dot said.

Em's spirits rose once they'd set off and they were away from the familiar streets of home. It suddenly felt like fun, an adventure, and Dot had brought a picnic! She and Molly skipped along, chattering away behind the two mothers.

'What if she's not in?' Cynthia said uneasily to Dot.

'Well, we'll have to wait till she is,' Dot said. 'Don't s'pose she'll go far.'

'I just hope Molly knows what she's on about after all this,' Cynthia said doubtfully. Molly was certain that the address was close to the park in Aston, because she had been on her way there that day she had spotted Daisy Dawson.

'It's quite a tall house,' she said. 'With a black front door and a big brass knocker.'

'All right, bab,' Dot told her. 'Well, we're counting on you.'

Em was impressed by Molly's sense of direction. Aston, to her, seemed a confusing place, stinking of vinegar from the sauce factory and with streets leading off in every direction, jam-packed with houses, and she was sure she would never be able to find her way back home from here. But Molly led them with hardly any hesitation towards Aston Park and off along a street of solid, respectable-looking terraces, bigger than they were used to seeing in Kenilworth Street, with little gardens at the front.

'You sure about this, Molly?' Dot said, looking anxious.

Molly nodded. She was walking faster now. 'It's just up 'ere, on the left.' She stopped suddenly, pointing.

'Well, I never,' Cynthia said. And then, 'Oh, I don't know about this...'

There was the black front door with its brass knocker. The house was three storeys and seemed to loom over them. At the front were a couple of sad, scrubby-looking bushes and the flower beds along the front of the house were neglected and choked with weeds.

'This doesn't feel right,' Cynthia said shakily. 'I don't know what I'm going to say...'

'You can just say what's happened. Polite, like. God knows, Cynth, you've got a right to know a bit about the woman. She's stolen your husband! Look, shall I come in with yer?'

'No – best not. It'll look like a gang turning up. You wait with the girls.' Cynthia took a deep breath and pulled her shoulders back. 'Oh – I don't know why I'm doing this. I must be off my head... Still–' there was a wry flicker of a smile – 'I have just come out of the asylum.'

'You'll be all right,' Dot said. She suddenly took each of the girls by the hand and they retreated even further and stood by someone's front gate. Em liked the feeling of holding Dot's hand, though she didn't enjoy the idea of her mother disappearing into this strange house.

They saw Cynthia look up and down the road then go to the front door. The sound of the knocker rat-tatted along the street. Then it went quiet.

'Come on!' Dot said. 'We'll just walk past.'

As they strolled along the street they were just in time to catch sight of Cynthia's back disappearing into the dark hall of the house. The door closed.

It seemed an age that they waited, walking round and round the block, not liking to go too far away in case Cynthia came out again. Dot was left with the task of jollying the children along in these odd circumstances.

'After this is over,' she said, 'we'll go and have our bit of picnic. Nice day for it.'

She chatted to the two girls, trying to make things sound calm and normal, and they brightened when she promised them some sweets as well. But every so often she'd say in a worried voice, 'Oh my goodness, I wonder what on earth's going on...'

At last, when they had done another turn-about of the roads close to Flossie's sister's house, rounding the corner past the little shop, which was by now coming to seem familiar after several laps, they saw Cynthia coming along towards them.

'Mom!' Em broke away and ran towards her.

'You've been ages!' Dot cried, as she and Molly ran to catch up. 'Are you all right? What did she say?'

It was then that they all took in the stunned expression on Cynthia's face. She was shaking her head as if she could not find the words.

'It wasn't a she,' she gobbled at last, pointing back, wide-eyed, at the house. 'It was a he. That man in there is Flossie Dawson's husband – and she's still married to him.'

Fifty-One

They sat at the edge of the park, with the Jacobean edifice of Aston Hall looming grandly at the top of the slope in front of them. But none of them took much notice of this, or even of the bread and cake, because they were all desperate to hear Cynthia's story.

'He seems quite a nice bloke really,' Cynthia said, her bewilderment still plain in her face. Behind it they could sense a deep excitement which was hard to fathom as yet. 'I mean, he's angry all right, but otherwise he seems quite decent. Quite a bit older than her, I'd say. I think he still loves her, in his way... He's still keeping her, despite it all. And Daisy must be fond of him to keep going and seeing him.'

'Well, what the hell's she playing at, then?' Dot erupted, desperate to know the whole picture.

'You might well ask. It's a queer story all right.' Cynthia swallowed her mouthful and, seeing the rapt faces all round her, her face suddenly broke into a delicious grin which made the rest of them smile. They could see she was bursting to tell them what she'd found.

'Flossie Dawson's been married to him *for fourteen years* – only his name's not Dawson – that's her maiden name. He's a Welshman, his name's Dai Owen. He's a gentle, dithery sort of bloke – wouldn't say boo to a goose. He works in a bank.'

'Goodness,' Dot said. 'Well, they're not too poor, then – the house is big enough.'

'He said he'd inherited it from his mom and dad,' Cynthia said.

'Never mind the house – go *on!*' Dot insisted, impatient as a child.

'He said Flossie and he got wed just after the war. He's a good bit older, fifteen years or so. Everything went all right at the start, only they were trying for a babby. Time went by and nothing seemed to be happening and she started to get very down in herself over it. She started blaming him to begin with, but in the end she went to the doctor and they had a look at her up the hospital because they couldn't seem to find what was wrong. But there's summat the matter with her – I don't know what – and she can't have children...'

Em and Molly looked at each other and frowned, not sure of the implications of this.

'But...!' Dot's mind was racing round these fragments. 'What about Daisy? And that means... Christ, Cynth – she can't be expecting your Bob's babby!'

The girls gasped. 'She's a liar and a cheater!' Em burst out. 'She's a wicked, wicked woman!'

'Daisy's not theirs,' Cynthia said. 'Flossie got in such a state over not being able to have her own that they decided to take in a child from the orphanage, and they got Daisy when she was just about three. When you think of it, she's nothing like Flossie... Any road, that was all right for a bit. She spent a couple of years wrapped up in having Daisy. But then, he said – he seemed quite keen

394

to pour it out to me, surprising really – then Daisy went to school, and that was when things went down the pan even further. Flossie got very funny about men. I s'pose you girls oughtn't to hear all this, but still – I'll say it short, like...' Cynthia took a swig of tea from one of the bottles. Giving Dot a meaningful look she went on, 'She started to wander, if you know what I mean, and she weren't too fussy either, apparently, even with her being quite respectable. Mr Owen said it was like a kind of drug to her – she had to have men. As if she wanted to cast a spell over them, that was what he said. And of course she's a looker, got summat about her that hooks them in.'

'Blimey,' Dot said. 'I wonder he stood for it. So he threw her out?'

'No, not straight away. Course, it upset him terribly, you could see, but he's a kindly soul. He's not the ruling with a rod of iron sort, and I don't think he knew what to do, especially seeing the kind of men she was going for – you know, not her class. He thinks she likes to lord it over them. He turned a blind eye so far as he could and kept hoping she'd just stop it. And he's ever so fond of Daisy. Flossie didn't leave home, but she was in and out, playing about... He said it would stop for a time and things would go back to normal, but then it would all start off again. He said she was like two people: his loving wife and a prostitute all in one. That was his words. He put it down to her not being able to have a babby of her own, that it had turned her head somehow. Anyway, this went on for some years until about eighteen months ago he'd had enough. Said he couldn't stand any more. He'd see her all right but she'd got to go. He said he didn't know where she went first of all, but then of course she came to our neck of the woods.'

'And started on your husband, the handsome so-and-so.'

Cynthia nodded. Her eyes shone with a mixture of deep hurt and great hope. She looked at Em and Molly, and stroked Em's head for a second. 'I'm sorry you had to hear that, girls. But I know you've already been forced into seeing what kind of person Mrs Dawson can be.'

Em gave a quick smile, but her eyes remained sad. She still didn't know what any of this meant. Would it bring Dad home again?

'You and Bob have always been good together,' Dot said, laying a hand on her friend's shoulder for a second. 'That woman's cast a spell on *him*. That's just how it feels. But she's deceived him every step of the way!'

Cynthia sighed, staring longingly at Dot. 'Well, I hope so. I just don't know now whether he can break the spell, even if he finds out the truth, or if it's too late.' She looked unbearably sad. 'Maybe it's her he really wants now.'

'What, when she's lied to him and led him up the garden path with all her carry-on and her tall tales! He's not going to want to stay with her now, when there's no babby for her to hold over him!'

Suddenly the strain of it all became too much for Cynthia and she clasped her hands over her face.

'Oh God, Dot!' she said, dissolving into tears. 'I

just want my husband back. I just want things to be the way they used to be!'

Dot put her arm round her friend. Em and Molly watched, wide-eyed.

'Come on, love, it'll be all right. Let's just get back. We could wait till tomorrow to go round. It's all a bit much for you, isn't it?'

'No.' Cynthia wiped her eyes and looked fiercely at Dot. 'I've got to do it, face up to it. I've got to know one way or another.'

Fifty-Two

It was Flossie who opened the door. For a second she looked shocked when she saw who was outside, but covered it up with an insincere smile which glinted with triumph.

'Oh, I'm surprised to see you,' she said, looking at Cynthia and pretending to ignore Dot. 'Was there something you wanted?'

'We want to come in,' Dot said brusquely. 'Is Bob here?'

Flossie affected to look shocked and gave a little laugh. 'What's that to you? And why would I want to invite *you* into my house?'

'Look, bab, just step out of the way before I make yer.' Dot pushed in past her, with Cynthia following. 'There's a few things poor Bob needs to know.'

'What the hell's going on?' Bob said, looking extremely worried when he saw them crowding through into the back room. 'Cynth, Dot, what're you doing?'

Dot didn't waste a second. 'We've come to tell you a few home truths about Mrs Dawson here,' she said loud and clear. 'Or rather, *Mrs Owen.*'

There was an immediate shocked intake of breath from Flossie and an ugly blush spread over her face. Her eyes narrowed viciously.

'What're you going on about?' She tried to cover up, giving another little laugh. 'Bob, I've really no idea what they're talking about! Some spiteful story they've cooked up between them, no doubt. Tell them to leave my house, will you, please, dear?'

'Bob,' Cynthia went to him urgently, 'don't listen to her! She's not what she seems at all – she's been lying to you all along. What she said about being a widow, it's all lies. All this time, she's still married. Her husband's in Aston. Dot and I went to see him.'

'Yes, the poor bugger,' Dot put in, standing with hands on hips. 'If ever anyone had a fool made of him it's Dai Owen.'

'What are you doing, spreading all these ridiculous lies!' Flossie cried shrilly. She was panicking and quickly losing control of herself. 'Bob, make them get out! They're just vicious gossip-mongers. They're lying to you. You know your wife's not right in the head. Get out, the pair of you!'

So saying, she grabbed Cynthia's arm and tried to drag her away.

'Get your filthy, deceiving hands off me!' Cynthia cried as Dot, by far the strongest of the three women, intervened, seizing Flossie round the waist and dragging her away from Cynthia.

'You come over 'ere and shut yer cake'ole for a minute – we've heard enough from you to last a lifetime. Go on, Cynth, tell him!'

Bob looked utterly bewildered, not knowing who to believe about anything.

'Bob, listen, for God's sake,' Cynthia gabbled, grasping Bob's arm in her urgency. 'Daisy's not her real daughter. She's married but she can't have children, so she's not expecting your babby now. She's not capable of it!'

'No-o-o!' A terrible, shrill wail poured out of Flossie. 'Don't say that! It's not true. It's all lies. She's just trying to come between us, Bob.'

'You know it's true,' Dot said, still holding onto her tightly. 'You know damn well you're not expecting his child and you've wheedled your way into this family and bloody nearly wrecked everything, you scheming little bitch. Go on, tell him the truth for once. You're not having a babby, are you? Because you're barren, and you're not a widow. In fact you're not anything you seem to be. Everything about you is a bloody sham!'

Bob looked stunned but they could see he was starting to believe them.

'It's not true!' Flossie crumpled, starting to shake and sob. 'I can have a baby with you, Bob, I know I can,' she pleaded. 'If we keep trying I know it'll happen. It's different with you. It was Dai who couldn't have children. I should never have married him.'

'Oh yes, and what about all the other men you've been with?' Dot flung back at her. 'I

399

suppose it was all their fault as well?'

'Is it true?' Bob said quietly. 'Floss – tell me the truth. Have you been lying to me, all this time, about everything?'

'Yes, she flaming well has!' Dot said, her impatience getting the better of her. 'And you swallowed every word of it, you bleeding idiot.'

'Floss?' He spoke quietly.

Flossie didn't say anything, not then. She couldn't even look at him. It was obvious from the state of her, the way she crumpled within Dot's grasp, that they had exposed all her strange pretence, and she seemed to have no fight left in her. Dot propelled her to a chair where she bent over, sobbing hysterically.

'You can't do this to me! Don't leave me, Bob. We'll be happy together, we will have a child, we *will!*'

Cynthia's emotion welled up in tears. 'Bob, you're my husband and I want you home – we all do. It's not all your fault. I wasn't myself and I frightened you away. But come home now, come and be with your family, please!'

Bob looked in anguish from one weeping woman to another, seemingly unable to think what to do. After a moment he broke away from Cynthia.

'Christ, I can't stand this. I've got to get out – just let me out...'

He rushed from the house and they heard the front door slam behind him.

Cynthia and Dot returned to eighteen Kenilworth Street, leaving a sobbing Flossie Dawson.

Em, Sid and Joyce's faces were all anxiously at the window. Molly was waiting with them.

'Where's our dad?' Sid burst out as they came in. Em had told them she thought he'd be coming home with them.

'I don't know,' Cynthia said wearily. Violet was crying and she went to her and picked her up. 'He just went off.' She hadn't the strength to think up any other excuse that would soften the blow.

'Your dad just wanted to think things out a bit,' Dot told them, hardly able to look at the children's faces, especially Em's, so deep was their disappointment. She knew Em felt everything so keenly, was so desperate for her family to be together the way they used to be.

'He's got to come back,' Em said, backing towards the door.

'I expect he will,' Dot was saying, but Em was already on her way out of the house.

'He's *got* to!' she cried, gone before anyone could stop her.

Fifty-Three

Em tore along the street, dodging the flying skipping ropes, with groups twirling and chanting rhymes.

Someone called to her, but she took no notice. She could only think of one thing and it felt like the most urgent and important thing in the

401

world. She had to find her dad, *had* to, her thumping heart told her over and over again as she dashed past the Prices' shop and the timber yard and on and on along the neighbouring streets.

The rubber soles of her shoes slapped on the pavement and her long cotton skirt with the blue and white checks swished round her skinny legs... *Dad, my dad...* She ran so hard it felt as if her lungs would burst.

'Steady on!' With the bright sun in her eyes she almost collided with a man turning the corner but she ignored him, barely aware of anyone else, so intent was she on her mission.

Almost certainly she knew where he would be. She ran on along the side of the power station, its cooling towers smudging the spring sky with its manufactured weather. She had to stop for a moment to catch her breath, hearing the chuff-chuff of a train shunting in the goods yard on the other side of the road. Grit blew into her eyes and she blinked hard, then she ran on, limping now as her too-small left shoe was chafing her little toe.

Soon she saw him, where she'd hoped he would be when he needed to try to think straight: on the little bridge close to the tube works where you could look over the cut. He was a dark, hunched figure in the sunlight, his head bent, eyes fixed on the water, so lost in thought that he didn't notice her coming.

Her heart thudding, she went up to him and touched his arm.

'Dad?'

Bob jumped, startled. His expression was very grim, but softened a fraction on seeing her.

'Oh, Em – it's you.' He seemed dazed and suddenly she was tongue-tied as well. They stood staring at one another. Then he looked down again into the murky water. 'I've made a right ruddy mess, haven't I?'

Em examined his profile. He looked worn, and older. Although he was still her good-looking king of a father, there was a sad droop to his cheeks. 'Come home, Dad,' she said at last.

Bob's blue, watery eyes rested on her face in a troubled way, and for a moment he couldn't seem to speak.

'I don't know if I can,' he said at last. 'I–' He drew his head back, looking over towards the power-station chimney with its flag of smoke. 'I don't know if ... if yer mother's all right, if I can do it. I don't know how I could've been such a fool. Flossie lied to me – lied to me so bad. I don't even know what's right any more... I don't know nothing...'

'Dad, *please*...'

Hearing the tears in Em's voice he turned to her properly again.

'Just come home, that's all. We all want you home. Can't we just be together again like before?'

He looked down, ashamed, shaking his head. 'I'm sorry, Em. I was frightened of your mother – of the way she was. I was weak...You were right, I *was* stupid. I don't even know what I was doing.' He shrugged. 'Not much of a father to yer, am I?'

Crying now, tears that never seemed to stop, Em went to him and tugged at his coat. She

403

turned her wet face up pleadingly to him. 'Come on, Dad.'

After a moment, he reached down and took her hand.

'Is everyone home?' he asked, as they walked along, and she told him they were. They didn't say anything else.

She felt proud, walking back along Kenilworth Street, holding her father's hand. When they reached the house, he said, 'Here goes,' and she could hear from his breathing that he was scared stiff.

Cynthia was in the scullery, but she heard them and came through.

'Em?' she said, with worried eyes.

'Dad's here,' Em said.

She saw her mother take in the sight of him, standing humbly just inside the door, his hat between his hands. There was silence for a few seconds. Bob cleared his throat.

'I've come back home,' he said. 'If you'll have me.'

Em saw in her mother's face the depth of her relief. Quietly, calmly, Cynthia said, 'Yes, Bob, I'll have you. Course I will.'

Only after the children were asleep were the two of them able to be alone. They had all sat round the table together for tea as a family, and the children were all happy and excited that both their mom and dad were home together and things looked hopeful. Cynthia sat there, with Violet in her arms, gazing round at her family, hardly able to believe it. It was all so fragile, but it was right – at last.

'You won't go away again, Dad, will yer?' Joycie said before she went sleepily up to bed.

'No, bab. Now come 'ere and give us a kiss.'

Cynthia watched Bob say goodnight to each of them in turn, holding them as if they were the most precious things ever. Then he got up. 'I'll come and tuck you in. Let yer mother have a rest.'

'I ain't half missed them,' he said sheepishly, when he came down.

It was on the tip of Cynthia's tongue to say something nasty about how he'd gone off to replace their children with Daisy Dawson, but she bit the words back. They hadn't had a chance to talk yet – it was no good spoiling a new start with angry accusations.

Getting ready for bed in their candlelit room, it was with the sudden shyness of newly-weds. Cynthia turned away from him to unfasten her blouse, almost as if Bob was a stranger to her.

'Cynth...' He spoke softly, coming round the big wooden bed to her.

She turned, her breasts half exposed, pulling the sides of her shirt together again.

'No, don't,' he said. 'Let me see yer.'

He spoke so sweetly that even after all her pain and anguish she felt very tender towards him. He was nothing but a boy in some ways, a frightened, hurt boy who needed her, deep down, far more than he knew.

'I'm all skinny now,' she said apologetically. 'Not much there.'

Taking his hand she pulled him to her and sat

down on the edge of the bed. He gave a sob, 'No – Christ – you're so beautiful, Cynth.' For a second he gazed at her, as if about to kiss or caress her breasts, but then he knelt beside her, burying his head in her lap, and broke down in tears.

'I'm sorry.' The words choked out brokenly. 'I've been such a fool. I don't know how I can've done what I did. That woman, she bewitched me. I couldn't seem to think straight.'

Cynthia sat, bare-breasted, the warmth of his head in her lap, stroking his dark hair, the curling bits at his neckline, gently trying to reassure him. She felt overwhelmed with tenderness.

'I've been no good to yer,' he went on. 'I know I should've been better – but when you were bad you were like someone else. I couldn't seem to think what to do. It felt as if I'd lost you! I couldn't stand it, Cynth. It was like being in the Boys' Home all over again, with no one to care about yer. You were my wife, but you're like a mom to me an' all, I know that now. And when you were poorly it was as if you'd died like she did...'

He raised his head, seeming bemused by what he had just said.

'I didn't mean to leave you,' she said. 'I don't know what happened to me. What with the babby, then our Joycie going missing, everything got on top of me. It was like the floor opening and there being nothing underneath to catch you. D'you get me?'

He stared ahead, then nodded. 'I think I do. A bit, anyhow.'

Her eyes were frightened. 'I feel different. As if

I'll never be who I was before, not ever completely.'

'But you're better?'

'Better than I was, yes.' She gave a faint smile. 'You won't go back to her, will you – that woman?'

Bob grasped her hand. 'Course not. Here's where I belong. It's like I went blind for a bit and couldn't see. She's a scheming bitch, I can see that now an' all, but God knows, she had me taken in. There's summat not right with her.' He got to his feet, taking her hand. 'You're my wife, and by God I need yer, Cynth. I want to hold yer close and stay here – in our house where we belong.'

Gently, he pulled her to him and she felt his warm, strong chest against her bare breasts, and his heartbeat and the hard strength of him, and she longed to take him to her and love him and begin to make everything right.

Fifty-Four

A few days later, Molly was absent from school and Em decided to go and see if she was all right. She had to dare herself even to go anywhere near the Foxes' yard, but Molly was her pal now, after all they had been through together.

Her heart thudding, she crept along the entry, but even before she reached the house she could hear the sound of someone weeping unrestrainedly. The loud, aggrieved bawling was coming out of the door of Molly's house, which as usual was not closed. Em peeped in and was met by the sight of Iris Fox's immense form crouched on the chair by the fire, which was where the old man usually sat. Her hands were over her face and she was rocking back and forth and wailing fit to burst.

Em was fascinated by the sight, but didn't know what to do. She could just see Molly's dad's feet sticking out opposite Iris, and not wanting to interrupt this scene she dithered outside the door. But as she stood there Molly came charging out and knocked right into her.

'Ow!' Em rubbed her forehead.

Molly looked taken aback. 'What're you doing 'ere?'

'I came to see why you weren't at school.' She was taken aback to see that Molly looked tear-stained as well. 'What's up?'

'It's my grandad,' Molly said, closing the door on her distraught mother. 'They've taken him off up the hospital. They said he won't last long – he's got poison in his blood.'

'Oh,' Em said. 'Is that...?' She'd been about to ask if that was why he stank so bad. The last time she'd been to the house the smell had been appalling

'He lost his toes on one foot and then it was all through him,' Molly said miserably. 'Septi – septi something.'

'Oh,' Em said, not sure about this. 'I've got a penny our dad gave me. Want to get some sweets?'

'All right,' Molly said, cheering up visibly.

The girls hurried along to the Miss Prices' shop and chose as many sweets as they could get for a penny. Molly chose a gobstopper and Em had some sherbet. Then they popped in to see Mr and Mrs Button, Molly's home from home, and Mrs Button was kind about Molly's sick grandfather.

'Come and see me tomorrow, won't you?' she said, as they ran out into the sun.

The pavements were busy with children and a group were swinging a long rope right across the street in a big skipping game. Two of the eldest were turning the rope, and everyone was chanting together.

'I like coffee, I like tea...'

'Hey, Em, Molly – come and play!' a voice shouted. Molly's eyes lit up. 'Come on, Em,' she said.

And they launched themselves into the game as the rope rose high over the road, ready to jump as it swung round.

George Washington never told a lie
He went into the larder and stole a cherry pie...

The girls chanted with the rhythm of the rope. Molly's cheek was bulging with the gobstopper and Em had her little bag of sherbet in her hand as she skipped. She looked at Molly, beaming with happiness. Mom was at home, and so was Dad now, and things were beginning to get back to normal, blessed ordinary – normal. Flossie Dawson had disappeared from her house – she and Molly had been to see – and the place was deserted. Flossie had vanished from the area. She was gone gone *gone*. Without trace! Em beamed, celebrating with every jump at the thought, and she felt so happy and tireless and in tune with the rhythm, as if she could never make a mistake.

Fifty-Five

Though the family had its ups and downs as usual, things started to settle, and as the summer arrived the Brown children got back to their routine and began to try and forget all the sad things that had happened. Sid's bed gradually became dry at night, Joycie didn't have so many tantrums and Em started to fill out a little. Dot and Cynthia went back to their friendly routine of helping each other out.

One evening after dark, though, there came an unexpected caller at the door. Bob went to open up.

'Ah, Mr Brown! I've something for you!'

The children, recognizing the voice, looked at each other in amazement and crowded into the front room to look. It was one of the Miss Prices, Madeleine, they realized, because of the mole. They were full of curiosity. They had scarcely ever seen one of the Miss Prices outside the shop, let alone calling at their house!

'It's a very strange thing,' Miss Price began in her dithery way. 'And I'm sorry to disturb you, only a lady has just called into the shop. Of course we were closed, but she was very determined. In fact she kept hammering on the door. She asked me to give you this – it's to be delivered to you.'

In her hand was an envelope which she held out to Bob Brown.

'Well, who was she? Why didn't she just come here?' Bob said, taking the envelope from her.

'Ah, well, this was it, you see, she didn't know where you were. She said she knew you lived in this street but she didn't know the number of the house. And she asked me to be discreet, you see. So I've brought it *straight* across to you. She wouldn't tell me who she was, I'm afraid, though I've an idea she might have been someone's maid, by the way she was dressed.'

Bob looked up and down the street, bemused.

'Where's she gone now, then?'

'Oh, she disappeared straight away. Seemed most eager to get back.'

He thanked Madeleine Price and, frowning, brought the letter through to the back. Cynthia was still sitting at the table with Violet asleep on her shoulder.

'What was all that about?' she asked. It was remarkable for the family to receive any letters.

'I dunno.' Bob sank down at the table and slid his knife along the flap. They all watched him as he slowly read. Em felt her chest tighten with dread, until she saw his expression alter from puzzled to astonished as he did so He raised his head, looking round at them all, speechless.

'What is it, Bob, for goodness sake!' Cynthia demanded. 'It's not bad news, is it?'

He shook his head. 'Hardly – read that out. I can hardly take it in.'

Cynthia took the letter impatiently. 'Should I –

411

is it all right for the kids to hear?'

'Yeah, go on.'

She read:

Dear Mr and Mrs Brown,

I have had it on my conscience to write to you for many months, but have not been able to find the courage until now.

It was I, foolish, foolish woman, who took your lovely little girl, Joyce, with me to visit my house last summer, and she stayed the night with me, as I'm sure she told you. It was a great pleasure to me and I cared for her so very well, but it has grown on me how much distress I must have caused you, and I realize that I did a terrible thing. But I was not myself in those days. I have not been well.

You see, I had a daughter once. Her name was Alice, but my little darling went to rest in the arms of her Saviour when she was only just twelve months old and I have had no children since. Alice would have had her fourth birthday just before I met your beautiful daughter Joyce and I'm afraid the great longing to be in the company of a little one such as her overtook me completely and I was led into temptation. She is such a darling child! And I reasoned that a child from such a poor area would be glad of a better home. Of course, when my husband came home I was discovered. I had my maid bring her back to you, hoping and praying that no damage was done and that I could be forgiven.

I hope you will accept the enclosed as a token of my repentance and good will towards your family. And I do hope you can find it in your hearts to forgive me, a broken-hearted mother. I meant no harm by it,

please believe me. I would have loved her as my own.
Yours sincerely.

Cynthia's voice grew increasingly full of wonder as she read and she looked up at last, deeply shocked.

'She was going to keep our Joyce, if she hadn't been found out, the evil cow...' She reached out and pulled Joyce to her, cuddling her. 'God, the poor woman losing her babby – but if she ever came anywhere near here again I don't know what I might do to her...' She looked across, seeing Bob opening the other little fold of paper which had been inside the envelope. 'What's in there?'

Bob pulled out several notes and, looking even more amazed, counted them up.

'Christ – twenty-five pound!' He jumped up excitedly. 'She's sent us bloody *twenty-five pound!*'

'No!' Cynthia cried. 'Are you sure?'

Em caught the enormous excitement and felt a grin start to spread across her face, which grew even more as Bob went to Cynthia, waving the notes at her, then pulled her up, still holding Violet, and started dancing with her round the back room as if they were carefree children, both of them giggling in amazement. All the children laughed, loving seeing their mom and dad so excited. Joyce's little face puckered up in a grin of sheer delight and Sid bounced, roaring, on his chair. They hadn't seen a scene as jolly as this in a very long time.

'Eh, Joyce – we'll have to get you taken away more often!' Bob joked, picking her up and swinging her in the air, while she let out gurgles of laughter.

'Oh, don't say that!' Cynthia protested, but she was chuckling too.

'Well, kids, we're in the money. You can all have a treat. What's it going to be?'

Sid and Joyce immediately thought of little toys they wanted, only small things: a model aeroplane for Sid and a little doll for Joyce that you could dress in her own clothes.

'Em, what about you?' Bob squatted down, his beaming face close to hers.

Em squirmed with pleasure but she knew she must not ask for too much.

'Can I have a packet of chalk?' she said daringly. 'So we've got our own chalk to play hopscotch?'

Her father laughed, and stood to pick her up by the waist, twirling her round until she giggled.

'Oh, I think we can run to that. A packet of chalk it is! That'll keep you going for the whole of the summer, won't it?'

'Yes,' she gasped as the room spun round her. 'All summer and next summer as well!'

The publishers hope that this book has given you enjoyable reading. Large Print Books are especially designed to be as easy to see and hold as possible. If you wish a complete list of our books please ask at your local library or write directly to:

Magna Large Print Books
Magna House, Long Preston,
Skipton, North Yorkshire.
BD23 4ND

This Large Print Book for the partially sighted, who cannot read normal print, is published under the auspices of

THE ULVERSCROFT FOUNDATION